Worlds COLLIDE

OTHER BOOKS AND AUDIO PRODUCTS BY TRACI HUNTER ABRAMSON

UNDERCURRENTS SERIES

Undercurrents

Ripple Effect

The Deep End

SAINT SQUAD SERIES

Freefall

Lockdown

Crossfire

Backlash

Smoke Screen

Code Word

Lock and Key

Drop Zone

Spotlight

Tripwire

Redemption

Covert Ops

ROYAL SERIES

Royal Target

Royal Secrets

Royal Brides

Royal Heir

GUARDIAN SERIES

Failsafe

Safe House

Sanctuary

On the Run

In Harm's Way

Not Dead Yet

DREAM'S EDGE SERIES

*Dancing to Freedom**

An Unlikely Pair

*Broken Dreams**

Dreams of Gold

*The Best Mistake**

Worlds Collide

FALCON POINT SERIES

Heirs of Falcon Point

The Danger with Diamonds

STAND-ALONES

Obsession

Deep Cover

Chances Are

Chance for Home

Kept Secrets

*Twisted Fate**

Proximity

*Entangled**

Mistaken Reality

A Change of Fortune

*Sinister Secrets**

The Fiction Kitchen Trio Cookbook (Coming March 2023)

*Novella

from best-selling author

TRACI HUNTER ABRAMSON

Worlds COLLIDE

of the DREAM'S EDGE *series*

Covenant Communications, Inc.

Cover image: *Figure Skating Couple* by Artur Didyk © courtesy of istockphoto.com

Published by Covenant Communications, Inc.
American Fork, Utah

This is a work of fiction. The characters, names, incidents, places, and dialogue are either products of the author's imagination, and are not to be construed as real, or are used fictitiously.

Name: Traci Hunter Abramson
Title: Worlds Collide / Traci Hunter Abramson
Description: American Fork, UT : Covenant Communications, Inc. [2023]
Identifiers: Library of Congress Control Number Number 2022941700 | ISBN: 978-1-52442-260-8
LC record available at https://lccn.loc.gov/2022941700

Printed in Mexico
First Printing: February 2023

30 29 28 27 26 25 24 23 10 9 8 7 6 5 4 3 2 1

Priase for Worlds Collide

"I don't find a lot of ice skating books, so I am always happy when I have the opportunity. *Worlds Collide* by Traci Hunter Abramson is absolutely wonderful. Tyler and Amaliya are loveable characters, and their determination on the ice had me in awe of their talent. It's easy to see the deep research the talented Abramson does by the details throughout the book, not only with figure skating but with the details of Russia and the KBG. I was glued to this book, especially when the story got to Canada. I was familiar with the Canadian part of it but knew nothing about the Russians and the KGB. It's all still buzzing around in my head, and it will stay there for a good long while.

"Abramson knocks it out of the park on this one. She had no trouble keeping my attention, and the characters were fabulous in playing their parts as they developed so well throughout the story. If you enjoy ice skating, and especially pairs figure skating, you will love this book, and you will get a little lesson on Russia along the way."

—Readers' Favorite five-star review

"In *Worlds Collide*, the newest and final book in the Dream's Edge series, author Traci Hunter Abramson keeps suspense, mystery, and excitement high as this page-turner continues the story of pairs figure skaters Tyler and Amaliya following their 1984 Olympic gold victory. With danger around every corner and the menacing presence of the KGB watching their every move, Tyler and Amaliya wonder if the future they hope for is just an impossible dream. Captivating and engaging from the first page to the last, *Worlds Collide* is one book you don't want to miss."

—Michele Ashman Bell, best-selling author of *The Crown of Rosemund*

Praise for the Dream's Edge Series

"The author creates fabulously realistic scenes and characters that seep through every page of *Dreams of Gold*!"

—*InD'tale Magazine*

"A thrilling story packed with various aspects of the very different worlds of the main characters, ballet, hockey, and ice skating, all with their own disciplines."

—Readers' Favorite five-star review

"Traci Hunter Abramson's ability to create realistic scenes and characters that any reader would admire seeps through every page of *Dreams of Gold*. Even for the reader who knows nothing about ice skating, this plot-driven story ensures that everyone has a warm seat at the front row of all the excitement and nerve-racking moves that come with the sport. One cannot help but keep rooting for the pair and, surprisingly, the coach who is fighting a couple of fears too. The secrets that Amaliya unearths during their journey add an exquisite thread to the overall beauty of the book."

—Crowned Heart Review, *InD'tale Magazine*

"Abramson has the ability to create characters that are both believable and somehow larger than life. Readers will find themselves cheering on these two young skaters both in their sport and in the relationship growing between them. Her parents' battle with horrible injuries and paralysis is a story in its own right. The assistance and support of friends is another important element of the story. The settings in Washington D.C., New York, and Connecticut are well done. Most of the action takes place in skating arenas and homes. The story not only advances following a comfortable plot arc, but there is a second arc showing the emotional growth that takes place in the hearts and minds of Amaliya and Tyler."

—*Meridian Magazine*

Praise for Traci Hunter Abramson

"When it comes to creating stories that blend suspenseful and romantic notes into symphonies that keep readers riveted (and wanting more), Traci Hunter Abramson is an absolute virtuoso."

—Stephanie Black, author of the Natalie Marsh Mystery series

"Traci Hunter Abramson is a master of her craft, an auto-buy author who never disappoints."

—Sarah M. Eden, *USA Today* best-selling author

"As an admirer of Traci Hunter Abramson's prolific talent, I once asked her how she does it. Her answer blew me away. She said, 'I write as I work out on my treadmill.' Now that's devotion. Is it any wonder that this amazing author crafts one award-winning novel after another? Kudos to her as her writing journey continues with yet another awesome series."

—Kathi Oram Peterson, author of award-winning *Treacherous Legacy*, 2021

"Heart-stopping action, unexpected plot twists, brave and gallant heroes, warm humor, and sweet romance. It's no wonder readers—especially this one—love everything Traci Hunter Abramson writes. Her books have it all!"

—Sian Ann Bessey, author of best-selling Georgian Gentleman series

for Sarah Eden

Thank you for the roads you've paved and for
the joy you spread everywhere you go.
Your friendship is a gift I will always treasure.

Acknowledgments

As this series comes to a close, I want to thank everyone who has been so supportive of this project and who has helped my first-ever novel come to life. Thank you to Samantha Millburn for the countless hours you've spent on the Dream's Edge series, especially for always being able to find those few minutes to help me uncover the answers when my characters stop talking to me. Thanks to Ashley Gebert, Jessica Bybee, Amy Parker, and the rest of the Covenant family for all your efforts in helping me get my work out into the world.

Thank you to Mandy Biesinger and Lara Abramson for sharing your beta-reading skills, and thanks to the many critique partners who helped me polish this book in the early stages, especially Kyla Beecroft, Paige Edwards, H. Y. Gregor, Connor Olsen, Kori Pratt, Daniel Quilter, Eliza Sanders, and Ellie Whitney.

Thanks to Sian Bessey for helping me keep my sanity through the writing process, and thanks to my family for sharing me with my fictional worlds.

Also, thank you to the many members of my Traci's Friends Facebook group who are always so willing to help me remember character names and details, and thank you to the readers who have supported me in my writing journey. I appreciate you more than I can ever express. And a special thanks again to Lucetta Allen Lilly for letting my borrow your parents' names when these characters were created.

Chapter ONE

February 1984

THE STEADY VIBRATION OF THE plane's engines should have lulled Tyler to sleep, but over the past six hours of the transatlantic flight, he had managed only a few moments of fitful slumber. So much had happened over the past two weeks while he and his fiancée had been in the Soviet Union.

His fiancée. He liked the sound of that, even though he hadn't yet been able to call her that in public.

Amaliya shifted slightly, her beautiful profile barely visible in the dim airplane cabin. Dark eyelashes against flawless skin and a natural beauty that went far deeper than her appearance. Love flowed through him, along with a sense of gratitude. How had he gotten so lucky?

The glow of the reading light from the passenger in front of them spilled onto Amaliya's bare hand. Her diamond engagement ring would remain out of sight for another day or two until Tyler spoke with her father, Robert.

Just the thought of facing Robert sent a whirlwind of nerves and anticipation whipping through Tyler. For months after Tyler and Amaliya had started dating, Robert had opposed their relationship. Even though the tensions between them had eased, the possibility that Robert would object to their marriage was far higher than Tyler would have liked. Nearly as concerning was the prospect that he would kick Tyler out of the apartment over the garage and essentially leave him homeless.

Tyler's chest tightened uncomfortably. If Robert objected, they would not only have to wait to get married until they could make enough money to support themselves, but they would also have to deal with the very real ramifications of trying to prepare for the world championships in the midst of family strife. Never a good combination. Especially if he ended up without a place to live.

Sitting on the other side of Amaliya, their coach, Gordon, leaned forward and looked at Tyler. Though the older man had already lived half a century, he could still skate circles around most people, and he had experienced the ups and downs on the world stage of ice skating.

"You didn't get much sleep," Gordon said.

"I got some."

"Too much adrenaline still rushing through you?"

Tyler glanced at Amaliya's bare hand again. "Something like that." He tried to push the practicalities of their relationship aside. Surely, Robert would want his daughter to be happy.

And at the moment, she was happy. So many things over the past two weeks in Leningrad had brought both of them joy. They were coming home with the Olympic gold medal in pairs figure skating, they were excited about their future together, and Amaliya had met her long-lost uncle and his family.

What would Amaliya's mother think about the news? Katerina had been a Soviet defector nearly twenty-five years ago, and now, if all went well, she would get to reunite with the family members she had left behind.

A stewardess, who wasn't much older than Tyler's twenty-three years, stopped beside their aisle. "Sorry to disturb you, sir," she began, speaking to Gordon. "I've been asked to relay the message that once we land, security would like you to wait on the aircraft until the other passengers deplane."

"Why?" Gordon asked.

"Apparently, there are quite a few reporters waiting at the gate," she said.

Tyler repeated the stewardess's words in his mind. Reporters. Waiting for them. Even though he'd expected attention after their win, he hadn't anticipated they would receive it quite so soon.

"We want to make sure the others can get past the crowd before the excitement begins," the stewardess continued.

"That's understandable." Gordon glanced briefly at Tyler before he spoke to the stewardess again. "Just let us know when we're good to go."

"Of course, sir. Thank you for your understanding."

"I didn't expect that we would have a crowd at the airport," Tyler said.

"Everyone is proud of you," Gordon said. "Olympic gold medals are a big deal."

"Yeah, you're right." Tyler still couldn't believe that he and Amaliya had won. The years of hard work, of overcoming injury and frustration, had paid off, and now here they were, arriving at Washington Dulles International Airport as the best pairs figure skaters in the world.

In the seat beside him, Amaliya stirred, and her eyes fluttered open. "What time is it?"

Gordon checked his watch. "It's almost four o'clock in DC. We should be landing soon."

Amaliya pressed a hand to her stomach. "I'm nervous. Why should I be nervous?"

"No reason to be," Gordon said. "You are returning home as champions."

"Does that mean you'll let us have our phones back?" Tyler asked. Right after they'd qualified for the Olympics, Gordon had taken away the phones in their rooms and restricted their access to TV and radio.

"You still have a few more weeks before that will happen. You aren't done training yet, not until after the world championships."

"I bet no one else's coach took away their phones and TVs."

"Yeah, but how many of those other skaters are coming home with gold medals?" Gordon asked.

"He's got us there," Tyler said.

"I'll still let you talk to your family on Sundays."

"I guess that's better than nothing."

Gordon motioned to Amaliya's left hand. "When are you going to put your engagement ring back on?"

Surprise illuminated Amaliya's face, and Tyler swallowed hard. How did Gordon know about their engagement? Tyler had asked Amaliya to marry him only a few days ago.

As though reading his thoughts, Gordon shook his head and said, "Amaliya may have been wearing gloves when we went to the bobsled competition, but it wasn't hard to figure out there was a new piece of jewelry on a very important finger."

Amaliya glanced at Tyler. "Sorry. I guess I should have locked my ring in my room after all."

"Why the secrecy?" Gordon asked. His eyes narrowed, and he focused on Tyler. "You haven't asked her dad for permission yet, have you?"

"You told us to avoid stressful situations when we were training for the Olympics," Tyler said. "Talking to Robert would have definitely been stressful."

Gordon chuckled. "I'll give you that."

The plane came to a stop, and the seat belt sign turned off. Amaliya held up her hands and wiggled her fingers. "I'm not wearing a ring right now, so we don't have a problem."

"*You* don't have a problem." Tyler grabbed his backpack from beneath the seat in front of him. "I still have to talk to your dad."

"It won't be long before that conversation is behind you." Amaliya laced her fingers through his, but the intended comfort didn't come.

"Robert wants Amaliya to be happy," Gordon said. "You make her happy."

"It's true." Amaliya squeezed Tyler's hand.

"When are you going to talk to him?" Gordon asked.

"I don't know," Tyler admitted. "We have a lot we need to talk to him about besides our plans to get married."

"Do you think your dad already told your mom about Viktor?" Gordon asked, referring to Amaliya's uncle.

"I don't know," Amaliya said.

Tyler rolled his shoulders to stretch out the stiffness that had settled there. "We'll find out soon enough."

The stewardess returned. "You can get off the plane now."

"Thank you." Gordon stood and fell in line behind the last of the other passengers.

"Why did we need to wait to get off the plane?" Amaliya asked.

"Apparently, we have a welcoming party that includes more than just your parents," Tyler said. "A bunch of reporters are waiting for us too."

"Really?"

Gordon glanced back at them. "Enjoy this moment. You've earned the attention you're about to receive."

Tyler couldn't help but smile as the magnitude of what they had accomplished washed over him. He and Amaliya gathered their belongings and followed Gordon off the plane onto the Jetway.

Gordon slowed his pace when they were halfway to the exit. "You ready for this?"

"I'm ready to be home," Amaliya said.

Tyler took Amaliya's hand. "So am I."

Amaliya stepped off the Jetway to flashing cameras and a burst of cheers. Were all these people really here for her and Tyler?

Her gaze swept over the crowded airport lobby, the sea of humanity blocking her view of the rest of the terminal. American flags and signs with her and Tyler's names on them waved among the frenzy of television cameras and photographers.

Several reporters surged forward, their questions tumbling over each other.

"Tyler, Amaliya," a man called out. "Can we talk to you for a minute?"

A female reporter shoved a microphone in front of Amaliya. "Did you expect to win the gold?"

"What happens next?" another man asked. "Will you compete in the world championships?"

The crowd seemed to press in on her, the wall of bodies edging closer. Amaliya took a step back, suddenly needing space.

Tyler's hand lifted to rest on her waist, a reminder that she wasn't alone.

Gordon stepped beside her and spoke in a low voice. "Smile for the cameras. The sooner they get what they want, the sooner they'll leave us alone."

Amaliya forced a smile, her eyes searching for her parents. A hand waved behind one of the television cameras, and a moment later, her father pushed to the front, clearing a path for her mom.

Joy shimmered through Amaliya, and she rushed into her mother's embrace. Instantly, her father's arms wrapped around them both. The comfort of home swept through her despite the buzz of people crowding in on them.

Her parents released her and stepped to her side.

"Give them some room," her dad demanded.

Several of the reporters eased back, creating a loose half circle around them.

Tyler and Gordon edged forward.

"Now, one at a time," her dad said. Instantly, hands rose as each reporter vied for their turn. Her dad pointed to one in the center.

"How does it feel to be the Olympic gold medalists?" the reporter asked.

"It still hasn't sunk in yet," Amaliya said.

Her dad pointed at a woman to their left.

"What about the world championships?" she asked. "Will you compete in Toronto?"

Tyler answered this time. "Yes, we will."

"Any plans yet on whether you'll go pro or try for the 1988 Olympics?" the next reporter asked.

The question stirred through Amaliya. Until this moment, she hadn't considered what would come after the world championships. She and Tyler had been so focused on getting to Leningrad for these Olympics that she hadn't looked much beyond that finish line. Overwhelmed by the uncertainty that lay beyond next month, Amaliya tried to picture what her skating future would look like but couldn't.

Tyler's hand squeezed her waist as though he sensed her sudden turmoil of emotions. "For now, we're focusing on the world championships. After that, we'll see."

"Gordon, what are your thoughts?" the reporter asked, pressing the issue. "Are you hoping to keep these two on the amateur circuit for the next four years?"

"Like Tyler said, we're only looking a month out right now. After worlds, we'll have time to take a breath and discuss what they want next for their future."

Only four weeks until the world championships. Four weeks to prove they really were the best skaters in the world. Were they the best? Or had they gotten lucky?

They had considered ending their competition season after winning at the Olympics rather than pushing to prepare for yet another event. Ultimately, the possible benefits of traveling to Canada had outweighed their concerns that they wouldn't be able to repeat as gold medalists. Now the pressure was on to prove they not only deserved their Olympic gold medals but also that they could win again.

Amaliya glanced at her mother, and new emotions swirled inside her as the main reason for their competing in worlds pushed to the forefront of her mind—her mother and Uncle Viktor could be in the same place for the first time in twenty-four years. Excitement and anticipation bubbled inside her.

Someone pushed closer, and a flurry of cameras flashing blinded Amaliya momentarily. Hadn't these photographers taken enough pictures? She needed to talk to her mom without an audience.

The interview continued for a few more minutes, but thankfully, Tyler and Gordon answered the majority of the questions. When they were asked about their future for a fourth time, irritation shimmered through her.

As though reading her thoughts, her dad stepped forward and spoke with the authority born of coaching a professional hockey team for the past decade. "Thanks, everyone, but I'm afraid that's all we have time for."

A few more reporters shouted questions, but her dad simply put his hand up to indicate they were done. Then he put a protective arm around her mom and led the way through the edge of the crowd.

Amaliya followed, with Tyler and Gordon flanking her on either side.

More cameras flashed as they worked their way through the crowded space. It wasn't until they had collected their luggage at baggage claim and made their way to the exit that they finally found some breathing room.

"I thought we were never going to escape," Gordon said.

"Be grateful we didn't have to wait long for your bags," her mom said. As soon as they reached the car and loaded the luggage into the trunk, she turned to Amaliya. "How were the Olympics? How was Leningrad? I want to know everything."

Anticipation pulsed through Amaliya. She glanced at her dad. "Did you tell her?"

He unlocked the car and shook his head. A little smile pulled at his lips. "It's your story to tell, not mine."

"What are you talking about?" Her mom's Russian accent thickened.

Amaliya couldn't keep her own smile from forming. "We found Viktor."

Confusion illuminated her mom's expression, quickly followed by shock. "Viktor?" Her eyes widened, and she reached out to grip Amaliya's hand. "My brother, Viktor?"

Amaliya's excitement burst inside her. "Your brother, Viktor." Her grin widened. "My uncle."

"How? How did you find him?"

"It was a miracle." Amaliya put her free hand over their joined ones. "It was an answer to my prayers."

Tears surfaced in her mom's eyes, and she looked from Amaliya to her dad. "You knew about this?"

"Amaliya told me, but I never got to meet him." A tinge of regret colored her dad's words. He opened the car door. "We can talk about this on the way home. Let's get out of here before more reporters track us down. This isn't a conversation we want to risk being overheard."

They all climbed into the car, Amaliya's father behind the wheel and her mom in the passenger seat. Amaliya took the spot in the center of the back seat, between Tyler and Gordon.

As soon as her dad pulled out of the airport, her mom twisted around in her seat so she could see Amaliya. "How was he? And how did you find him?"

"He's doing well," Amaliya assured her. "We ran into him at the practice rink. His daughter, Sonya, was competing in the Olympics too. She won the bronze."

"I watched the competition." Wonder filled her mom's voice. "I had no idea she was my niece. The reporters here in America didn't say a thing about the connection."

"I'm surprised," Tyler said. "A lot of people were talking about it at the Olympics."

"That's true," Gordon added. "It's a good bet that the Soviet crowd learning about Amaliya's heritage was one of the reasons they welcomed Amaliya and Tyler so openly."

"Did you get to spend any time with Viktor? Did you meet his family?"

Amaliya explained the chain of events that led to her finding her mother's family and described the evening spent in her mother's childhood home with her aunt, uncle, and two cousins.

"Viktor and Ursula only have two children?" her mom asked, a hint of panic lacing her voice. "There should be at least three."

"How do you know that?" Amaliya asked. "I thought you hadn't communicated with Uncle Viktor since leaving the Soviet Union."

"I haven't, but Sonya is too young to be the child Ursula was carrying when I left home." Her mom pressed her lips together as though trying to control her emotions. "They should have another child, one who would be turning twenty-four this November."

"I'm sorry, Mama, but they didn't say anything about any other children." Amaliya squeezed her mom's arm. "I wish you could have been there so he could have told you everything."

"Me too, milaya," her mom said, using a familiar Russian endearment. Her voice turned wistful when she added, "I would have given anything to see you compete in person. If I could have trusted the Soviet government to let me come home to the United States, I would have been there. And the chance to see my brother again . . ." Her voice trailed off. "That would have truly been a miracle."

A new wave of enthusiasm burst through Amaliya. "We're hoping to make that miracle happen next month."

Her mom's eyebrows drew together. "I don't understand."

"Sonya is competing in the world championships." Hope rose within Amaliya. "According to Viktor, he will be there too."

Chapter TWO

Katerina couldn't have heard her daughter right. She gripped the back of her seat and focused on Amaliya. "Viktor will be in Canada?"

"He told me to bring you to worlds."

Hope sprang inside her. Her brother. Her only remaining relative from her childhood. "I get to see Viktor?"

Amaliya grinned. "Yes, in only a few weeks."

The dreams of the past many years flooded through Katerina, her excitement rising. Then reality surfaced, and her hope and excitement were quickly extinguished by the skepticism bred into her during her early years in the Soviet Union. Even if Viktor came to Canada, so would the KGB and the Soviet security forces. And her brother would be watched closely. Viktor wasn't just the father of an Olympian. He was also the brother of a defector. "I seriously doubt my brother will be allowed to leave the country, especially to come to North America."

"Wouldn't the parents of a star athlete be allowed to travel to see their child compete?" Tyler asked.

"Sometimes a parent or sibling would be permitted, but even that is rare," Katerina said, remembering her own experience when she had traveled to Canada for the first time. "With Viktor being my brother, he would not be trusted."

"What's the difference between Viktor coming to Canada and Sonya traveling there?" Amaliya asked.

"History. Sonya doesn't know me, and she has a reason to be in Canada."

"Viktor works with her coach. Maybe that's why he's being allowed to come," Amaliya suggested.

"Perhaps, but even if he is permitted to leave the Soviet Union, he and Sonya will both be closely guarded," Katerina said. Memories of her own escape flashed through her head. "The KGB will not let any of us get close to Sonya or Viktor."

"Sounds like we need to recruit some help," Robert said.

"What kind of help?" Katerina spoke the words before her thoughts caught up with her husband's meaning. "Miles and Linda?"

"They helped you escape," Robert said, referring to the Donnellys, the couple who had been their dearest friends since she'd defected. "Maybe they'll be willing to help us orchestrate a meeting between you and Viktor."

Though everything inside her yearned to connect with her brother, to see for herself the man he had become, to apologize for not returning home, she shook her head. "It's too risky. I escaped. He would never be able to leave without jeopardizing the lives of whatever family he leaves behind."

"We aren't talking about Uncle Viktor defecting," Amaliya said. "We're just trying to let the two of you see each other."

Again, her dreams warred with reality. "It's a lovely thought, Amaliya." Her voice trembled, and she swallowed hard before she continued. "But I can't risk my brother's safety."

Everyone fell silent. After a moment, Gordon asked, "Robert, is there any chance Amaliya and Tyler can get some rink time tomorrow at the Capital Centre?"

"Sorry, we're not going to have much open ice time, but I already called the local rink for you. I suspected these two wouldn't be quite ready to hang up their skates."

"You scheduled practice time for us?" Amaliya asked.

"I did. The more time you spend on the ice before worlds, the better," Robert said.

Gordon nodded. "I couldn't agree more."

Katerina listened half-heartedly as everyone else discussed Amaliya and Tyler's practice times for the rest of the week. The guilt she had long since buried rose within her with a vengeance. Had Viktor suffered because of her actions? Had his family? What had happened to the child Ursula had been carrying when Katerina had left Leningrad? Had they suffered a loss that was her fault?

The desire to see Viktor battled with the fear that rose beside it, not only for her brother and niece but for herself too. The KGB could recognize her. They could try to take her back to the Soviet Union. They might even succeed.

Robert turned onto the George Washington Parkway, the Potomac River flowing alongside them. Several minutes passed before their home came into view. The stately manor with pillars in the front, trees lining the driveway, the lawn a rolling hill that ended at the parkway that separated their property from the river.

When Katerina had first arrived in America, she hadn't believed people could live like this. Now she had come to expect such luxuries as a view of the water from her bedroom window and a private dance studio on the main level of her home.

What would Viktor think of this life she and Robert had created for themselves? And how did Viktor feel about her after all of these years apart?

Robert pulled into the driveway and parked in the garage. Yes, Katerina had truly been blessed, but she had no idea what her brother had suffered for her to enjoy a life filled with love and freedom or if he would ever forgive her for leaving him behind.

Viktor Petrov removed his fur cap as he entered the utilitarian-gray building with its functional lines. A chance meeting with the niece he hadn't known existed until days before the Olympics had put him on the KGB's radar. Now, only weeks before his family was to travel to Canada, the KGB's suspicions could take everything away.

For nearly twenty-five years, he had stood by while the Soviet government had sectioned off the land that had once belonged to his family. Josef, his oldest, had been forced to work in the glass factory instead of attending university like so many others of his intellect.

Despite Josef's long hours at the factory and Viktor's job at the skating rink, they worked countless hours farming what land they had left only to have the government commandeer their crops before Viktor could take them to market.

Sonya's grace and talent had saved her from menial labor, but even she had suffered the stigma of being the relative of a defector. The Leningrad Choreographic School, where Katerina had studied ballet, had refused Sonya entry when she had been younger, insisting she was too tall. Viktor knew better. She wasn't too tall; she had the wrong last name. Thankfully, her skating ability had been too stellar to ignore.

Viktor made his way down the grim hallway to the travel office for the world championship team and knocked on the door.

A man's voice called out, "Enter."

Viktor walked inside. Two desks overflowed with files. Behind one, a man in his early thirties shuffled papers from one part of his mess to another. The other was occupied by a man in his late forties.

"What do you want?" the older of the two barked out.

Viktor's grip tightened on his cap. "I am here to pick up travel papers for my daughter and my family."

"Name?"

"Viktor Petrov." Both men looked up. They knew who he was. This wasn't good. "My daughter is Sonya Petrova."

The older man stood and moved across the room to a battered metal filing cabinet. He pulled open the third drawer. After he rifled through several files, he pulled one out. "Ah, yes. Here we are."

Nerves tangled inside Viktor, but he remained rooted to the spot in front of the man's desk.

The official passed a single sheet of paper to Viktor. "This is the information for your daughter. She will depart with the rest of the athletes in three weeks."

"What about me and the rest of my family?"

The man feigned ignorance. "Your family?"

"Yes. The arrangements were made over a month ago," Viktor said. "We were granted permission to accompany Sonya to Canada."

"There is no mention of this here."

Disappointment swamped over him, but Viktor kept his expression neutral. "Who do I need to speak with to get this corrected?"

"It came from the field support office. You need to talk to the director or one of his aides."

The runaround. Viktor knew it well. He nodded and left the office.

Gathering his courage, he made his way to the appropriate office, bracing for what would come next. His contact with the Americans had cast a shadow of suspicion over him. Now he needed to find a way to dispel the concerns. If he didn't, he would never be able to see his sister again.

He went to three offices before he finally found the person who could make decisions on who could travel with the athletes to the world championships. Unlike his first stop, this office contained a single utilitarian desk that was empty except for a single notepad and pen.

"You say you were granted permission to travel with your daughter?" Grigori Lenkov asked, his voice clipped and impatient.

"Yes, sir."

"Why would the whole family need to go to Canada?" Grigori looked up and pushed his glasses more firmly onto the bridge of his nose. "Your daughter is sixteen. The team chaperone can tend to her without your assistance."

"I assist my daughter's coach, Pavel Turgenev, and my wife is a seamstress. She helps with the costumes for my daughter as well as the other skaters."

"And your son?"

"A translator." Viktor didn't mention that Josef had learned English and French by using books hidden beneath the floorboards in his bedroom.

"How did a boy who has never gone beyond secondary school get selected as a translator?"

"Coach Turgenev wanted someone who already had a knowledge of the skating team," Viktor said, not expounding further.

"I will have to speak to him before making any changes."

He didn't say no. Not yet, anyway. Viktor clung to that fact as he took a step back. "Thank you for your help."

"Mr. Petrov."

"Yes?"

"Don't think I am unaware of who your family is." He waved a hand through the air. "Even if you are granted permission to accompany your daughter, don't expect to spend any time away from the team."

"Of course." Viktor nodded. He left the office, his heart sinking. Which was worse? Remaining in Leningrad while Sonya traveled to Canada alone? Or making the trip, knowing he could end up in the same city as his sister and not get the chance to see her? His little sister, his best friend. His heart twisted in his chest as pain rose within him. Along with it came a flood of determination. He had told Amaliya to bring Katerina to Toronto. He had to do everything possible to be there too.

Chapter THREE

Tyler took his time unpacking despite the fact that most of his clothes went straight into the hamper. Then he stored his suitcases in the closet. He debated where to display his gold medal—was the shelf by the couch better, should he hang it on the wall, or should he protect it by hiding it out of sight? His sock drawer won that debate.

Next, he cleaned out the refrigerator in his tiny kitchenette. He checked the cabinets and made a grocery list. What he didn't do was go search out Robert to ask permission to marry Amaliya.

Tyler's insides seized, much like when he had been waiting to step onto the ice before he and Amaliya had competed in the Olympics, but this time, he didn't have Amaliya by his side, her hand in his. No, the uncertainty that pulsed through him was something he had to bear alone.

Tyler set his grocery list aside and stared at his front door. All he had to do was walk downstairs, pass through the garage, walk into the main house, and face the man who had only months ago seen Tyler as the enemy. Tyler suspected Robert would disapprove of any man who was dating his daughter. How would he feel now about the idea of his little girl getting married?

Nerves and a touch of nausea twisted inside Tyler. Not sure which was worse, the thought of facing Robert or the act itself, Tyler forced himself to move toward the door. He could do this. He hoped.

He made it as far as the kitchen in the main house before his footsteps slowed and he debated how to approach his future father-in-law.

Possible greetings were still rolling through his mind when he reached the living room at the same time Robert walked in from the entryway.

"Hey, Tyler. Have you seen Amaliya?"

"No. Sorry. I've been in my apartment."

Robert grabbed his coaching briefcase from where it lay on the couch. "If you see her, can you tell her we have reservations at Gadsby's Tavern for Saturday night to celebrate?"

"Sure." Tyler swallowed and forced himself to ask, "Do you have a minute? I wanted to talk to you about something."

Robert glanced at his watch. "Sorry, but I have a game tonight. I'm already running late for my team meeting."

"Oh." Relief and regret fought for dominance.

Robert passed him and headed for the door leading to the garage. "I'll see you tomorrow."

"Good luck tonight."

"Thanks."

Robert was barely out the door when Amaliya came down the hall. "Was that my dad?"

"Yeah. He said to tell you he made reservations for Saturday night to celebrate."

Amaliya glanced over her shoulder before she crossed to him and lowered her voice. "Did you already talk to him?"

"I tried, but he was running late for a meeting."

Disappointment darkened Amaliya's face.

"I'm sorry." Tyler headed into the living room, glancing back as he added, "I'll talk to him tomorrow."

"When?" Amaliya followed him. "We have early practice, and Papa will be at his practice by the time we get back."

"Maybe I'll have time before dinner." A new wave of anxiety rushed through Tyler, and he gripped the back of the couch.

"Maybe."

"I'm sorry. I should have come over earlier," Tyler admitted. And he meant it. He would love to be on the other side of the conversation with Robert instead of still having the uncertainty running through him.

"Why didn't you?"

"I was stalling."

Amaliya fisted her hands on her hips. "I thought you said my dad didn't intimidate you."

A conversation from last year repeated in his mind. "No. I said I wasn't going to let him chase me away," Tyler corrected. "Your dad is plenty intimidating."

"You need to talk to him." Amaliya closed the distance between them and reached up to kiss him.

The moment her lips touched his, Tyler's nerves of a moment ago settled and faded into the comfort of the familiar. His hands lifted to tangle in the silkiness of her hair. His pulse thickened, and a deep yearning seeped through him.

Tyler drew her closer, his desire to have Amaliya in his life growing until it threatened to overwhelm him. He wanted Amaliya to be his wife; he wanted to be the man she could always rely on. She deserved nothing less than to know she could count on him for anything, including facing her father.

She pulled back, and her gaze met his. "I really would love to share our dreams with our parents."

"I know." A new resolve rose within him. "Trust me, I want to have this conversation behind me as soon as possible."

"You just said you were stalling."

"I was." He took her left hand and lifted it to his lips. "But I'm ready for the world to know how lucky I am. Part of that is making sure you can wear your ring without your father grabbing a shotgun."

"He owns a rifle, not a shotgun."

A new bout of nerves tangled inside Tyler. "I really wish you hadn't reminded me of that."

Amaliya laughed and kissed him again. "It'll be fine. I promise."

Artyom Belsky was doomed. Or he would be if he achieved the same results as his predecessor. The Soviets had entered the Olympic Games with skaters ranked in the top three spots in every figure skating event, and they had the advantage of competing at home, yet they had managed only two medals, neither of them gold. The former director of amateur ice skating had been relieved of his post within hours of the final competition.

"A silver medal? A bronze?" Grigori Lenkov slashed his hand through the air, his imposing stature making the gesture that much more threatening. "Competing in Leningrad was supposed to give us a competitive advantage."

Artyom stood at attention in front of his superior and nodded solemnly. "Yes, sir."

"What happened?" He planted his hands on his massive wooden desk and leaned forward, his glasses slipping halfway down his nose. "Why did our athletes fail?"

"Many reasons." Artyom swallowed hard, uncertain if his assessment was wanted. Despite Grigori's position as executive director of the Olympic

Committee, Artyom doubted the man had paid attention to anything at the Olympics beyond the medal count and his precious hockey team.

Several seconds passed in silence before Grigori pushed his glasses back in place and let out an impatient huff. "Well?"

Artyom started with the least offensive challenge. "Our top ice dancing pair suffered from a bout of the flu as the Games began."

"I'm aware of their inability to overcome the physical challenges they suffered, but what of the others? Popov and Sidrova were expected to win, as was Zakharova." Grigori picked up a newspaper and waved it for emphasis. "Had Sonya Petrova not done well, we wouldn't have even medaled in the women's event."

"Zakharova's coach believes his skater suffered from nerves." Artyom braced for the next verbal attack. "They are working together on correcting the problem."

"Perhaps we should focus more on elevating Sonya Petrova's difficulty so she will have more potential to score higher and move up in the standings."

"I will address that with Coach Turgenev."

"Good. And what of this American pair who won? They had never even placed on the world stage, much less been expected to win."

Artyom swallowed. He didn't want to contradict his superior, but in truth, the American pair had been on his radar since they'd placed in the Americans' national competition. "Actually, they nearly won at the world championships last year. Their accident took them out of competition."

"The accident Popov and Sidrova were blamed for?"

"Yes, sir." Artyom forced himself to share the rest of Linden and Marcell's background. "We now know that Amaliya Marcell is not only the daughter of Soviet defector Katerina Petrova, but she also benefited from her mother's influence in creating her routines."

"Katerina Petrova." Grigori spat out her name as though he were expelling poison. "The woman has taken what was given her and has used it as a weapon against us."

Eager to direct Grigori's anger anywhere but at him, Artyom nodded vigorously. "Yes. She must have been behind the decision to use a Russian folk song for their short program. The choreography was, in essence, a modification of a dance all Soviets are familiar with."

"They used our own culture to capture the crowd."

Perhaps Grigori had watched some of the ice-skating competition after all.

Grigori dropped the newspaper he held onto his desk and paced to the window behind him. "What can be done to interrupt their success at the world championships?"

"I don't think there is anything we can do." Artyom curled his fingers into his palms to keep from fidgeting. "After the accident last year, the event organizers will surely keep Linden and Marcell in a different practice session than our skaters."

"It would be best if any ill fates can't be traced back to us anyway." Grigori gazed out the window for a long moment. "Surely other skaters would benefit if Linden and Marcell were no longer part of the competition."

Artyom's jaw clenched. Elevating his athletes through training and steroids when necessary was one thing, but causing physical harm to the competition wasn't a skill he cared to develop. "Surely there must be another way."

"If you are not able to follow through with what must be done, I will find someone else who can."

Panic skittered through him. Failure at his job could mean being demoted to a much less desirable position or even banished to Siberia. He didn't want to go to Siberia. He would never see his grandmother again, not to mention he would never survive a winter there. With his asthma, he wasn't sure he would last more than a few months regardless of the season.

Artyom grasped for the right words. "I simply meant an accident could still be blamed on us even if we are careful. Perhaps another means of distracting the American pair would be more effective."

Grigori pursed his lips as though deep in thought. "You say Katerina Petrova is involved in her daughter's skating career?"

"We believe so."

"Then perhaps it is time for Katerina to be removed from the equation."

Kill a former Soviet citizen on foreign soil? Dread filled him. "You don't mean . . ."

"There are more ways to take care of a problem than ending a life," Grigori said, clearly understanding where Artyom's thoughts had gone. "Our skating program would benefit from such a talent, don't you think?" Grigori settled into the chair behind his desk. "And it would be a boost for our nation's morale to see one of our former ballet stars choose to return to her homeland after suffering for so many years living in America."

"You think Katerina Petrova would be willing to come home?"

"I believe she could be persuaded."

Persuaded or forced? Artyom swallowed hard. Grigori's tone suggested it would most certainly be the latter.

Chapter FOUR

Despite her fatigue from the long day of travel, Amaliya made her way into the dance studio where she had studied ballet for most of her life. The high ceilings and mirrors on the walls enhanced the generous space, the three framed photos on the far wall adding the personal touch that always inspired Amaliya to be her best.

The photo with her and Tyler skating had been a recent addition, as had the one of her father playing hockey. It was the image in the center that drew her attention now: her mother as a young ballerina, her body graceful as she executed a grand jeté.

Her mother had been one of the premier ballerinas when she'd defected from the Soviet Union. She had kept her heritage alive by sharing her native language and her love of dance with Amaliya, yet there were so many details of her mother's early life that Amaliya still didn't understand.

She could only imagine the turmoil her mother had experienced when she had made the decision to stay with Amaliya's father. Two paths, two possible futures. Since the press interview at the airport, Amaliya had gained a new understanding of how difficult that choice must have been. Even though her own options for her future didn't include the danger of losing her freedom, Amaliya couldn't keep the weight of what would come next from filling her mind. What did she want to do after she and Tyler competed in worlds?

And what about their personal lives? Her parents had waited a few years before having her. Would Tyler be okay with giving them time to be a married couple before adding children to the mix? She hoped so.

Someone approached from the hall. Amaliya glanced over her shoulder as Tyler entered the room.

"Don't tell me you want to practice tonight," he said.

Amaliya shook her head. "I was just thinking."

"About your mom's reaction to your news?"

"Yes." Among other things. Amaliya crossed to the barre that stretched along one wall and ran her hand along it. "It's been so long since she lived in the Soviet Union, but every time I talk to her about her brother, it's like she's under Soviet control again."

"In a way, she still is." Tyler moved to stand in front of her, his hand resting on the barre so he mirrored her. "We got a taste of what her life must have been like when the KGB was following us around in Leningrad."

Amaliya's chest tightened at the memory. The constant presence of the man assigned to observe them, the knowledge that every move was being monitored, the fear that a single misstep would cause them to be deported before they were able to compete. All of it had combined to leave her unsettled and more than a little paranoid.

"Imagine having that feeling of being watched for your whole life," Tyler continued.

"I barely survived the two weeks we had to deal with it," Amaliya said. "Still, it's not like any of those people will have control over Mama in Canada. She's an American citizen now."

"Viktor isn't."

Tyler's words brought with them a wave of apprehension. "Is this a terrible idea, to try to help Viktor see my mother?"

"It's what Viktor wants," Tyler said. "I suspect deep down, it's what your mom wants too."

"I hate that this is so complicated." Amaliya lifted a hand and waved to encompass the room. "I've grown up with so much, and my family in Leningrad can't even sit in their living room in the winter without wearing coats and wrapping themselves in blankets."

"Maybe we can help with that a little."

"In what way?" Amaliya's eyebrows lifted. "It's not like the Soviets will let my parents pay for a new heating system for them."

"No, but a new coat, some long johns, even a few sweaters might help."

"Assuming we'll even be able to see them."

"You and Sonya will be using the same locker room," Tyler reminded her. "We'll find a way."

"I hope you're right." Amaliya shook out her arms in an effort to release the tension that had settled in her shoulders. "Enough about this. Let's go put on the hockey game."

"I'll probably fall asleep in the middle of it, but I'll watch with you for a while." He glanced over his shoulder before he leaned in and his lips met hers.

Amaliya surrendered to the kiss. The familiar attraction and the warmth of their friendship sparked. She slipped her hands around his neck, and tingles worked their way from her fingertips all the way to her toes.

She pulled back and smiled up at him. "How did I get so lucky?"

"I'm the lucky one." Tyler slipped his arm around her shoulders and guided her out of the studio.

As soon as they were settled in front of the TV in the living room, the game on the screen, the volume on low, Amaliya asked, "Have you thought about what we should do next?"

"Worlds, then marriage." He laced his fingers through hers. "That's my plan."

"But then what?" Amaliya angled her body so she could face him more fully. She tucked one leg underneath her before she continued. "Do you want to go pro? Or do you want to try for the '88 Olympics?"

Tyler's brow furrowed. "I guess I always assumed we'd go pro after worlds."

Amaliya tried to picture it. A new city every day or two, skating routines for entertainment rather than competition. A hollowness spread through her. "It's hard to imagine a life on the road like we would have if we join the Ice Capades or Disney on Ice."

"Both shows take a break for a few months every year."

A few months of freedom, nine months of the same thing over and over again, all of it spent skating for someone who wasn't Gordon. Amaliya tried to push those thoughts aside and forced herself to address another aspect of the life she hoped to build with Tyler. "What about once we have kids?"

"We're both still young. We can take a couple years before we decide when we want to cross that bridge."

Relieved that he wasn't in a rush to start a family, her mind wandered. They were still young, and as much as she looked forward to having children, if they waited until after the next Olympics, she would still only be twenty-four or twenty-five when they started having a family. They could still compete. They could keep skating for Gordon. She tried to push that possible future aside and align her wishes with Tyler's. Going pro might not be so bad.

Tyler jutted his chin toward the television, where the Washington Capitals and the Philadelphia Flyers were still scoreless in the opening period. "Your parents both had nontraditional careers, and they've made it work."

"I guess so." Despite her words, a seed of doubt sprouted.

"Don't worry." Tyler stretched his arm out and drew her closer. "Everything will work out, both for us and for your mom and uncle."

"I hope you're right."

Katerina waited outside the locker room as one hockey player after another streamed out. She greeted them automatically, memories pressing to the forefront of her mind of a similar scene when she used to wait for her brother rather than her husband after hockey games. Granted, her brother had been only eleven at the time, but that didn't diminish the sense of familiarity.

Thoughts of her childhood rushed through her head as she let herself be transported back in time. Her family had been more blessed than many in their little village outside of Leningrad. Grapes on the vines growing along their fence, vegetables in the garden, firewood from the field of trees that lined their farm as well as from the nearby woods.

The fear that her defection had stolen that life from Viktor had haunted her, but according to Amaliya, Viktor had been permitted to keep the family farm. Part of it anyway.

The locker room door opened, and several more athletes emerged.

"Hey, Mrs. Marcell," the goalie said when he reached her. "Coach said to tell you he'll be out in a couple minutes."

"Thanks, Travis." She offered him a smile. "Great game tonight."

"Thanks." He continued past. "Have a good night."

"You too." Katerina turned her attention back to the now-closed locker room door. How many days had this scene been reversed when Viktor had waited for her after she'd performed? Her career with the Kirov Ballet had kept her so busy that often the only opportunity she'd had to see her family was when they'd come to watch her dance.

From the age of ten, she had spent most of her childhood and all of her teenage years living first at the Leningrad Choreographic School and then in the housing designated to the Kirov.

The last time she'd seen Viktor had been several weeks before she'd left for her North American tour with the ballet. Would she even recognize him after all these years?

The door opened again, and Robert walked out, his coaching briefcase in his hand.

"Sorry I took so long." Robert leaned in for a quick kiss. "Stevens had an injury we needed to assess."

"His knee again?"

"It's his ankle this time. Looks like a mild sprain. Doc is sending him in for an X-ray just to be sure." Robert slipped his free arm around her waist, and they headed for the exit. "How are you doing with Amaliya's news?"

"I'm still trying to make sense of it all," Katerina said. "I was so afraid Viktor would lose the farm, or worse."

"I know." Robert gave her waist a squeeze. They walked in silence until they passed by the security guard and made their way to the car. When they were safely inside, Robert started the engine and waited a minute for the heater to start working. "Tell me what you're thinking."

Katerina didn't have to ask what he was referring to. He knew her too well. "I want so badly to see Viktor, but I'm afraid of what will happen to him if he's seen with me." Katerina swallowed hard. "I'm afraid of what will happen to me if I'm recognized."

"Katerina, he's your brother. You've prayed for this opportunity since the moment you escaped." Robert reached out and tucked a lock of hair behind her ear. "You can't let this pass."

"I can't risk Viktor."

"We've outsmarted the KGB before. We can do it again." Robert leaned in for a kiss. "I hate seeing you beat yourself up over your choice to stay in the United States. It's time to put that guilt to rest."

She couldn't deny that her concern for her brother and what he must think of her decision had festered inside her, creating a pool of guilt and regret that had caused her to avoid the mere mention of her family. "We barely escaped last time, and that was with help."

"So we bring in help." He leaned over and gave her another kiss, the connection between them every bit as strong as when they'd first fallen in love. Her blood heated despite the cold. When Robert pulled back, he settled into his seat. "I'll call Miles tomorrow. We only have a few weeks to make our plans for you to see Viktor."

A wave of anticipation, with a slice of fear, flowed through her. "I'm not sure any amount of time will be enough to find a way to get past the security that will surround Viktor and his family."

"They're your family too," Robert reminded her. "I'll make some calls to see if I can find out where they're staying."

"You don't have time for this."

"You're right." Robert put the car in gear. "We'll have Miles make the calls."

"Trying to get him to pay for the long-distance bill?"

"Nah." Robert backed out of his parking space and then pulled out onto the road. "That's just a side benefit."

Katerina couldn't help but laugh. "If I'm able to see Viktor while we're in Canada, we're paying the long-distance bill."

Robert glanced at her. "So, you're willing to try?"

Katerina ran her hand over the smooth leather of the seat. She had been so blessed here in America. If, perhaps, she could share some of what she had with her brother, even if it was only some money, it could make a huge difference in Viktor's life back in Leningrad.

She waffled for a moment between her overwhelming desire to see Viktor and the bone-jarring fear for his safety. "As long as we do everything we can to protect his safety, I want to try."

Robert reached over and put his hand on hers. "We'll find a way."

Another blade of fear sliced through her, but with it came a glimmer of hope. "I pray you're right."

Viktor turned his work truck onto the dirt driveway that led to what was left of his family property. The fields adjoining his land only made up five acres, as compared to the twenty-seven his family had once controlled before communism and his sister's defection had whittled away at their possessions.

He parked in front of the simple farmhouse that had been built nearly a century before. So many memories had been born here. Summers running through the fields with Katerina, picking berries and grapes, and eating them to their heart's content when no one was looking. Winters huddling by the wood stove while their mother read from the Bible or the storybook she kept hidden under the floorboard in what was now his bedroom. So many memories flowed through him, memories he had tried to re-create for his own two children despite the stigma that had come from being related to a known defector.

Everything had changed so quickly in his life. One minute, he and Ursula had been looking forward to the birth of their second child and Katerina had been one of the rising stars in the Kirov. And the next minute, in less than a month's time, Ursula had suffered a miscarriage and Katerina's fame had transitioned from a source of pride to a source of humiliation.

He pushed aside the old hurt that surfaced. Regardless of the fact that Katerina had let a Westerner influence her to stay in the United States instead of returning to her family in Leningrad, Viktor needed to see her. He needed to know for himself that she was safe and happy. He needed to know he hadn't failed his parents in his promise to watch after his little sister. Even more than that, though, he longed to hear her voice, to see her face, to hear her laugh. Despite the years that had passed, he still missed her.

He lifted the handle and used his shoulder to open the door. The blast of frigid air whipped into the truck and penetrated his threadbare coat. He quickly climbed out and hurried into the house.

The warmth of the wood stove welcomed him, but he kept his coat in place. Even though it was warmer inside the house, the old-fashioned heating system wasn't enough to eliminate the need for outerwear.

The scent of bread baking drew him through the narrow living room and into the even narrower kitchen. Ursula stood at the stove, a stained apron wrapped around her ample waist, a spoon in her hand as she stirred the stew.

She looked up and hope illuminated her expression. "Did you get the travel papers?"

"Not quite."

Skepticism replaced the hope. "What happened?"

"I have Sonya's travel information, but none of us are listed with her."

"Pavel promised he would let us come." Ursula set the spoon aside and put a hand on her hip. "Is this because of Amaliya?"

"I don't know." Viktor didn't share his suspicions that his niece's presence in their home had likely cost them the opportunity to see life outside their little corner of the Soviet Union. "I'll talk to Pavel at practice tomorrow."

The door opened, and Josef entered, carrying an armful of firewood. He set his load in the wooden box beside the stove.

"How much wood do we have left in the cellar?" Viktor asked.

"It should last the few weeks until we leave for Canada," Josef said.

"We'll need to cut some more tomorrow."

"Why?" Josef asked. "Leaving fuel here is asking for someone to steal it."

"I want to make sure we have some when we get home. We can hide some beneath the floorboards if we need to." Viktor didn't add that he wasn't sure any of them would be leaving their home for the trip to Canada after all. Josef already had enough hostility toward Americans, and he hadn't been thrilled when Viktor had had Amaliya visit their home two weeks ago. Had it really been only two weeks since he had met his niece and learned about his sister's life in America?

"Did you get the travel papers?" Josef asked. "I need to show them to my boss so I can have the days off for our trip."

"Not yet."

Josef's jaw tightened, and the muscle in his cheek jumped. "What happened?"

"Just a little mix-up." Viktor set out the bowls on the table.

Josef's dark eyes went almost black. "It's Aunt Katerina's influence again, isn't it?"

"You can't blame everything on my sister," Viktor said. "It's rare for an entire family to be approved for international travel."

"You can't let Sonya go by herself," Josef insisted. "What happens if some Canadian convinces her to stay like Robert did with Aunt Katerina?"

"Your sister is hardly old enough to decide to stay in Canada for a man." Viktor never should have let Josef read the letters Amaliya had given Viktor from his sister. While Viktor had taken comfort in learning of his sister's success and good fortune, Josef had scoffed at her excess and was convinced she had been coerced to leave behind their way of life. As a result, his anti-American sentiment had only deepened, as had his paranoia.

"She's old enough to say she wants to defect," Josef countered.

"That's enough," Viktor said sharply.

Footsteps approached from down the hall, and Sonya entered the room. "Who is old enough to defect?"

"No more talk of this," Viktor said.

Ursula walked in holding three bowls, one nestled into the crook of her elbow and one in each hand. "Sonya, go get the last bowl from the kitchen. The bread too."

Sonya crossed into the kitchen and returned with her dinner and a small, round loaf of bread.

"I'm sorry there wasn't more," Ursula said. "The store didn't have any meat today."

Viktor took a bowl from her and looked inside. Boiled potatoes. Again. "This is fine."

"Maybe in Canada, we'll have something to eat besides potatoes." Josef sat on one of the mismatched chairs closest to the stove.

"Be grateful we have food on our table," Ursula said.

"But not enough heat to be able to sit at it," Josef countered.

The complaint was one Viktor had heard before, but the sarcasm in Josef's voice had a sharper edge than Viktor was accustomed to. Viktor let his spoon clatter into his bowl, and he glared at his son. "What would you have me do?"

Josef pressed his lips together briefly before he spoke. "Nothing, Papa. Nothing at all."

Chapter FIVE

The disadvantage of living in a house with a dance studio was that Tyler never had an excuse to skip dance class. Not that he usually minded, but after traveling for so many hours yesterday, it would have been nice to have a few more hours off.

He made his way through the living room. The clock said daytime, and so did the sunlight streaming through the front windows, but his body still wasn't sure whether it was day or night.

Amaliya walked down the stairs as he approached the entryway. Her dark hair was pulled back in a tidy bun, and she wore a white leotard and sheer ballet skirt that showed off her legs. Okay, so maybe dance practice wasn't all bad.

Her face brightened when she spotted him. "Good morning." She descended the last few stairs and greeted him with a kiss.

"Morning." Tyler lifted his hand to hold her in place. After a quick glance around to make sure they were really alone, he leaned in for another kiss.

When Amaliya pulled back, she asked, "How did you sleep?"

"I feel like I should still be asleep."

"I know what you mean." They reached the studio and walked inside, where Katerina was talking to Gordon.

Katerina greeted Amaliya in Russian and then said in English, "You're just in time."

"In time for what?" Tyler asked.

"To redo your short program."

Tyler couldn't have heard her right. "Redo our short program? In less than a month?"

"We're not talking about a complete overhaul." Gordon held up a record. "But a change of music and a couple tweaks will go a long way."

"What kind of tweaks?" Amaliya asked, as though a change in routine were no big deal. But it was a big deal. They'd spent more than three months practicing their programs for nationals and the Olympics. To redo one with less than a month until their next competition was terrifying.

"Don't worry." Gordon put his hand on Tyler's shoulder. "We're just planning to change the opening to match the new music and add a different transition for your ending."

So they would be redoing a third of their short program rather than the whole thing. That wasn't much better.

Amaliya crossed the room and retrieved a notepad from beside the record player. "What else do you want to change?"

"I want to put a triple twist lift where the death spiral is and move the death spiral to where we have the fish lift."

"That's increasing our difficulty a ton," Amaliya said.

Tyler shook out his arms at the thought of adding such a challenging element into their short, especially knowing they would repeat it during their long program.

"It's a bit of a risk, but if we go into worlds expecting a repeat without making any changes, the odds will be stacked against you," Gordon said.

"If you knew we would need to make a change, why didn't you start prepping us for this before the Olympics?" Tyler asked.

"Because you needed to focus on the Olympics." Gordon cocked his head to one side. "Even though I told you a gold medal was possible, you didn't truly believe me until it happened. We also didn't know how much difficulty Popov and Sidrova had in their routines."

"That's true." The details of their Olympic competition played through Tyler's head. "If they had skated a clean program, they could have ended up with the gold instead of us."

"Don't second-guess your success," Gordon said. "This isn't about the Olympics. It's about the world championships. The judges appreciate knowing the athletes are treating worlds as a separate competition."

Don't second-guess your success. Tyler repeated the words in his mind but didn't manage to get them to sink in. Had their win at the Olympics been a result of the Soviet pair's mistakes? Or were he and Amaliya really the best pairs skaters in the world?

Amaliya jotted down a few notes.

Even though Tyler couldn't imagine them pulling off such a change in only a few weeks, he forced himself to ask, "Amaliya, what do you think?"

"We'll have to tweak a couple of transitions." She looked up at him, hesitation flashing in her expression before she masked it. "If we can pick our music quickly, I think it's possible."

"We already narrowed down the selections for you." Gordon removed the record he held from the paper sleeve and set it on the record player. "This is our first choice."

"What is it?"

"It's another Russian folk song, but this version has a bit more of a western European flare." Gordon turned on the record player and set the needle on the record.

Unfamiliar music filled the room, the tempo not dissimilar to the music they had used for their short program for the Olympics.

"It's got a good beat," Amaliya said.

Katerina nodded. "That's what I thought too."

Tyler tried to envision moving to this music. He could more easily than he'd expected. That was a good sign. "It's one the crowd can clap along to."

"Shall I show you the opening sequence I had in mind?" Katerina asked.

Amaliya set her notepad aside. "Let's see it."

Katerina explained the movements, both for Tyler and for Amaliya. The energy of the movements, the quick tempo—both would play well to the judges and the crowd.

Tyler tapped his fingers against his leg in time with the beat and tried to visualize skating to this music.

"Let's get you two warmed up so we can give it a try." Katerina motioned for them to take their positions at the barre. After they stretched, Katerina demonstrated the movements a second time, instructing each of them to follow along with her, their steps modified to adjust to practicing on solid ground instead of on ice. After two run-throughs, Katerina had them work together.

Amaliya took her position with her back to Tyler's. Gordon started the music, and they both went into motion. Tyler missed a step and got out of time with the music by the end, but overall, they made it through without any huge errors.

"Not bad." Gordon focused on Katerina. "What do you think? Do we have time?"

"Most certainly." Katerina nodded. "Especially if Amaliya helps me choreograph the final sequence."

"I'd love to."

"Great. We'll work on that later. For now, let's get this segment down." Katerina instructed them on the corrections they needed to make. She then motioned to the record player. "Gordon, start that again."

This time, the dance flowed smoothly, with only a few minor errors.

"Much better." Katerina nodded her approval. "Again."

Tyler took his starting position with Amaliya again, the events of the past half hour catching up with him. They were really moving forward with a new routine. They must all be crazy.

Amaliya scribbled notes in her sketchbook, ideas flowing on how she and Tyler could adapt their short program for the world championships. Exhilaration rushed through her as she considered the possibilities. The thrill of the challenge, the anticipation of the next competition welled up inside her, feeding the drive to show the world and herself that she and Tyler had what it took to be the best.

Tyler walked into the room from the kitchen. "Hey. What are you up to?"

"I was just playing around." She looked up as he sat beside her. "I want to come up with something different going into our triple twist so it doesn't feel like the same move as in our long program."

"What did you have in mind?" Tyler stretched his arm along the back of the couch, and she settled against him.

"I think we could do a version of the footwork section we're taking out of the later part of the program." Amaliya held out her sketch and pointed. "That would leave us several seconds going into our throw triple lutz to add another dance element."

"You're adding a lot of difficulty up front."

"We don't have much of a choice if we're adding the triple twist lift."

"What else do you have?" Tyler moved closer.

Amaliya explained her ideas and the resequencing of the elements they had discussed during their dance class that morning.

"You've really got a knack for this," Tyler said, admiration in his voice.

Warmth spread through her at the compliment. "Thanks."

"Between you and your mom, we may have our whole routine reworked by tomorrow."

"That's my plan." Amaliya tapped a finger on her sketchbook. "If Mama will work with us in the studio again tomorrow, we really could have the whole routine done by tomorrow night."

"That would be nice since we need as much time as possible to get used to the new sequencing."

"And the new music," Amaliya added.

"Yeah, that too."

Eleanor walked out of the kitchen. "Did you two want to eat some lunch before practice? I have some roasted chicken for you."

"That sounds great," Amaliya said.

Tyler stood up. "I missed being spoiled like this when we were in the Soviet Union."

"I thought they took good care of the athletes at the Olympics," Eleanor said.

"They did, but not the way you do."

"That's sweet." Eleanor's cheeks flushed as she smiled. "Now, come eat before it gets cold. I'm going to let Gordon know lunch is ready."

Eleanor took only a few steps before Gordon emerged from the hall.

"Is lunch ready?" he asked.

"It's on the table." Eleanor said.

Amaliya set her sketchbook aside and stood.

"Bring that with you." Gordon started toward the kitchen. "I want to see what you have planned for your short program."

"Were you eavesdropping on us?" Amaliya asked.

"No. Why?"

"Because we were just talking about possible changes to our short program."

"I figured as much," Gordon said. "I knew you wouldn't be able to stand it until you had the new routine sorted out. You are done with it, aren't you?"

"Just about." Amaliya grabbed her sketchbook and walked into the kitchen with everyone else, then sat at the table, where three plates were already set out for them. The men sat on either side of her.

"Show me what you've got," Gordon said, ignoring his food.

Amaliya handed him the sketchbook and outlined her suggested changes.

"You know, you could make a career out of choreography. You're good."

A sense of accomplishment washed over her. "Thanks."

Gordon studied the sketches a moment longer before focusing on Amaliya and Tyler again. "We'll work on the first half of the new routine at practice today."

"Can I just ask one question?" Tyler asked, the reservations he had shown earlier surfacing again.

"What's that?" Gordon asked.

"Have we all gone insane?"

"Nope," Gordon said without hesitation. "I have faith in you. To be honest, I think you'll do better by having some fresh moves to focus on."

"Why is that?" Amaliya asked.

"Complacency can lead to mistakes. The changes will force you to focus."

"You love throwing new challenges at us, don't you?" Tyler asked.

"It's what I live for." Gordon handed the sketchbook back to Amaliya. He lowered his voice to a whisper so Eleanor couldn't hear. "Besides, Amaliya needed something to keep her mind off the ring she isn't wearing."

Amaliya glanced down at her bare hand. She'd barely thought about her engagement since she'd started working on the new choreography. "You're good."

Gordon nodded. "Yes, I am."

Chapter SIX

THE ATTENDANT AT THE RINK entrance snapped to attention when Artyom walked inside, bringing with him a blast of arctic air into the already chilly interior. Music played through the overhead speakers, or, rather, the single speaker that still worked. And Grigori wondered why their skaters weren't rising to the top. If he put half the money into the practice rinks for the figure skaters as he did for the one reserved for his hockey players, they might very well win gold in every event.

Sonya Petrova executed a series of spins, her body every bit as graceful as her aunt's. Artyom had seen Katerina Petrova perform with the Kirov before she'd gone on the American tour that had stolen her away from the Soviet people. She hadn't yet been promoted to principal dancer at the time, but anyone in the audience could see she had the talent for a bright future.

Sonya's transition into her next move wasn't as smooth as Artyom would have liked. Her coach must have shared the sentiment because he stopped her to give her instruction.

She started the sequence again. It was better but still not perfect. Would she be able to gain the perfection needed in the sport if she had a choreographer added to her coaching staff? What would Sonya think of having her long-lost relative return?

Artyom shook that thought away. It didn't matter what the young skater thought. She would do what she was told and perform to the best of her ability.

A man emerged from a doorway near the entrance. Artyom studied him for a moment. Viktor Petrov, Sonya's father. He watched his daughter for a moment before he disappeared back the way he had come. Suddenly, the whir of machinery competed with the music playing, the grinding of metal on metal screeching through the air. Petrov must be sharpening skate blades.

The exterior door opened, and a taller and younger version of Viktor Petrov entered. He crossed to the office where Viktor had disappeared. A moment later, the machinery turned off.

Voices carried to Artyom, muffled at first and then becoming clearer as the younger man's voice rose in volume.

"This is my chance to do something with my mind," the younger Petrov said. "I don't want to spend the rest of my life working at a glass factory."

"Be grateful for what you have," Viktor replied. "I will visit the travel office again as soon as Pavel calls them."

"Thank you, Papa." The younger man reached into his pocket and handed over a set of keys. "And thank you for letting me borrow the truck."

Viktor nodded. "I'll see you tonight."

The son said something else Artyom couldn't hear and then headed out the exit.

Artyom focused once more on the athletes before him. The music stopped, and the other skaters moved to the side. Popov and Sidrova stepped onto the ice and glided to the center. As soon as the reigning silver medalists took their starting positions, the music from their short program started.

The couple began their routine, and Artyom continued forward until he reached the rink's edge. The pair truly was amazing. Each movement flowed into the next; each skill was performed with precision. They were the best in the world, and they needed to be recognized as such.

Their coach caught sight of him and skated over.

"They look good," Artyom said.

"They looked good in the Olympics too." Coach Kuznetsov's words were tight, disappointment and anger humming through them.

"Yes, they did." Artyom faced the unanswered question head-on. "Why do you think they didn't win?"

"The judges put too much emphasis on the Americans' signature lift."

The lift had been beautiful, one resembling a pair of ballet dancers rather than skaters as Tyler Linden had held Amaliya Marcell over his head, her body arched gracefully with her hands reaching back toward the ice. Artyom kept his appreciation for the Americans' artistic ability to himself. "Do you think the judges at worlds will react in a similar fashion?"

"The possibility is there." Kuznetsov focused on his skaters as they executed their double axels. "My skaters will be ready. It would help them tremendously if the Americans had some new obstacles to overcome." His gaze never wavered when he added, "We all know an ill-timed injury can happen to even the best of athletes."

"Yes, I am aware." Artyom's back stiffened at Kuznetsov's calculated tone and lack of remorse. "A possibility has been discussed."

"Good." He gave an approving nod. "My skaters will be ready to take their proper place when the medals are awarded at the world championships." Kuznetsov moved away as though he were the person in charge instead of Artyom. Perhaps that assessment was correct. At the end of the day, no matter what Artyom did behind the scenes to boost the Soviet skaters in the standings, it would be the athletes and the coaches who would be lauded, not him. It would never be him.

Tyler spun through the air, his arms crossed tightly against his chest. Two and a half rotations, his skate landing solidly on the ice, Amaliya mirroring his movements.

"Better." Gordon skated toward them, a satisfied nod following the single word.

Tyler blew out a breath. The short program was coming together, albeit slowly. "I get the feeling you want us to add to our gold-medal collection."

"You both said you want to go out on top."

Go out on top. The words repeated through Tyler's mind. Go out. What would life be like when preparing for the next competition was no longer part of their world? A needle of disappointment pricked at him, but he pushed it aside. This part of his skating career was coming to a close. It was time to step into the real world, where he would receive a paycheck and didn't have to rely on others to help him put food on the table or pay for ice time.

"Let's see the transition from the new segment into the middle section. Go through the double axels," Gordon said, breaking into his thoughts.

Amaliya slipped her hand into his. "Ready?"

Tyler nodded and counted them off. He worked through the new dance move, grateful that they quickly returned to the familiar part of their routine. Love flowed through him as he pulled Amaliya into his arms for a brief moment before their combined strength sent her flying through the air for her triple lutz. They continued the next steps and performed their side-by-side double axels.

As soon as they finished, they both turned to receive the expected corrections from Gordon.

Gordon tilted his head to one side before nodding. "That was gold-medal worthy."

"Wow." Tyler turned to Amaliya. "Do you have a tape recorder with you? We may need to have him say that again to prove it happened."

"Sorry. You missed your chance." Gordon shrugged. "If I tell you that too many times, it will go to your heads."

"Gordon, we won the Olympic gold medal a week ago." Amaliya fisted her hands on her hips. "I think if we were going to let winning go to our heads, it would have already happened."

"Maybe, but no reason to take chances."

"So you always tell us," Amaliya said.

"It would be nice to have our phones back though," Tyler added. "I haven't talked to my sister since we got home."

"Tell you what. I'll let you have your phone long enough to call her and your parents when you're ready to announce your engagement." Gordon focused on Tyler. "Remember how I told you I don't want you stressed?"

"I remember." But remembering didn't erase the tension that gripped him at the mere thought of talking to Robert.

"Good," Gordon said. "I want the two of you focused on practice and preparing for the world champions, not stressing over what Robert is going to say about your plans."

His emotions in turmoil, Tyler managed to nod. "I'll talk to him tonight."

"Best to get it over with," Gordon said.

"Easy for you to say," Tyler muttered.

"Enough distractions for now." Gordon pointed at the ice in front of him. "It's time to get this short program ready. Opening sequence. Let me see it."

Tyler reviewed the new moves in his mind as he and Amaliya took their positions and counted off the first segment. The steps they had mastered in the dance studio flowed for the first ten seconds. Then Amaliya's skate collided with Tyler's, and he slipped, falling onto the ice.

Gordon skated closer. "That's not what I had in mind."

Tyler pushed himself to a stand, his apprehension surfacing. "I guess that wasn't gold-medal worthy."

"Not yet," Gordon said, "but it will be."

Katerina must be crazy to consider putting herself in the path of Soviet security forces again. All day, she had rolled the possibilities over and over in her head, but each time, she came to the same conclusion: if Viktor was allowed to come to North America, she had to do whatever she could to see him, if for no other reason than to know for herself that he had survived the aftermath of her defection and to beg his forgiveness for not coming home.

The garage door rumbled open, and she wandered from her bedroom to the main level. She passed through the empty living room into the kitchen. Also empty. Eleanor must have gone grocery shopping.

The phone rang, and Katerina plucked the receiver off the base. "Hello?"

"This is Stan Delworth calling from Cambridge Insurance. I'm looking for Amaliya Marcell or Tyler Linden."

Another endorsement request. Katerina reached for the pad of paper she kept beside the phone. "I'm sorry, they aren't home right now. If you would like to leave a message, I can pass it on to them."

Stan gave Katerina his phone number. Fully aware Robert and Gordon wouldn't want Amaliya and Tyler to deal with negotiations themselves, she said, "Amaliya and Tyler are still in training, so they aren't going to be returning any calls until after the world championships."

"Oh. Well, this is quite time sensitive."

It always was. "This is Katerina Marcell, Amaliya's mother. If you are calling to offer an endorsement deal to them, I would be happy to take down the details and discuss it with them."

"I guess I can do that." Stan gave the additional information.

After Katerina managed to get off the phone, she moved back into the living room. Endorsement deals, her daughter training for the world championships, her brother possibly coming to Canada. She needed to talk to someone. With the house currently empty, she sat on the couch and picked up the phone on the end table to dial the long-distance code followed by Linda Donnelly's phone number. Two rings was all it took before her friend answered.

"I was hoping you were home," Katerina said.

"Katerina, how are you?"

"I'm not sure." The old paranoia of expecting someone to be listening in on her phone calls surfaced. "I have a few things I would love to talk to you about, but I'd rather not do it on the phone. Any chance you and Miles can come visit for the weekend?"

"Is everything okay?" Linda asked.

"I think so, but I may need your help with something. Miles too."

"Let me see what I can do to free up my schedule. As soon as I talk to Miles, I'll let you know our plans," Linda said. "What can you tell me about how things are going down there? How are our Olympic champions?"

"They're surprisingly the same as they always are." Katerina smiled slightly. "They're at practice right now."

"They did say they wanted to add to their gold-medal collection."

"So I've heard."

"I'm sorry. I know how hard that must have been on you to have to stay home while all of us were in Leningrad with Amaliya."

Katerina fought back the regret. "No, I'm glad you were there for her when I couldn't be."

"You know we love her like she's our own, and we're here for you too."

"Thank you." Katerina was counting on it.

The garage door opened again. "I'd better go. It sounds like either Robert or the kids just got home."

"I'll talk to you soon."

Katerina hung up the phone, and a moment later, Robert walked into the living room. "Was that another endorsement request on the kitchen counter?"

"Yes. I need to put it with the others before Amaliya gets home from practice."

"Maybe it's time we let her know about them."

"Do you really think that's a good idea?" Katerina asked. "I doubt Gordon will want us giving the kids any distractions when they're so close to competing."

"Only one way to find out," Robert said. "We can talk to him while the kids are doing their weight training. They pulled in right behind me."

The door leading from the garage to the kitchen opened and closed, and Gordon walked into the living room. "Robert, can I borrow your office for an hour or so? The lightbulb on my projector is out."

"No problem, but we wanted to talk to you about all these endorsements the kids are getting." Robert glanced at the door to the kitchen. "Are they already in the weight room?"

"Yeah." Gordon took a step forward. "What's the deal with the endorsements? Are you getting pressure to give answers?"

"Several want the letters of intent signed before worlds so they can capitalize on the publicity that will surround them then." Robert sat beside Katerina. "I also wonder if Amaliya and Tyler should understand their options before they hang up their amateur careers."

"It's a fine line we're walking right now." Gordon put both hands on the back of the chair in front of him. "If we protect them from all of the noise of the world, they'll miss some opportunities, but there's also the risk that they'll feel pressure to win if they see the dollar signs being thrown at them."

"How did you handle it?" Katerina asked.

"Irene and I decided before we competed in the Olympics that we would make that our last season." Gordon circled the chair and sat down. "We started our careers with an ice show a month later and stayed with that until I started coaching."

"Gordon, maybe you should be the one to explain their options to them," Katerina suggested. "You've lived this life. They're only beginning their careers."

"If we're going to have the conversation before worlds, it's best to do it sooner than later. That will give them time to work through any nerves it might give them." Gordon leaned forward and rested his elbows on his knees. "Plus, if they sign the letters of intent before worlds, that could take away some of the pressure to repeat as gold medalists."

"How much will it affect them if they don't win gold?" Katerina asked.

"The Olympics are a bigger stage, but if they don't do well at worlds, some of those offers could be withdrawn if they haven't already signed the contracts." Gordon shrugged. "I've seen it happen before."

"Do you want us there when you talk to them?" Katerina asked.

Gordon hesitated. "Maybe it would be best if I talk to them alone."

Robert fell silent in that way he always did when he was debating whether to do what he wanted or what was best. Finally, he said, "I'll write up the list of the offers for you while you're using my office. Might as well make it easy for them to see what's out there."

"Thanks, Robert." Gordon stood and moved toward the hall. "Once you have that and I get through the film I took today at practice, I'll talk to Tyler and Amaliya."

As soon as Gordon left, Robert asked, "Are you sure we shouldn't be there too when Gordon talks to them?"

"It will be best for Tyler and Amaliya if they can make their own decisions without us interfering." Katerina reached out and put her hand on his. "I'm sure Amaliya will talk to us before she makes any decisions."

"She'd better."

Katerina laughed. "Careful. You're sounding like an overprotective father again."

"It's my best career."

Katerina leaned in and kissed him. "And you're a pro at it."

Chapter SEVEN

Viktor stood at the edge of the rink and watched in awe. His little girl spun around, one skate in contact with the ice, her free leg stretched out gracefully behind her. She completed her last rotation and planted her toe pick before raising her arms in triumph.

With her dark hair pulled into a tight bun, Sonya looked so much like Katerina when Katerina had been sixteen—the heart-shaped face, the blue eyes, the stage presence and confidence. What would the future hold for Sonya now that she was an Olympic medalist? Would she receive more privileges and more freedom to visit home, or would her training intensify as she pursued more medals and more glory?

During the Olympics, Sonya had been permitted to live at home to make room in the Olympic Village for the foreigners, but she would move back to her room tomorrow, after the last of the athletes left Leningrad.

Pavel Turgenev, Sonya's coach, skated to Sonya's side. "More tilt in your chin. Show me again."

Sonya nodded obediently and repeated the move.

Pavel moved to the side of the rink beside where Viktor stood. "Did you get the travel papers?"

"For Sonya." Viktor lowered his voice. "The rest of my family is missing from the travel list."

Annoyance flashed on Pavel's face. "I put the request in myself."

"Grigori Lenkov said he would speak with you."

"I don't have time for this nonsense." Pavel focused on Sonya again and pointed at an open patch of ice. "Figures. Show me a double tree." Sonya moved to the far side of the rink, and Pavel returned to Viktor's side. "You need to look at the blade sharpener. It isn't working again."

Viktor's heart dropped. Was Pavel going to ignore the fact that his family was no longer approved to accompany Sonya to worlds? "I'll take care of it."

Pavel gave a sharp nod. He pushed off and glided two strides before he turned back. "If I don't hear from the travel office by tomorrow, I'll make a call."

"Thank you." Some of the tension in Viktor's neck and shoulders eased. He headed for the equipment office and turned on the machine he used frequently to sharpen skate blades. Nothing happened. His eyebrows drew together. He'd just used it this morning.

He went through his usual check: power cord, motor, the blades, the rotors. When the typical problems didn't present themselves, he grabbed a screwdriver out of his toolbox and began the labor-intensive task of disassembling the machine.

Nearly an hour later, he discovered the problem: a wire had frayed and come loose. Doubtful that he would be able to get a replacement wire, he removed the damaged one and used pliers to repair it as best he could. Forty-five minutes later, he reconnected the power source to the engine, plugged in the machine, and hit the On button. The power indicator lit up, and Viktor blew out a sigh of relief.

Footsteps approached. He glanced at the service counter behind him.

Sonya reached the other side of the counter and held up her skates. "Papa, can you sharpen these for me?"

"Of course, milaya." Viktor took the skates and proceeded to sharpen each blade. When he finished, he handed them back.

"Thanks." Sonya placed her skate guards over the blades.

Viktor turned off the machine. "Are you ready to go?"

"Yes, but Coach Turgenev said I have to move back to my room in the city today."

Though the question of why burned on his tongue, Viktor swallowed it. He couldn't afford to appear uncooperative right now. "We'd better get you home to pack, then."

"Coach Turgenev said someone already went to the house and had Mama pack my things for me."

Viktor's heart sank. So much for explaining the travel situation to his daughter.

He took a step forward so only the counter separated them and put both hands on her cheeks and kissed her forehead. "Get a good night's sleep."

"I will, Papa."

Pavel walked around the edge of the rink, his own skates dangling from his fingers. "Did you get it working?"

"Yes."

Pavel set his skates on the counter. "I need these sharpened." He motioned toward the door. "Sonya, your driver is waiting."

Sonya cast a quick glance at Viktor before she turned and headed for the exit.

Viktor ignored the sinking sensation inside him and proceeded to sharpen Pavel's skates.

When Viktor handed them back, Pavel said, "I also need you to run the Zamboni before you leave."

Viktor nodded.

Pavel retreated the way he had come, leaving Viktor with a new question: Was Pavel really planning to help him get to Canada with Sonya, or was he one of the obstacles standing in Viktor's way?

Tyler's muscles trembled as he gripped the bar and pressed weights over his head. The home gym really was the perfect setup. A weight bench, barbells, an exercise bike, a rack of hand weights.

Robert had been generous in allowing Tyler to use the equipment whenever he wanted. He hoped that generosity wouldn't disappear once Tyler announced his intentions. He let the barbell rattle into the rack above him and shook out his arms. He was nearly done with his workout, and Robert was home. It was time to get this dreaded conversation over with. As soon as he finished another set.

Tyler leaned back on the bench and put his hands on the barbell, then straightened his arms and methodically lowered the bar to his chest before pressing it back into the air. He repeated the movement, counting in his head as he did so.

Gordon walked into the gym, and Tyler pressed the weights above his head two more times before he set the bar on the rack.

"Where's Amaliya?" Gordon asked.

"I think she's in the dance studio." Tyler slid forward on the weight bench so he could sit up. "She stretched with me after practice, but she said she wasn't up to weightlifting today."

"It takes a couple days to fight off the jet lag," Gordon said. "How are you feeling?"

"A little off but not too bad."

"You should cut your workout short today. I don't want you pushing too hard and ending up with an injury."

Gordon didn't have to tell him twice. Tyler stood and shook out his arms. "I'm going to shower before dinner." And before talking to Robert.

"I'll meet you in the kitchen when you're done. I have a few things I need to talk to you and Amaliya about."

"What kind of things?" A streak of apprehension pulsed through him. "Don't tell me you want to change our long program too."

"Nothing like that." Gordon shook his head. "Just shower and meet me in the main house in a half hour." He headed for the door. "I'll get Amaliya."

Tyler nodded. He put his weights away and then walked through the garage and up the stairs to his apartment. He took a quick shower and had barely finished getting dressed when a knock sounded on the door.

He checked the time. It had been only twenty minutes since Gordon had left him in the gym.

Still barefoot, Tyler moved to the door and pulled it open. Gordon stood on the other side.

"I thought you said we were meeting in a half hour," Tyler said.

"I did, but you have a phone call you're going to want to take."

"You're letting me talk on the phone when it isn't Sunday?"

"Just this once." Gordon motioned him forward. "Hurry up."

Tyler slipped his shoes on and followed Gordon downstairs. When they entered the kitchen, Amaliya stood next to the phone mounted to the wall, the receiver pressed to her ear.

Excitement illuminated from her, and she smiled. "Here he is now."

Amaliya handed him the phone.

"Who is it?"

"Carolyn."

His sister. His very pregnant sister. "Hey, sis. How are you?"

"Tired but okay."

A tiny cry carried through the line. Was that a baby? "Was that—Did you . . . ?"

"If you're trying to ask if your nephew arrived, the answer is yes." Despite the three thousand miles between them, Tyler could hear her smile.

His own lips curved into a grin. "Congratulations! Tell me the details."

"Six pounds eleven ounces. Twenty inches long."

"And his name?"

"Grant Andrew."

"After dad. I like it."

"Dad is over the moon," Carolyn said. "He's going to fly out here right after the world championships."

"What about mom?"

"She got here yesterday," Carolyn said.

"That was fast. She only left Leningrad two days ago."

"She was only home long enough to do laundry and have dad drive her to the airport," Carolyn told him. "I told her she could wait a few days before she came, but now I'm glad she didn't listen."

"Me too."

The baby cried again but, this time, with more volume.

"I'd better go," Carolyn said. "It sounds like Grant may be getting hungry."

"Congratulations again," Tyler said.

After he ended the call, Tyler turned to face Amaliya and Gordon. "I'm an uncle."

"I know." Amaliya grinned. "Can you believe it?"

"Not really." Tyler shook his head. "Carolyn's only two years older than me."

"Depending on when you two tie the knot, that could be you in a couple years," Gordon said.

A child of their own? Tyler let that thought roll through his head for a moment, not sure how he felt about going from being a couple to a family so quickly.

"Come sit down." Gordon motioned toward the kitchen table. "We have some details we need to go over."

Amaliya eyed him suspiciously. "Don't tell me you're changing our long program too."

"That's what I said," Tyler said.

"Your long program is staying as is," Gordon said. "Everyone in Canada will want to see you perform that one in person to see for themselves why you're the gold medalists."

"Then, what did you want to talk to us about?" Amaliya sat down.

"What comes after worlds," Gordon said.

Tyler furrowed his eyebrows and lowered himself into the chair beside Amaliya. "I thought you didn't want us to worry about that until after we compete."

"Typically, that would be true, but you both have some opportunities that you need to be aware of before then." Gordon picked up a stack of papers that lay on the counter before he took a seat across from Tyler and Amaliya. "You have had several endorsement offers."

"So quickly?" Amaliya asked.

"Your parents have been fielding calls from companies since right after you won gold."

Tyler's interest piqued. "What companies?"

"Here's the list and the amounts they're offering." Gordon slid a single piece of paper across the table.

Tyler's eyes widened. He had expected three or four companies, but the handwritten list filled the page. Two shoe companies, a department store, a pizza place, a clothing line, a fast-food burger chain, an insurance company, and the list went on.

"Oh, wow." Amaliya leaned forward. "They really want to pay us this much?"

"Endorsements can give you a nice little income, especially while you decide what you want to do next. The amounts will be a bit different if they sponsor you rather than endorse you, but either way, you have options."

"What's the difference between endorsements and sponsors?" Amaliya asked.

"In an endorsement, the two of you say you like a company or its products and they pay you," Gordon said. "Sponsors basically ask you to use their products in public, and in exchange, they help offset your training costs and possibly provide athletic gear."

"We can't make any money off sponsorships," Tyler elaborated.

"That's right. Most of your living expenses would still be your responsibility."

Gordon held up the next page on his stack. "Speaking of which, the casting director for the Ice Capades has also reached out. If you're interested, you can join their spring show, but they would need you to start rehearsals a week after we get back from worlds."

"That's quick," Tyler said.

"They want to make sure they get you locked in before anyone else has the chance to sign you," Gordon said. "Technically, you can't accept any of these offers while you're still competing as amateurs, but if you decide to go pro, we can have the contracts ready for you to sign right after you compete in worlds."

Tyler scanned over the numbers listed beside the various offers. "How many of these can we accept?"

"You'll have to choose between the different shoe and athletic wear companies, but most of the others are in different industries, so you can probably negotiate to do most of them."

Tyler did the math. "That's enough money to buy a house."

"If you want to go that route," Gordon said. "My wife and I waited until after we finished touring with the Ice Capades before we settled down and bought one."

Tyler studied the older man across from him. Gordon had lived so many of the experiences he and Amaliya now had laid out before them. The only difference was that Tyler and Amaliya had won gold, while Gordon and his late wife had just missed making the medal stand.

Gordon had made a life in the ice-skating world. Tyler and Amaliya could do the same.

"What do you think, Amaliya? What do you want to do?" Tyler angled his body so he could see her better. Before she could answer, he added, "Which companies do you like best?"

Amaliya shrugged, her face devoid of the excitement currently pulsing through him.

"What's wrong?" Tyler asked.

"It's a lot to think about," Amaliya said.

"You don't have to make any decisions now," Gordon said, "but I wanted you to be aware of your options."

"Thanks, Gordon." Tyler picked up the list of offers. "Can we hold on to this?"

"That's fine. Robert wrote the list for you."

Amaliya stood. "I'm going to find Mama and tell her about Carolyn."

Tyler watched her leave, unsettled by her odd reaction. "She didn't seem very excited about the possibilities."

Gordon shook his head. "No, she didn't."

Chapter EIGHT

Amaliya couldn't explain the tightness in her chest or the unsettled sensation that rippled through her every time she tried to picture herself moving forward with the plans Tyler was making for them. Or, more specifically, the plans he wanted to make for them.

Life on the road, one city after another, one hotel room after another. She struggled to picture it. Instead of practice sessions spent with Gordon, trying to improve her skills at every turn, she would only strive to maintain the ability to perform whatever choreography was assigned to them.

She wandered down the hall, past the empty dance studio, to the library, where light burned from within and spilled onto the hardwood floor. She walked inside to find her mom sitting at the little desk on the far side of the room.

Her mom turned and greeted her in Russian. "What are you up to?"

"I was looking for you." Amaliya circled the library table and sat in the chair closest to her mother. "Carolyn just called. She had her baby."

Her mom's face lit up. "Oh, that's wonderful."

"She has a little boy. Grant Andrew."

"And everyone is healthy?"

"Yes." Amaliya smiled. "Everyone is healthy." She shared the details, trying to imagine what it would be like to have a little one of her own. Was she even ready for motherhood? How long did Tyler want to wait after they got married to have children? Did he even want children?

"What's on your mind?" her mom asked.

"It's just hard to imagine how much will change in the next few years. Carolyn is only five years older than me, and she's already been married for three years, and now she has a baby."

Her mother reached out and took both of Amaliya's hands. "You're trying to picture your future with Tyler."

Amaliya let the truth spill out. "Yes." She tilted her head in the direction of the kitchen. "He's talking about what we can do with our endorsement money and how soon we can start working with the Ice Capades."

"I gather Gordon already talked to you."

"Since you aren't surprised by Tyler's plans, Gordon must have talked to you too."

Her mom nodded. "He spoke to me and your papa this afternoon."

Even though her insides were still churning with unidentified emotions, Amaliya asked, "What do you think about all of these opportunities?"

"I think it's wise that Gordon make you aware of all your choices," her mom said.

When she didn't continue, Amaliya asked, "But?"

"But none of us can make those decisions for you."

"What did Papa think?"

"About you touring around the country where he can't protect you?" Her mom laughed. "What do you think?"

"Since he wasn't thrilled about me joining the ballet when I was still in high school, I doubt he'll be happy about this prospect either."

"That was only two years ago."

"Yes, but there's a big difference between being almost eighteen and still in high school and being twenty and an Olympic champion."

"Maybe, but sometimes your papa struggles with the idea of you growing up and moving on with your life," she said. "At least he's finally gotten used to you dating Tyler."

"Thank goodness." Needing to test the waters, Amaliya asked, "How do you think he'll be when we decide to get married?"

Her mama laughed. "Before or after he banishes you to your room until you're thirty?"

Amaliya slipped her hands into the pockets of her warm-up pants. "I guess that means he isn't ready for that yet."

"He'll get there eventually." She narrowed her eyes. "Are you and Tyler already talking about getting married?"

"Maybe." But maybe it was best to keep that to themselves until after they competed. Her father's temper, when combined with his protective streak, was unpredictable, at best.

"Papa will think you're too young, but I know better. A lot has changed in the past couple of years." Her mom leaned back in her chair as though studying Amaliya from a new angle. "The question is, What do you want the next year or two to look like?"

Or the next four. The thought popped into Amaliya's head with unexpected clarity.

"It's something you need to think about," her mom continued. "You won't be happy if you fall in line with someone else's plans. You need to make sure your future is one you choose."

"You're right." Amaliya glanced at the small framed photo on her mom's desk of her mother's family from when she was a child. Her mother had been only about seven or eight when the picture was taken, Viktor a few years older. "I'm sorry seeing Viktor can't be part of your future."

"Papa and I have been talking about that." Her expression softened, and a glimmer of hope shone in her eyes. "If Viktor really does come to Canada, I want to see him."

"You do?"

"If I can talk to him without risking his safety."

"You don't really think anyone would try to hurt him for talking to you, do you?"

"Oh, milaya." Her mom rested her hand on Amaliya's knee and shook her head. "There are so many things you don't know about life on the other side of the Iron Curtain, experiences I hope you don't ever have to know."

Amaliya couldn't deny that she had been uneasy when the KGB had followed her and Tyler around Leningrad and when various amenities had stopped being available to them before they'd competed. She suspected her mother had suffered far worse.

"I have a better idea since visiting the Soviet Union," Amaliya said. "And I don't have to know everything to help. We need a plan."

"Your father said the exact same thing."

A tremor worked through Viktor when he entered his frigid living room. Why was it as cold inside as it was outside? He crossed to the wood stove and held out his gloved hands. No warmth radiated from within.

"Ursula?" he called, the scent of boiled potatoes carrying to him. "Why is the fire out?"

She appeared in the doorway from the kitchen, a quilt wrapped around her shoulders, a knit cap on her head. "When Vera came to pick up Sonya's clothes, they also took our firewood."

Fury spurted through him. "All of it?"

"Everything but the two pieces we had hidden beneath the floorboard. I thought it best to save those for tonight."

"Where is Josef?"

"He's not home yet." Ursula shivered. "He must have had to work late."

Viktor fought against his frustration. This wasn't the first time a Soviet official had taken advantage of the natural resources available to Viktor and his family. "I'll go chop some more."

Viktor retrieved the axe from behind the wood stove.

"Be careful."

Viktor nodded, then walked outside, the wind slicing through him.

His hand tightened on the wooden axe handle, and he prayed he would be able to cut enough wood to survive the night before he lost the feeling in his fingers. He grabbed the handle of the wooden hand cart beside the front porch and pulled it toward the woods.

His boots crunched on the snow-covered ground, his big toe going numb where it poked through the hole in his sock. The branches that had fallen in the last storm had already been picked over by his neighbors and whoever else dared travel this far from the city to find fuel for their fires.

In the fading light, Viktor identified a fallen tree that was too large for the city dwellers to scavenge without an axe or a chain saw. He raised his axe and used his strength to hack at the end of the thick tree. His efforts repeated until he was able to chop several pieces of wood off the fallen log.

Footsteps crunched in the snow, and Viktor turned, hopeful his son was coming to help. The man who approached was similar in height to Josef, around one point eight meters, but the thick coat and the fur hat were far too new to belong to anyone in Viktor's family.

"Mr. Petrov." The man's cool, blue eyes assessed Viktor. "I suspected I would find you here."

Viktor froze. The dark coat, the eerily calm voice. Was this man with the police? Or worse, the KGB?

"Taking more wood than you have been allotted without permission. That isn't wise."

Viktor's grip tightened on the handle of the axe. "Our wood was shared with the athletes. I am only trying to replace what we gave away."

"I see." The man drew closer, his face shrouded in darkness. "I understand you plan to visit Canada with your daughter."

Viktor fought the urge to question who this man was or why he was asking about his plans. If he knew about their planned travel, he was connected to the government somehow. "My plans are still unsettled."

"Perhaps I can help you."

"How?" The question escaped before Viktor could stop it.

"Your sister."

"I haven't seen my sister in over twenty years."

"Yes, but you could see her again." He took another step. "If you go to Canada."

"What is it you want of me?" Viktor clenched his teeth together to keep them from chattering.

"Wouldn't you like to have your sister home again?"

Even though Viktor wanted Katerina back in his life, he knew what happened when defectors were returned to the Soviet Union. A protectiveness for his little sister welled inside him. If the KGB let her live, she would become a prisoner with even less freedom than she'd had before she'd left the Kirov. "She no longer has a home here."

"That could change." The man didn't speak for a moment. Then he leaned down and picked up several pieces of wood out of Viktor's pile. "I suggest you get out of the cold."

Viktor debated whether to gather the rest of the wood before following the stranger's instructions. When the man turned and moved toward a vehicle parked on the road, Viktor gathered the firewood and loaded it into his cart, one hand still gripping his axe.

He returned to his house as someone approached from the opposite direction. Viktor slowed his steps. Relief flowed through him when he identified Josef.

"Why are you chopping wood? I did that yesterday."

"Mama had to share it today when Sonya's chaperone came by to gather her things."

Josef scowled, but he didn't address the unfairness of someone taking what should have been theirs. "Is this all you cut?"

"I'm afraid so." Viktor grabbed two pieces of wood from the cart, leaving the last three for Josef.

Josef opened the door, and they walked inside. Viktor set the axe aside and dropped the wood in the woodbox.

"Why were you so late tonight?" Viktor asked.

"My bus didn't come. I had to wait for the next one." Josef set down the firewood he had brought in and eyed the small stack. "This won't last us through the night. I'll go cut some more."

Apprehension rippled through Viktor. What if someone was still watching for them? He shivered again. They didn't have a choice. If they didn't get some heat, they would freeze to death. "I'll get some more," Viktor finally said. "You start the fire."

"Are you sure?" Josef asked.

"Yes." Viktor took the axe. "Take care of your mama."

"I will, Papa."

Viktor strode back into the cold and faced the uncertainty of what he would find in the dark.

Chapter NINE

Amaliya sat on the window seat in her bedroom and stared into the darkness. The fatigue from traveling on Monday still lingered, but she hadn't yet adjusted to sleeping as late as she normally did at home.

The faintest glimmer of light glowed in a long streak along the horizon, but daylight wouldn't arrive until she, Tyler, and Gordon were already at the rink.

For two years, she had spent six days a week learning and then perfecting the skills needed to become a competitive ice skater. Before that, she had spent her practice time in the dance studio in preparation to become a professional ballerina. A position with the Ice Capades would be similar to what she had expected to experience with the ballet: rehearsals followed by performances. So why was it that every time she thought of stepping into that life, a ball of lead sank to the bottom of her stomach and festered there? Could it be that with the ballet, she would have spent the majority of her time in one city? Or was it the idea of moving away from home in general? Or maybe it was the thought of skating without Gordon coaching her.

And then there were the endorsements. Smiling for cameras, putting herself on display, allowing the public into her private life.

She really didn't want to live like that, with people always interested in the minute details. She supposed the gold medals she and Tyler had won would garner interest regardless of what they chose next, but she rather liked the way the public forgot about them from one championship season to the next.

A heaviness settled in her chest, and she struggled against the sensation. She didn't have to make any decisions today. For the next three weeks, she could focus on the next competition and the expectations to do her best. Another knot of tension formed at the base of her neck. Their best would mean another gold medal. Anything less and they would fall short. And now it wasn't just their hopes and dreams on the line. It was the hopes and dreams of an entire country.

Pressure mounted inside her, and she rolled her shoulders in an attempt to fight against it.

She glanced at the clock. Nearly an hour of staring into space, yet she wasn't any closer to understanding her emotions or knowing what she wanted for her future. If they won gold again, perhaps that would prompt Tyler to change his mind about going pro. Maybe he would remember the thrill of winning and want to continue forward with their amateur career.

She stretched her arms and tried to shake away the uncertainty still humming through her. She slipped on her shoes and headed downstairs in search of breakfast.

When she reached the kitchen, Tyler was already sitting at the table with a yogurt and a banana in front of him.

"Is that all you're eating?"

"I already ate some scrambled eggs and a piece of toast." Tyler motioned to the stove. "There are more eggs in the pan."

"Thanks." Amaliya popped a piece of bread into the toaster before she retrieved a plate and scooped some eggs out of the skillet. Once she had her breakfast, she joined Tyler at the table.

Tyler glanced at the doorway before he leaned forward and kissed her. "Good morning."

Some of Amaliya's earlier anxiety faded. "Good morning yourself. Did you sleep okay?"

"I keep waking up early."

"Me too." Amaliya stifled a yawn.

Tyler hooked his arm around the back of her chair and leaned closer. "You know the best part about talking to your dad about our plans?"

"I didn't think there was a good part."

"Okay, the best part about after I talk to him?"

"What's that?" Amaliya asked.

Tyler peeled the foil off the top of his yogurt. "I won't feel like he's going to grab a gun every time he sees me kiss you."

Amaliya scooped a bite of eggs onto her fork. "I hate to break it to you, but I doubt Papa will ever get used to me kissing you."

His eyebrows rose. "Not even after we get married?"

"Not even then."

"I'm sorry I didn't talk to him last night like I'd planned. After the excitement about Carolyn's baby and then the endorsement offers, I got distracted. By the time I tried to go talk to him in his office, he was on the phone with his assistant coach, and it didn't sound like things were going well."

"They had a key player get injured last night. I'm sure they're trying to decide who to replace him with." Amaliya rubbed her thumb along the inside of her ring finger. As much as she wanted her engagement ring to reside there, her mom's comment about her dad's potential reaction had her reconsidering their timeline. "Are you sure you want to talk to Papa before worlds? Maybe it would be better to wait."

"I thought you wanted to be able to talk to your parents about what comes next."

"I do, but we just have so much going on right now, and I don't know how Papa will react." Amaliya shrugged. "Maybe waiting wouldn't be such a bad thing."

Tyler's eyebrows lifted. "You aren't having second thoughts about marrying me, are you?"

"No, not at all." Not about the marriage, anyway. She struggled to find her words. "With the stress Mama is under about seeing Viktor and with the pressure on us to win gold again, maybe now isn't the best time."

Tyler didn't say anything for a moment. Then he reached out and took her hand. "If that's what you want."

Relief flowed through her. "Thanks."

Tyler gave a slight nod before he released her hand and picked up his spoon. He motioned to her plate. "You'd better eat something."

Amaliya bit into a piece of toast. Too bad she couldn't have french toast or pancakes instead. Only a few more weeks of Gordon dictating her diet and her sleep schedule. That thought should fill her with joy, not regret. She looked over at the cookie jar on the counter. Something was seriously wrong with her.

The moment the doorbell rang, Katerina rushed to the door and pulled it open. Gratitude and relief swirled through her as she greeted Linda and Miles, her first American friends. She embraced Linda, the cold air sweeping over them both.

"I'm so glad you made it." Katerina stepped back and motioned them inside.

"Linda said it was important." Miles waited for Linda to walk into the house before he followed with their suitcases in hand.

As soon as Miles closed the door, Katerina reached out a hand. "Let me take your coats."

Miles set the suitcases down, and he and Linda both shrugged out of their coats. After Katerina hung them in the hall closet, she said, "Come in by the fire and warm up." She led the way into the living room, where flames licked at a thick log in the fireplace.

Linda sat on the couch. "Are you going to tell us what you were afraid to talk about over the phone?"

"It's about my brother." She lowered herself onto the couch across from Linda and Miles.

"Amaliya told us she met him in Leningrad. Such a miracle."

"Amaliya is hoping for another miracle in Canada." Despite the heat emanating from the fire, a chill worked through her. Katerina fought back the deep-rooted fear and clasped her hands. "I am too."

"Viktor is going to be at the world championships?" Miles asked, piecing the details together.

"That's what Amaliya said. I want to see him, but I don't know how I'll be able to get past the KGB. Not to mention, I don't want to risk Viktor's safety."

"What can we do to help?"

"I'm not sure, but I hope together we can find a way for me to see Viktor, if only long enough to tell him I'm sorry."

A wrinkle formed on Linda's brow. "How does Robert feel about you putting yourself in the path of the KGB? Are you at all worried about what they might do if they see you?"

"It's been almost twenty-five years. I'm not sure anyone would recognize me after all this time. That was half a lifetime ago."

"I hate to break it to you," Miles said, "but you haven't changed much since we first met you."

Her body tensed in the same way it had when she had been under Soviet control and had dared to stay up late to see Robert before they were married. Would she be noticed? Would anyone who knew her accompany the Soviet team? Questions circled through her head.

"What do you have planned so far?" Linda asked.

"Robert is going to take a week off from work to make sure I'm not alone."

Miles's eyebrows shot up. "He's volunteering to miss more games? He already missed two when he went to the Olympics."

"We got lucky. Robert's only game during the world championships is against Montreal, so he'll meet his team there and then come back to Toronto," Katerina said. "His assistant will run practices for him while he's away."

"How do you plan to see Viktor?" Linda asked. "Getting close to the Soviet team isn't going to be easy."

"I know." Had it not been for the adjoining balconies at her and Robert's hotel, she likely would never have had any contact with any Westerners.

Miles leaned forward. "We found a way to sneak you out of the ballet, past dozens of people who were supposed to prevent that. You only want to talk to your brother."

"Yes, but we still have to get past security." She fiddled with her wedding ring, twisting it back and forth.

"Leaving your brother behind has been your biggest regret since I've known you." Linda reached out and put her hand on Katerina's arm. "This is a chance you can't afford to miss taking."

"Linda's right," Miles said. "We'll find a way."

The band around Katerina's heart eased slightly. "I hope so."

Artyom approached Grigori's office, his steps slowing as he grew nearer. The conversation about Katerina Petrova still made him queasy, and the possibility of Grigori handing the task off to him of "returning" her to the Soviet Union had his heart pounding and his palms sweating despite the cold draft sweeping through the narrow hallway.

Disobedience wasn't an option. Artyom reminded himself of that when he reached the door. More than once, he had seen neighbors disappear after voicing opinions that went against the government. His own wife had been taken in for questioning after one of her friends had started spouting off complaints about not enough food at the market.

She had survived that encounter but not the flu epidemic that had spread through the city a few months later. The familiar ache of loss swept through him.

Forcing himself back to the present, Artyom knocked on Grigori's office door.

"Enter," Grigori barked out.

Artyom opened the door and walked into the room. Grigori sat behind his massive desk, and a second man occupied the single chair across from him.

Dark clothes, cold blue eyes, a faint scar on the left side of his forehead. Artyom suppressed a shudder. Everything about this man screamed KGB.

"Close the door." Grigori waited for Artyom to comply. "We need your help."

Though he wasn't sure he wanted to know the answer, Artyom forced the question from his mouth. "Help with what?"

The man in the chair leaned back and studied Artyom openly. After an uncomfortable moment of silence, he spoke, his voice deep and eerie. "I believe Katerina Petrova will be more cooperative if her family is involved."

"You want them to convince her to come back to the Soviet Union?" Artyom asked. If the woman was willing to leave them behind in the first place, it was unlikely she would choose to return to them now.

Grigori jutted his chin toward the man. "Budimir has been tasked with the recovery of Katerina Petrova and reintegrating her back into our society."

Reintegrating. This time, Artyom couldn't stop the shudder that worked through him.

"I spoke with her brother," Budimir said. "He wants to see her but is afraid to admit it."

"Which is where you come in," Grigori said. "You have access to the Petrov family. Talk to them. Find out where their weaknesses are and who is most likely to help us."

Artyom's intrinsic sense of integrity rose briefly, but he shoved it firmly aside. He didn't have a choice. The KGB didn't take no for an answer. "What exactly am I asking them to do?"

"We simply need their help in facilitating a meeting between Katerina and the family in a place where we can discreetly take care of the matter of Katerina's citizenship."

A kidnapping. They wanted him to help plan a kidnapping.

"The travel papers for the family have already been suspended. As soon as you identify who would benefit our efforts the most, we will determine how to proceed."

"Travel papers for the whole family?" Artyom asked. "I'm surprised they were approved to travel, knowing they're related to a defector."

"Coach Turgenev seems to think Sonya Petrova needs family support to perform her best," Grigori said as though he were trying to expel a bad taste in his mouth. "Find out how true his assessment is and how we can best take advantage of those desires."

Though Artyom had no idea how to go about the task laid at his feet, he nodded.

"How well do you know the Petrov family?" Budimir asked.

"I have a nodding acquaintance with Viktor. He is a hard worker, loyal."

"And the rest of the family?" Grigori picked up a paper from his desk. "Ursula, the wife, and their son, Josef?"

"I don't know the wife," Artyom said. "I've only seen the son a few times. He came to the rink yesterday when I stopped by."

"What was he doing there?"

"It appeared he was returning his father's car keys." Artyom took a moment to recall the brief conversation he had overheard. "He may have also been checking on the status of their travel papers. He seems quite eager to move into a new career, but I didn't catch what it was."

Budimir's eyes brightened. "That is good to know."

"I believe that is all we need for now." Grigori waved absently toward the door. "We will speak soon."

"Yes, sir." Artyom left the office, his mind whirling. Was he really willing to be a part of this master plan to bring Katerina Petrova back into the country? And would he be able to forgive himself if he did?

She had made it to the land of the free. He had heard stories of what it was like on the other side of the Iron Curtain. They were folktales, words spoken in whispers by people who remembered life before Lenin had come into power. Artyom's grandmother immediately came to mind. What would she think of his dilemma? And were the stories of her childhood real? Or were they all imagined?

Chapter TEN

Tyler worked through figures, drawing the intricate designs in the ice using his blades. When Amaliya's turn came to perform the same skill, his mind wandered to this morning's conversation. He should have been relieved that Amaliya wanted him to wait to talk to Robert. He should have been. It wasn't until she'd spoken the words that Tyler had realized how much he had been looking forward to getting that task behind him.

That was what he got for stalling on their first day back. He'd had the opportunity to ask Robert's permission to marry Amaliya, and he had let it slip past him.

"Tyler, your turn," Gordon called out. "Back change loop."

Tyler pushed off and created the intended design in the ice. He focused on the task at hand, but that didn't stop the distractions from creeping in. The job offer with the ice show, the endorsement requests, Amaliya's change of heart on when to talk to her father.

Tyler's focus shifted slightly as he completed his figure, his gaze landing on Amaliya.

Gordon approached. "You're leaning too much into the top of the figure."

"Sorry."

"Let's go through them again." Gordon motioned to Amaliya, who went first this time. Twenty minutes of drawing on the ice with their blades and, finally, Gordon gave them a break.

Tyler skated beside Amaliya to the nearest opening in the rink wall, and they made their way to the drinking fountain.

"How long do you think it will take for Gordon to start having us go through our complete programs again?" Amaliya asked.

"A day. Two tops," Tyler said. "As soon as he thinks we're adjusted to this time zone, we'll be back to business as usual."

"For the next few weeks anyway."

"It's hard to believe how much will be changing for us after worlds." Tyler glanced back at the rink. "Can you believe people will be paying us to skate instead of us having to work to pay for rink time?"

"Not really." Amaliya's tone lacked the enthusiasm Tyler was accustomed to hearing from her.

"Is everything okay?"

Before Amaliya could answer, Gordon approached the rink wall barrier. "Okay, you two. Time to see how your timing is. Long program."

"The whole thing?" Amaliya asked.

"That's right. We only have fourteen more days until we leave for Canada, only seventeen more days until you compete." Gordon held up his clipboard. "After that, we'll work on the new short program."

"These back-to-back competitions are brutal," Tyler said.

"They are, but we'll make sure you're ready for the next one," Gordon said. "After that, you can have a nice, long rest."

"Not if we start working for the Ice Capades," Amaliya said.

"We will be able to eat cookies again though." Tyler couldn't remember the last time he'd been able to walk into the kitchen and eat anything he'd wanted. "Speaking of which, you promised we could have a cookie after the Olympics."

"How about we go double or nothing?" Gordon asked.

"You make it sound like we're betting."

"Think of it more like a reward. You two win another gold medal, and I'll let you have twice as many cookies afterward."

"Did you tell Eleanor not to make cookies so we wouldn't be tempted?" Amaliya asked.

"Maybe." Gordon wiggled his eyebrows. "Or maybe your dad and I have been eating them all before you get the chance."

Some of Amaliya's earlier tension eased. "I wouldn't put it past either of you."

"Come on. We'll talk diet later." Gordon pointed at the center of the ice. "For now, I want to see you deliver a gold-medal performance."

"You're getting demanding again," Tyler said.

"I may not have much more time to boss you around," Gordon said. "I'm taking advantage of these last days while I've got them."

Gordon's words struck Tyler. "Have you thought about what will come next for you?"

"I already have plenty of couples asking for auditions, but I won't deal with any of that until after you two go pro." Gordon shrugged. "For now, my focus is on preparing you for worlds . . . and keeping you out of the cookie jar."

Tyler stepped onto the ice. "I'd say I was going to miss you monitoring my diet after we go pro, but I'd be lying."

Gordon's lips quirked slightly, but he fought back the smile trying to form. He pointed at the rink again. "Long program. Now."

Tyler took Amaliya's hand. "Yes, Coach."

Amaliya sat at the dinner table, her family and friends surrounding her. The goal of the day: find a way to reunite her mother with her uncle.

"What's the plan?" Tyler asked. "Do you have any idea how to even find Viktor?"

"We spent the afternoon calling hotels in Toronto," Miles said. "No luck yet."

"I'd hate to see your long-distance bill," Tyler said.

"It isn't my long-distance bill." Miles jerked a thumb toward her dad. "It's his."

Her dad picked up a roll and broke it open. He slathered butter on the inside. "Maybe you should save me some money by picking the right hotel the first time."

"Yeah, I'll get right on that." Miles rolled his eyes.

"Let's assume we can find out where Viktor is staying," Amaliya said before her dad and Miles could continue the banter that would most certainly derail the conversation. "What then?"

"We need to find a way to communicate with him." Her mom glanced at her before turning back to everyone else. "Maybe there's someone in the hotel staff who can help us pass messages to him."

"You know that isn't going to work." Linda passed the breadbasket to Miles. "Amaliya is our best chance at making contact."

Amaliya read the doubt on her mother's face and put two and two together. She would share a locker room with Sonya. Sonya would logically see Viktor at some point during the championships. If they could find a place where Viktor and her mother could meet, it would be as simple as having a single conversation. Maybe. The memory of her time in Leningrad rolled through her mind.

"At the Olympics, there was always an attendant in the locker rooms." Amaliya took a bite of her dinner and pondered for a moment. "Do you think the Soviets will have someone watching Sonya in Canada too?"

"I'm sure they will." Her mom's fingers tightened on her water glass before she took a sip. "And if they see you talking to her, they'll make sure she doesn't get the chance again."

Amaliya set her fork down. "Then we need to figure out a way to make it look like I'm not really talking to her."

"How do we do that?" Tyler asked.

Amaliya shrugged. "I have absolutely no idea."

"Passing notes was what saved us when we were in Canada." Her dad plucked another roll out of the breadbasket. "Maybe we can use the same ploy."

Ignoring what was left of her dinner, Amaliya asked, "How would I pass a note to Sonya without being noticed?"

"Maybe Amaliya could slip it into her skating bag," Tyler suggested.

"But Sonya would need to know to look for it," Amaliya's dad said.

"It's a catch-22." Frustration hummed through Tyler's voice. "The note won't be of any use unless Sonya knows about it, but we don't have any way to tell her to look for it without her reading the note."

"Maybe I can say something to her in the locker room," Amaliya said. "I would only need a minute."

"They know about you." Fear and concern illuminated her mom's face. "We can't even be sure her chaperones will let you anywhere near her."

"Let's not worry about how to communicate with Viktor for now." Miles picked up the water pitcher from the center of the table and filled his glass. "Instead, we need to know what we want to communicate."

"You mean where I'll be able to see Viktor," her mom said.

Her dad grabbed another roll and held it up as he spoke. "We need a place where we can keep Katerina protected."

"And where Viktor would have access," her mom said. "That will limit our options."

Amaliya played through a typical competition in her head. Practices at a practice rink, the locker room, the staging area before they competed, the bleachers where they could watch the other skaters after they performed, their hotel rooms, the restaurants where they ate dinner.

"What about trying to pass a note at dinner?" Amaliya asked. "The Soviets have to eat at some point."

"Yes, but they often have food ordered in, and they eat as a group," her mom said. "At least, that's how it worked when I was on tour with the ballet."

Her dad leaned back in his chair. "Amaliya may be on to something. I was able to talk to you when I was delivering your food."

"Yes, but you were working at the theater at the time," her mom said. "We don't even know where the Soviet team is staying, much less where they'll be eating or who will be providing their food."

"I'll keep working on finding their hotel, but we probably won't be able to make any decisions on how to get Katerina and her brother together until after we see what the Soviets' security looks like," Miles said.

Her dad nodded. "We'll find as many potential opportunities as we can, and hopefully one will work out."

"It shouldn't be this complicated to plan a family reunion," Amaliya said.

Her mom put her hand on Amaliya's. "I couldn't agree more."

Artyom knocked on the door to his grandmother's tiny one-room apartment. A minute passed without any indication that anyone was home. He knocked again. This time, a shuffling sound carried to him.

Another moment passed. Finally, the locks clicked, and the door opened a crack. Only a flicker of light shone from within, but it was enough to illuminate his grandmother's hunched figure. A scarf covered her head, and she had a blanket wrapped tightly around her shoulders.

"Ah, my boy." Her words were barely distinguishable beneath the hoarseness of her voice. She coughed. "Come in. Come in." She shuffled back a step, and Artyom walked inside.

A thick, short candle burned on a plate on the tiny table beside what his granny liked to call her kitchen. The narrow refrigerator, tiny sink, and minuscule counter that held her hotplate hardly counted as a kitchen.

His grandma moved slowly to the nearest chair, an old wooden rocker with a homemade cushion on the seat. She lowered herself into it and coughed again.

He turned on the lamp beside his grandmother's chair and studied her frail frame and pale skin. "Are you ill?"

"It's nothing." She wrapped her blanket tighter around her. "What brings you by on a Wednesday night?"

"I wanted to see you." When his grandma simply lifted an eyebrow, he added, "And I needed a distraction."

"From what?"

He sat on the wooden chair beside her. "The new job is different from what I expected."

"The more responsibility you gain, the more complicated life becomes."

"You used to tell me stories about life before it became complicated."

She lowered her voice to a whisper. "Before Lenin."

"Yes." He leaned forward and rested his elbows on his knees. "Was it real? The picture you painted?"

"Ah, it was real." A wistful expression stole over her face. "Our family was among the lucky ones. We lived in the country and had fertile ground to farm. Things were not so good in the city, where food was hard to find."

"Like now."

"Yes. Many things have changed since I was a young girl, but many things have remained the same." She shivered.

Despite the chill in the air, Artyom shrugged out of his coat and laid it across his grandma's lap.

She accepted the offering and snuggled beneath the added layer. "You're a good boy. Your parents would be so proud of you."

Artyom knew better. When they were still alive, his parents had shared the sense of integrity they had passed along to him. And if his grandmother knew what he had been asked to do, she wouldn't approve either.

As though reading his thoughts, she asked, "What has you troubled?"

"Have you ever had to do something you didn't agree with?"

"We all have to make choices."

"But what if you don't have a choice?" Artyom asked.

Her eyes seemed to sharpen as she gazed at him. "My dear boy, there is always a choice."

Chapter ELEVEN

Katerina stirred Robert's favorite soup while Linda slipped a batch of rolls into the oven. Over the past several days, they had gone over one idea after another on how to contact Viktor, but with every possibility, they couldn't even begin to create a plan until they uncovered where the Soviet skating team would be staying. Unfortunately, none of the hotels would admit to hosting the group.

Katerina lifted the spoon and tasted the steaming broth. Almost perfect. She lifted the salt shaker and added a bit more to the pot.

At home in Katerina's kitchen, Linda retrieved a stack of bowls and set them on the table. "There has to be something we can do to help you see Viktor."

"I don't know what," Katerina said. "At this point, the only way to be sure where Sonya is staying will be to follow her back to her hotel."

"We can do that."

"One of you can if the KGB doesn't stop you," Katerina countered. "And even if you find my niece, we have no guarantee that Viktor will be staying in the same hotel." She stirred the soup again and set the spoon aside, then looked around the large kitchen: the long wooden table by the window, the pristine counters, the stools lining the island. "I have so much. I wish there were a way to pass along some of what I have been blessed with to my brother."

"Maybe there is a way."

"But how?" Katerina asked. "We can't even find him, much less find a way to contact him. We don't even have a plan to get a message to him."

The garage door rumbled open. A moment later, Amaliya and Gordon walked in.

"It has to be in my room somewhere," Amaliya said.

"What are you looking for?" Katerina asked.

"My USA team jacket from the Olympics. I know I wore it yesterday, but I have no idea where I put it."

"I haven't seen it," Katerina said.

"We may have to do another search," Gordon said. "You need it for worlds."

A quick knock sounded on the door to the garage, and the door opened an instant later. Tyler walked in and held up the missing jacket. "I found it."

Relief filled Amaliya's expression. "Thank you. Where was it?"

"It was in my skating bag. I must have picked it up, thinking it was mine."

"Are you two about ready for lunch?" Linda asked. "It'll be on the table in about ten minutes."

"I'm going to change, but I'll be back in a few minutes." Tyler disappeared the way he had come.

"And I need to put my skates away," Amaliya said. "I'll be right back." She left the room carrying the jacket. Gordon followed.

"The jacket." Katerina stared after her daughter.

"What about it?" Linda asked.

"What if we hide a note in the pocket of a jacket?" Excitement rose within her. "If we could switch jackets with Viktor when he's at his daughter's practices or competitions, we could get a message to him."

"Most people do take their coats off when they're inside watching the performances," Linda said. "But how would we know what kind of coat Viktor would have?"

"He wouldn't have a lot of choices," Katerina said. "If I buy a couple of simple wool coats in black and brown, one of them would likely be similar to what he owns."

"We can go shopping after lunch."

"I should buy him some gloves too."

"You're going to put a message in his gloves?"

"It would be a good place to hide a note, but I was thinking it would be something he may be in need of."

"Why would you think that?"

"In the Soviet Union, one always needs a new pair of gloves."

For three days, Viktor went through his normal routine without a word to anyone about the mysterious stranger who had met him in the dark. He worked at the skating rink. He tended to the needs of his daughter and the other skaters who practiced there. He watched helplessly as Sonya attempted to increase the difficulty in her routine, her coach pressuring her to improve her standing at worlds. Each night, he went home and scavenged for firewood to keep his family warm. And with every outing, he braced for the man in the dark coat to come back.

Hoping to avoid another confrontation, he gathered a third load of wood and carried it to the house. Ursula and Josef had already filled the space beneath the floorboards with yesterday's surplus in case they received another official visit.

The wind gusted. Snow swirled around him. Viktor's breath caught, a stabbing sensation seizing his chest. Fighting through the pain, he quickened his steps.

He reached the front door and took a quick glance over his shoulder. Alone. He was still alone. Maybe the man would decide bringing Katerina home wasn't worth the effort after all. Or perhaps he altered his plans to no longer include Viktor.

A sickness spread through him at the thought of Katerina being dragged back to the Soviet Union against her will, of the life she would have here if that happened. If he could accompany Sonya to Canada, maybe he could warn her. Or perhaps Sonya could get a message to her through Amaliya.

He slipped inside the house, where Ursula stood beside the woodstove, a log in her hand. She laid it on the fire and closed the stove.

Viktor leaned down and dropped the wood into the half-empty woodbox.

Ursula wrapped a quilt around his shoulders. "That's enough for tonight. It's too cold for you to be out any longer."

Viktor held his gloved hands out to thaw them out. Two fingertips poked out through the latest holes.

"Any news today on our travel papers?" Ursula asked.

Though he ached to confide in his wife about his visitor three nights ago, he didn't dare. If the KGB was watching him, they could also be listening. "I'm sorry, milaya. Nothing yet." He gathered her close and lowered his voice. "We'll pray I will get the answers we want when I go to the travel office next week."

"If you can't go, you won't be able to see—"

Viktor dipped his head and kissed his wife before she could speak Katerina's name. He slid his hands to her shoulders and held her in place when he pulled away. "We will work through whatever happens."

Ursula nodded.

The door opened, and Josef walked in. He tugged off his gloves. His new gloves.

"Where did those come from?"

"I was paid today." Josef kept his eyes on the stove in front of him as he tucked his gloves beneath one arm and held out his hands to warm them.

Viktor opened his mouth to object to Josef buying such an item when they had other things they needed just as much, including new shoes for Ursula, but Ursula squeezed Viktor's arm. "They look like fine gloves," she said.

"Thank you, Mama."

Ursula stepped toward the kitchen. "Dinner is ready. Josef brought home some bread to go with our stew."

Only slightly mollified that Josef had also shared some of his income for something that would benefit them all, Viktor tugged off his own gloves. "That is good, but a bag of flour would be better."

"The store was out of flour again, but the baker arrived as I was passing by," Josef said.

"Josef, help me bring the food to the table."

"Yes, Mama." Josef set his gloves on a nearby chair and disappeared into the kitchen.

Viktor's eyebrows drew together. "I thought Josef didn't get paid until next week."

"He must have been paid early." Ursula shrugged and followed their son into the kitchen. A moment later, they both returned with their hands full. Josef set his bowl at his place at the table and lowered the bread basket beside it. An entire loaf of black bread lay inside.

"Sit, Viktor." She set their dinner down and took her seat.

Viktor claimed his chair and picked up his spoon. "Is this beef in the stew?"

"Yes." Josef picked up his spoon. "Yaroslav down the road traded me some meat for a few logs of firewood."

"Why did he not chop some down himself?"

"He said his axe blade needs sharpening," Josef said. "He asked for so little in return, I thought you would approve."

Viktor broke off a hunk of bread and dipped it in his soup. He took a bite, savoring the taste of rye and beef flavoring.

Meat, fresh bread, and new gloves. What was going on here? And would their good fortune last through his next visit to the travel office?

Endorsement contracts, job offers, travel plans. Was Tyler really ready to handle all of these things on his own? He leaned back on the couch in his apartment, his mind churning. Planning for the future should be an exciting venture, but with Amaliya's engagement ring still tucked away out of sight and his needed chat with Robert still looming, he was struggling with his continued roller coaster of emotions. Even worse, it was starting to affect his skating. Not a good sign if he planned to make money off his athletic abilities.

The mistakes were minor, but with each passing day, he and Amaliya seemed to be falling more and more out of sync. Between the decisions they had to make about their future, the very real possibility that Robert could object to their wedding plans, and the pressure to repeat as gold medalists, they were both struggling.

The official offer from the Ice Capades had arrived in the mail just today, which included not only the pay he and Amaliya would receive but also the touring schedule. A very busy touring schedule.

With the offer letter gripped in his hand, he headed to the main house. He couldn't help but smile when he reached the living room, where Amaliya sat on the couch, the contents of today's mail scattered all around her.

Tyler leaned in for a kiss, his world settling for that brief moment his lips were on hers. "You reading through the offer letter too?"

"Yeah. It's so much to think about." Amaliya tossed the paper she held aside and tucked her legs underneath her. "Employment agreements, health insurance, travel schedules. It's all making my head spin."

"Mine too." Tyler sat beside her. "I looked at the pay. It's enough that it would cover a mortgage if we want to buy a house with our endorsement money."

"Yeah, I guess."

"Don't you think so?"

"It's hard to imagine moving out on our own, buying a house, doing all of those grown-up things."

"Getting married is a grown-up thing."

She tilted her head to the side, and her lips quirked up. "You're right." She leaned into him. "I guess I'm still trying to sort out what I really want. I didn't expect so many options."

"It is a lot to take in."

"What do you say we watch a movie?" Amaliya asked. "It would be nice to relax for a while."

"That sounds good." He glanced around the empty room. "Where is everyone?"

"Eleanor is upstairs, Gordon is in his room watching film, and everyone else is at the hockey game." The doorbell rang. "And that should be our dinner."

"Our dinner?" Tyler asked as Amaliya pushed to a stand.

"I convinced Gordon to order Chinese food."

"It's not all steamed vegetables again, is it?"

"I hope not." She lowered her voice. "If we get lucky, there might be some fortune cookies though."

"Ooh, I like those." Tyler moved toward the door.

Gordon emerged from the hall and beat him to it. "I've got it." He opened the door and exchanged cash for a brown paper bag.

The scents of cooked vegetables, meat, and Chinese spices wafted toward Tyler. Was that beef and broccoli he smelled?

After Gordon thanked the delivery man, he closed the door and carried the bag to the kitchen. "Let's eat. I'm hungry."

Tyler and Amaliya retrieved plates and silverware while Gordon set out the food. Sure enough, when he dumped out the last remaining items from the bag, three fortune cookies spilled out with the sauces. Gordon scooped up both the cookies and the sauce packets.

"I should have been faster to the door," Tyler muttered.

"Trying to beat me to the fortune cookies again?" Gordon asked.

"Maybe."

"I wanted the sweet-and-sour sauce." Amaliya sat at the table.

"I let you have beef and broccoli." Gordon opened one of the containers and set it in front of Amaliya. "Be happy with what you've got."

Amaliya offered a sweet smile, but her words carried a hint of sarcasm. "Thank you, Gordon."

"That's a little better."

"What did you get me?" Tyler asked.

"Chicken with vegetables." Gordon pointed to Amaliya's food. "The two of you should share. You need some beef too, and she needs more vegetables."

"I can live with that," Tyler said.

Gordon scooped some lo mein onto his plate and picked up a pair of chopsticks that had come in the bag. "I saw something in the mail from the Ice Capades. I assume that was the official job offer."

"It was. The offer is decent, but I'm not crazy about having to start so soon after worlds."

"Amaliya, what do you think about all this?" Gordon asked.

"I already decided what was for dinner." Amaliya speared a piece of broccoli with her fork. "The only other decision I want to make tonight is which movie to watch."

Tyler took a bite of his own meal and glanced at his fiancée. Was Amaliya avoiding making a decision because she was just as overwhelmed as him, or was there some deeper issue she had yet to mention? Either way, their time was running out. They had to make a decision. Soon.

Chapter TWELVE

Artyom spotted Budimir the moment he reached the hallway leading to Grigori's office. Budimir stood outside as though he were standing guard. Perhaps he was.

The fleeting thought of turning around and heading in the other direction popped into his mind but was quickly discarded. Budimir would know how to find him. He would certainly know where he lived. Artyom forced himself to continue forward. Adopting a professional air, he asked, "Did Grigori ask to see you too?"

"No. I asked to see him." Budimir opened the door and held it for Artyom.

Feeling much like a criminal being escorted into an interrogation, Artyom forced his feet to move. He entered the empty office.

"Where is Grigori?"

"He had another meeting." Budimir closed the office door and motioned to the single chair positioned opposite the desk. "We have already discussed what needs to happen next. He doesn't need to be here for this conversation."

Artyom swallowed hard and lowered himself into the seat.

Budimir moved to the front of Grigori's desk and leaned against it. "It appears your instincts about the Petrov boy was correct."

His brow furrowed. "My instincts?"

"I arranged for some good fortune to fall his way. Josef Petrov appears to be someone who is anxious to improve his situation in life."

"What sort of good fortune?"

"An early paycheck, the chance for a few items that he needed."

A bribe disguised as something else. Was the young Petrov too naive to recognize the "good fortune," as Budimir called it, for what it was, or was he desperate enough to take advantage of the situation without knowing what would be asked of him?

Artyom swallowed again. "Have you already spoken to Josef? Does he know what you want him to do?"

Budimir nodded. "Josef doesn't have any particular fondness for his cousin or his aunt, nor does he appear to trust Americans."

The boy was willing to betray his own family? Artyom reminded himself that he was supposed to be on Budimir's side. "That bodes well in your favor."

"Yes, as in yours. Once we are in Canada, he will share information with you," Budimir said. "You will then pass it along to me."

"Wait. You want me to be Josef's contact?" His voice rose a decibel on the last word.

"Who better?" Budimir patted his chest. "Viktor knows me. It won't do for him to see his son speaking with a man he doesn't trust."

Artyom let out a resigned sigh. "But he trusts me."

"Yes." Budimir pushed away from the desk, now towering over Artyom. "Be sure to speak to the Petrov family at the airport. You need to be certain Viktor knows you are acquainted with his son."

"Of course." Artyom's eyes narrowed. "Are you allowing the whole Petrov family to travel?"

"Not quite. One will remain behind to ensure they will all come home."

The silent threat hung in the air. "I understand."

"So will they."

Amaliya sat beside her mother and Linda as her mother's shopping list continued to grow. Coats, gloves, hats, scarves. At the table across from them, Gordon sat with the sports section open in front of him, a plate of cookies at his elbow.

Linda flipped through the Sears catalog on the coffee table. "What else would be helpful for Viktor and his family?"

"Even if we buy things for Uncle Viktor, how would he take any of it back with him?" Amaliya asked. "Swapping out a coat will be hard enough. I don't know how he would be able to get much else past security."

"Plan for the best. Prepare for the worst," Gordon said, contributing to the conversation for the first time.

"He's right," Linda said. "Katerina, think back to when you lived in the Soviet Union. What would you have wanted then?"

"So many things." Her mom sighed. "Fresh fruit, clothing from Europe or America, books that weren't censored."

"Fruit is something that won't travel well, but clothes are easy enough to buy," Linda said. "I heard Levi's can be sold for quite a bit of money in the Soviet Union."

"That's true, but if we can't find him, it won't matter what we do."

Amaliya heard the despair in her mother's voice. "We'll find him. Even if we have to pass things through Sonya, we can find some way to help him."

Her mom let out a sigh. "At least he has the letters I sent him."

"That's right." Amaliya reached out and put her hand on her mom's arm. "He knows how much you miss him."

Miles rushed into the room, his face and hands animated when he spoke. "I think I found it."

"Found what?" her mom asked. "The hotel?"

"Yes. And you aren't going to believe this."

"What?"

"It's the same hotel as the one we stayed at when you met Robert."

Her mom shook her head. "That doesn't make sense. That's the first one we called."

"I know. I decided to check again, but this time, I talked to security instead of the front desk." Miles grinned. "Turns out the Soviets reserved the entire fifth floor."

"That gives us something, but we won't have any way of knowing what room Sonya is in."

"Or Viktor, if he's staying there too," Amaliya added.

"We know the first question we need to ask when we try to contact Sonya at her practice session."

"The best way to pass information to Sonya is if Tyler and I can practice at the same time as her."

"I wish we knew someone who could fix that for us."

"I know someone." Gordon set the newspaper aside.

"You do?" Amaliya asked.

"Archie Benton is on the U.S. Olympic Committee. He has to know someone in Canada who can help us." Gordon moved to the phone hanging on the kitchen wall. "If you don't mind another long-distance charge, I'll call him now."

"Go. Call him," Amaliya said.

Gordon looked past Amaliya to her mom.

"Yes, Gordon. Please call."

Gordon picked up the phone and dialed. Everyone fell silent while they waited for him to chat with his old friend. After several minutes, Gordon turned toward them and grinned. "Thanks, Archie. I appreciate your help." He paused. "Yes, I'll wait for your call."

"Well?" Amaliya asked.

"He's going to make some calls for us, but he thinks he can adjust our practice schedule to match Sonya's." He grinned. "Not only that—I know what day the Soviets have their first reservation at the rink in Toronto."

"When?"

"A week from today."

"The day before we're supposed to get there." Amaliya looked at her mom. "Any chance we can get to Canada before the Soviet team?"

"I think that's an excellent idea." Her mom glanced over at Miles. "And I know exactly which hotel I want to stay at."

A seed of concern sprouted within Amaliya. "Mama, are you sure you want to be where the Soviet security people will be staying?"

"No, but it's my best chance for seeing Viktor."

A look of determination flashed on Miles's face. "We won't let anything happen to you."

"And we'll make sure you aren't ever alone," Linda added.

Gordon picked up the phone again. "I'll call the travel agent. We'll leave Saturday."

"I guess I'd better go tell Tyler that our plans have changed."

"And we should get back to Connecticut so we can make arrangements to leave early as well," Miles said.

"You're coming to Toronto early too?" Amaliya asked.

"We are." Miles nodded. "Like Linda said, we aren't going to let your mom face any Soviets alone."

"I appreciate that, but you should stay through breakfast tomorrow. That will give us time to sort out some more details."

"And go shopping," Linda said.

"That too."

Levi's, sweaters, thermal underwear, socks, shoes. Katerina could remember all too well what it was like to go without, to enter a store with enough rubles to buy something but to find the shelf bare. She didn't know how she would get these new items to Viktor or Sonya, but she was going to be ready in case the possibility presented itself.

"What are you going to put all of this in?" Linda asked. "Maybe we should buy an extra suitcase."

"That's a good idea." Katerina paid for her latest purchases, then she and Linda made their way to the luggage section of the department store. She passed the designer bags, instead focusing on the ones without any distinctive tags. She picked up a large brown case that appeared sturdy enough. "What about this one?"

"It's simple."

"It's perfect." Katerina picked it up and motioned to the matching bag beside it. "Let's get that one too."

"Are you planning to give suitcases to your brother?" Linda asked skeptically. "I doubt he will have much need for them."

"He won't, but Sonya will." Katerina shrugged. "These are just a way to carry what we purchase. How we use the rest of the clothes we bought remains to be seen. I don't even know if my brother's sizes are correct."

"With what Amaliya told us, we should be close."

"I hope so." Katerina and Linda carried the suitcases to the checkout counter. When they reached it, Katerina asked the clerk, "Can you hold these for us until we're done shopping? I still need to look at coats."

"Of course. Would you like to leave your other bags here too?"

"Yes," Linda responded without hesitation. "Sorry, Katerina, but I didn't plan on this much of a workout today."

"Neither did I." Katerina handed her bags to the clerk, who tucked them behind the counter. "Thank you."

The clerk pointed to her left. "The coat section is that way."

"Thanks." Katerina led the way to the racks of coats that lined an entire section by the wall. Clearance signs topped several of them. "Looks like we are buying at the right time of year."

"They must be making room for the spring lines." Linda moved to one of the clearance racks and plucked one off the rack and held it up. "This looks like it might work."

Katerina studied the simple coat. "It does, but how warm is it?"

Linda turned it inside out to reveal the coat wasn't lined. "Not warm enough." She replaced it on the rack. "I'll keep looking." Linda pulled another off the rack before replacing it as well. "There is one more thing I wanted to talk to you about."

"What's that?" Katerina asked.

"I know Amaliya and Tyler have been offered some sponsorships and endorsement deals." Linda held up a blue coat, studied it, and then draped it over her arm. "Do you know yet what they're going to do?"

"They still haven't decided. Why?"

"I'm pretty sure I can get my father's company to help fund their living expenses if they decide to keep competing."

"Seriously?" Katerina's grip tightened on the hanger in her hand. "Your dad would do that?"

"He donates to the arts every year. The amount in his budget far exceeds what Amaliya and Tyler would need."

"That would be incredible." Katerina shook her head in disbelief. The additional funding could be exactly what Amaliya and Tyler needed to move forward without stress.

"I wonder, though, if I should wait to tell Amaliya and Tyler about it until they decide what they want to do next." Linda moved to the next rack. "I don't want to influence them in their decision. Money shouldn't be the deciding factor."

"I'm afraid money may be one of the things driving Tyler's decisions."

"Which is why I don't want to complicate things further. They need to consider every aspect of their future—what's really going to make them happy—and not just the dollar signs sitting in front of them. And these funds would only be available to them if they remain amateurs."

After watching Amaliya and Tyler struggle with their options, Katerina could see the wisdom in Linda's suggestion. "That's actually a really good idea."

"I'll wait, then. Let me know when they decide."

"I will."

For the next ten minutes, they searched through the racks until they found two simple wool coats for Viktor, one in brown and one in black, and a coat for Sonya in navy blue.

Katerina studied her selections. "I think we're done for now."

"Good. Let's pay for these and the suitcases. Then we can pick up some Kentucky Fried Chicken on our way home."

"That sounds like a great idea, but Gordon won't approve."

Linda let out a sigh. "I hate it when your daughter's diet interferes with mine."

"Maybe we should just go to the restaurant down the street. They have plenty of options Gordon will let the kids eat."

"No cooking and no dishes. I approve of this plan." Linda led the way to the counter and laid the purchases down. She then pulled out her credit card.

"What are you doing?" Katerina asked. "I'm paying for these."

"Consider this my little contribution to the cause." Linda handed her card to the clerk. "The three coats and both of those suitcases."

"Yes, ma'am."

"Linda . . ."

"Let me do this." Linda pointed at the pocketbook in Katerina's hand. "It's a small token. Besides, that will let you save some money you can give to your brother. You mentioned giving him some cash."

"Yes, assuming I can find a way to slip it to him without it being noticed."

"I've heard hard currency can be quite helpful on the other side of the Iron Curtain."

Katerina had heard the same thing, but she had never lived those challenges. As a premier ballerina, her needs had always been met. She suspected the same was true for Sonya. Viktor, on the other hand, lived an existence she knew little about. She hoped that would change soon. Very soon.

Chapter THIRTEEN

Something had to change soon. Tyler's timing was off on his footwork. He stepped out on his double axel. He fell on his triple lutz. Twice. Anyone looking at him would never believe he had an Olympic gold medal tucked away in his sock drawer.

The new short program had come together much faster than he had anticipated. Executing it was another story. He pushed to a stand after the most recent fall.

Amaliya approached. "Are you okay?"

"Yeah." It had been a full week since Amaliya had announced she wanted to wait for him to talk to her dad, and every day, the mistakes were getting more and more significant.

Gordon approached. "What's going on with you?"

"Just a lot on my mind." Like facing a protective father and asking for his daughter's hand in marriage.

"You still haven't talked to Robert, have you?"

"Amaliya thought it best to wait." Although now Tyler wasn't so sure falling in line with Amaliya's wishes was the best course for either of them.

"Why?" Gordon asked.

"Maybe because he nearly kicked me out of the house last year for dating her."

"It wasn't quite that bad," Amaliya countered. "He just had to get used to us being a couple."

"He's used to it now, so why wait?" Gordon asked.

Tyler looked at Amaliya. Why were they waiting again?

When Tyler didn't answer, Amaliya said, "I'm just not sure how my papa will react. My parents are under a lot of stress right now, especially with them trying to plan how to communicate with Viktor."

"You don't think Robert will approve?"

"I think he still considers me his little girl," Amaliya said.

"Fathers always do," Gordon admitted.

"I learned that the hard way." Tyler rolled his shoulders in an attempt to work out some of the tension that had settled there. "It was a rough couple months when we were all first living together."

"We don't have months for you to work through your stress this time." Gordon blew out a breath. "I hate to say it, but if anticipating that conversation is affecting you on the ice, you aren't doing yourself any favors by waiting."

An unexpected surge of determination flowed through him. Gordon was right. It was time he spoke with his future father-in-law. No more waiting. He turned to Amaliya. "What do you think? Are you okay with me talking to your dad tonight?"

Doubt flitted across her face.

Before she could respond, Gordon spoke. "The two of you need to get your rhythm back if you're going to be competitive in Toronto. I'll even give Tyler his phone back when we get home so you can call Tyler's family tonight."

Amaliya hesitated a moment, clearly debating their options. Finally, she gave a little shrug. "It would be kind of nice to be able to talk to my mom about our plans too."

Another wave of relief swamped through Tyler. "I'll talk to him tonight."

"And I'll hide his rifle," Gordon added.

The blood drained from Tyler's face. "Do you think that's really necessary?"

"Probably not, but it's better to be safe than sorry." Gordon gripped his shoulder and squeezed. "We only have fifteen minutes left of practice. Let's call it a day."

Amaliya's eyebrows rose. "You're ending practice early?"

"Until Tyler gets through these nerves, it's best to keep his feet on the ground."

"Right." Tyler blew out a breath. Then he turned to Amaliya. "You sure you don't want to just elope?"

Amaliya's eyebrows lifted. "You really think talking to my dad after eloping would be better than facing him now?"

A quick fictional conversation of that scenario played through his mind. He shook his head. "We really would need to hide his rifle."

Gordon squeezed his shoulder again. "I'll pray for you."

Tyler swallowed hard. "Thanks."

Viktor drove the Zamboni over the ice, the sweepers creating a glassy surface. Across the rink, Sonya stood beside her coach, her right arm lifted gracefully above her head while Pavel bent her elbow slightly to show her the position he wanted her to emulate.

Pride rose within Viktor. The Petrova grace his sister had so often demonstrated had passed down to Sonya. What would it be like for Katerina and Sonya to meet? Would that even be a possibility? Should he dare allow his daughter to meet the sister who had opted for love and freedom over family and duty?

He had read the stack of letters his niece had given him multiple times, letters Katerina had written over the course of the past twenty years.

No matter how much Viktor missed her, he couldn't deny that within those pages, Katerina painted a picture of creating a new family and a new life he could barely imagine.

The yearning to see her again surged inside him, but along with it came the fear—fear for himself and fear for his sister. What he didn't understand was why the Soviets wanted to bring Katerina back to Leningrad now after all this time and what they would do if they got her here.

Despite his concern that the KGB planned to use him as bait, he had checked with the travel office twice last week, but the story still remained the same. The travel office insisted they needed Pavel to approve his family as part of the skating team's travel party, and Pavel insisted he had granted permission and that the request simply hadn't been processed.

Time was running out, and Viktor's hope was quickly extinguishing. He needed to warn Katerina, and he couldn't very well do that if he never left the Soviet Union.

Viktor parked the Zamboni. A moment later, the skaters returned to the ice.

Sonya glided past and raised a hand in greeting. They hadn't been given the opportunity to communicate beyond a simple greeting for days. He missed his little girl. And he missed his sister.

Pavel started Sonya's music for her long program and moved to the side of the rink closest to where Viktor now stood. "Have you heard from the travel office?"

"They continue to tell me they need your permission."

"This is preposterous." He shook his head. "Go again tomorrow. Tell them I need to know if they require me to replace any of your family."

Viktor swallowed hard. "Perhaps that comment should come directly from you."

"And when would I go?" Pavel asked. "The office is only open when I am at practice."

Resigned, Viktor nodded. "I will go tomorrow."

"Good. Go first thing in the morning so we can get this settled." He focused on Sonya. "It is best not to upset Sonya in the days before we travel. If your family is not approved, I want her to know right away."

Viktor held back another sigh and the fear surging through him. "I understand."

Anxiety coursed through Tyler as imaginary conversations repeated through his mind. In some, he played out an elaborate monologue about how much he loved Amaliya and the plans they had for their future. In others, simplicity ruled.

All throughout dinner, he let the different possibilities roll over and over through his mind, his nerves tangling into a knotted mess until he could barely eat the chicken and rice dish before him.

"Thanks for dinner, Eleanor." Robert pushed back from the table. "I hate to eat and run, but I have some film I need to review before tomorrow night's game."

Tyler watched him go. Everyone else was still at the dinner table. Robert would be alone for the next few minutes. This was Tyler's chance.

He didn't move. If he didn't still have half his dinner on his plate, he would have added more to avoid the task before him.

From her seat beside him, Amaliya nudged his arm. He glanced over at her, and she lifted her eyebrows.

"I know." Tyler sighed. "I need to get this over with."

"Get what over with?" Katerina asked.

How did Tyler respond to that question? He didn't want to lie to his future mother-in-law, but he also didn't want to have the can-I-marry-your-daughter conversation twice. He opted to sidestep the question entirely. "Thanks for dinner, Eleanor."

"You hardly ate anything," Eleanor said. "Are you okay?"

"I'm fine." Great. Now he was lying to the Marcells' housekeeper. He pushed back from the table. "If you'll excuse me."

Amaliya motioned to his plate. "I'll clear your plate for you."

"Thanks." Tyler escaped the kitchen and headed for Robert's office before anyone could ask why he wasn't staying to help with dishes or heading for his apartment.

He passed through the living room, and his footsteps slowed when he turned down the hall and approached the open office door. Tyler stopped a few feet before he reached it, drew a deep breath, and squared his shoulders. He could do this.

Tyler took two steps forward and knocked on Robert's open door. "Mr. Marcell, do you have a minute?"

Robert kept his focus on the film he was loading into his projector. "Sure. What's up?"

Tyler stepped through the doorway. "It's about Amaliya."

Robert clicked the reel of film into place and looked up. "Is something wrong?"

"Actually, something's right." With a true sense of bravery, he closed the door. "I wanted to talk to you about Amaliya's future. About our future together."

"I already heard about the job offer with the Ice Capades." Robert lowered into one of the lounge chairs that faced the screen and motioned for Tyler to sit.

Tyler somehow managed to take the few steps necessary to reach the offered chair. He sat down.

"I can't say I'm thrilled with the prospect of Amaliya being on the road for nine months out of the year," Robert said.

"It's a different kind of life, to be sure, but we would both be able to do what we love."

"Is this really what Amaliya wants?"

Tyler ignored that question and pressed forward. "It's actually not the job offer I wanted to talk to you about." Tyler drew a deep breath and spit out the words that had been bottled inside him for the past two weeks. "I'm here to ask for your permission to marry Amaliya."

Robert's expression of fatherly concern disappeared and was replaced by a resolute refusal. "Absolutely not." Robert shook his head adamantly. "Amaliya is barely twenty. Neither of you have a real job. You need to find your future before you can start talking about marriage."

Tyler straightened his shoulders. "We were just discussing the possibility of the Ice Capades. We can provide for ourselves."

"Together you'd be able to pay your bills, but what kind of life would that be for the two of you? More importantly, what kind of life would that be for Amaliya?" Robert didn't give Tyler the chance to answer before he pressed on. "You two perform as a team. What happens when you want to start a family? How will you provide for her then?"

The question was a good one, one Tyler couldn't answer.

"And where do you plan to live? Do you expect my daughter to live like a nomad her whole life, moving from one hotel room to another?"

"With the endorsement money we've been offered, we could buy a place of our own." Tyler waved a hand to encompass the large office. "It wouldn't be as grand as this, but we'll be able to manage."

"I don't want my daughter to have to manage. She deserves better than that."

Tyler's patience stretched thin. "She deserves the best. I don't know why I've been lucky enough for her to want to be with me, but I do know that I make her happy. That's all I want now. I want your permission to make her happy."

The tension in Robert's posture eased slightly. "I don't doubt you have good intentions, but you aren't in the kind of career that has any longevity. Look at Gordon. Every time he has to move from one couple to another, he takes a financial hit while he's waiting for the next paycheck."

"Gordon and his wife built a life they could be proud of," Tyler said, finding it easier to defend his coach than himself. "They raised a daughter in a loving home. I want the same opportunity."

"But are you ready for that opportunity?"

"Yes, sir. I am." Tyler jutted his chin toward the hall. "You and Katerina didn't have traditional careers, and look at all you've built for yourselves. Amaliya and I deserve the chance to find our own way, to build our own life together."

Robert blew out a breath. "I hear what you're saying, but I can't in good conscience agree to this, not when Amaliya is so young and your career options are still so unsettled."

"With all due respect, shouldn't you consider what Amaliya wants?"

"Amaliya is still a child."

"No, sir. She is quite grown." Tyler stood. "Please don't ask her to choose between us."

Robert fell silent for a moment. "I'll think about it, but don't expect me to change my mind anytime soon."

Tyler's jaw clenched, and he fought the words swirling through his mind, words that would demand Robert to open his mind and allow Tyler and

Amaliya the freedom to build their life together without interference. Instead, he turned and left the office, a storm of emotions flooding through him. Maybe Amaliya had been right. Maybe he should have waited until after worlds.

Chapter FOURTEEN

AMALIYA FOUGHT THE URGE TO stand up and pace around the kitchen. How would her dad react when Tyler asked to marry her? What would he say? The fear of a negative outcome had been enough for her to postpone this moment. She prayed her fears were unfounded.

Too restless to sit still, she pushed back from the table and cleared her and Tyler's dishes.

"Are you sure Tyler is okay?" her mom asked for the second time in the past three minutes.

"I'm sure he's fine." Nervous but fine.

Her mom followed her to the sink. "Things are okay with you two?"

"They're fine."

Amaliya took her mom's plate from her and rinsed it. "Mama, I can clear the table and do the dishes."

"Thank you, milaya." Her mom moved toward the doorway leading into the living room. "I need to make some calls."

"And I'm going upstairs to my room," Eleanor said. "My show is coming on soon."

Amaliya had no idea what show Eleanor was talking about, but it was probably some sitcom. Amaliya had stopped trying to keep up with their housekeeper's viewing choices a long time ago. Too bad Amaliya and Tyler couldn't watch TV yet. That would change soon enough.

Following that thought came the kaleidoscope of possibilities for her future. If she and Tyler really did join an ice show, would they have the chance to sit down at night and watch a TV show or a movie? Would they be able to have dinners at home? Or would every night be filled with getting ready for the next performance, all of their meals coming from a restaurant or room service?

Amaliya slid her mom's dish into the dishwasher and proceeded to put away the leftovers.

She glanced at the clock. Tyler had been gone for a few minutes now, and she hadn't heard any yelling from her dad's office. That was a good sign. Right?

Just as she thought that, Tyler walked into the kitchen, his jaw set.

"Uh-oh. Was it that bad?" Amaliya asked.

For a moment, Tyler didn't speak. "Besides believing you're too young for marriage, your father doesn't seem to think I'm capable of providing for our future."

Surprise and sympathy stirred together. It was even worse than she anticipated. "He said that?"

"Pretty much."

"Tyler, I'm sorry. Maybe we should have waited."

"It wouldn't have mattered. He's pretty set on keeping you his little girl."

"But I'm not a little girl."

"You are to him." Tyler shrugged. "At least I don't have to wonder what your dad is going to say anymore."

Amaliya dried her hands on the nearest dish towel and then embraced him. "I'm sorry."

"I'm sorry too." Tyler's drew her close and rested his chin on top of her head. "I'd hoped that conversation would go way better than it did."

"I guess you were right to be worried." And she had been right to want to wait.

"Can we get out of here for a while?" Tyler asked.

Amaliya pulled back so she could see him more clearly. "Where do you want to go?"

"Let's skate."

"You know that we already skated for seven hours today, right?"

"Yeah, but that was work. We could use some play time."

Amaliya smiled. She had met Tyler when they'd both gone ice skating one Saturday afternoon. Maybe a Tuesday night at the rink would lift both of their spirits. "I think that's a great idea. I'll grab my skates and let my mom know where we're going."

"I'll meet you at my car."

The oddity that Tyler didn't want to meet her in the living room like usual wasn't lost on her. She reached up and gave him a quick kiss. "I'll see you in a minute."

Tyler headed for the door leading to the garage, and Amaliya went in search of her mother. She only had to go as far as the living room, where her mom sat on the couch, a phone pressed to her ear.

"No, that's okay. Thank you for your help." Her mom hung up and looked at her. "Tyler looked upset when he came through here a minute ago. Are you sure he's all right?"

Amaliya wanted to share the problems with her mom, but an urgency to get out of the house overrode the desire. "It's been a rough day. Are you okay if we go to the rink and skate for a bit?"

"Of course, but don't stay out too late."

"We won't. Thanks, Mama." Amaliya hurried to her room and grabbed her skating bag. A few minutes later, she slipped on her coat and walked out to where Tyler's car was parked at the edge of the driveway.

The car was already running, with Tyler sitting behind the wheel. She slid into the passenger seat.

"You told your mom where we'll be?" Tyler asked.

Amaliya clicked her seat belt into place. "I did."

Tyler started down the driveway and turned onto the parkway.

"Are you going to tell me any more about what Papa said?"

"Pretty much what I already told you. He thinks you're too young to get married, and he doesn't think I can take care of you."

A trickle of doubt rose within her about the future career Tyler had planned for them, but she focused on the more important detail. She still wanted to marry Tyler. "Whether Papa wants to admit it or not, I am a grown adult. If we want to get married, he can't stop us."

"No, but neither of us wants to start a marriage without the support of our families."

"You're right, but what does Papa expect us to do? Wait until he's ready for grandchildren to grant his permission?"

"Maybe if he knows this is what you want, he'll change his mind."

"Maybe." Amaliya contemplated what such a conversation would look like if she were the one having it with her dad instead of Tyler. "I think for tonight, we need to put all of this out of our heads and have some fun."

"Fun." Tyler turned off the parkway and reached a stop sign. "I'm not sure I know the meaning of that word."

Before he could pull forward, Amaliya reached over and turned his head toward her. She leaned closer until her lips brushed his. Tyler's hand lifted to cup the back of her neck. The music from the radio faded into the background, and the warmth of the air blowing from the heater vents rippled over her skin.

Tyler changed the angle of the kiss, and her stomach fell away as though she had just crested the top of a roller coaster and started on the downward freefall.

A horn honked, and they broke apart.

Amaliya glanced at the headlights shining through their rear window. "I guess we'd better save the good-night kiss for later," Amaliya said.

"As long as it's not where your dad can see us," Tyler said. "He hasn't said anything about kicking me out yet, but I don't want to press my luck."

"He'll come around." Amaliya gave his hand a reassuring squeeze. "I'm sure of it."

"I'm sure the kids will be back well before curfew," Katerina said. She didn't know what had gotten into Robert, but the minute he'd found out Amaliya had left the house with Tyler, he'd been on a rampage.

"She should have asked me before she left."

"Why?" Katerina asked. "She talked to me. She knows that Gordon expects her and Tyler to be in their rooms by ten."

"Did they tell you about their plans?" Robert paced the length of the living room and then returned to stand a short distance from where Katerina sat on the couch.

"I just told you they said they were going skating."

"I'm not talking about those plans." Robert's voice rose. "I'm talking about them getting married."

"Married?" Katerina repeated. Surprise came first. Acceptance wasn't far behind. Katerina couldn't think of anyone she would rather have for a son-in-law than Tyler. The fury and frustration on her husband's face revealed he didn't share her sentiment.

"Can you believe they think they're old enough to be out on their own?" Robert paced the room again. "She's barely twenty years old."

"She is twenty years old," Katerina said. "Only two years younger than I was when I met you."

"There's a big difference between twenty and twenty-two," Robert shot back.

"It seems to me that had I met you two years earlier, we would have followed a similar path to the one we chose."

"That's different." Robert waved his hand in the general direction of Amaliya's room. "She's had a much more sheltered life. She doesn't know what the world has to offer her."

Katerina stood and stepped into Robert's path before he could circle the room again. "Our daughter is an Olympic gold medalist. She has traveled to both Finland and the Soviet Union without us. She has a promising career ahead of her."

"Yeah, a career that requires her to work to put food on the table."

"There was a time when we benefited greatly from the extra income I was able to bring in."

"But you chose to dance. Tyler is roping Amaliya into this Ice Capades thing."

"Is he?" Katerina asked. "Have you asked her what she wants?"

"No, but I doubt Tyler has either."

"Whether they've talked about it or not, it is their life."

"Their *lives*," Robert corrected. "Two people, two futures."

"You know that isn't true." Katerina slipped her hands around his waist, partially to show her support and partially to keep him from making her dizzy. "Amaliya loves Tyler. And clearly, Tyler loves Amaliya. Who are we to stand in the way of their happiness?"

Robert pulled back and tucked his chin so he could see her more clearly. "You approve of them getting married?"

"I approve of them having the chance to make their own choices," Katerina said. "We have raised Amaliya to understand what a gift she has been given to be born in a country where she is free. How can we justify taking away the very freedom we chose to give her?"

Robert looked away, his gaze focused across the room.

"Look at me." Katerina reached up and touched his cheek until his gaze met hers once more. "I gave up my family and my country to marry you. I loved you that much, and I've never regretted my decision. Tyler isn't trying to take Amaliya away from us. He's asking for the chance to make her happy."

Robert didn't speak, but degree by degree, the tension in his body drained.

"Trust Amaliya to do what is right for her," Katerina said softly.

"She's still so young."

"She's grown up."

Robert looked down at her now, his emotions raw on his face. "How did we let this happen?"

"I don't know." Even though her sympathy stirred, she couldn't keep a grin from forming. "I guess even the great Robert Marcell can't hold back the clock."

"That's not funny." He linked his hands around her waist.

"You need to talk to Tyler when they get back."

"And say what?"

"Tell him you'll give him your blessing."

Robert let out a heavy sigh. "Can't it wait for another day or two while I get used to this idea?"

Katerina stepped out of his embrace. "Put yourself in Tyler's shoes for a minute. How would you feel if you had asked my father's permission for my hand and been told no?"

"Your father had already died before I met you."

"Yes, but you can imagine how difficult that was for Tyler to talk to you," Katerina said. "And also how respectful it was that he felt the need to do so."

Robert's jaw tensed. "So I'm the bad guy in this?"

"No, you're the father," Katerina countered. "And as a father who wants his daughter's happiness, it would be best for everyone if you speak to Tyler tonight."

"What time does the rink close?"

"Nine o'clock."

"I'll talk to him when he gets back."

"Good." Katerina reached up and kissed him. "In the meantime, you said you had film to watch."

"It can wait until later."

Katerina shook her head. "Oh no you don't. I'm not going to have you blame me or anyone else if you go into tomorrow night's game unprepared."

Robert blew out a breath. "Fine."

"Don't worry, I'll tell you when the kids get home."

Robert leaned down and kissed her again. "I don't like it when you talk sense into me."

Katerina grinned. "I know."

Chapter FIFTEEN

The conversation with Robert circled through Tyler's head over and over again as he and Amaliya skated. Even though it was a Tuesday night, several kids weaved in and out as they raced across the ice. Teenagers held hands and circled on unsteady blades. A few older couples also skated to the music coming through the speakers overhead.

Amaliya glanced at her watch. "It's almost nine. We should probably head back home."

"Let's wait until the last couples' skate," Tyler said. "If we're lucky, the rink will clear out enough that we can play a bit."

She cocked an eyebrow. "You mean work a bit."

"I want to see if talking to your dad helped my timing at all."

"You were more upset after talking to him than you were before."

"Maybe skating mad will be good for me."

The current music stopped, and a male voice came through the loudspeaker to announce the couples-only skate.

Tyler squeezed Amaliya's hand. "Dance with me?"

Her smile radiated back at him, and humor lit her eyes. "You know, if you hadn't asked that exact question two years ago, I wouldn't be a competitive skater now."

"You wouldn't be an Olympic gold medalist right now," Tyler corrected.

"That too." She reversed direction so she was skating in front of him. Then she put her hand on his shoulder.

They made a revolution around the rink, bypassing an older couple and four sets of teenagers.

"It's not very crowded," Tyler said. "Double lutzes?"

"Sure."

Tyler released Amaliya and fell into step beside her. They circled halfway around the rink before they reached a space where they had enough room for their jumps. Tyler counted them off, and he launched himself into the air in time with his partner. He made the required two revolutions, and his blade connected solidly with the ice. When he glanced beside him, Amaliya was at his side, mirroring his movements.

"What about our pairs spins?" he asked.

"Which one? Long program?" Amaliya asked.

Tyler nodded.

Again, they worked together, performing a series of intricate spins that they performed together while changing positions several times.

Someone clapped and was joined by several others. Tyler glanced around only to realize the other couples had cleared the ice and were now watching them.

He couldn't help but smile. "Looks like we have an audience. How about we give them something to watch?"

"What did you have in mind?"

"Long program sequence starting with the throw triple lutz."

"I'm game." They circled the rink until they gained the right position and speed. Then Tyler's hands were at Amaliya's waist and he threw her into the air.

A collective gasp sounded from the dozen people watching. When Amaliya's skate connected solidly with the ice, the crowd burst out in applause. They moved into a dance sequence followed by another set of jumps and another spin. Then the song ended.

More applause, this time accompanied by someone's whistle of approval.

Amaliya laughed. "I hope the judges react this favorably when we perform at worlds."

"Me too."

A voice came over the loudspeaker requesting everyone clear the ice—meaning Tyler and Amaliya because they were the only ones out there.

"I guess it's time to go," Amaliya said.

Tyler let out a sigh. "You don't think your dad has changed the locks on me, do you?"

"Even if he tried to lock you out, it wouldn't work. We would just have you stay with Gordon in his room."

"That would be weird."

"Yes, but I guarantee that given a choice between you living in the main house or the apartment, Papa would choose for you to be in the apartment."

"I'm sure you're right."

They changed out of their skates and left the rink. As they drove toward home, Amaliya said, "We were pretty good out there tonight."

"Yeah. It was nice not having to worry about anything beyond having fun," Tyler said.

"I think it's time we get back to having fun at practice," Amaliya said. "We're already the Olympic champions. Maybe we should mix things up a bit."

"Mix things up how?"

"I just think we need to remember that we're skating because we love it," Amaliya said. "You were struggling at practice all day today, but tonight, you didn't make a single mistake."

"Maybe thinking about talking to your dad really was causing me to mess up. Of course, we didn't try any triples."

"We can work on those tomorrow," Amaliya said.

"Gordon will make sure we do." They drove in silence for a minute, his conversation with Robert rolling through his head again. "What do you want to do about your dad?"

Amaliya held up her left hand and spread out her fingers. "Seems to me that now that Papa knows what we are planning, I can wear my ring again."

Tyler's heart warmed, the sensation spreading through him. "I do like seeing it on your finger."

She lowered her hand to his and squeezed. "So do I."

He pulled into the driveway and parked. He turned his hand over and laced his fingers through hers to hold her in place before he leaned closer. His lips settled on hers, and his free hand lifted to caress her cheek. He drew out the kiss, reveling in the softness of her skin beneath his fingers.

Though tempted to extend their time alone, he pulled back. He was already on Robert's bad side. The last thing he needed was for Amaliya's father to catch them together in a parked car.

"We'd better get inside. We only have a half hour until curfew."

"It sounds so ridiculous when you say it that way, like we're sixteen instead of in our twenties."

"Gordon doesn't care much about the ages of his skaters. I suspect if we skated for him through the next Olympics, he'd still give us a curfew every night." Tyler climbed out of the car and circled to open Amaliya's door for her. She was barely out of the vehicle when the front door opened and Robert stepped onto the brightly lit porch.

"Uh-oh," Tyler muttered under his breath. "Looks like Gordon isn't the only one watching to make sure we're home on time."

"Come on. We have to face him eventually." Amaliya put her hand in his and tugged.

"Maybe it would be best if I go to my apartment through the garage."

"Avoiding him isn't going to help your stress level. It'll only make it worse."

Amaliya was right. Tyler squared his shoulders and lifted his chin. With some effort, he started forward, Amaliya's hand warm in his.

"Hi, Papa."

"Come inside." Robert pulled the door wide. "I want to talk to both of you."

The muscles in Tyler's neck and shoulders tightened. Was Robert about to repeat his concerns in front of Amaliya? Surely once in an evening was sufficient to make his feelings known.

Tyler released Amaliya's hand when they reached the door and waited for her to walk in first.

Robert held the door wide until they both passed through and then followed them into the living room. He waved at the couch opposite his favorite chair. "Have a seat."

Tyler and Amaliya sat together.

Robert focused on Amaliya. "I assume Tyler spoke to you about the conversation he and I had this evening."

"Yes," Amaliya said.

Robert fidgeted in his seat. "You can understand my concerns given your age."

"Papa, I'm twenty years old. I think it's time you trust me to make my own decisions."

A wistful expression flitted across his face, leaving Robert with a raw vulnerability Tyler hadn't ever seen before. "It's hard to believe you're so grown up, that you're ready to start a life that won't include me and your mother."

"You and Mama will always be a part of our lives. So will Tyler's parents and his sister."

"Have the two of you talked about your plans? About the timing of when you want to get married?" Robert asked.

Katerina walked in from the kitchen. "I want to hear their plans too."

Tyler waited until Katerina sat on the loveseat before he answered. "We didn't expect the Ice Capades to want us to start so soon after worlds, so we would have to look at when we would be able to take a couple weeks off work."

"I've talked to Gordon about how the Ice Capades operate. That's likely going to keep you busy for nine to ten months before you'll get a break."

Tyler tried to imagine waiting so long. An ache started in the back of his throat and spread outward. "Truthfully, our biggest focus so far has been talking to you about our plans."

"Can you support our decision, Papa?" Amaliya asked. "We don't want to begin our life together without your blessing. Please don't make us have to do that."

Robert's eyes narrowed fractionally. "You're getting married whether I agree or not, aren't you?"

Tyler didn't answer. Neither did Amaliya.

"My wife has encouraged me to support your decision . . ." Robert said.

"Thank you, Papa." Amaliya leaped up and crossed the room to hug him.

Robert's arms came around her briefly before he nudged her away. "I'm not finished."

Amaliya reclaimed her seat. "We're listening."

"First, Tyler explained his plans to join the Ice Capades and possibly use the promised endorsement money to create a home for the two of you."

"That's right," Tyler said.

Robert focused on his daughter once more. "Amaliya, is that what you want? Do you want the life Tyler has planned for both of you?"

Amaliya put her hand on Tyler's arm. "I want to marry Tyler."

Robert glanced at Katerina before he spoke again. "I don't doubt that you love Tyler and that you want to marry him, but that isn't what I asked." He leaned forward, his elbows resting on his knees. "What I asked is, Do you want to live the life Tyler has planned for you, or are you simply going along with what he wants?"

Tyler turned to Amaliya. Her eyes met his, and doubts reflected in the deep blue.

For the first time since the professional offers had been presented to him and Amaliya, a new question surfaced. He had asked what Amaliya wanted, but had she ever answered? Had he given her a chance to express her opinion? And had he been foolish to assume she wanted the same things he did for their future?

Amaliya looked from Tyler to her father and back again. What should she say? Did she want to give up competing? Not particularly. Did she want to join the Ice Capades and spend most of her year on the road? Not at all.

She clasped her fingers in her lap. That action alone belied how disconnected they were at the moment. Her typical reaction when she was nervous was to reach for his hand.

"Amaliya?" Tyler put his hand on top of hers. "What do you want?"

"I want you to be happy. If going pro is what will give you that, then I can do that too."

"That isn't what I asked." Tyler didn't have to look at her parents to know they were staring. "And I'm sure your parents don't want you to make your choices based on what I want either."

"I don't know what I want." Both shoulders lifted. "It's hard to imagine skating without Gordon coaching us or spending practice sessions trying to maintain our skills instead of expanding them."

"Wait." Tyler shifted back so he could see her more clearly. "Are you saying you want to keep competing after worlds?"

Compete after worlds. The Ice Capades. Or something different entirely. She mulled the possibilities over in her mind.

"Think about where you want to be a week after we return home from Canada," her mom said gently. "What do you want that day to look like?"

"I guess I picture us living here like we are now, getting up and having Gordon coming with us to practice, creating new routines to compete next fall."

Tyler's gaze intensified. "So you do want to keep competing."

Clarity suddenly filled her. "I'm sorry, but yes, I do." She let out a sigh. "If it were only me I had to think about, that's what I would choose."

"What about you, Tyler?" her dad asked. "Could you be happy if you remained as an amateur athlete for another year? Or more?"

"I don't know. I always assumed that after the Olympics, we would take advantage of the opportunities being offered to us."

Her dad stood, and so did her mom. Tyler followed suit.

"I was hasty in refusing to give you my blessing, but I do believe some of my concerns were valid."

"So it seems," Tyler said solemnly.

"We'll leave you two to talk," her mom said.

"And when you sort out how you want to build your life together, you both have my blessing." Her dad stepped forward and offered his hand to Tyler.

Tyler shook it. "Thank you."

Tyler sat back down beside Amaliya, but he didn't speak until after her parents had left the room. "Why didn't you say anything?"

"I don't know. I thought maybe I just needed to get used to the idea of skating without Gordon, of performing instead of competing." Amaliya looked down at her hands. "You were so excited about the possibilities. I didn't want to disappoint you."

"I would have preferred to be disappointed than to sit in front of your parents and find out that you were afraid to tell me how you really felt."

"I'm sorry." Amaliya looked at him now. "I didn't want to get in the way of your plans."

"You're the only part of my plans that I'm not willing to bend on." Tyler took her hand again. "I love you. I want you to be happy too."

"I am happy." Amaliya hesitated a moment, then forced herself to ask, "Have you ever thought about competing beyond worlds? Is that even something you would want to do?"

"I don't know." Tyler drew a deep breath and let it out slowly. "It's hard to imagine staying with it unless we wanted to try for the next Olympics."

"Nicole and Andrew competed in back-to-back Olympics," Amaliya said.

"Wait." Tyler released her hand and stood. "Are you saying you want to compete in the '88 Olympics?"

Amaliya stood as well. "What if we did? I'd only be twenty-four. You'd be twenty-seven. That's still young enough to compete and have a shot for another medal."

"But how would we live?" Tyler asked. "I'm sorry, but teaching skating lessons at the rink isn't going to give us enough money to pay our training fees and pay for rent somewhere."

"I know. It's just . . ." How could she put her feelings into words? How could she explain that sinking feeling that crashed over her every time she thought of joining the Ice Capades? Finally, she said, "We don't have to decide anything tonight."

"What were you going to say?" Tyler asked. "It's just what?"

"When I try to imagine what life would be like with an ice show, I feel this squeezing in my chest, like I can't breathe." Amaliya blew out a breath.

"But you do want to keep skating?"

"Yes. I love skating." She stepped closer and slipped her hands around his waist. "I love skating with you."

"But you don't want to skate with me as part of a show."

Slowly, she shook her head. "No. I'm sorry, but I really don't."

"This changes everything."

"Not everything." She tilted her chin up, her gaze meeting his. "I still love you. I still want to marry you."

"I want to marry you too, but your father was right. I don't have a way to provide for you. Not anymore."

"Tyler, wait . . ."

He leaned down and gave her a quick kiss. "It's getting late. We both need our sleep."

She didn't release him. "We need to talk first."

"We'll talk tomorrow." Tyler stepped free of her.

Amaliya touched the back of his arm. "I love you."

Tyler smiled, but it didn't reach his eyes. "I love you too."

Amaliya stood in the living room and watched him go. She let out a sigh. Her father had given his blessing, but now everything was even more unsettled than before. Was this what she had in her future, always balancing what she really wanted with what was best for Tyler? And should she have gone along with his plans instead of admitting to her own desires?

The 1988 Olympics. Four more years of training. Four more years of getting up early, of curfews, of not eating cookies.

The last item on her list gave her pause, but she moved past it. The certainty of her situation flowed through her. She did want to compete, even more than she wanted Eleanor's homemade chocolate chip cookies. But she was also a pairs figure skater. She wanted to compete, but she couldn't do it alone.

Chapter SIXTEEN

Tyler kicked off his shoes and left them by the door. He dropped his skating bag on the couch, and he strode across the modest living room. The one-bedroom apartment was adequate for his needs, but he had been looking forward to moving into something bigger, something that would give him a real kitchen and maybe a second bedroom for when he and Amaliya started a family.

The thought of creating a family beyond him and Amaliya startled him, and his emotions pitched again. Even as he tried to wrap his brain around the idea of becoming a father, the timeline for the Olympics stretched out before him. Four more years of training meant four more years of putting their lives on hold. It meant four more years of putting off having children.

Then again, if he and Amaliya joined the Ice Capades, he would lose his job as soon as she got pregnant, or at least as soon as she was too pregnant to perform. He wanted the stability the job would give them, but he couldn't do it alone. He was a pairs figure skater. Pairs meant two.

His thoughts still whirling, he stripped off his shirt and tossed it at the hamper. He missed, and the shirt crumpled onto the floor. Frustration welled within him and threatened to overwhelm him. He needed to talk to someone, and it was too late to call his parents.

Taking advantage of the three-hour time difference between Virginia and California and the phone Gordon had returned earlier so he could call his family with his news, Tyler picked up the receiver and dialed his sister instead. Two rings later, Carolyn's greeting came over the phone.

"Hey, sis."

"What are you doing up so late? Gordon is not going to be happy."

"Yeah, well, I doubt he'll be happy regardless of when I go to bed if I don't get my act together."

"What's going on?"

"I asked Amaliya to marry me."

"You're getting married?" Excitement rang over the line. "Congratulations."

"Thanks, but our future is a little uncertain right now."

"Tell me what's going on."

Tyler explained the offers from the Ice Capades and the endorsements, along with Amaliya's revelation tonight about her desire to continue competing.

"Wow, that's tough," Carolyn finally said. "How do you feel about the possibility of competing for another four years?"

"Even with sponsorships, I can't support a wife on part-time work," Tyler said. "Where would we even live?"

"What's wrong with your apartment?" Carolyn asked. "Amaliya's parents agreed to let you live there while you're training."

"Yes, but when we made that agreement, we were talking about me living here for two years, not six," Tyler said. "Besides, I'd rather not live another four years without a real kitchen."

"Does that really matter?" Carolyn asked. "The Marcells let you use their kitchen any time you want. And they have that great dance studio for you to use."

"I know, but it would feel too much like living with Amaliya's parents."

"And?"

"And what?" Tyler asked.

"What else is bothering you?"

"I don't know." Tyler twisted the phone cord around his finger. "I guess this is really the first time that Amaliya and I don't want the same things."

"And it's coming at a time when you're trying to create a path together."

Her words rang true. "Yes. Exactly."

"I hate to say it, but the only right answer is the one you come up with together."

"This is feeling a little too much like when you retired," Tyler said, the pain of that memory surfacing. "Amaliya and I can't have our dreams unless we can agree on the same path." He ran his hand over his face and let out a sigh. "How did you know for sure that it was time to walk away from skating?"

"It was when the joy of my family became more to me than the joy of skating," Carolyn said. "I kept getting this overwhelming desire to have a baby, and no matter how much I tried to convince myself to wait, I couldn't make the feeling go away."

"I wish my emotions were that clear-cut."

"You can't compare your life to mine. We're different people in different situations," Carolyn said. "I was only married a little over a year before I decided to try for a baby. That might not be right for you."

"But we will want to have a family eventually. How am I supposed to provide for Amaliya once we start having kids?"

"Maybe the person you should be talking to right now is Gordon," Carolyn said. "He's been in your shoes before, more than any of the rest of us have."

"That's true." Tyler dropped onto his bed. "I'll try to talk to him tomorrow."

"Good plan, but for now, get to bed."

"Now you're sounding like my coach."

"Hey, any day I get to boss my baby brother around is a good day."

Some of Tyler's earlier stress melted away. "You're so easily satisfied."

"Right now, all I want is to sleep for eight hours straight." A baby squeaked in the background. "That's Grant. He must be ready for his next feeding."

"I'll talk to you later," Tyler said. "And thank you."

"You're welcome. Let me know what you decide."

"I will." Tyler hung up the phone and flopped back on his bed. Maybe if he got a good night's sleep, the answers to his questions would be easier to find in the morning.

Artyom spent half the morning in meetings and the other half fielding calls about travel. This had to stop. He didn't have time to do his job *and* everyone else's. They were leaving for Canada in six days, and nearly a quarter of the permissions had yet to be granted. Ridiculous.

With the latest travel request in his hand, this one for the meal coordinator, Artyom pushed back from his desk and headed for the travel office. He reached the two-person office and held up the paper. "Which one of you idiots denied the travel request for Izolda Rogova?"

The younger of the two men looked up, a guilty expression on his face. "She didn't have the proper approval."

"Grigori Lenkov's signature is right here." Artyom stabbed at the spot on the bottom of the page where the approval had been granted. "I want this processed. Now."

The man at the adjoining desk stood. "We have dozens of these requests to work through. We will get to it in due time."

"At the rate you're going, half of the travel staff won't be on the plane next week." Artyom shook his head. "I'm tired of fielding calls for your ineptitude." He took a step forward. "Now, unless you would like me to forward these complaints to the director, I suggest you take care of this and the others that you are 'working through' for this trip by the end of the day."

Someone stepped up behind Artyom, and both men stiffened. Artyom turned. Behind him, Budimir stood with a piece of paper in his hand, Josef Petrov beside him. Both men wore their coats as though they had just come in from the cold.

Budimir stepped forward. "While you are taking care of the issues Mr. Belsky has brought to your attention, please process this one as well. I expect Mr. Petrov will be by later today to pick up his papers."

The older of the two men reached out and took the offering. "Of course. We'll take care of it."

"Thank you." Budimir turned to Artyom. "Mr. Belsky, I was hoping to speak with you."

Artyom forced himself to keep his posture straight and his composure intact. He handed his paperwork to the other clerk and followed Budimir into the hall.

Budimir pulled the office door closed behind them. "Artyom, I believe you have met Josef Petrov."

"I have seen him around." Artyom shook the younger man's hand and addressed him. "I'm surprised to see you here today."

"We needed to have a brief discussion about his role in Canada." Budimir moved farther down the hall before stopping. "Since I will be busy with security, it would be best for Josef to communicate with you when he has any information for me."

Josef's gaze darted to the floor briefly before he asked Budimir, "Should I wait and get the travel papers myself?"

"No. Let your father take care of that task." Budimir pulled his gloves from his coat pocket. "I have another errand to run. Artyom, perhaps you can show our young friend the way out."

"Of course." Why Budimir didn't escort Josef to the exit if he was leaving anyway, Artyom couldn't explain. He waited until Budimir walked away before he started down the hall in the same direction. "I understand you are to be one of our translators in Canada."

"Yes, sir." Josef walked beside him.

"And you will also be providing information to our friend."

"Yes."

Artyom's sense of integrity surfaced, and he tried to comprehend what would cause this young man to turn on his own family. Though he knew he should limit his involvement as much as possible, Artyom couldn't help asking the question burning through him. "What exactly have you been asked to do?"

"Simply to make sure my father and my sister don't fall under the influence of my American cousin."

Artyom furrowed his brow. "And what information has our friend asked you to give me?"

"I am to tell you if they speak to one another or if they plan to meet."

"That's all?"

"Yes, sir."

The boy didn't know. He didn't have a clue that he was being used.

"What has been promised to you in return?" Artyom turned down the next hall.

"A chance to travel to Canada and perhaps continue working as a translator."

"And?"

"A new heater," Josef said as they approached the door.

"A heater?" Artyom repeated.

"Yes." Josef pulled out a new pair of gloves from his pocket. "It has been a cold winter."

The door opened, bringing with it a gust of frigid air. Artyom caught his breath. "Yes, it has."

Viktor pushed the table against the wall to make space as Josef pulled his mattress into the living room. Despite the supply of firewood he and Josef had managed to store, the subzero temperatures were too much for the little woodstove in the living room. The bedrooms were no longer habitable and wouldn't be until this cold front broke.

"I'll get the other mattress." Josef headed back toward the bedrooms.

Ursula shivered and huddled closer to Viktor. "You never told me if you visited the travel office today."

"I will go in the morning." Viktor debated whether to share the rest of what Pavel had said.

"What aren't you telling me?"

Leave it to his wife to sense when something was wrong. "Pavel said if the travel office doesn't process our papers, he will have to find others to take our places."

Disappointment flashed in her eyes, but her words were matter-of-fact. "We always knew something like this might happen."

The edge of a mattress appeared in the hallway opening at the same time it started to tip. Viktor grabbed it before it toppled forward.

"Push it over here." Viktor guided the mattress to the open spot beside the stove and eased it onto the floor.

"I'll get the blankets." Ursula disappeared and returned a moment later with the rest of their bedding. She shivered despite the hat and coat she wore.

Viktor tugged his own hat lower on his head. "Josef, put another log on the fire."

"Yes, Papa." Josef did as he was told and then climbed beneath his blankets.

Viktor waited until Ursula spread out her covers and climbed into bed, coat and all, before he turned off the light and made his way to his side of the bed.

Like his wife, he left his coat on when he slid beneath the covers.

Ursula snuggled closer. "With your next paycheck, we should buy more blankets."

"We need better heating," Josef said. "Maybe it's time to invest in another stove for the bedrooms. Or better yet, central heating."

"That all costs money," Viktor said. "Money we don't have."

"And our turn has not come," Ursula said.

"Sonya won an Olympic medal," Josef said. "That should help us move to the front of the line."

"Perhaps, but until we receive the papers to let us buy what we need, we will have to get by with what we have." Viktor tugged the blankets tighter around him. "For now, try to sleep. We have work in the morning."

"Yes, Papa. That we do."

Chapter SEVENTEEN

Tyler didn't know what to say to Amaliya. Hardly a word passed between them on their drive to practice on Wednesday morning, Gordon generating what limited conversation they did have.

"Tonight when we get home, I want you to start going over your packing list," Gordon said.

They wouldn't leave for four more days, but Gordon was a firm believer in being prepared.

"Is our packing list as bad as when we went to Leningrad?" Amaliya asked.

"Not quite." Gordon made the turn into the rink parking lot. "At worlds, we won't have to worry about the Soviets trying to sabotage you by limiting your supplies."

"I know we're trying to change our practice time to match Sonya's," Amaliya said. "We aren't going to have to deal with Popov and Sidrova, are we?"

"No. I already requested that they be assigned a different time. After the accident they caused in Helsinki, it wasn't hard to get that issue taken care of."

"Good. I'm sorry, but I really don't like being around those two."

"It isn't much worse than dealing with Andrew and Nicole," Tyler said, referring to the other top American team, a team Gordon had previously coached.

"Don't worry. Andrew and Nicole aren't in your practice session either." Gordon parked, and a sparkle flashed in his eyes. "In fact, they got the same draw as Popov and Sidrova."

"I actually feel sorry for them," Amaliya said.

"As long as we don't have to deal with either of them, I'm good," Tyler said. But he wasn't good. His whole life plan had crashed down around him last night, and he had no idea how to fit the pieces back together.

Gordon parked the car and climbed out. "You two, stretch."

"I don't know why you tell us that every day," Amaliya said. "I think you have us trained by now."

"I'm making sure you don't forget. It won't be much longer before you're going through your routines without me."

They walked inside, and the rink manager approached.

"Hey, Bruce," Gordon greeted him.

"I have another stack of messages for you." Bruce handed Gordon a half dozen pieces of paper the size of a small notepad. "A couple of them are repeats."

"Some of these skaters are persistent." Gordon flipped through the messages. "This one is new."

"You're already interviewing new skaters?" Amaliya asked.

"Not yet, but I need to start making plans. You two only have another couple weeks until your competition season ends." Gordon folded the messages in half and stuffed them in his pocket. "If you really go pro, that means I need to find new skaters and a new place to live."

"The house won't be the same without you," Amaliya said.

"The house won't be the same without you either," Gordon countered. "You'll be on the road shortly after I leave."

"Maybe," Tyler said under his breath.

Gordon must not have heard him because he continued forward. "You two get your skates on and stretch. I'm going to cue up your music."

As soon as he left, Amaliya sat on the bench and pulled out her skates. "I'm sorry about last night. I didn't mean to say anything about our plans with my papa there." She kept her eyes on her boot as she slipped her foot into it and laced it up. "But I didn't want to lie to him either."

"I understand you not wanting to lie to him, but why were you lying to me?"

Her head lifted, and her eyes met his. "I wasn't."

"You didn't tell me that you wanted to keep competing."

"You never asked."

"I asked," Tyler countered. "You never answered."

Amaliya fell silent, as though replaying their previous conversations. "You're right. You asked, and I didn't know what I wanted yet, so it was easier to just go along with your plans."

Tyler played through the conversation when Gordon had outlined their offers and the options those created for them. "I assumed you wanted the same thing I did."

"I kept trying to convince myself that I did." She tied the laces on her second skate before she angled her knees toward him. "I'm still trying."

Maybe if Tyler could understand her motivations, he would be able to help her make the transition. "Why don't you want to join an ice show?"

"I don't know. Maybe it's all of the changes happening at once." Amaliya let out a sigh. "Living out of a hotel room doesn't sound terribly appealing either."

"We would get to travel all over the country. We could see so many places."

"We'd see a lot of hotel rooms, ice arenas, and highways," Amaliya said. "We wouldn't see much else."

"You don't know that."

"Tyler, when I was little, Mama and I went with Papa on all sorts of road trips," Amaliya said. "We sometimes went to see the sights, but Papa could rarely come with us because he was so busy practicing and preparing for the next game. I have to think touring with an ice show would be similar."

"Maybe, but we could try it out for a season and see how it goes," Tyler said. "A year on the road wouldn't be so bad."

"And then what?" Amaliya asked.

"I don't know."

"Once we accept a job offer, we can't go back to amateur status."

She was right. The moment they cashed their first paycheck, their course would be set.

She reached for his hand. "Maybe we both need to decide what happens after skating."

"What do you mean 'after skating'?"

"I mean after we are no longer able to compete or perform or whatever it is we choose to do next." Amaliya pushed to a stand. "What happens when putting skates on every day isn't part of our lives?"

"I can't imagine not putting my skates on every day," Tyler said.

Amaliya tilted her head as though pondering his words. "Right now, neither can I."

It was going to take a miracle. Viktor trudged through the biting wind, his worn boots crunching on the icy sidewalks as he approached the administration building. He had lost count of how many times he had visited in search of his family's travel papers.

This was his last chance. If he didn't find success today, he wouldn't be accompanying Sonya to Canada, and the chance to see his sister would be lost. Unless the KGB brought her back, but what would happen then? Would

Katerina even survive life here in Leningrad if she were forced to return? Would she be allowed to see him and his family?

Terrifying possibilities cartwheeled through his mind. Despite the years that had passed, Katerina was still his baby sister. He needed to protect her. He needed to get to Canada.

He reached the door and hurried inside to escape the frigid weather. He took several steps before he stopped in the empty hallway and sent a silent prayer heavenward. He couldn't be sure there was a God, but he preferred that possibility to the idea that life ended once one died. Hope could be a good thing, as long as the government didn't know about it.

He finished his silent prayer and let a blanket of hope surround him. Surely God hadn't dangled this opportunity in front of him only to rip it away. The yearning to see his sister magnified, and he forced himself forward. Today was the day of truth.

Viktor bypassed the main office and went straight to the director's office. He was nearly to his destination when someone emerged from within. The man carried a dark coat over his arm, and there was something familiar in the way he moved.

Preferring to stay anonymous, Viktor slowed his steps to give the other man time to leave. The man glanced at Viktor only to look quickly away.

Did Viktor know him? Or more importantly, did the man know Viktor? And why would Viktor be of any interest to someone outside the skating world?

The flash of memory surfaced of the night in the woods. The man walking rapidly away from him now was the same height and build as the one who had spoken to him in the dark. It could be the same person, but if he wanted Viktor's assistance, why hadn't he ever come back? Maybe he'd known Viktor couldn't betray his own sister or that bringing Katerina back to the Soviet Union would serve no real purpose.

Viktor waited a minute longer, until the man disappeared down the hall and into a stairwell. Then he moved to the director's door and knocked twice.

"Come," Grigori Lenkov called.

Viktor walked inside. "Sir, I'm sorry to bother you, but I've come back to inquire about my family's travel papers."

"Ah yes. The Petrov family." He reached into a stack of files on his desk, shuffling papers until he came up with the ones he wanted. "I believe this is what you are looking for."

Viktor fought to keep his face expressionless despite the joy that leaped inside him. He stretched out a hand and took the proffered papers. "Thank you." He scanned through the top one, a travel authorization with his name on it. He then shifted it and looked at the next one. This one bore Josef's name. He shifted the papers once more. He had only two. "I'm sorry, sir, but there should be one more."

"Your daughter already has her papers. A copy has been sent to her coach."

"Yes, I picked Sonya's up almost two weeks ago, but I was referring to my wife, Ursula Petrova."

The director shook his head. "Mr. Petrov, you can't honestly expect me to approve your whole family to travel to Canada, not with your family's history."

"We were all approved some time ago."

"Then that was a mistake." Grigori motioned to the papers in Viktor's hand. "We cannot approve both you and your wife to go. When evaluating the skaters' needs, we determined a seamstress was not necessary."

"But you are allowing my son to accompany me?" The words spilled out, and Viktor quickly wished he could take them back. What if their travel party shrank further?

"Your son's services as a translator will be needed."

Though disappointment swirled inside him, Viktor nodded. "Thank you for your assistance."

"I suggest you remember what and who you are leaving behind while you are in Canada," Grigori said. "Mercy was given to your family once. Do not expect it a second time."

Viktor swallowed. "I understand."

Chapter EIGHTEEN

Amaliya glided around the ice, mirroring Tyler as they approached the center where they would come together for their pairs' spin. She glanced at him, but he wasn't quite where she expected him to be. Had she missed a cue, or was their timing off again? She tried to speed up so she would meet Tyler in the right spot.

They were only two yards apart when Gordon's voice rang out over their music. "Stop. That's enough."

Amaliya abandoned her approach into the move, veering away from Tyler. Tyler spun out in the opposite direction.

Gordon glided between them. "What's the problem?"

"Sorry. I think my timing was off," Amaliya said.

"It wasn't just you." Gordon backed up so he could look at both of them at the same time. "You messed up equally. Tyler made the turn too fast. Amaliya's approach was too slow."

"Where do you want us to pick up from?" Tyler asked.

"Before we start again, I'll repeat the question: What's the problem?" Gordon looked pointedly at Tyler. "Did you talk to Robert last night?"

"Yes."

"And?" Gordon's eyebrows drew together. "Don't tell me he said no."

"He did at first."

"But he changed his mind after Mama talked to him," Amaliya said.

"Sort of," Tyler muttered.

Gordon's eyebrows lifted. "Did he or didn't he object to the two of you getting married?"

"Yes," Tyler said.

"No," Amaliya said in the same instant.

"Which is it?"

The muscle in Tyler's jaw twitched, a sure sign he was fighting his frustration. Resigned that he wasn't going to answer, Amaliya said, "My papa brought up some concerns about us getting married." She wanted to leave it at that, but she forced herself to give Gordon the rest of the story. "Tyler wants to join the Ice Capades as soon as we finish competing at worlds."

"I already knew that." Gordon looked from Tyler to Amaliya. Understanding dawned on his face. "You aren't ready to go pro."

"I don't know. It's a lot to think about."

"Regardless of what you decide to do two weeks from now, the two of you need to get in sync today. You can't compete when your communication is off."

The muscle in Tyler's jaw twitched again. "We'll work on it."

"Good. In the meantime, let's move to figures. We'll save the program work until this afternoon."

A woman's voice carried to them. "Is that him?"

Gordon turned, and irritation flashed in his eyes.

The woman waved.

"Do you know her?" Amaliya asked.

"She's the mother of fifteen-year-old twins who are looking for a coach." Gordon turned his back on the woman. "She stopped by a few days ago to see if she could hire me."

"If you stay on the ice, you won't have to talk to her," Tyler suggested.

"Our rink time ends in forty-five minutes."

"Okay, so you'll be able to put off talking to her for a little while," Tyler said.

"I don't want an audience during your practice." Gordon waved in the general direction of the water fountain. "Take five."

Amaliya considered getting a drink for about a half second. She followed Gordon across the rink.

Tyler chased after her. "Where are you going?"

"I want to make sure Gordon doesn't abandon us."

"We were already planning to abandon him," Tyler said. When Amaliya turned her head, her gaze meeting his, Tyler amended his comment. "Okay, so I was planning to move on."

"Sorry. I'm selfish." Amaliya held her hands out before she let them drop to her side. "I want Gordon all to ourselves, at least until we decide for sure what comes next."

Gordon came to a stop beside the rink wall, the barrier now all that separated him from the woman with the brassy blonde hair and ridiculously long red fingernails.

"Mrs. Wagner, what are you doing here?"

"I was in the neighborhood, and I wanted to see when we can set up a time for you to audition Mark and Michelle."

"As I already told you, I'm not considering any auditions until after the world championships."

"That's next week. Surely we can set a time for after your return."

"Mrs. Wagner, I have a job to do now. I have no interest in looking for the next one until my current skaters decide on their future."

"But . . ."

Tyler pushed forward until he was standing beside Gordon. "Mrs. Wagner, is it?"

"Yes."

"I'm sorry, but I'm afraid you'll have to find another coach."

Mrs. Wagner looked down her perfectly straight nose at Tyler. "But Gordon hasn't even seen my children skate."

"I realize that, but we don't intend to stop competing anytime soon." Tyler tilted his head toward Gordon. "Gordon already has a job."

Amaliya searched Tyler's face for any hint of deceit. Was he saying that to protect Gordon from an overeager skating parent, or had he changed his mind about going pro? Her mind was still reeling when Gordon nodded at the woman.

"Well, there you have it. Looks like I'm not available to coach after all." Gordon glided back a step. "Have a nice day."

Gordon turned and left the woman at the rink wall, her pretty red lips forming a pout.

The three of them returned to the center of the rink before any of them spoke again.

"Did you just change your mind about going pro?" Amaliya asked.

"No, but Gordon didn't want to work for that woman anyway."

"You've got that right," Gordon said. "Thanks, Tyler. I owe you one."

"No problem."

"Wait a minute until she leaves. Then the two of you should get some water," Gordon said. "After that, we'll do figures. And over lunch, we'll talk through what we can do to get you back in sync."

Amaliya watched the woman leave and then led the way to the drinking fountain. They didn't need these distractions right now. It was time to focus. She and Tyler had experienced the magic of everything falling into place before. They could do it again. She hoped.

Viktor studied the travel papers. Only four days until he and Josef would leave to accompany Sonya to Canada and Ursula would be left behind with no protection. Could he really leave her behind? Would she be safe if he did?

He sat in his truck for several minutes until the numbness started creeping into his hands from the below-freezing temperatures. Resigned that he would have to tell Ursula eventually, he tugged his hat lower on his head and climbed out of the car. He had barely made it inside before the scent of meat sizzling tantalized his taste buds. Josef sat in his usual spot at the table, which had already been set. A basket of bread and a bowl of boiled potatoes were already in the center.

"Papa's home," Josef called out.

"Oh good." Ursula's voice carried to him before she appeared in the doorway, holding a platter stacked with shashlyk, the scent of the skewered meat making Viktor's mouth water. "Dinner is ready."

"Where did this food come from?"

"Yaroslav killed a deer, and he shared a roast with us."

"Why?"

"I cut more firewood to sell," Josef said.

"How are you finding time to chop firewood when you are also working at the factory?" Viktor asked.

Josef took a piece of bread from the basket in front of him. "I got off work early today."

"What will that do to your paycheck?"

"It was only by an hour. I will go in early tomorrow to make it up."

"Good. We can't afford to lose what income we have, especially now."

"Why especially now?" Ursula asked.

"Let's eat while the food is still hot," Viktor said.

Ursula's expression sobered, but she set the platter of meat on the table and sat beside him. After the blessing was said and the food dished out, she said, "Tell me the news."

Viktor took a bite of the tender meat and chewed slowly. "I went to the travel office today."

"They didn't approve us, did they?"

"I'm sorry, milaya. They approved only me and Josef."

Tears glistened in her eyes, and she blinked rapidly against them.

"I'm so sorry."

Ursula swallowed hard. "I always wondered why we were all approved in the first place. It never made sense that the government would trust all our family to travel to Canada together."

"I thought the same thing, but I hoped we could make it happen."

Ursula swiped at an errant tear. "It's best you're the one who can go. You need to see Katerina."

The fear of being overheard surfaced, and Viktor chose his words carefully. "My focus will be on keeping Sonya safe and making sure we all come home to find you are well when we return."

"I'll be fine." She motioned toward the kitchen. "I have potatoes still in the root cellar and enough firewood to last another week."

"Josef and I will cut some more tomorrow night." Viktor looked at his son now. "And see if Yaroslav will trade any more meat so we can leave your mama with enough to eat."

"Yes, Papa." A combination of excitement and wariness shone in his eyes. "When do we leave for Canada?"

"In four days. We will have to find something to carry our clothes in."

"I have the satchel I made for Sonya," Ursula said. "The skating team gave her a new one to travel with for this trip."

"I can stop on my way home to see if I can buy a suitcase," Josef offered.

The likelihood that Josef would be able to find what they needed at a price they could afford wasn't high, but Viktor kept that opinion to himself. "Try on your way home tomorrow."

Josef nodded before taking another bite of his meat and bread.

"If he can't find one, I'll sew something for you," Ursula offered.

"With what material?"

"I have some scraps I can use."

"If you are thinking of turning one of our quilts into scraps to take care of us, you can erase that idea right out of your mind." Viktor scooped some potatoes onto his plate and cut through one. "I am not happy about leaving you here. The blankets we already have will stay here so you can keep yourself warm."

"I'll be fine." Ursula lifted her chin. "I am a Russian woman. I know how to take care of myself."

"You're right." Viktor's tension eased slightly. "You are a strong woman."

"Yes." Ursula wagged her fork at him. "And don't you forget it."

Chapter NINETEEN

Tyler sat across the kitchen table from Gordon, feeling much like a school kid who had ended up in the principal's office. Beside him, Amaliya clasped her hands together.

Eleanor set a plate of sandwiches and a bowl of fruit salad in front of them. "I'm going to eat up in my room," she said. "Help yourself to the carrots in the fridge if you need another snack."

"Thanks, Eleanor." Gordon cast her an appreciative glance. He must have told her he needed to speak with Tyler and Amaliya alone.

Gordon ignored the food before them. "Are you ready to talk about what's really going on with you two?"

"We already told you," Tyler said. "I assumed we would go pro after worlds. Amaliya just said last night that she wants to keep competing."

"I haven't ruled out going pro," Amaliya countered.

"Let's back up." Gordon held up his hand to stop her. "If you didn't know what Tyler wanted, what would you want to do?"

Amaliya looked at Tyler, her hesitancy obvious.

"Be honest," Tyler said. "What do you really want?"

"I love our life like it is now. I like skating for Gordon. I love competing."

"And living with your parents?" Tyler asked.

"I enjoy spending time with them, so yeah, I guess."

"Okay, now what about you, Tyler?" Gordon asked. "When you envisioned your future, before you talked with Robert yesterday, what did you see?"

Tyler didn't have to hesitate. The vision had formed in his head the moment the opportunities had presented themselves last week. "Me and Amaliya getting married, joining the Ice Capades, maybe buying a house of our own with the endorsement money."

"Let me rephrase the question." Gordon grabbed a sandwich and put it on his plate. "After you and Amaliya first got engaged, before we got home and back in our routine, what did you envision?"

Tyler furrowed his brows. "I'm not sure there was a difference."

"At the time, you didn't already have an offer from the Ice Capades. You didn't know about the endorsements. I suspect when you bought the ring, you didn't even know if those opportunities would be given to you." Gordon lifted his sandwich but didn't take a bite. "When you bought Amaliya's engagement ring, what did your future look like?"

"I don't know. I just cared about us being together."

Gordon used his free hand to pick up a serving spoon to scoop some fruit salad onto his plate. "Then that's where you start."

"Start what?"

"Your plans for the future." He set his sandwich back on his plate. "You have a lot of decisions to make, but the first is whether you want a future together as a couple. After that, you need to decide whether you have a future as a professional pair."

"Did you and your wife ever face these kinds of decisions, or did you both always want the same thing?"

"Irene hoped that we would start having children shortly after we competed in the Olympics." He shrugged. "Life didn't turn out the way we planned. Instead, we ended up going pro and working until after she had her second miscarriage."

"Is that when you started coaching?"

"I taught lessons first and eventually moved up to managing a rink," Gordon said. "Then I met the first pair I ended up coaching."

"I always assumed you went straight from skating to coaching," Tyler said.

"I'm going to give you the advice my wife always gave me," Gordon said. "Talk about what you want, and then both of you pray about what will be best for you. My wife and I would probably have kept performing had she not struggled with keeping a pregnancy."

"Even after having kids?" Amaliya asked.

"Irene loved the travel; she loved the crowds." Gordon's voice grew wistful. "But once we walked away from performing, she loved making a home and eventually becoming a mom. You have a lot of life in front of you. Don't let what comes over the next few years derail what you're capable of building together."

A warmth speared through Tyler's chest and radiated outward.

"One of the reasons I worried about talking to you both about the job and endorsement opportunities is because I didn't want to distract you from your training, but you need to be aware that there is a decent amount of money to be made if you go pro."

"And if we don't?" Amaliya asked.

"Like I mentioned before, several of the companies offering endorsements would be willing to sponsor your training."

"Unfortunately, we can't receive any kind of income from sponsors," Tyler said.

"But they could reduce our costs," Amaliya said. "And we wouldn't have to stand up in front of any cameras in exchange for money."

"That's true," Gordon said. "The biggest issue the two of you are dealing with right now is time. You only have a few more days before we leave for Canada. Most of these companies will want you wearing their products while you're at worlds."

"Is it possible that we could agree to do the sponsor side of things with those companies, and then change the agreements to endorsements if we go pro?" Amaliya asked.

"That's a good question," Gordon said. "If you pick out which companies you are most interested in associating with, I can call and find out."

Though Tyler wasn't crazy about delaying their decision indefinitely, some financial help was better than nothing. "Thanks, Gordon."

Gordon pushed back from the table and picked up his plate. "I'm going to eat in my room. You two have a lot to talk about. The sooner you let yourselves be honest about your dreams, the better it will be for all of us." Gordon carried his plate from the room.

"He's right." Amaliya turned so she was facing him. Her eyes glistened with tears. "So where do we go from here?"

"We do what Gordon said. We start from the beginning." Tyler reached out and took her hand in his. Her bare left hand. "Forgetting about our skating lives for a minute, do you still want to marry me?"

A tear spilled over, and Amaliya nodded. "I do."

"Then we should start by having you put your ring back on your finger." Tyler lifted her hand to his lips. "Even though it wasn't easy for your dad, he did give us his blessing."

Amaliya offered a watery smile. "Yes, he did."

Tyler dipped his head and captured her mouth with his. Amaliya's hand lifted to grip his arm, and she leaned into the kiss. The spark between them flashed, the rightness of what they created together flowing through him. Here they were, sitting in her parents' kitchen with a simple lunch before them, but this, this was what he wanted. He wanted the spark and the joy and the struggles. He wanted everything life had to offer them. And somehow, they were going to find a way to choose their path together.

Amaliya didn't wait to eat lunch before she rushed upstairs to her room to put her ring on her finger. She slipped it in place and held out her hand. The diamond sparkled beneath the light flowing through her bedroom window.

Finally, she could move forward with her life with Tyler. Or rather, she could start planning for it without hiding anything from her parents and those close to her.

She returned to the kitchen, where Tyler sat, a half-eaten sandwich on his plate. He glanced at her ring finger. "That's better."

She held up her hand. "I agree."

"Are you up for calling my parents with me tonight?" Tyler asked.

"I'd like that." Amaliya leaned over and kissed him before she sat back down. "We still do have a lot to talk about though. You know your parents will be asking questions we don't have the answers to yet."

"I know." Tyler took another bite of his sandwich and chewed slowly. Was he stalling?

"Why are you so anxious to go pro?"

"The money, mostly." He waved a hand to encompass the kitchen. "Your parents have a beautiful home, but it's theirs, not ours. I don't want to feel like they have to support us indefinitely. Not to mention, my parents have been paying part of my training fees. They never planned for that to go beyond this month."

"But if we can sign on some sponsors, that could offset what your parents were paying and probably a whole lot more."

"It could, but that still leaves us barely scraping by for our living expenses."

"I have some money that Uncle Miles and Aunt Linda gave me," Amaliya said. "Well, it's in stocks, but it would be enough to pay for a deposit on an apartment and a few months' worth of rent."

"You should keep that for an emergency fund, or for when we start having children."

Tyler's words struck her, and new questions arose. Was she ready to start a family? The answer to that came in an instant: no. As much as she wanted children at some point, she wasn't quite ready to add that dynamic to her world now.

She forced herself to ask the difficult question. "How soon did you plan on us having kids?"

"I assumed we would wait a couple years before we started thinking about that," Tyler said. "Whether we go pro or stay amateur, you can't skate for long once you're pregnant."

"I'm glad we agree on that." Amaliya scooped some fruit salad onto her plate and took a bite. She speared her fork through a strawberry and asked, "What about getting married? Any thoughts on when you want to take that step?"

"I was so worried about getting your dad to say yes, I hadn't really planned anything beyond getting through that conversation."

"Regardless of what we decide, worlds is only a week and a half away. The soonest we would probably be able to pull off a wedding would be late summer."

"If we do go pro, we would be on tour right then," Tyler said.

"What about Christmas?"

"The shows go through the holidays. We wouldn't get a break until January." He tapped a finger on the table. "That was the one huge downside to joining an ice show, that we would have to start so soon and we wouldn't get a real break for almost nine months."

"Which would mean we would have to either rely on our families to do most of our wedding planning, or we would have to pick a date that would be right before we would go back on tour."

"We've been dating almost two years," Tyler said. "I don't know about you, but I don't want to wait that long to get married." He took a sip of juice. "Since we haven't signed any contracts yet, maybe we would be able to take a few days off to get married."

Amaliya's shoulders tensed at Tyler's renewed assumption that they would follow his plans. As much as she hated confrontation, she forced herself to call him on it. "You're back to assuming we're going pro."

"Sorry. You're right."

"So back to the real question: If we didn't have anything else getting in our way, when would you want to get married?" Amaliya asked.

"Next weekend."

Amaliya laughed. "We aren't getting married at worlds."

"We could get married the day after worlds." Tyler wiggled his eyebrows and leaned in for another kiss. "Short engagements can be good, right?"

"They can if both people already know what they want," Amaliya said. "I'm afraid we still have some plans to sort out. Besides, we should give your sister some time to recover from having her baby before we get married."

"I guess you're right." Tyler stood and crossed to where the calendar hung on the kitchen wall. He flipped a few pages. "What about May? That would give us a couple months to plan our wedding. And Carolyn would be able to fly by then."

"That's still pretty fast."

"June, then?" Tyler asked hopefully.

Amaliya tried to picture their perfect wedding. Exchanging vows in the local church, tables and chairs spread out in their yard, the Potomac River flowing in the background. She balanced those images against the heat and humidity in Virginia during the summer. "What about September?"

"September?" Tyler counted out the months on his fingers. "Six months. That's still a long time."

"It's long enough for us to make sure we aren't rushing things but still plenty of time to put together our wedding without anyone getting totally stressed out."

"September could work. You're worth waiting for."

"I'm glad you think so." She smiled. "Now, what about our skating?"

"I don't know." His voice grew serious. "Why are you so set against going pro?"

"I don't know. I guess I just don't like the whole moving around thing."

"You said that before, but you mentioned before that you used to travel with your dad for his games when you were younger. What's the difference between that and traveling with an ice show?"

"I think it's because when I was a kid, Mama and I always had a choice of whether we wanted to go with Papa. With this, we would spend most of the year on the road and we would have no control over our lives." Amaliya took a bite of her sandwich.

"You realize that if we keep training under Gordon, we don't have much control over our lives anyway."

She looked down at the well-balanced meal on her plate. "Okay, the whole no-sweets thing can get pretty old, but Gordon has trained us so well, we would probably hear his voice in our heads every time we ate something we shouldn't anyway."

"Maybe, but I wouldn't mind having the chance to find out."

Amaliya couldn't blame him there. Taking a different tactic, she asked, "If money weren't an issue, what would you want to do?"

"That's not a fair question," Tyler said. "You may have grown up with all of this, but I didn't. We need money to live. And when we get married, it's only fair that we find a way to take care of ourselves."

Amaliya glanced around the spacious kitchen and the enormous backyard visible through the window. Tyler was right on that count. Money was a necessary element to how they would build their future, and it was something she had never before needed to consider.

"How about we narrow down which sponsors we want to work with?" Amaliya suggested. "If we know who would be interested in sponsoring us, we can make our decision and know how much money we'll actually have."

"I guess it can't hurt." Though skepticism laced Tyler's voice, he pushed back from the table. "I'll go get the list. We can look it over while we eat."

Amaliya reached out and took his hand before he could leave. "I love you."

The usual joy didn't sparkle in Tyler's eyes, but he leaned down and kissed her. "I love you too."

Chapter TWENTY

Back to basics. Tyler should have expected Gordon to revert to working on individual skills after the disaster of this morning's practice, but with only four days until they left for Toronto, Tyler couldn't keep the ticking clock from sounding in his head.

After their time together at lunch, he and Amaliya now had a solid list of who they wanted to work with, but if they couldn't perform well at worlds, those companies might very well rethink their offers.

"Tyler, focus," Gordon said. "Side-by-side combination jumps. Triple salchow, double toe loop."

Tyler let his concerns spill out. "Shouldn't we work on timing our programs? We're running out of time."

"Tomorrow, we will go through your programs during both practices, but for now, you two need to get the basics down."

Amaliya reached out and took his hand. "We can do this."

Tyler glanced down at her fingers in his. This was what they had been missing this morning, and for the past week even. They needed to let the simplicity of the connection between them rule their movements on the ice.

Reminiscent of their early days together, Tyler squeezed her hand. "You'll help me up if I fall?"

"That's my line." Amaliya laughed. "But yes, I'll help you up if you fall."

"Don't fall," Gordon countered.

"You heard him." Amaliya fell into step beside Tyler. They circled together and executed their jumps in unison.

"That's what I'm talking about." Gordon bridged the space between them. "Much better."

Energized by their success, Tyler asked, "Now what?"

"Show me the dance sequence in your short program through your death spiral."

"Got it." Again, Tyler and Amaliya followed Gordon's instructions. A dance sequence, a double lutz, a separation followed by Tyler taking Amaliya's hand and pivoting while Amaliya stretched her body out over the ice in a perfect death spiral. Tyler pulled her hand to bring her upright beside him, both of them moving as they had only two weeks ago in the Olympics.

"Much better." Gordon moved onto lifts, followed by jumps again. When practice time ended, he nodded his approval. "Glad to have my skaters back."

"Um, it looks like you have more than just the two of us vying for your attention." Amaliya nodded toward the edge of the rink.

Mrs. Wagner was back. And she wasn't alone. Two teenagers, a boy and a girl, stood at her side, both of them wearing workout clothes and ice skates.

"You've got to be kidding me," Gordon said.

"Hey, you can't blame her for trying," Amaliya said. "You are the coach of the Olympic champions."

"She's right," Tyler said. "The story about Amaliya not being able to do a double axel when we started with you only makes you more impressive."

"We never should have broadcasted that." Gordon shook his head.

"Maybe you should just give them a tryout," Tyler suggested.

Gordon huffed out a breath. "I guess it's either that or deal with them for the next few days while we're trying to focus the most."

Tyler caught the quick flash of panic that appeared on Amaliya's face before she managed to control it. He put his hand on Amaliya's back. "Come on. We can watch from the side."

"Oh, no." Gordon shook his head. "If Bruce can't keep Mrs. Wagner out of here, the least he can do is give us some extra ice time. You two get to demonstrate for me."

"What? Us?" Amaliya asked.

"Yes, you." Gordon nodded firmly. "Get a drink of water and then meet me back on the ice."

Tyler led the way to the water fountain and took a long swallow. He stepped back to make room for Amaliya, but she was still at the edge of the rink, watching Gordon talk to Mrs. Wagner.

"Hey, you should get something to drink before Gordon wants us back out there," Tyler said.

"You don't think he would really coach those two, do you?" Amaliya asked. "That mother is so overbearing."

"If we retire from competition, it will be up to Gordon who he coaches next." Tyler nudged her toward the drinking fountain.

She took a quick sip but then returned to her previous spot beside the rink opening.

Gordon spoke to the teenagers, and both of them stepped onto the ice and circled the rink twice. When they came to a stop beside Gordon in the center, Gordon motioned to Tyler and Amaliya.

"That's our cue," Tyler said.

"I don't know what he expects us to do," Amaliya said.

"We're about to find out." Tyler's hand found hers, and they glided to a stop beside Gordon.

"Tyler and Amaliya, this is Mark and Michelle."

The foursome exchanged greetings.

"Mark and Michelle, show me your side-by-side camels."

The two nodded and pushed off, Mark on his left skate and Michelle on her right. They were halfway around the rink before they corrected their footwork.

"Not a promising beginning," Gordon muttered.

They went into their side-by-side camels.

"Mark's leg is too low," Gordon said.

"Their rotation is off too," Tyler added.

"Good eye." Gordon waited for the young pair to complete the move before he approached and gave them their corrections. When they started again, this time, they both pushed off on their right foot. Mark's leg wasn't quite in the correct position in his spin, but it was better.

"The spin rate will take longer to correct," Gordon said. "Let's have the two of you show them how it's done." He waved at the younger skaters. "Mark, Michelle, come over here. I want you to watch Amaliya and Tyler."

Tyler's hand pressed against Amaliya's waist, and the two of them skated to the center of the rink. They proceeded to perform their side-by-side camels, careful to rotate at the same speed.

"Excellent." Gordon nodded his approval. "Now, let's see your double axels."

Again, Amaliya and Tyler executed the requested task. When Gordon shifted his attention back to Mark and Michelle, Amaliya looked skeptically across the rink at Mrs. Wagner. "Do you really think you'd be okay dealing with their mom?"

"If I agree to take them on, I'll have a contract drawn up. I don't allow spectators at practice."

"You never objected to when our parents came to watch," Tyler said.

"With your parents, I never had to. They let me do my job without interruption."

"True."

Gordon sent Mark and Michelle into the next skill while Tyler and Amaliya watched.

"I'm not sure I want to be here while Gordon evaluates our replacements," Amaliya said.

Gordon gave Mark another suggestion, and an unexpected twinge of jealousy rose within Tyler. He watched Gordon interact with the younger skaters, and a sigh escaped him. "I'm not sure I do either."

Katerina folded her purchases and laid them neatly in the new suitcases. The coats alone filled half of the available space. She tucked the boots, gloves, and scarves on the other side before layering several pairs of Levi's and four wool sweaters on top of them.

Robert walked into the bedroom, his hair disheveled from the wind, a white shopping bag in his hand. "We don't leave for three more days."

"These aren't my clothes. They're for Viktor."

Robert peered over her shoulder. "For someone who wasn't sure she even wanted to see her brother, you look pretty optimistic that it's going to happen."

"I feel a lot better about the possibilities now that we know where the Soviet team is staying."

"Are you sure you want to stay in the same place as the security forces?" Robert asked.

"I would prefer to avoid it, but my best chance of seeing Viktor is if I'm where he is."

"That's true, but we could try to set up a meeting place."

Katerina fisted both hands on her hips. "Do you remember when we first started dating and you wanted to take me for a picnic?"

Robert slowly nodded. "I wanted to sneak you out of the hotel, but you were too afraid to go."

"Yes, and you can't assume Viktor will be able to get out of the hotel by himself, much less that he'll be willing to try," Katerina said. "The only two logical meeting places are at the rink and at the hotel. Staying at the hotel doubles our opportunities."

Robert raked his fingers through his hair, combing it into submission. "If the Soviets lock down their floor, the hotel won't be an option anyway."

"But we'll be able to see them coming and going."

"You won't, but the rest of us will," Robert said. "I don't want you anywhere near the Soviets."

"Miles and Linda arrive the same day we do." Katerina folded another sweater and set it in the suitcase. "I wish I could be sure Viktor would be able to take all of this home with him."

"Maybe we should pick up a few extras in case he needs to share."

"Share?" Katerina's eyes widened. "Don't tell me you're planning on bribing the KGB agents."

"Not necessarily the agents, but I'd rather go in prepared." Robert lifted the bag he held into view. "Speaking of being prepared, I picked this up today."

Katerina's eyes widened when Robert pulled out a box with the image of a Polaroid camera on the outside. "You bought me a new camera?"

"Your other one is fine for most things, but if you do see Viktor, you'd be able to take pictures and send some photos home with him."

"That's wonderful. Thank you." Katerina gave him a hug.

"You're welcome." He drew her close for a moment before he motioned to the open suitcase. "Did you buy anything for Viktor's children?"

"Only a coat for Sonya. I'm sure she is given what she needs by the athletic committee, and there should be enough here for Viktor to share with Josef."

"What about for Ursula?"

"I didn't even think about it." Katerina focused on the folded coats. "I haven't seen her in so long. I have no idea what size she is now."

Robert crossed to the bedroom door. When he reached it, he called out, "Amaliya?"

A moment later, footsteps approached, and Amaliya entered the room. "What do you need?"

"We need your memory," Robert said. "Any idea what size Ursula would be in clothing?"

"She's a little taller than me." Amaliya held her hand above her head to show her aunt's height.

"And her size?" Katerina asked. "When I saw her last, she was a little bigger than me. Maybe a medium?"

"She's about the size of Mrs. Hernandez down the street."

Katerina and Robert looked at each other and spoke in unison. "Large."

"Are you going shopping again?" Amaliya asked.

"I think I'll need to." Katerina looked at her watch. "Springfield Mall doesn't close for a couple more hours. Maybe I'll go over there."

"Can I come?" Amaliya asked.

"Don't you have packing of your own to do?"

"Yes, but I could use a break."

"Grab your shoes. We'll leave in five minutes."

"Okay." Amaliya headed for her room.

"I wonder what that's about," Robert said.

"What?"

"She wants to go shopping with you when she could stay home with Tyler."

"Maybe she wants to help pick out clothes for Ursula."

"Maybe." Robert leaned down and kissed her cheek. "While you're shopping, you should pick up something else for Sonya. If we do find a way to send all this stuff home with Viktor, you don't want your niece to feel left out."

Katerina nodded. "You're absolutely right."

Amaliya sat in the passenger seat as her mother navigated her way toward the nearest mall.

"Is everything okay?" her mom asked. "Have you and Tyler sorted out what you want to do next?"

"We know we want to get married. We're thinking about September."

"A fall wedding. That would be lovely."

Amaliya smiled. "I think so too. Do you think Papa would be okay with us having the reception at our house?"

"I'm sure we can persuade him." She looked at Amaliya. "I hope you aren't planning on looking at wedding dresses tonight though. We'll want to plan a lot more time than an evening out to shop for that."

"No, I think we can save the wedding-dress shopping for when we get home from worlds." Amaliya studied her mother for a moment. "Unless you still have your dress."

Her mom pulled up to a red light and turned her head. "You want to wear my dress?"

"I've seen pictures. Your dress was beautiful." Amaliya shrugged. "And we are about the same size."

Her mom's eyes misted, and she smiled. "You can try it on when we get home."

"Really?"

"Unless you'd rather wait until we get back from Canada."

"Maybe sooner would be better," Amaliya said. "It might help Papa get used to the idea of me getting married if he sees us making plans."

"What about your other plans?" Her mom made the turn into the mall parking lot near JCPenney.

"Tyler and I are still talking about what comes next, but we realized we need to focus on worlds first."

"That's wise." She parked, and they both climbed out of the car. "Your papa and I had a lot of discussions on how to balance our careers."

Surprise surfaced. "You did?"

"Oh, yes." Her mom led the way into the department store. "When your papa got traded to the Washington Capitals, I had just been cast to dance the lead in *Giselle*. Losing that opportunity wasn't something I let go of easily."

"Did you step down?" Amaliya asked. "I thought you did dance the lead in *Giselle*."

"We negotiated."

"How?"

"Your papa agreed to keep our house in Canada for an extra six months, and I promised that I would audition for the Washington Ballet after the show ended."

"You lived apart for six months?"

"Not exactly. Papa was traded in March. After his season ended in May, he moved back to Canada." She stopped at a rack of women's sweaters and began searching through them. "Papa came out and did some house hunting a couple times that summer. When he found out a piece of property overlooking the river was up for sale, he snatched it up. We broke ground on our house a month before we moved back to Washington."

"Tyler and I don't have the option of going separate ways when it comes to our careers."

"That's true. You are very much a team when it comes to that part of your life." Her mom held up a blue sweater. "What do you think of this one?"

"I like it."

Her mom draped it over her arm and led the way to the women's department. "Have you and Tyler talked about what you want?"

"Yes. Tyler said the main reason he wants to go pro is because of the money."

"And what's your reason for not wanting to?"

"I want to make a home, not live out of a suitcase all the time."

"If money is the only issue, you know you and Tyler could always live in the apartment over the garage."

"Thanks, Mama, but I think Tyler wants us to get out on our own." She shrugged. "We wouldn't really have that living there since there's not a real kitchen."

"I suppose so, but it would be nice to still have you so close."

"I'd like that too."

Chapter TWENTY-ONE

Tyler checked his watch. Amaliya should be back any minute. He hoped. Even though he had already convinced Gordon to let him call his parents tonight to share the news of his engagement, he didn't want to make that phone call without Amaliya by his side. Despite the decisions that still lay ahead of them, he couldn't help but smile. He and Amaliya were getting married. And now, finally, they could include all their family in their plans.

Looking for both a distraction and a snack, he crossed to the small refrigerator in his kitchenette and pulled it open. A jar of strawberry jam, a half a bag of celery, and some mayonnaise. He pulled out the celery and moved to the cupboard. The contents weren't much more promising: three slices of bread, a can of tuna, a can of chicken noodle soup, but no peanut butter. How was he supposed to eat his celery without peanut butter? That was one thing he needed to get better about, especially once he and Amaliya got into their own place. They needed at least a three-month supply of the essentials.

He carried the celery with him to the main house. The lack of vehicles in the garage told a story: Robert was still at his game at the Capital Centre, and Amaliya was still with her mother at the mall.

Even though only Eleanor and Gordon were home, Tyler gave his habitual courtesy knock before he walked into the kitchen. Empty.

Tyler crossed to the pantry and hunted for the peanut butter, which he found tucked behind a jar of spaghetti sauce.

The garage door rumbled open, and a moment later, Amaliya walked in with her arms full. Katerina followed, equally heavy laden.

Tyler set the celery and peanut butter on the counter. "I'm afraid to ask this, but is there anything else?"

"Just one more bag," Amaliya said. "I dropped it on my way in."

Tyler went into the garage and found the shopping bag on the concrete floor. He returned to the kitchen and closed the door behind him. "Is all of this for Viktor?"

"No." Amaliya set the bags on the table. "Most of it is for Sonya and Ursula. We picked up a couple things for Josef too."

"I hope they have a way to take it all home with them," Tyler said.

"We can always return anything they don't want or can't use," Katerina said. "Can you two help me carry this up to my room?"

"Sure, Mama." Amaliya gathered the bags again.

"Here. Let me take some." Tyler took two bags from Amaliya and three from Katerina.

Together the three of them carried everything upstairs and placed the bags by the new suitcases.

"Thank you." Katerina settled the last bag on the floor.

"Amaliya, are you up for calling my parents?"

"Sure," Amaliya said. "I'd say we could use the phone in my room, but Gordon still has it hidden."

"Mine is still in my apartment." Tyler lowered his voice. "He actually forgot to take it away after he let me have it back yesterday."

"Maybe he trusts you."

"Either that, or he's figured out how to disconnect my phone line some other way."

Katerina motioned to the latest purchases. "I can sort this on my own. You two make your call."

"I'd actually like to call Uncle Miles and Aunt Linda too."

Katerina motioned to the phone beside her bed. "Tyler, go ahead and take my phone there. It's better if my husband doesn't find out Amaliya was in your apartment."

"True," Amaliya said.

"You should have plenty of privacy in the living room. Papa's game won't end for another hour," Katerina said.

"Thanks, Mama."

Tyler led Amaliya downstairs to the living room. Excitement surged. "I can't believe we're finally going to be able to tell my parents that we're getting married."

Amaliya held up her left hand. "It still feels like a fairy tale to me."

"Not quite a fairy tale. That would include an easy happily ever after."

Amaliya tilted her head to the side. "Even though Disney wants us to think otherwise, I suspect all of those happily ever afters took some work and some compromise."

"You're probably right." Tyler plugged in the phone and sat on the couch. "I assume you're okay with calling my parents first."

"Of course. And we should call Carolyn too before we call the Donnellys."

"Carolyn already knows."

"She does?" Amaliya sat beside him.

"I was talking to her last week about how she decided it was time to retire."

"What did she say?"

"She said she knew when spending time with her family gave her more joy than ice skating."

"That's great that she was able to come to the right decision for her and Dan," Amaliya said. "I think our decision is a bit more complicated than that."

"I guess." Tyler ignored the sudden heaviness in his body and dialed his home phone number. His mom picked up on the third ring.

"Hey, Mom."

"Tyler. Is everything okay? It's not Sunday."

"Everything is fine." Tyler put his hand on Amaliya's knee. "Everything is better than fine, actually. Amaliya and I are getting married."

"What? You are? When?"

"We are." Tyler grinned. "And we're thinking about this fall."

"Oh, congratulations, sweetie! I couldn't be happier for you." She took a breath and called out to his dad. "Here's Dad. You need to tell him yourself."

In the background, Tyler's dad's voice came over the line. "Tell me what himself?"

"It's Tyler. Talk to him," his mom said.

Then his dad's voice came through clearly. "Hey, Tyler. What did you want to tell me?"

"Amaliya and I are getting married."

"Well, that is something. Congratulations. Any idea when or where?"

"We're thinking this fall in Virginia."

"Sounds like we'll have a lot to talk about when we see you at the world championships," he said. "I'm happy for you, son."

"Thanks. Fair warning though. I'm sure Gordon won't want us focusing on wedding plans until after we compete."

"True. Well, we'll have a nice celebratory dinner after you win your next gold medal."

"We hope we can win again." The expectation weighed on him, but he pushed it aside. With the way their past week of practices had gone, they might be lucky to make it onto the medal stand at all.

He chatted with his parents for a minute longer, handing the phone over to Amaliya so they could offer their congratulations to her as well. After they hung up, Tyler blew out a breath. "That was exhausting."

"Just one more phone call to make and all of the most important people in our lives will have heard the news."

"Does that mean we can get away with having a small wedding?"

Amaliya pursed her lips, clearly considering. "A small wedding here in my backyard would be beautiful."

"And simple."

"And not too expensive."

Tyler leaned over and kissed her. "I'm sold."

"We just need to pick a date and find someone to officiate." Amaliya held her hand out and took the phone. "I don't know why everyone thinks weddings are so stressful."

Tyler shrugged. "Me neither."

Katerina laid the oversized box holding her wedding dress on her bed and removed the top. Amaliya moved closer as Katerina pulled back the tissue paper the gown had been wrapped in to keep it protected.

Amaliya helped free the gown from its wrappings to reveal its simple silk. "It's gorgeous."

"Try it on." Katerina helped Amaliya pull it out of the box. "It's yellowed a bit, but we can take it to the cleaners to see what they can do with it."

Amaliya carried it into the master bathroom and closed the door. A moment later, she walked out, the gown flowing around her. Katerina's little girl was getting married and looking far too grown up.

"Can you help me zip it up?"

Tears filled Katerina's eyes.

Amaliya's eyebrows rose. "Mama?"

Katerina lifted her hand to her lips. "Sorry. You just look so lovely."

Amaliya smiled. "Thanks."

"Here. Let me help you." Katerina stepped behind Amaliya and pulled the zipper up the rest of the way. She took a step back to take a better look. "It fits you beautifully."

Amaliya moved in front of the dresser so she could see herself in the mirror. She gasped. "Oh." Her eyes met Katerina's in the mirror. "It's perfect."

"Yes, it is." Katerina checked the dress for wear, but other than a bit of discoloration, it was still in great condition. "Go ahead and take that off. I'll take it to the cleaners tomorrow."

"Thanks, Mama." Amaliya changed out of the gown and checked the time on the bedside clock. "I'd better get to bed."

"Good night."

Amaliya moved to the door before turning back. "Thank you."

"You're welcome, milaya."

Amaliya left the room, and Katerina returned the dress to its box.

From the hall, Robert's voice carried to her as he said good night to Amaliya. A moment later, he walked into their bedroom and closed the door behind him.

"What's that?"

"That is my wedding dress." Katerina sniffled back the last lingering tears. "Soon to be our daughter's wedding dress."

Robert crossed to the bed and ran a hand over the silk. "Amaliya's really getting married."

"She is." Katerina turned into his arms. "How did she grow up so fast?"

"I don't know." Robert pulled her close.

Neither of them spoke for a moment. Finally, Katerina stepped from his embrace and placed the lid on the wedding dress box. Thoughts of her earlier conversation with Amaliya played through her mind. "How hard would it be to remodel the apartment over the garage to expand the kitchen?"

"Why would we need to do that?" Robert asked. "Tyler hardly ever eats in his apartment."

"Yes, but after they get married, wouldn't it be nice to keep them close?"

"You're assuming they're going to keep competing."

"Whether they do or not, they could keep living here as their home base after they get married if they had a real apartment."

"It sounded to me like Tyler wants for them to have their own space."

"I think it's more accurate to say that he wants them to have their privacy." Katerina lifted the box off her bed and set it aside. "Not that I can blame him. Newlyweds need their space."

"We do have enough room on that back wall to expand if we wanted to . . ." Robert trailed off. "Do you think Tyler will convince Amaliya to join an ice show?"

"Amaliya has a good head on her shoulders. If that's what she decides to do, it will be her choice."

"Is it selfish to hope that she chooses to keep competing?"

"I don't know, but if it is, we're both guilty of being selfish."

Robert sat on the edge of the bed. "I'm not ready for her to be gone for so much of the year."

Katerina sat beside him. "Neither am I."

Chapter TWENTY-TWO

Viktor packed his two spare pairs of pants in the cloth shopping bag he was using to carry his belongings. Neither he nor Josef had managed to find a suitcase for sale, though they hadn't had time to look much further than the shops nearest their home and where they worked.

Ursula walked into their bedroom, a pair of his socks in her hand. "I repaired the holes in these. They should last until you come home."

"Thank you." Viktor added the socks to the bag.

"You will come home, won't you?" Ursula asked.

"Of course I'll come home." Viktor understood her question and the fear that fed it. He linked his hands around her waist. "Our life is together. As long as you are here, there is nowhere else I could possibly call home."

"And you'll bring Josef and Sonya home with you?"

"Yes. In a couple weeks, we will all be together again." Viktor leaned down and kissed the woman he had fallen in love with nearly three decades ago. Despite his deep desire to see Katerina, worry and doubts pressed to the forefront of his mind. "Maybe I shouldn't go."

She shook her head. "No, you need to go. I don't want our children out in the world alone, and you can't miss this chance to see your sister."

Viktor lowered his voice to a whisper. "She may not even be there."

"Amaliya will bring her." Ursula rested her hand on his chest.

"She is from another world now," Viktor said. If the KGB got ahold of her, he wasn't sure she would even want to be part of his world again.

"That may be, but she is your family every bit as much as I am. You need to know who she has become."

Viktor couldn't deny that his sister's absence had left a hole in his life that had never been filled by another. His children helped ease the pain, especially when Sonya had been selected to train as an elite athlete. What would Katerina think of her niece? And her nephew for that matter? Even though Katerina had met Josef before she had defected, he had been only a toddler at the time, too young to remember his aunt.

Viktor glanced toward the hall. "Is Josef home from work?"

"Yes. He's packing his clothes right now."

"I'd best check on him." Viktor left his room and knocked lightly on his son's bedroom door. Not waiting for Josef to answer, he pushed it open and walked in.

Josef quickly stuffed a sweater into the satchel on his bed before he turned to face Viktor. "I'm almost finished packing."

Viktor looked down at the bulging bag. "What all do you have in there?"

"Only my clothes."

"You have that many clothes?" Viktor had purchased Josef some new pants and socks several months ago, but his wardrobe didn't contain many more items than Viktor's did.

"What is it you need, Papa?"

"I came to see if you needed help."

"I am a grown man." Josef cocked his head to the side. "I am capable of packing a bag by myself."

The hint of arrogance caught Viktor by surprise, as did the claim. Josef had never traveled anywhere overnight before.

Viktor studied his son more closely. Josef looked away and stuffed his gloves into the satchel.

"Best leave those out for our drive to the airport tomorrow."

A knock sounded on the front door.

Concern flashed across Josef's face.

"Are you expecting anyone?" Viktor asked.

"No." Josef closed the satchel.

Viktor left his son's room and made his way to the door. He tightened his coat around him before he answered.

A man in a pale-gray coat stood on the porch, a brown suitcase gripped in his gloved hand. "Mr. Petrov?"

"Yes?"

"This is for you." He held out the case.

"Who sent this?" Viktor accepted the offering.

"Coach Turgenev said he wished for his team to be represented well." The man took a step back. "Safe travels."

"Thank you." Viktor closed the door and set the suitcase down. He flipped open both latches and lifted the lid. Inside were two thick sweaters with CCCP across the front and two small Soviet flags attached to little sticks.

"Josef, come look at this." Viktor lifted one of the sweaters.

Josef and Ursula both came into the room.

"Where did that come from?" Ursula asked.

"Pavel." Viktor picked up the other sweater and handed it to Josef. "This one must be for you."

"Thank you." Josef held it up to measure the size.

Ursula waved at the open piece of luggage. "And now you have a suitcase."

"It will be a mostly empty suitcase."

"That is okay. Maybe you will find something to bring home as a . . . What do you call it? A souvenir?"

"We will bring something back for you, Mama," Josef said.

Ursula smiled. "As long as you come back safely, I will be happy."

Tyler plugged the phone into the wall in his bedroom and sat on his clothes-covered bed. He had finished his laundry an hour ago but hadn't bothered to put anything away. After all, it was just going to be packed into his suitcase anyway.

Only one more day until he and Amaliya would leave for Toronto. Only ten more days until their competitive skating career could be over.

A knot twisted inside him, the heaviness there uncharacteristic of his pre-competition jitters. He picked up the phone and dialed his sister's number.

Carolyn answered on the first ring.

"Were you sitting by the phone, waiting for my call?" Tyler asked.

"I was sitting by the phone and had to grab it so it didn't wake the baby," Carolyn said in a low voice. "I didn't think Gordon would let you have your phone back once you told the family about your wedding plans."

"He never took my phone back after I talked to you last," Tyler said.

"Wow. He must really trust you."

"Maybe." In truth, Tyler had kept his phone unplugged between calls to his sister.

"When do you leave for Canada?" Carolyn asked.

"Tomorrow." The word came out on a sigh.

"I can't tell if you sound relieved or excited."

"I'm not sure what I am." He paced across the room as far as the phone cord would allow. "I'm ready for a new beginning, but it's hard to figure out if that new beginning should only be in my personal life or if it should be in my professional life too." Tyler paced back to the bed, the tension in the phone cord easing.

"What's holding you back from making a decision?"

"Amaliya mostly. At least, that's what started the problem," Tyler said.

"And now?"

"Gordon had a tryout a couple days ago."

"That's understandable considering you're thinking about going pro."

The jealousy Tyler had experienced during the tryout came back full force. "I hated seeing him with those other skaters."

"Were they any good?"

"Their mother was awful, but they had potential," Tyler admitted. "And they seemed coachable enough."

"Tyler, you can't make your decision based on being jealous of your potential successors," Carolyn said. "How you spend the next four years, or even the next four months, needs to be based on what's right for you and Amaliya."

"I keep telling myself that, but I don't know what's right for us." Tyler told her about his most recent conversation with Amaliya, about his financial concerns compared to the challenges for keeping his amateur status for the next few years.

When he finished, Carolyn asked, "If money weren't a concern, what would you want to do?"

"Amaliya asked me the same thing, but it's hard to answer since money is something I need to consider."

"Obviously you need money to live, but don't forget that you and Amaliya are the Olympic champions. If you both have the desire to compete in the next Olympics, I'm sure there is a way to make that happen. You could look for some sponsors instead of signing endorsement deals."

"Amaliya and I already narrowed down the list, and Gordon is reaching out to our top choices," Tyler said. "He seems to think some of the companies will want us to wear their clothes when we're in Canada, but we're still sorting out which ones would be willing to sponsor and which ones are only interested in endorsements."

"At least you have options."

"I guess."

"You're thinking too much. You need to figure out how you feel," Carolyn said.

How did he feel? He let that question roll through his mind, but the answer didn't come.

"Have you and Amaliya made any plans yet for when you're getting married?"

"We're thinking about September here in Virginia."

"What are you going to do between worlds and September? You know if you stay amateur, regionals are the first weekend in October."

"I hadn't really thought about that."

"Maybe you are ready to go pro."

"I don't know. Maybe." He let out a sigh. "Honestly, it would probably be easier to work around regionals than the schedule with the Ice Capades."

"Sounds like a conversation you should be having with Amaliya."

"Yeah. You're right." Tyler turned to the mound of clothes on his bed. "That conversation may need to wait until after we're through competing in worlds."

"Why is that?"

"I don't want to create any more stress between us, especially when we have other things we'll be juggling when we're in Canada."

"What other things?" Carolyn asked.

Tyler opened his mouth to confide in his sister about the plans to find Viktor, but he couldn't get the words out. What if Katerina's paranoia was well-founded? What if someone was listening to this conversation right now? "It's a long story," Tyler finally said. "I'll tell you all about it when I get back."

"I'm holding you to that."

"Deal."

Artyom sorted through his sweaters and sweatshirts that bore his country's logos on them, debating which one to wear on the plane tomorrow and which ones to pack. During his time in Canada, he would be a representative of the Soviet Union, and as such, he needed to dress appropriately. He added dress shirts and ties to the mix along with the coordinating trousers. Folding each item carefully, he loaded his clothing into his suitcase.

The telephone rang, and he abandoned his packing to pick up the phone from where it sat on the small table beside his couch. "Hello?"

"Mr. Belsky, this is Varvara from Gorodskaya Mariinskaya Bol'nitsa."

The hospital? "Is everything all right?"

"I'm afraid it's your grandmother. Polina Belsky passed away this morning from complications from pneumonia."

"What?" Artyom's hand tightened on the phone receiver, his knuckles turning white. "I visited her only a few days ago."

"I'm sorry, Mr. Belsky. She was admitted yesterday, but there was nothing we could do."

His grandmother was gone? Artyom dropped onto the couch, the voice of the woman on the phone buzzing in his ear. The details she shared barely registered until she mentioned something about burial services.

"I am to leave the country tomorrow for three weeks."

"Is there another family member you would prefer me to work with?"

"No." Artyom lifted his free hand and rubbed it over his face. "I'm the only family she has." The only family she had. The words repeated in his mind. Artyom was now truly alone.

"I'm afraid we cannot hold the body that long. I can put in the request to have her buried. You will be notified of her location by mail."

"But—" Artyom started to protest but stopped himself. He had a choice—stay home to bury his grandmother or go to Canada and get a glimpse of life outside the Soviet Union.

His grandmother's words echoed through his mind. *There's always a choice.*

What choice would she have him make?

He hated the idea of his grandmother being buried without him there, but she wouldn't want him to stop living. Quite the opposite. She wanted him to experience life.

"Mr. Belsky?"

"Please arrange for my grandmother's burial."

"Yes, sir. I'm sorry for your loss."

"Thank you." Artyom hung up the phone, his fingers numb from gripping the handle so tightly. He stared blankly at his modest apartment. His position had granted him some improvement in his situation in life, the one-bedroom unit a vast improvement over his grandmother's drafty apartment that was only half the size of his. Maybe she would still be alive if he had been granted enough space to have her live with him.

He shook that thought away. She hadn't wanted to lose her independence any more than he'd wanted to sacrifice his privacy. He moved back to the bedroom and stared at the half-packed suitcase. Tomorrow he would get on a plane bound for Canada. But he had one stop to make before he could start that journey. His grandmother may not have had much, but he didn't want to leave her wedding ring sitting in her apartment while he was gone. For all he knew, her apartment would be cleaned out long before he returned.

He grabbed his keys and his wallet. Grief shot through him as he headed for the door. Time for a trip down memory lane.

Chapter TWENTY-THREE

Viktor handed the keys to Ursula as they stood at the airport surrounded by athletes, coaches, and KGB agents. His heart raced, but he wasn't sure if it was fear coursing through him or excitement.

"You be safe." Ursula kissed him before turning to her children. "Josef, be a help for your papa. And, Sonya, skate your best."

"I will, Mama." Sonya hugged her, tears shimmering in her eyes. "I wish you could come too."

Ursula blinked back her own tears. "I know, milaya."

Viktor took Ursula's hand, needing to feel the connection while he could. "We'll see you soon."

Ursula pressed her lips together and nodded. Then Josef tugged at Viktor's sleeve. "It's time."

Viktor pulled his hand free of Ursula's, and soon he was walking across the tarmac to a set of stairs on wheels.

Sonya tucked her hand through his arm. "Can you believe we're going to Canada?"

"No, milaya. It is quite a miracle."

They boarded the plane, Josef looking wide-eyed as he entered the plane.

Viktor understood the sensation. Only once before had he been on a plane, when he had accompanied Sonya to the European Championships in Budapest.

Sonya led the way to their seats, claiming the window for herself.

Viktor motioned to Josef. "Take the seat beside your sister so you can see out the window too."

"I don't know if I want to see out the window."

"Come. Sit." Sonya set her purse beneath the seat in front of her and tugged on Josef's arm. "It's not scary. I promise."

Josef complied, but the tension in his body indicated he was far from ready for this part of their journey.

Viktor sat beside his son and patted his arm. "It's safe. We'll be fine."

Josef gave a curt nod.

"Fasten your seat belt." Sonya demonstrated how to clip the two pieces of the seat belt together. Josef mimicked the action until his seat belt was securely around him.

Within minutes, a voice came over the intercom, instructing them on how to fasten their seat belts as well as where to find the emergency exits. As the safety instruction continued, the tension in Josef's body increased steadily.

Sonya reached into the seat pocket in front of her and pulled out a folded bag and handed it to her brother.

"What is this?" Josef asked.

"It's for if you get sick." She gave him a haughty look. "I don't want you to throw up on me."

"I'm not going to get sick."

"You will if you don't relax," Sonya said. "Breathe."

Josef sucked in a breath. An instant later, the plane started to move. Josef dropped the bag Sonya had given him and gripped both arm rests.

Sonya leaned forward to look at Viktor. "You'd better give Josef your bag too."

A sense of nostalgia washed over Katerina when she stepped off the plane in Toronto. Canada had been the first country she had ever visited outside of the Soviet Union, and it would always have a special place in her heart. English and bits of French blended together as their group made their way through the terminal. She could speak both now, but for her first years with Robert, French had been their common language.

She glanced behind her at Amaliya, who had embraced all her heritage—American, French Canadian, and Russian. If only Katerina could have traveled with her daughter to the Soviet Union and visited the country of her birth.

She pushed that thought aside. This was her life now. She was free to do what she chose—except return to her homeland.

Robert laid his hand on her waist. "Baggage claim is this way." They made the walk through the terminal to the baggage claim. As soon as they reached the carousel, Robert turned to Gordon. "Can you and Tyler grab the bags? I'm going to pick up our rental car."

"That's fine." Gordon motioned toward the exit. "We'll meet you out front."

Forty-five minutes later, they were all loaded into the large sedan, the backpacks and small suitcases that wouldn't fit in the trunk resting on their laps.

"Katerina, you may have gotten a little carried away with bringing things for your brother," Robert said.

"There are so many more things I wish I could have bought for him." Katerina glanced over her shoulder at Amaliya. "Maybe we can do more shopping while we're here."

"Oh, no." Gordon shook his head. "These two need to focus on their skating."

"Linda will be here tomorrow. Maybe she can help." Katerina pursed her lips as she debated what else she could send home with Viktor. "Amaliya, what do you think they could need that I haven't already bought?"

"Blankets," Tyler answered for her. "Warm blankets."

Amaliya nodded. "He's right. That woodstove in the living room doesn't keep their house very warm."

"Let's focus on finding Viktor before we buy any more stuff for him," Robert suggested.

"Fine." Katerina looked down at her watch.

"Any idea what time the Soviet team arrives?" Tyler asked.

"Linda checked with her travel agent to find out what time flights were arriving in Toronto from the Soviet Union," Katerina said. "There are a couple of possibilities since all of the flights stop somewhere along the way, but the travel agent seemed to think they would get here around ten tonight."

"Seven hours from now." Amaliya looked from Katerina to Robert. "I know one of you is going to stay up and watch for Viktor. Who's it going to be?"

"Me." Robert glanced sideways at her. "I don't want you anywhere near the lobby when the Soviets arrive."

As much as she hated sitting around and waiting, Katerina couldn't deny that Robert's protective streak was warranted.

"Maybe I should be the one to watch for them," Gordon said. "I know what Viktor looks like."

"By the time they get here from the airport, it will be after eleven."

"That's okay. I can take a nap after dinner." Gordon glanced sideways at his skaters. "Assuming you can keep the kids out of trouble."

"We can do that on our own," Tyler said.

"I don't think he trusts us." Amaliya lowered her voice into a mock whisper. "There must be desserts in the hotel restaurant."

Katerina's smile bloomed on her face. "Pretty amazing desserts, if I remember correctly."

Robert glanced at Gordon in the rearview mirror. "Maybe I should wait downstairs with you. You can point Viktor out to me, and it will look more natural to have two of us sitting in the lobby talking rather than one person waiting alone."

"That's not a bad idea." Gordon nodded.

"I wish I could be the one waiting," Katerina said.

"I know," Robert said. "I'd take the Polaroid down there and take a photo for you, but I'm afraid that might look a bit too suspicious."

"You're probably right."

Robert kissed Katerina on the forehead. "Don't worry. If all goes well, it won't be long before you'll get to see him for yourself."

"Let's hope."

Amaliya lugged her skating bag and the smaller of her two suitcases into the hotel lobby.

"You could have left that out in the car," her dad said. "We can have a steward bring our luggage up to our rooms."

"Thanks, Papa, but Gordon doesn't like us to leave our skates and costumes in anyone else's hands."

"I have you trained." Gordon reached out and took Amaliya's suitcase. "You can trust me not to lose anything though."

"Thanks."

"I'll get us checked in." Her papa crossed through the quaint lobby, past the sofa and chairs that created a conversation area. Several more chairs were clustered beside a fireplace on the far side of the room, along with potted plants and occasional tables.

When her papa reached the hotel clerk, he spoke in a low voice before reaching into his pocket and slipping a bill free. Amaliya couldn't tell what denomination it was, but the clerk pocketed it and quickly proceeded to retrieve their room keys.

When her papa returned, he handed each of them their keys. Amaliya noted that she and Tyler were as far apart as possible. "Let's carry what we have up to our rooms now. Gordon and I can come back for the rest."

They all made their way to the elevator, and as soon as the doors slid closed, Amaliya asked, "Papa, why were you tipping the clerk?"

"I was hoping to improve our chances of seeing your uncle."

"How?"

"Our friend at the front desk confirmed the Soviets will be on the fifth floor," her papa said. "Our rooms are spread out on the fourth."

"How will that help us?" Amaliya asked.

"It may not, but having our balconies right below the Soviets could prove useful," her dad said.

Tyler stopped when he reached his room. "Want me to meet you back at the elevator to help with the luggage?"

"Sure." Gordon stopped at the next room. "Robert, we'll see you in a minute. Amaliya, I want you to stretch when you get to your room."

"Yes, Coach." Amaliya continued onward.

When her parents stopped at their room, her mama asked, "What room are you in?"

"Four seventeen."

"Wait a minute and I'll walk you to your room," her dad said.

"Papa, I'm fine going into my room alone."

"Indulge me. It never hurts to be careful." Her dad unlocked the door to his and Mama's room, which was located a few doors away from the stairwell. He opened it and escorted her mom inside.

Even though she knew her father was being overprotective, Amaliya followed her parents into their room. A kitchenette lined one wall, and a small table was situated by the sliding-glass door across the room. From where she stood, the bed wasn't visible, but there was a seating area with a couch, a chair, and a desk that filled the open space before her.

Her dad did a quick check of the room, including the bathroom and closet. "Okay, I'll walk you down now."

Amaliya led the way into the hall. "I know we talked about being careful, but the Soviets aren't even here yet. Don't you think you're being a bit paranoid?"

"We can't be sure there weren't some security people who came early." Her dad put his hand on her back. "Your mom risked a lot to stay with me. I'm not going to risk her safety now."

Despite her father's serious tone, Amaliya smiled. She really was lucky to have parents who still adored each other. They walked past several hotel rooms until they reached Amaliya's door. She slid the key into the lock and opened the door.

Her dad escorted her inside and crossed the simple room. He opened the balcony door and stepped outside. "I was afraid of this."

"What?"

"Your balcony adjoins the two on either side."

"So?"

"So, I don't like the idea of you having strangers with access to your back door." His brow furrowed. "Maybe I should see if we can get you into the room next to mine."

"Papa, it's not like some handsome stranger is going to sweep in and steal me away. I'm already engaged." Amaliya reached the balcony and looked out. The skyline of Toronto lay directly in front of her, a wrought-iron railing separating her small balcony from the ones on either side. "Besides, I know how to lock my door." She turned and looked back at her modest room. "And I'll be sure to keep my curtains closed at night."

"I don't know . . ."

"Papa, I'm a grown woman. I'm engaged to be married." Amaliya held up her left hand. "Maybe you need to trust me to take care of myself."

He scowled, a battle clearly waging within him. Finally, he huffed out a breath. "If you end up with a neighbor you don't feel comfortable with, I want to know right away."

"I promise."

He moved back inside, and Amaliya followed. When he reached the door leading into the hall, he pointed back at the balcony. "Keep that door locked."

Feeling like she had won a small victory, she smiled. "Yes, Papa."

Chapter TWENTY-FOUR

White tablecloths, low lights, muted classical music. Katerina took in the elegant surroundings of the French restaurant and breathed in the scents of freshly baked bread, rich sauces, and cooked meat.

"This place is something," Gordon said as they followed the maître d' through the main part of the dining room to a table in a private alcove.

"This is the last time Katerina will be able to leave the hotel for the next few days," Robert said. "I wanted to make sure she enjoyed it."

Amaliya grinned. "We don't mind."

Robert pulled out a chair for Katerina, waiting for her to sit before he claimed the spot beside her. She couldn't help but smile when Tyler followed the same ritual with Amaliya.

The maître d' passed out their menus, and Gordon opened his, but instead of focusing on the contents, he looked at Amaliya and Tyler. "I shouldn't have to remind you that you can't order just anything off the menu. You compete in four days."

"I'm sure we can find something we can agree on," Amaliya said.

"I doubt there's anything here we wouldn't like," Tyler agreed.

"It smells heavenly." Katerina scanned the menu, taking her time to read the descriptions before making her decision and setting her menu aside. She took in the lovely atmosphere again, appreciating these last moments of freedom. Nearly twenty-four years of freedom, yet with her decision to stay in the same hotel as the Soviets, she would once again be a prisoner.

She pushed that thought aside, determined to enjoy the moment.

As soon as the waiter took their orders, Robert said, "I have an idea of where we can have Katerina and Viktor meet."

"Where?" Katerina asked.

"We have a couple of options. Both our suite and Gordon's room have adjoining rooms. If we can somehow pass a key and room number to Viktor, he would be able to let himself into the connecting room and meet with you."

Katerina was still processing Robert's idea when Amaliya spoke. "You would willingly risk someone knowing where Mama is staying?"

"If somehow the key is intercepted by someone else, we'll change to a different floor," Robert said.

"How would this work? Even if we manage to get the key and room number to him, Viktor may not be able to get away at a specific time to meet me," Katerina said.

"We give him a note with the room number and tell him to call the hotel front desk. We can have the front desk forward the call to our room," Robert said. "That way we aren't risking someone finding the note and knowing what room we're in."

"That could work." Gordon picked up his glass. "And if you use the room next to mine, I can listen for someone coming in."

Anxiety rose within her, Katerina's chest tightening. Meeting Viktor was a risk. Was she willing to take the next step? She drew a deep breath. "We should use the room next to ours."

Robert looked at her skeptically. "Are you sure?"

She nodded. "If we do the one adjoining ours, I won't have to go out in the hotel and risk being seen in case he's followed."

"That is the big advantage of using the one next to us."

"And like you said, if someone else ends up with the note, we can switch rooms. Since there aren't room numbers on the hotel key cards, we don't have to worry about being found if just the key gets intercepted by someone else."

"I'll let the hotel staff know I want that extra room when we get back."

"Now, how are we going to pass the note?" Gordon asked.

"I'll do it," Amaliya said. "Viktor is more likely to trust me than anyone. Or I can pass it to Sonya."

"They both know me and Tyler too," Gordon said.

"Handing the key and note off at practice makes the most sense," Robert said. "But you need to be careful."

"Don't worry, Papa," Amaliya said. "We will."

Tyler couldn't sleep. No matter how many times he rolled over in bed, he couldn't quiet his thoughts. The job offers, the endorsements, the skaters

Gordon had auditioned, the financial requirements to continue training, wedding plans.

He stretched out on his bed and folded his hands beneath his head. Six months from now, he and Amaliya would be husband and wife. Or would they? Would Amaliya change her mind about a September wedding if they decided to compete for another year? He could guarantee Gordon wouldn't be happy if they added the stress of a wedding to the weeks before a major competition. As reigning US and Olympic champions, they could bypass regionals this year, but would they want to? The chance to iron out the kinks in their programs wasn't one they would often want to pass up.

Tyler pushed out of bed and crossed to the balcony. He stared out at the Toronto skyline, the lights twinkling before him. Possibilities circled through his head again. Could he and Amaliya find contentment living together in the apartment over the garage after they got married? He supposed there were worse things than having to share a kitchen with his in-laws. Not to mention that having Eleanor fixing a good number of their meals would take some of the pressure off them while they were training. Still, the lack of privacy, especially when it came to Robert hovering, wasn't a challenge to be ignored.

An engine rumbled through the darkness, a pair of headlights cutting across the parking lot. The vehicle took shape as it moved forward. A bus.

Tyler straightened. Could this be the bus bringing the Soviet team from the airport? He slipped his feet into his tennis shoes, put on his jacket, and stepped out onto the balcony. The cold air swept over him, and his breath plumed out.

The bus pulled to a stop beside the main entrance, which was only two rooms over and four floors down from where he now stood. He couldn't have asked for a better view of the people coming and going.

The doors whooshed open. Two men stepped out, followed by a third. Each was dressed in a long dark coat and wore a cap lined in fur.

The man wearing glasses waved at the other two as though issuing some sort of orders. The shortest of the three men walked into the hotel while the other moved toward the far end of the building. When he reached the corner, he disappeared from sight.

Several minutes passed, the glow of the hotel's outside lights shining on the silver bus. Finally, the man who had disappeared around the side of the building came back into view, but this time from the other direction. He was nearly back to the bus when the other man returned from inside.

The men spoke briefly. Then two of them walked back onto the bus, leaving the third to stand guard outside.

Several more minutes passed. Then the man with glasses stepped off the bus again, but this time, he was followed by a line of others: two men who looked to be either KGB or some sort of Soviet security, a woman wearing a thick knit cap, another man, and a young woman. Sidrova. Popov appeared behind her. Tyler remembered the pair well. They had been their main competition at the Olympics and would undoubtedly pose the greatest threat to him and Amaliya at the world championships.

The parade of people leaving the bus and walking into the hotel continued. Finally, Sonya stepped off the bus. When the next person emerged, Tyler narrowed his eyes. Was that Josef?

The man looked around. It was definitely Amaliya's older cousin. But where was Viktor? Tyler's heart sank. Had Katerina made all these plans to see her brother only to have him not show up?

Two more people followed Josef until a man with a fur cap stepped off. Unlike Josef, he didn't stop to look around. Instead, he carried two pieces of luggage into the hotel, his head down as he passed into the building. Could that have been Viktor? The man was the right height and build, but from this angle, Tyler couldn't be sure.

He watched the last few Soviets enter the hotel and stayed on his balcony long enough for several of the men to return to retrieve more luggage.

He shivered. Even though he wanted to wait outside until the bus pulled away, he returned to his room and locked his balcony door. He was hanging his coat in the closet when voices sounded in the hallway. Tyler pulled his door open and poked his head out. Gordon and Robert were both walking past.

"Did you find him?" Tyler asked.

Gordon scowled at him. "What are you still doing up?"

"I couldn't sleep." Tyler focused on Robert. "Did Viktor come with Sonya?"

Robert nodded. "Viktor is here."

Relief flooded through Tyler. "So is Josef."

Chapter TWENTY-FIVE

Viktor carried his and Josef's suitcases down the hall and searched for the correct room number. For the past forty-five minutes while Josef had translated for the hotel staff, Viktor had helped bring in the athletes' luggage and deliver it to their rooms. Now, finally, he was free to find his own room and his own bed.

Perspiration dotted his brow, and a trickle of sweat dripped down the center of his back.

He passed by Oleg, one of the guards assigned to Sonya, and continued halfway down the hall until he reached the correct door. Though his room key was in his pocket, rather than set down the suitcases, he used his elbow to knock on the door.

Josef opened it an instant later. "Sorry, Papa. I was about to come down to help you."

"It's okay. This is the last of it." Viktor walked into the room that they would share during their time in Canada. Warmth greeted him.

Josef relieved him of his suitcase and set it on the floor. "I just finished interpreting for Mr. Belsky and the hotel manager. Breakfast will be brought to our floor in the morning at nine. We will need to deliver the food to everyone's rooms."

Viktor pulled off his gloves and moved past the bathroom to his left. Two beds, each with thick down comforters, a long dresser across from them, a small table with two chairs beside it.

He set down his suitcase and stripped off his coat, hat, and scarf. The simple act brought with it a pang of regret. Standing inside without having to wear a coat. Ursula should be here to experience the sensation with him.

He crossed the room to where heavy drapes covered the window opposite him and pulled aside the curtains to reveal a large glass door leading to a small balcony. Two wrought-iron chairs occupied the space, both crusted in a layer of ice and snow.

Snow outside, yet he was sweating inside. He used his sleeve to wipe his brow.

His gaze lifted to take in the city lights twinkling in the darkness. So many lights, as though people could keep their curtains open despite the cold. Perhaps they could.

After all, here he was in March, and he wasn't wearing a coat.

Was Katerina's home like this too? Her letters were filled with images of warmth, beauty, and opportunity. How much of that was real, and how much was imagined? More importantly, would he have the chance to ask such questions in person? Or ever?

He returned to where he had left his suitcase and opened it. His CCCP sweater lay on top, the newness contrasting against the ragged clothing that lay beneath. Despite his weariness, he pulled open a drawer and transferred his meager belongings into the dresser.

After he retrieved his sleeping clothes, he said, "We should go to bed."

"I'm not tired."

"You will be come morning."

"At home, it is morning," Josef said.

"True, but you didn't sleep that much on the plane."

"It was hard to with Oleg snoring and Popov and Sidrova talking about how they were going to beat Amaliya and Tyler."

Viktor's eyebrows lifted. "You didn't seem terribly fond of your cousin when she visited us in our home."

"I don't know Amaliya," Josef countered.

Viktor closed the dresser drawer and set his suitcase beside the wall. "But you didn't like Popov and Sidrova talking about beating them?"

"People know she is our family."

"Ah, so it's our family pride that's at stake."

Josef traded places with Viktor and unpacked his clothes into the second drawer. The third drawer remained empty. They didn't have enough clothes to fill even the first two. "People will be talking about the connection, and I will be helping translate for those media interviews. I don't look forward to the ones with Popov and Sidrova."

"Wait." Viktor straightened. "You're doing the media interviews? I thought Samuil was taking care of those."

"He is, but there will be a few times when there will be press conferences going on at the same time in the early rounds of competition, so we may both be needed."

"You will be able to attend your sister's competitions, won't you?"

"Coach Turgenev has asked that I be there for all of Sonya's performances."

"Good." Viktor started to ask about Amaliya's as well, but he didn't dare. If anyone was listening, it wouldn't do for either of them to express any special interest in connecting with her again. Instead, he said, "Best get ready for bed."

"In a bit." Josef's gaze wandered to the skyline that illuminated the darkness. "Can you believe we're here?"

"No." Never had Viktor considered he would be permitted outside of his homeland, much less eastern Europe, yet here he was in the land of the free. Or maybe that was the United States. Regardless, he was on the same continent as his sister for the first time in nearly twenty-five years. He let the sense of wonder sweep over him. Was Katerina here yet? And if so, where was she? And would he be able to find her?

Katerina paced her room until the doorknob turned. She barely let Robert walk in the door before she asked, "Did you see him? Is Viktor here?"

Robert slid the security bolt into place. "Viktor is here."

Tears sprang to her eyes, pure joy rushing through her. Her brother was here in the very same hotel as her. So many years, so many prayers that she would see him again could truly be answered.

Robert reached out and brushed away a tear that spilled over. "I hope those are happy tears."

She swallowed hard and nodded. "You really saw him?"

"Gordon pointed him out." Robert toed off his shoes. "Sonya too."

"I can't believe they're really here."

"It's not just them. Josef came too."

Katerina pictured the toddler who had barely been learning to walk the last time she'd seen him. He must be twenty-five or twenty-six now. Had Sonya really been permitted to bring her whole family? "Did Ursula come as well?"

"I don't know what she looks like, but Tyler didn't see her," Robert said.

"Tyler?" Katerina's eyes narrowed. "What was he doing with you?"

"He wasn't with us. He watched from the window and then came out and talked to me and Gordon when we came back upstairs."

The errant thought that Gordon wouldn't be happy about one of his skaters being up so late flitted through her mind, but Katerina focused on the purpose of why she was still awake at nearly one in the morning. "How did Viktor look?"

"Good, as far as I could tell." Robert shrugged. "You were right about him needing new gloves, but other than that, he looked like everyone else walking through the hotel lobby: serious and exhausted."

"Serious?"

"Yeah." Robert sat on the side of the bed. "Why is it that Soviets always seem so serious?"

"I'm not."

"Maybe not now, but you were when we first met."

Katerina let the memories flow over her from her and Robert's early days together. "I was in danger of being sent home if anyone found out I was talking to you."

"Maybe they're all worried about the KGB or their security people or whoever is watching them."

"They're wise to be worried. So are we." Katerina sat beside him. "Is it selfish of me to risk Viktor's safety just so I can talk to him?"

"That's not selfish. That's normal," Robert said. "Besides, from what Amaliya said, Viktor is every bit as eager to see you as you are to see him."

"I hope we can find a way for it to happen."

"We'll find a way." Robert leaned in and kissed her. "But until we do, we're keeping you out of sight."

"Your protective streak is coming out again."

"You should be used to it by now."

Katerina cocked an eyebrow. "As a matter of fact, I am."

Artyom stood in the hotel hallway, his body so tired he could barely move, much less think. Unfortunately, one of his many responsibilities tonight was to ensure everyone made it safely to their rooms and that no one was left unaccounted for.

In front of him, chaperones knocked on doors, checked on athletes and staff, and reported to Kirill, the security officer tasked with tonight's bed check.

With so many people present to make sure everyone was safely in their rooms, Artyom didn't know why his presence was necessary, but Grigori had assigned him this task. Artyom wasn't about to disobey an assignment only hours after arriving in Canada.

The blur of the past forty-eight hours tumbled through his mind. The arrangements for his grandmother's burial, the last-minute details as he'd left for the airport, the long flight, and the tension of knowing his role in Budimir's plans.

Artyom had made a point of chatting with the Petrov family on the plane. Unfortunately, that also meant he needed to make conversation with all the other athletes as well to make sure nothing looked amiss.

He didn't want to think about the paperwork he had planned to review during the flight. By the time he had checked in with everyone traveling with him, he had been unable to focus on anything beyond taking a nap. He couldn't imagine where he would be now if he hadn't given himself that luxury.

He held out a hand. It trembled. He needed sleep. Soon.

Someone approached from the elevators, and instantly, Artyom's blood turned to ice. Budimir.

"The stairwells have been secured," Budimir said. "The last guards are checking the grounds one last time before they relieve the men by the stairwell doors and the elevators."

Artyom didn't know why Budimir was telling him this. His only role with security was making sure they knew who was supposed to be leaving the hotel and when. "The bed checks are almost done."

"And the practice schedules for tomorrow are taken care of?" Budimir asked.

"It's all set." Artyom swallowed and tried not to think about what his involvement might mean to the Petrov family. "Unless a change was made while we were traveling, Sonya is practicing at the same time as her cousin."

"Good. If we give the Americans a way to communicate with Viktor, it's only a matter of time before he tries to meet with his sister."

"How do you expect to get her out of Canada?"

"Simple. We will take her to the Soviet embassy. Once she is inside, there is nothing the Americans can do," Budimir said. "And the Canadians will not want to get on our bad side."

"They are allies with the United States."

"Yes, but Katerina Petrova is first and foremost a Soviet citizen."

A Soviet citizen who had spent half her life in the United States. Was she really still Soviet? Or was she an American now?

Eager to have this conversation end, Artyom said, "I'd best see if Kirill is done. I need to get some sleep."

"Good idea." Budimir shot him a knowing look. "We have a big day tomorrow."

"My day will be spent juggling paperwork and transportation schedules," Artyom said, needing to distance himself from the end goal Budimir had planned.

"All of us must do our part to ensure our athletes' success."

"That success will start with allowing everyone to sleep in tomorrow," Artyom said.

Budimir motioned in the general direction of the elevator. "The breakfast arrangements have been scheduled accordingly."

Kirill approached carrying his clipboard. "Everyone is accounted for."

"Thank you." Artyom initialed the bottom of the form Kirill offered him. "Now, if you'll excuse me, I'm going to bed." He left the two men and made his way to his room. He used the flat key card and slid it into the lock. The moment he closed the door behind him, he kicked off his shoes and changed into his night clothes, then flopped onto his bed and gave a fleeting thought to reviewing the latest practice and transportation schedule. He closed his eyes and let his body relax. Tomorrow. He would review the schedules tomorrow.

Chapter TWENTY-SIX

ANTICIPATION FLUTTERED INSIDE AMALIYA, AS if she were about to compete in the Olympics rather than go to practice. Her empty breakfast dishes lay on the desk, evidence that her father and Gordon were taking every precaution to make sure the Soviets didn't know they were staying at the same hotel as them.

What would happen if they were seen? Or more specifically, what would they do if the Soviets saw her mother? A healthy dose of fear rippled through her.

When her uncle mentioned bringing her mother to Canada, Amaliya had been thrilled at the prospect of her mom reconnecting with the brother she had missed for so long. Now she couldn't help but question whether the risk was worth it.

A sharp rap sounded at her door. She startled and lifted her hand to her chest. Another knock.

She willed her pulse to settle and peeked through the peephole in the door. Tyler and Gordon stood on the other side.

She pulled the door open.

"Are you ready?" Tyler asked.

"Come on in. I just need to put on my shoes." Amaliya retrieved her boots from the closet and sat on her bed.

Tyler moved to the balcony door. "Nice view."

"Too bad you won't be here much to enjoy it," Gordon said.

Amaliya pulled on her boots, her earlier thoughts circling through her head. "Is this really worth it?"

"Is what really worth it?" Tyler asked.

"Staying at this hotel, risking Mama's safety so she can see her brother." Amaliya stood. "They've already lived a whole lifetime apart. What will it matter if they see each other now?"

Tyler's eyebrows rose, and he looked at her incredulously. "This coming from the girl who was ready to risk anything to find her uncle at the Olympics?"

"Yeah, but I'm an American citizen. It's not like the Soviets could have really done anything to me while we were in Leningrad."

"It sure felt like they could do whatever they wanted," Tyler muttered.

"Tyler's right," Gordon said. "Having an agent following us around was nerve-racking."

"Yes, but when we were there, I was trying to find out if Viktor was even still alive, to help my mom learn what happened to him after she defected." Amaliya stood. "I already did that."

"You did do that," Gordon agreed. "But your mother still hasn't experienced that closure. She hasn't seen for herself that her brother survived her choices."

"But we've told her he's okay."

"Yes, but family ties run strong," Gordon said. "If it were your mom or dad you hadn't seen in twenty-plus years, wouldn't you need to see them for yourself?"

She couldn't deny it. Even the drive to find her uncle had been born of some intangible link to her family and her heritage. "I'm worried about my mom."

"Your dad will make sure she stays out of sight," Tyler said.

"Speaking of staying out of sight, it's time to go." Gordon motioned to the door.

Amaliya retrieved her coat from her closet and slipped it on. As soon as she lifted the hood into place, Gordon opened the door and led the way to the stairwell, where they descended the four flights of stairs to the ground level.

"Where are you parked?" Tyler asked.

"Right outside the door." Gordon reached the door. "Wait here for a minute. I'm going to unlock the car before you come out." He pushed the door open, and a blast of arctic air rushed inside. Amaliya shivered.

As soon as Gordon disappeared outside, Tyler pulled the door closed. "I'm suddenly missing Virginia."

"It's cold in Virginia too."

"Yeah, but not this cold."

Amaliya couldn't help but laugh. "And we spend most of our time inside an ice rink."

"Okay, so we're both a little crazy."

"A lot crazy is more like it." She blew out a breath. "I'm nervous about today."

"About what? Trying to see Sonya, or what might happen here at the hotel while we're gone?"

"Both."

"Maybe we should just concentrate on skating today." Tyler leaned down and kissed her. "Or we can start planning our honeymoon."

"We have a few months before we have to decide on that."

"Doesn't hurt to think ahead." Tyler pulled the door open a crack and peered through. Another gust of frigid air blasted inside. "I vote for somewhere warm."

Amaliya shivered again and put her hand in his. "I agree."

Anticipation flowed through Tyler as he approached the practice ice and removed his skate guards. The pairs competition would begin in three days, as would the women's competition.

Amaliya stepped beside him and looked around. "I don't see Sonya anywhere."

Tyler glanced behind him. Except for the Canadian men's champion, the rink was completely empty. "It's already seven. Maybe the Soviets are letting their athletes sleep in today."

"Maybe."

Gordon approached with his skates dangling from his fingers. "I checked with the rink manager. We have to share with the Canadian for a half hour, but after that, we'll have the ice to ourselves."

"Really?" Tyler asked. "How did that happen?"

"Yeah. I thought Sonya was practicing with us."

"The Soviets aren't coming in until this afternoon." Gordon sat on a nearby bench and took off his shoes. "You two go warm up. I'll meet you out there."

Tyler stepped onto the ice and took Amaliya's hand. He didn't miss the look of disappointment on her face. "I'm sure we'll see her later."

Amaliya pressed her lips together and nodded.

A short distance away, the Canadian performed a triple lutz. He stepped out on his landing and stumbled toward them. Amaliya gasped and quickly came to a stop. Tyler turned to put himself between Amaliya and the Canadian. The Canadian whipped by them, missing Tyler by inches.

"Sorry!" the other skater called out as he regained his balance and continued onward.

Tyler looked down at Amaliya. "Are you okay?"

"Yeah."

Tyler blew out a breath. "That is one thing I won't miss if we decide to go pro."

"What?"

"Having to worry about other competitors getting in our way at practice."

"Um, have you ever been to an ice show?" Amaliya pushed off to continue warming up. She waited until he took his place beside her before she continued. "They have tons of people on the ice for their performances. I imagine their practices won't be much different."

Tyler tried to fish back in his memory to the handful of times his parents had taken him and Carolyn to various ice shows. A few solo performances mixed among a crowd of chorus skaters. Amaliya was right. The number of skaters was excessive.

Gordon skated to the center of the ice and waited for them to finish another lap. As he had done a thousand times, Tyler kept Amaliya's hand in his and cut across the ice to meet their coach and receive instruction.

Their coach.

The image of Gordon going through this routine with someone else surfaced, but before it could take hold completely, Gordon spoke.

"I know we planned to work on figures this morning, but I think we need to take advantage of having the rink to ourselves."

"Are we going through both programs?" Amaliya asked.

"We'll start with the short. You need to gain more confidence with that one," Gordon said. "Let's start with your side-by-side spins."

Tyler and Amaliya lined up and followed Gordon's instructions. Another set of spins followed and then several dance sequences.

When the Canadian exited the ice five minutes early, Gordon said, "I'll cue up your music. Let's see how your short program looks today."

"Okay." Amaliya shook her hands at her side.

"Are you as nervous about this one as I am?"

"More."

"More?" Tyler's eyebrows lifted. "How do you figure?"

"I'm the one who choreographed most of the changes." Amaliya rolled her shoulders. "If it doesn't work, it's my fault."

"Hey, we're a team. Win or lose."

"I think Gordon would prefer we win."

Tyler couldn't help but laugh. "You've got that right."

"Come on." Amaliya led the way to the center of the rink. "We're supposed to be having fun, remember?"

"It doesn't seem like that long ago when I was telling you the same thing."

She grinned. "It wasn't."

They took their starting positions. Have fun. He could do that.

Their new music started, and they both went into motion. They danced the new opening sequence and then came together for the triple twist lift. Strength, timing, magic—all three combined as Tyler sent Amaliya into the air and she twisted three times above his head. He grabbed her waist as she came down, and her arms lifted in victory.

Her grin was instant, and Tyler smiled back as the music moved through him. They transitioned into the next portion of their routine, jumping, spinning, and dancing together.

A step out on Amaliya's double axel, a choreography error as he came out of their combination jumps, but overall, the routine was solid. The question was, Could they get it to gold-medal worthy within the next few days?

They reached their final poses, and applause sounded from the side of the rink.

Tyler turned, his smile widening when he spotted his parents. He closed the distance between them. "Mom. Dad. What are you doing here?" He gave them each a hug despite the rink barrier that separated them.

"We just got in," his mom said. "Linda and Miles seemed to think we might be able to help with a few things if we came early."

A few things. As in helping Katerina reconnect with Viktor.

Amaliya reached his side, and his parents greeted her warmly.

"Congratulations to both of you on your engagement," his mom said. "We're so excited for you."

Gordon skated to where they stood. "I hate to break this up, but we still have work to do."

"Sorry." His mom raised a hand apologetically. "We'll see you back at the hotel."

"Aren't you going to stay and watch?" Tyler asked.

"We just wanted to take a look around the facility here," his dad said.

Out of the corner of his eye, Tyler caught a glimpse of Miles talking to someone near the top of the bleachers. It appeared his parents really were involving themselves with the plot to reconnect Katerina with her brother. Concern for their safety surfaced briefly before Tyler took a good look around. They were in Canada, not the Soviet Union. The Soviets had no authority here. His family was safe.

Chapter TWENTY-SEVEN

Katerina stood to the side of the glass door leading to the balcony, her gaze scanning the parking lot below. A single bus stretched across six spaces beside the copse of trees that bordered the lot.

The Soviets must have opted to give their athletes the morning off. Katerina's first morning after arriving in Canada with the Kirov had been a late start too.

Memories flooded through her of her first days in North America. Arriving at the hotel late one evening, marveling at the sensation of standing on a continent so far from her homeland, walking onto her balcony and meeting a handsome stranger, who hadn't remained a stranger for long.

Robert emerged from the bathroom, his hair still damp from his shower. He was still handsome. Katerina smiled.

Robert retrieved his watch from the dresser and slipped it onto his wrist, then glanced at her. His eyebrows drew together. "What are you smiling at?"

"You." Katerina abandoned her post by the balcony and crossed to him. She slid her arms around his waist. "I was just thinking about the night I first met you."

"Really?" He leaned down and kissed her. "I was thinking about two nights after that."

More memories rushed through her. The candle on her balcony table, the fresh strawberries and cream Robert had brought her, the hours they'd spent talking. "That was a pretty great night."

"It was." Robert dipped his head for another kiss, his lips firm against hers, a spark working through her, this one born of familiarity rather than the promise of new love.

A knock sounded on their door, and Katerina startled.

"Don't worry." Robert stepped out of her embrace. "That's probably just our breakfast."

A little ripple of fear snaked through her. "Check first."

Robert complied by peeking through the peephole before pulling the door open.

A man stood in the hall, a food-service tray in his hand. "Room service."

"Right on time." Robert reached into his pocket and pulled out his wallet. He fished out a couple of bills and exchanged them for the tray that held three covered plates, a carafe of orange juice, and two glass goblets.

"Thank you, sir." The man pocketed the tip.

"Thank you." Robert closed the door and carried the tray to the table in the corner of the room.

"When did you order breakfast?" Katerina asked.

"When you were in the shower." He set their food and drinks on the table and set the tray aside. "I'm afraid it's too cold to eat outside, so this will have to do."

"What did you get me?" Katerina lifted the lid of the first plate. Croissants. She lifted the next cover. An arrangement of meat and cheese. "This looks wonderful, but it's more than we can eat for breakfast."

"Miles and Linda are coming over in a little while. Linda said she'd bring some Ziploc bags so we can store what we don't eat and save it for later."

"Making sure you aren't without any snacks?"

"Something like that." Robert put his hand on the lid of the last plate cover. "I have a feeling we'll want to eat this while it's fresh though." He lifted the lid.

"Strawberries and cream?"

"Just like we had on our first date." Robert set the cover aside.

Katerina's heart warmed, and she leaned in for another kiss. "Thank you. This is wonderful."

"You're welcome." Robert settled into his chair and waited for Katerina to sit across from him. "I know this week will bring up a lot of emotions. I wanted to make sure you had some happy memories."

"I have a lot of happy memories from our time here."

"Me too." Robert picked up a strawberry and swirled it in the bowl of fresh cream before he held it out to her.

She leaned closer and took a bite. The sweetness exploded on her taste buds. "Mmm. Yep. This is still one of my favorite treats."

Robert leaned in for another kiss. "I was hoping you would say that."

Artyom sat inside his hotel room, his half-eaten breakfast on the table before him and the empty sensation of grief filling his chest. He was thirty-seven years old, a widower with no children, and now had no living family he could call his own.

His hand lifted to the necklace hanging from his neck and the rings that adorned it. His wife's wedding ring, his parents', and now his grandparents' jangled together. Despite the two years that had passed since losing his wife, his own wedding band remained on his right hand, the three interlocking rings signifying the past, present, and future. He couldn't return to the past, he didn't want to live with the pain in his present . . . and the future? What would that hold? Day after day of never knowing if he would be left to do his work in peace or be subjected to his superiors' latest whims? Living alone in his one-bedroom apartment with no time to move beyond the painful losses of the past, much less try to create new relationships?

Loneliness swamped through him.

He pushed away from the table and crossed to the balcony. Despite the cold, he opened the sliding-glass door, stepped outside, and breathed in the fresh air. The scent of cooked meat wafted on the breeze, along with the telltale odor of a nearby body of water. Not the ocean, like in Leningrad, but fresh water. A lake. If his geography lessons served, Toronto bordered a Great Lake.

In the parking lot below, a gray-haired couple crossed to a large car. A man pushing a luggage cart followed behind them. The older man unlocked the car, and the valet proceeded to load the suitcases, all five of them, into the trunk. Did these people really own that many clothes?

Artyom took another step forward. His breath plumed out in front of him, and he shivered.

The door to the balcony beside him slid open, and Viktor emerged. Viktor caught sight of Artyom.

"I'm sorry." Viktor took a step back. "I didn't mean to disturb you."

"It's fine." Artyom waved absently toward the couple below. "I was just taking in what a different world we are in right now."

"Different how?" Viktor asked.

"That couple down there." The woman climbed into the car while the man tipped the valet. "Five suitcases for the two of them."

Viktor's eyes widened. "Five?"

"Have you ever heard of such a thing?"

"Only in stories." Viktor stuffed his hands into the pockets of his coat. The sleeves were threadbare at the elbows, and a small hole had formed on the edge of the pocket, likely from his using the pockets to protect his hands from the cold.

Artyom gazed out at the skyline. "We will have many stories to tell when we return home from here."

"Yes, we will." Viktor took a step back. "I'd best start collecting the breakfast dishes."

"Are you accompanying Sonya to her practice this afternoon?"

"Yes. Coach Turgenev wants me to supervise the skaters' equipment and ensure that the ice is groomed properly."

"It's an important task," Artyom said.

"A necessary one anyway." Viktor moved to the door. "Enjoy the rest of your morning."

Artyom shivered again but remained where he was. At least the cold proved that he could still feel. Or perhaps he was just numb inside and out. He couldn't tell.

Viktor pushed the room-service cart down the hall and knocked on Sonya's door. He had deliberately collected the dirty dishes from the other rooms first so he would have a moment to speak with his daughter alone. Not that they would really be alone, not with the listening devices security had planted in all the athletes' rooms. Why else would the security team have taken the time to check everyone's rooms before allowing them to enter last night?

He had hoped to speak with Sonya when he and Josef had handed out everyone's breakfast, but one of the female chaperones had insisted on delivering the meals to the female athletes.

The door opened, and Sonya's face lit up. "Hi, Papa."

"Are you finished with your breakfast?"

"Yes." She waved him forward. "Come in."

Viktor was halfway inside when he sensed movement.

"Zoya and I were just stretching."

"Your coach will be pleased." Viktor reached the main area of the room where Zoya was standing in the open area beyond one of the beds, her arms lifted above her head.

He glanced at the two beds, both of them made but slightly rumpled. "Are the two of you roommates?"

"Yes." Zoya lowered her arms and cast a haughty look his way. "Security no longer allows anyone to have their own room. Something about past trouble with defectors."

The verbal dart hit home. Clearly, Zoya was referring to Katerina. Ignoring the comment, Viktor asked, "Do either of you need anything before you leave for practice?"

"We're fine, Papa." Sonya stacked the dirty dishes on the food-service tray they had been delivered on and handed the tray to Viktor. "You're coming to watch me at practice, aren't you?"

"I'll be there." He would be working rather than watching, but Sonya would likely be too busy on the ice to notice.

"Good." Sonya motioned to the door. "Let me get that for you."

"Thank you." Viktor carried the tray to the door and waited for her to open the door for him. When she did, he set the dishes on the cart and gave her a hug. He lowered his voice and whispered, "If you see your cousin, ask if her mother is here."

"I will," she whispered back.

When Viktor released her, he studied her face. Excitement illuminated her expression, but he didn't sense any trace of fear. Was she too naive of the dangers facing her if she wasn't careful? Too much time spent with a Westerner or an overheard conversation could bring her to the attention of the KGB in a way neither of them wanted.

Viktor leaned closer to warn her, but before he could utter a word, Oleg called out. "Viktor, Grigori wishes to speak to you."

"I will be right there," Viktor said. He turned back to Sonya.

"Now." Oleg approached. "I will have these sent back to the kitchen."

Sonya took a step back. "I'd better finish stretching. See you later."

"Be good," Viktor said, offering the only warning he could in front of Oleg. After Sonya disappeared back into her room, he asked, "Where is Grigori?"

"In his room. It's number 523."

Viktor made his way down the hall and knocked on Grigori's door.

Grigori opened it a moment later. "Oh good, you're here." He escorted Viktor into his room. Unlike Viktor's room or his daughter's, this was much grander, a single large bed along one wall and a kitchen space that stretched along another wall. Apparently, not everyone had to share a room.

"Did everything go smoothly this morning with delivering breakfast?" Grigori asked.

"Yes. I was just picking up the last of the dishes." Viktor glanced around the room again. Even though he knew he shouldn't question the man who was in essence his boss, he asked, "Is it wise to have Sonya rooming with her biggest competition?"

"All of the athletes have roommates. It's standard procedure."

"Wouldn't it make sense to have others room together instead?"

Grigori's eyebrows rose. "Are you going to tell the officials accompanying us that they should share a room?"

"No," Viktor said, instantly repentant. The last thing he needed was to upset the man running things here in Canada.

"Arrangements have been made for you to be trained on the equipment at the practice rink." Grigori took a seat in the center of the couch but did not invite Viktor to sit with him. "After Sonya's practice tomorrow, you will need to stay for Popov and Sidrova's session. Sidrova needs her skates sharpened before she returns to the rink on Wednesday."

"Why didn't she have them sharpened before we traveled?"

"She is very particular about consistency. She sharpens her skates every twenty-four hours she is on the ice. It had only been eighteen."

Viktor swallowed his opinions about the pampered skater. Not for the first time, he hoped Amaliya and Tyler would beat the arrogant Soviet pair. "Is there anything else?" he asked.

"Yes. Day after tomorrow when the athletes are at practice, you will need to help with the laundry." He waved a hand absently through the air. "I don't know why people can't last more than three days without having their clothes cleaned, but one of the chaperones is insisting it is necessary."

Viktor didn't mention that it was probably because they didn't have enough clothes to last more than a few days without washing them—he fell into that same category. "I'm happy to help wherever I can, but my wife is the one who does the laundry in our house."

"The women simply need your help collecting the clothes and hauling them down to the washers." He waved toward the door. "Best finish with your tasks. The bus will be leaving in five minutes for practice."

Viktor nodded and backed out of the room. He had come to Canada to watch his daughter compete and to connect with his sister. Not just connect with her but also to warn her. Fear for her safety rose within him. Would he find the opportunity to see Katerina, to make sure she remained safe, or would the next two weeks be filled with chores and distractions that would erase any possibility of achieving his deep-seated desires?

Chapter TWENTY-EIGHT

Amaliya and Tyler took their time stretching for their practice session, Amaliya's gaze constantly sweeping over the entrance to the practice rink.

"They might not be here this afternoon either," Tyler said.

"I know, but I keep hoping."

Gordon approached, his skates already on his feet. "I spoke with the rink manager. As far as he knows, the Soviets are supposed to be here." Gordon turned to Amaliya. "Do you have the key and the note?"

"Yeah." She patted the pocket in her workout pants where she had tucked the note from her mother.

"Best let me hold on to those for now," Gordon said. "I don't trust the Soviets to stay out of our stuff, and you don't want to have anything flying out of your pocket when you're practicing."

Amaliya reached into her pocket and passed the note and the hotel key to Gordon. "Thanks."

"Finish stretching." Gordon slipped both items into his pocket. "I have your music for your long program already cued up."

The door opened, and a dozen people walked inside. Amaliya's heartbeat quickened when she spotted Sonya near the front of the crowd. Her coach stood on one side of her and a man in his thirties on the other.

Her coach, Turgenev, said something Amaliya couldn't hear. In response, Sonya and another skater moved to a nearby bench. As soon as they sat down, Amaliya spotted her uncle and Josef.

"Viktor and Josef are here too."

"Maybe you won't need to pass a note through Sonya," Gordon said quietly. "You may be able to speak to him directly."

After so much planning and worrying, could it be that simple?

Viktor caught sight of Amaliya. She started to lift her hand to wave but fought against the instinct. Would drawing attention to her connection to her uncle cause problems?

The man with Viktor and Josef motioned them both toward the skating office. They disappeared inside.

"Best get warmed up," Gordon said. "We'll give you a break if we see an opening for you to talk to him."

"Thanks."

"You stay focused out there though," Gordon warned.

"I will."

"Come on." Tyler took her hand. "Maybe we'll get the chance to talk to Sonya while we're on the ice."

Amaliya doubted it, but she could hope. She fell into step with Tyler, the note in Gordon's pocket at the forefront of her mind. What if the Soviets demanded Sonya change to a different practice time? What if she wouldn't get to talk to her cousin at all while she was in Canada? More importantly, could she find a way to communicate with Viktor so he could meet with her mother?

"Hey, relax." Tyler let go of her hand and slipped his arm around her waist.

"Sorry."

"The best thing we can do is go about our practice like usual," Tyler said. "If the KGB doesn't think we're trying to talk to your family, they're less likely to cause problems for us later."

"You're right." She leaned into him and followed his lead to the center of the rink, where Gordon waited.

"Let's go through the long program now before we have other skaters on the ice," Gordon said.

Tyler released her and shook out his hands. "Okay. Let's do this."

Amaliya moved to her starting position, struck by how much more confident she and Tyler had been only a month ago at the Olympics. She forced thoughts of everyone else out of her mind and placed her hand in Tyler's. They were the Olympic gold medalists. Now they just had to skate like it.

She lifted her chin, willing herself to find the same connection with Tyler that she'd had when they'd competed in Leningrad.

Tyler gazed down at her, the love in his eyes clear. She squeezed his hand in a silent signal of encouragement. The music began, and together they moved.

They danced through the first sequence and performed the triple twist lift without error. The thought flitted through her mind that they were crazy to do such a difficult move in both programs, but when Tyler took her hand for their death spiral, she forced herself to focus.

A combined spin, a minor timing error on their landings when they executed their double axels. Her muscles burned as they continued through each move, her focus remaining on her partner.

The moment they finished, the sound of skates on ice carried to her. She straightened from her final pose and couldn't stop her grin from forming when Sonya reached her side.

"That was wonderful!" Sonya gave her a hug.

"Thank you." Amaliya lowered her voice. "My mother is here—"

That was as far as she got before Turgenev's voice cut through the rink. "Sonya, get back over here."

Sonya startled and turned toward her coach. "I'll talk to you later."

Sonya skated off before Amaliya could make another attempt to pass information.

Tyler put his hand on her back. "I don't think her coach is going to let the two of you spend time together."

Amaliya sighed. "We suspected that would be the case."

Gordon glided to them. "Put your family out of your mind. Double axels. Your timing was off."

Amaliya watched Sonya begin her warm-up as she and the other Soviet skater circled the rink opposite each other. She forced herself to focus on Gordon once more. "Tell us what we need to fix."

They needed a few minor corrections, but their programs were coming together. Tyler blew out a breath, for the first time in weeks gaining the confidence that he and Amaliya might be able to repeat their gold-medal performances. Maybe another trip to the top spot on the medal stand would create more opportunities for sponsorships.

"Not too shabby." Gordon joined him at the side of the rink after they finished going through the last of their figures. He lowered his voice. "I'll see if I can pass the note to Viktor while the two of you change out of your skates."

"Maybe I should . . ." Amaliya began.

"They're already watching you," Gordon said, his voice low. "Take your time putting your shoes on. Maybe you'll get lucky and you'll be able to talk to Sonya again."

Amaliya glanced across the rink, where Sonya stood beside her coach. "I doubt that's going to happen."

Tyler put his hand on the small of her back. "Come on. We'll take a few laps to cool down before we put our shoes on."

"Good idea." Gordon left them and skated to the edge of the rink.

Tyler took Amaliya's hand, and they started their first lap around the outside of the rink. They approached where the Soviet coach stood, both Sonya and the other skater working on their jumps.

As soon as they passed them, Amaliya asked, "What do you think the chances are that Sonya will be in our practice time again tomorrow?"

"It's hard to say." Tyler was tempted to look at the Soviet coach and skaters, but the presence of several Soviet security people positioned around the edge of the rink was enough to deter him. He lowered his voice. "We'll find out tomorrow."

"If I can survive that long."

"You need to relax." Tyler squeezed her hand. "We're here to win a medal, remember?"

"Yeah, I remember."

Gordon appeared at the edge of the rink and motioned to them.

"Looks like our cooldown is over." Tyler guided Amaliya to the opening in the rink barrier.

"Did you see Viktor?" Amaliya asked, her voice low.

"He's learning how to use the blade sharpener in the office, but there were so many people in there, I wasn't able to get close to him." Gordon reached into his pocket and retrieved the note and key. "Take these. Maybe you can slip them into Sonya's skating bag."

"It's worth a try." Amaliya took both items from Gordon and tucked them into her pocket.

Tyler glanced around to make sure none of the Soviets were nearby. One had taken position near the entrance, another stood outside the office door, and a third waited beside the bench where the Soviets had left their bags. "I'm not sure we'll be able to get near their bags."

"I guess I'd better hope Sonya needs to use the restroom, then." Amaliya tugged on Tyler's hand. "I'm going to change out of my skates in case I get the chance to see her in the locker room."

Tyler tensed. Amaliya alone with Sonya was one thing, but the stocky woman who had accompanied the skaters into the rink still stood nearby, and she didn't look like the friendly sort.

Amaliya retrieved her shoes and sat on a bench next to where the Soviets had left their bags. Tyler followed her lead.

A moment later, Sonya and the other skater left the ice. Sonya made it only two steps toward them before the Soviet woman who had come with Sonya picked up the two skating bags and carried them to a bench that was on the far side of the seating area. The nearest Soviet security officer joined her.

"So much for gaining access to your cousin's bag," Tyler muttered under his breath.

Amaliya quickly exchanged her skates for her shoes. Tyler took his time so they would have a reason to remain where they were.

Only a few minutes passed before Sonya stood up, her shoes on her feet. Almost immediately, the guard positioned himself beside her. The five Soviets, Sonya included, then moved toward the door.

Tyler and Amaliya could do little more than watch as the group passed by, the security officer and Sonya's coach creating a human shield between them so they couldn't even see more than a glimpse of Sonya.

As soon as they left, two more of the Soviets exited behind them.

Gordon approached. "Looks like we're going to have to come up with another plan."

"Viktor is still here."

"Yes, but he's got as many people watching him as Sonya did," Gordon said. "The best chance we have for seeing Sonya again tomorrow is leaving now so we don't look like a threat. If Sonya isn't in our practice session, we can always send Miles to watch for an opening to pass a note to Viktor."

Tyler sensed Amaliya's hesitation. He laid a hand on her knee. "We have three days before we compete, and the women's competition ends a day after ours. We still have time."

"You're right." Amaliya stood. "But I really wish I could have had a minute longer with Sonya."

"I know." Tyler stood and grabbed his skate bag.

"For now, let's get the two of you back to the hotel. We're having dinner in your parents' room with them and the Donnellys in a half hour, and then we have a meeting an hour after that."

"A meeting with who?" Amaliya asked.

"Nike." Gordon lifted his own bag and slipped the strap over his shoulder, then headed toward the door. "One of the representatives arrived this morning. He has merchandise for the two of you to try on."

"Free clothes?" Tyler shook his head. "This is so weird."

"The rep also brought the offers for the sponsorship in case you decide to go that route." Gordon's eyebrows lifted. "I'm curious to see what they have in mind."

Tyler pushed open the door. "Me too."

Katerina sat on the edge of her bed with Robert beside her. Amaliya, Tyler, and Gordon sat on the couch across from her as they recounted the events of their afternoon practice.

"I was so close," Amaliya said. "A few more seconds, and I could have given her the room number to pass along to Uncle Viktor."

"The hotel room was just one possibility," Robert said.

Someone knocked, and Robert stood to answer the door. He pulled it open, and Miles and Linda walked in, each carrying a food-service tray.

"What did we miss?" Miles set his tray on the table.

"Viktor, Josef, and Sonya were all at Amaliya and Tyler's practice today, but they weren't able to pass the note to any of them," Robert said.

"How frustrating." Linda set her tray beside the one Miles had carried in. "I'm afraid I didn't have any luck with the hotel catering staff either. They're letting us bring the food up to the fifth floor, but then the Soviets take the food to the rooms."

"This isn't working at all how we hoped." Katerina sighed.

"Nancy and Grant are eating downstairs in the hotel restaurant to see if any of the Soviets come in there," Miles said, referring to Tyler's parents.

"We'll try again tomorrow at practice," Gordon said. "Although, I think we should write several notes so we all have one. You never know who might get an opportunity."

"That's smart, but we only have two keys to the extra hotel room," Amaliya said.

"I'll see if the front desk can code a third one for me after we finish dinner," Robert said.

Linda started unloading their dinner from the serving trays.

"Oh, if your father could see you now," Miles teased Linda. "He'd have my hide for letting you wait tables."

"I'm not waiting tables. And we established long ago that as much as I love my parents, they're both still snobs."

Miles laughed. "It's true. But it is nice that they let us use their house in the Hamptons when we want to go to the beach."

Linda handed Amaliya her plate. "You know, I bet I can get my parents to let you use their summer house for your honeymoon if it's open when you decide to get married."

"That would be amazing."

Her little girl getting married. Her brother here in the same hotel. Katerina's head was spinning. Eager for a distraction, she stood and took one of the trays from Linda. "Here, let me help you with that."

"This table isn't big enough for all of us to eat at it," Linda said.

"I don't need a table to eat," Miles said.

"Me neither." Gordon identified his dinner and settled his plate on his lap.

Katerina helped Linda pass out the rest of the food.

"How many security officers were with Viktor and Sonya?" Katerina asked.

"They had two guards with Sonya," Amaliya said.

"Or three," Tyler said. "There was that woman who was with them."

"She was probably the chaperone," Katerina said. "What about with Viktor?"

"It was hard to tell who was security and who was just meeting with the people at the rink," Gordon said. "They had a half dozen people in the office when I went in there. Josef was translating for them."

Katerina's eyebrows rose. "Josef is a translator?"

"Looked that way to me." Gordon broke off a piece of his roll. "His English was decent, and he's the only one I heard speaking anything but Russian."

Robert sat back down on the bed, his plate balanced on his lap. "If Josef speaks English, either me or Miles might be able to pass a message to him."

"Assuming he will pass the message to Uncle Viktor," Amaliya said. "He didn't seem to like Americans very much."

"Then we try to use him as a distraction," Miles said.

"How?" Tyler asked.

"I don't know yet, but if we can find a way to pull the security officers away from Viktor by having Josef translate between one of us and them, someone might be able to pass the note to Viktor."

"What are the chances Viktor will even be able to sneak down to the extra hotel room to see Mama?" Amaliya asked.

"It's the best chance we have unless we wait until the competitions start," Robert said.

"I wish Mama could just come with us to the practice rink."

"So do I, milaya." Katerina let out a sigh. "So do I."

Chapter TWENTY-NINE

SHOES. PRACTICE CLOTHES. WARM-UPS. AMALIYA looked through the dozen items of clothing that hung from a portable clothes rack on the side of the room.

"We can pick any of this?" Amaliya asked.

"All of this is for you." Lou Hollis, the representative from Nike, set four boxes of shoes on the table in the center of the room. "These are the selections from our current line. Once you sign the paperwork, you'll receive new product each season to showcase."

On the other side of the conference room, Tyler browsed through the men's selection Lou had brought him.

Gordon flipped through the paperwork. "Is this correct?"

"What?"

"The length of the agreement." Gordon held up one of the pages. "This says it's a two-year agreement."

"Two-year, renewable up to four." Lou motioned toward the agreement in Gordon's hand. "You'll see that if you win gold at the world championships, the dollar amount will increase by 30 percent."

Gordon flipped the page and let out a low whistle. He looked up. "This is generous. It's enough to cover your coaching fees, rink time, travel expenses, and your equipment."

Tyler looked up from the warm-up jacket he was holding. "So we really would only have to pay for our living expenses."

"If you win gold," Gordon said.

If they won gold. The pressure to perform well increased.

As though Gordon sensed Amaliya's sudden tension, he added, "Don't forget there are other potential sponsors out there."

"Actually, with this sponsorship, it would need to be exclusive."

"They can't take on any other sponsors?" Gordon asked.

"Technically, they can accept other sponsorship money, but they can't sign with any other product-based companies or anyone else who will be using them in their advertising."

"Which basically eliminates all the other offers," Gordon said. "The whole reason companies do sponsorships is so they can have their products showcased."

Amaliya's chest tightened. Win gold, and they could keep competing. If they didn't win, they would need another source of income. They discussed the other points of the agreement, including the company's willingness to sponsor them through the 1988 Olympics if they chose to keep competing.

Tyler moved to the table and scanned through the agreement. He glanced over at her. "You ready to sign?"

"This won't take away our amateur status?" Amaliya asked, needing that extra confirmation.

"No. It's only a sponsorship agreement now with the promise of an endorsement if we choose to go pro."

"In that case, where's a pen?"

Lou retrieved a pen from his pocket. "Here you go."

Tyler took the pen and signed his name on the two copies before him. He then handed it to Amaliya. She scanned through the terms of the agreement and signed her name beside Tyler's.

"Here you go." Amaliya handed both signed copies to Lou.

"This one is for you to keep." He handed one back. "Now that we've taken care of the paperwork, I'll have a bellboy bring the clothing up to your rooms. Try on what you like, and let me know if you need me to change out any sizes, but I think it should all fit."

Tyler slipped on a warm-up jacket. "This is great."

"Glad you like it." Lou held up a pair of shoes. "From now on, the only shoes I want to see on your feet are Nikes."

"I think we can live with that." Tyler sat down and tried on the shoes Lou offered him.

After Amaliya and Tyler verified that their shoes did indeed fit, Lou slid the paperwork into his briefcase. "If you don't need anything else from me, I'm going to head upstairs. I have an early flight tomorrow."

"You aren't staying for worlds?"

"I'm afraid not. I have a basketball player I need to meet with in Chicago tomorrow."

Tyler shook Lou's hand. "Thanks for everything."

Lou nodded. "We'll be in touch."

"That we will."

"I'll walk you out." Gordon led the way to the door.

"Good luck, you two." Lou waved before he disappeared from the room with Gordon.

As soon as Gordon and Lou left, Amaliya leaned forward in her chair and examined her new shoes. "Can you believe this?"

"It is pretty amazing." Tyler held out his arms to model his new jacket. "It makes all those early mornings worth it."

"I think the gold medal made the early mornings worth it," Amaliya countered. "Besides, you love skating."

"It's true."

"And from what Lou said, with the sponsorship, we really could keep competing." Amaliya hesitated before adding, "That is, if we keep living with my parents."

Tyler sighed. "I know that's what you want, but I really think we need our own space."

"If we live in the apartment, we'd have our own space."

"But we would have to go into your parents' house several times a day." Tyler shook his head. "Sorry, Amaliya, but I want to have our own home, one that allows us the freedom to come and go as we please without having your parents constantly checking up on us."

Amaliya tried to see their situation from Tyler's point of view. "It really is too bad the apartment doesn't have a full kitchen."

"Yeah. If there were space to expand the kitchenette into a real kitchen, it might work, but the apartment really isn't big enough."

"I know." She let out a sigh. "I guess having a free place to live after we get married would have been too perfect, huh?"

"We'll figure out what's perfect for us." Tyler held up the box of new shoes that lay in front of him. "And we'll be dressed in style when we do."

Amaliya laughed. "Yes, we will."

Artyom answered the knock at his hotel room door to a scowling Budimir. Artyom took an automatic step back. He would have liked to consider himself immune to the influence of the KGB, but he knew better. No matter how far up in the government he might reach, he would never be safe. No one was. He knew it, and so did Budimir.

Without invitation, Budimir pushed his way into Artyom's room and closed the door behind him. "What were you thinking?" He continued deeper into the room before he whirled and faced Artyom. "The whole reason to have Viktor Petrov here is to bait Katerina."

That wasn't the only reason for Viktor's presence, but Artyom didn't dispute the other man's claim.

Budimir lifted a hand and slashed it through the air. "No one will be able to make contact with Viktor if he's surrounded by guards."

"Which is why we planned to leave him unguarded during his niece's performance."

"That's too late. We need Katerina before the pairs competition begins." He slashed his hand through the air again. "Or at least before it concludes. We can't be sure Katerina will act the first time she sees her brother accessible."

"We can't be sure Katerina will attempt to contact him at all." Artyom wasn't sure he himself would risk it, not with the fear the KGB instilled in him by simply existing. "Besides, if we had left Viktor and Josef unescorted today, everyone would have been suspicious."

"The cousin is already here." Budimir continued farther into the room. "There's a good chance Katerina is as well."

Artyom hadn't expected their presence so soon. A lump formed in his throat at the very thought of what his actions could mean to the woman who had been living in America for so many years. He swallowed and forced himself to ask, "Where are they staying?"

"We don't know yet."

Another knock at the door. For a moment, Artyom froze. Should he answer it? Who could it be, and what would the person on the other side of the door think if he or she saw him with Budimir?

Budimir motioned Artyom forward. "Open the door."

Artyom complied. In a near repeat of Budimir's arrival, Pavel Turgenev stormed inside. "Did you know Sonya's cousin would be practicing with us?"

"Amaliya Marcell?" Artyom feigned surprise. He waited until Pavel walked in before he closed the door.

"Yes, Amaliya Marcell." Pavel acknowledged Budimir by repeating his question. "What of you? Did you know the Americans would be in Sonya's practice session?"

Budimir evaded the question. "I'm not in charge of practice assignments."

"Neither am I," Artyom said quickly. "Those are randomly assigned by the meet coordinators."

"Then you need to talk to the meet coordinators," Pavel said, his voice rising in volume. "I am not going to have Sonya influenced by a Westerner."

"Did they talk?" Budimir asked before Artyom could voice the question.

"Sonya is a sweet girl but naive. She went right up to her cousin and gave her a hug." Pavel shook his head. "Had I not intervened, they likely would have had plans to meet later."

A pang of envy rose within Artyom. What would it be like to still have family, even if that family were from the outside world?

"I don't want my skaters distracted," Pavel continued.

"I'm certain the distraction came from seeing her cousin unexpectedly. Tomorrow, Sonya will know her cousin will be there."

Apparently not intimidated by Budimir, Pavel took a step forward. "You know who her family is. I'm not going to lose an athlete on my watch."

"I assure you, Sonya will be well guarded," Budimir said, undeterred. He shifted his gaze to Artyom before he added, "And when we leave, none of our athletes will remain behind."

Viktor lowered himself into the chair beside the balcony door, his mind whirling. Amaliya was already here. And she was practicing with Sonya.

Had the KGB known that would be the case? Is that why he and Josef had been escorted by as many guards as the athletes had?

His hotel room door opened, and Josef walked in. "Everyone is in their rooms for the night." He dropped onto the side of the bed and kicked off his shoes. "The breakfast delivery will be at four thirty, but we only have to set it up in one of the extra rooms."

"We have extra rooms?"

"The KGB didn't want anyone else on our floor. They are using two of the adjoining rooms for our eating area for breakfast since the athletes will be eating at different times," Josef said.

Menial tasks in the morning, laundry during Sonya's practice. Would he be able to see his niece tomorrow? Or would the security team force a change in Sonya's practice schedule to keep them apart from their American relative?

"What else have they tasked you with tomorrow?" Viktor asked.

Josef wrinkled his nose to convey his distaste. "Tomorrow is helping Izolda finalize the menu selection for the meals for the rest of the week. The next day, I will be translating with the hotel staff to oversee the laundry."

"It seems they will have us working together again." Viktor leaned forward in his chair and let the truth spill out. "I don't like Sonya being at the rink without us."

"You worry about her being with Amaliya?" Josef asked.

"No. Amaliya is not a threat to her." Viktor didn't dare verbalize that the true threats were the guards watching her. What would they do if Sonya tried to talk to Amaliya again?

"I don't trust her."

"Josef, sometimes there is more to the stories that you read about in your studies," Viktor said. "Life isn't black-and-white."

"I'm learning that." Josef stood. "I'm going to take a shower." Josef retrieved a change of clothes from the dresser and disappeared into the bathroom.

Desperate for fresh air, Viktor put on his coat and stepped out onto the balcony. The brisk wind nipped at his skin, contrasting the warmth of his room. He shut the door behind him and stared out at the skyline. Ursula should be here with him to share this view. She should know what it was like to eat meals she didn't have to prepare, to see a piece of the world outside Leningrad. Of course, if she were here, she would likely be one of the women tasked with the enormous duty of tending to everyone's laundry. He didn't look forward to his part in that responsibility.

The door beside him opened, and Artyom emerged from inside. He glanced at Viktor. "Did you need to breathe in the fresh air too?"

"I am not accustomed to so much time indoors," Viktor admitted. "And I was wishing my wife were here to see this."

A wisp of sadness flitted across Artyom's face. "That is good that you have a wife back home waiting for you."

"You are not married?"

"Not anymore." Artyom focused on the city in front of them. "My wife died two years ago."

"I'm sorry."

Artyom lifted his chin in acknowledgment but didn't speak. Was Artyom missing his wife right now? Or was there something else causing the sadness surrounding him?

Something in the other man's demeanor compelled Viktor to ask, "Do you have other family waiting for you at home?"

"No." Artyom's breath plumed out in front of him in a long, steady breath. "No one at all."

"I'm sorry."

"Thank you." He stood in silence for a long moment before he turned back the way he had come. "Have a good night."

"You too." Viktor remained where he was, more questions running through his head. Was Artyom really alone in the world, without family? A new thought surfaced. Katerina had defected, but she hadn't been alone. Everything in her letters spoke of her happiness with her new husband and eventually with Amaliya. It was only her regrets that darkened the tone of the words she had written to him. He suspected that despite the years that had passed, she would still very much be the sweet, driven little sister he remembered.

Chapter THIRTY

Tyler grabbed his skate by the blade and pulled his leg up behind him to stretch out his quad. Beside him, Amaliya mirrored the motion.

"Do you think Sonya will be here?" Amaliya asked.

This conversation had repeated a dozen times since yesterday afternoon's practice. Tyler offered his standard response. "We'll find out soon enough."

"Focus on your skating," Gordon said.

"I'm sorry." Amaliya let out a sigh. "I don't mean to be distracted."

Tyler lowered his voice. "It's hard not to be distracted when we're all carrying notes for your uncle."

Gordon and Amaliya also carried extra hotel room key cards in their pockets. Tyler doubted the rep from Nike had planned to help them in their objective, but the new workout clothing he and Amaliya wore included zippered pockets. Quite convenient when trying to keep something safely tucked away while they were working out.

"If we see Viktor and Sonya, let me try to pass the note and key off first," Gordon said. "You two need to stay focused. We only have a few more days to perfect your short program, and one of those days will be the figures competition."

The familiar surge of adrenaline flowed through Tyler. Figures on Thursday, their short program on Friday, and their long program on Saturday. By this time next week, they would know if their gamble on the new routine had been the right one or not. They would also cement whether their sponsorship would be the higher amount that would allow them to keep competing without the extra financial pressure of paying for rink time.

The group of skaters in the practice session before them left the ice.

"Finish warming up," Gordon said. "I want you to go through your short program before the rink gets too crowded."

"Got it." Tyler stepped onto the ice. As soon as Amaliya put her hand in his, they pushed off together.

They were completing their second time around the rink when the main door opened, and Amaliya glanced over her shoulder.

"Hey, focus." Tyler squeezed her hand. "Remember?"

"Right." Amaliya lowered her voice. "It wasn't them anyway."

They circled the rink once more.

Gordon approached, and they met him in the center of the rink. "Your music is cued up. You should have the rink to yourselves long enough to go through it."

The door opened again, and Sonya walked in with her coach and the other Russian skater competing in the ladies' event. Amaliya grabbed Tyler's arm when Viktor came into view.

"They're here. Both of them."

"Josef too," Tyler said, spotting him beside one of the other two men who accompanied the group.

"You two skate your short program," Gordon said. "I'll try to get to Viktor."

"I'm more nervous about what you're about to do than about this entire competition," Amaliya said.

Gordon lowered his voice. "The best thing you can do right now is capture everyone's attention."

"We'll do what we can." Tyler glanced in the direction of the Soviets before turning his attention back to Amaliya.

"Ready to put on a show?"

Amaliya took a deep breath and blew it out. "I'm ready to do my best."

"That's all I can ask." Tyler took his position beside her.

Gordon reached the rink barrier. The music started, and Tyler spun Amaliya around. Time to nail their short program and finally complete the next step of bringing Katerina and Viktor together.

Viktor watched the young pair skate. Amaliya truly was her mother's daughter: beautiful, graceful, athletic. He stopped beside the edge of the rink and couldn't help but stare.

Tyler threw Amaliya up into the air, and her body twisted three times before Tyler helped her back to the ice. Incredible. Truly incredible.

Josef stopped beside him, Kirill only a short distance away. "They look good."

"Yes, they do," Viktor said as Sonya and Zoya stopped to watch.

"Get your skates on and stretch," Pavel demanded as though his skaters hadn't already been trained to follow his practice routine to the letter.

Sonya and Zoya moved to the benches and sat down.

Tyler and Amaliya skated past them before launching into side-by-side jumps.

"Viktor."

Viktor turned at the sound of his name, and his heartbeat quickened. Gordon, Amaliya's coach, was walking right toward him. Viktor cast a quick glance at Kirill, but the man's gaze was on the rink rather than on the American approaching.

Gordon greeted him in English. At least, Viktor was pretty sure the words were a greeting. He may not have recognized all the words Gordon spoke, but he understood the gesture when Gordon offered his hand.

Viktor shook his hand, surprised when paper met his palm instead of skin. Gordon placed his second hand over their joined ones, evidently to give Viktor the chance to grip the paper he had passed to him.

Gordon said something else in English, and Josef translated.

"He said it's good to see you," Josef said in Russian before he responded in English.

Gordon released Viktor's hand and stepped back. He spoke again, more words Viktor didn't recognize.

"He said he needs to go back to work, but he hopes to see you later," Josef said.

Viktor closed his fist. "Tell him I look forward to it."

Josef complied, and Gordon headed back toward the opening in the rink wall.

Viktor glanced down at the folded note in his hand as Tyler and Amaliya's music ended. Quickly, he stuffed it into his coat pocket, but something fell to the floor as he did so.

Kirill stepped closer and leaned down before Viktor could bend to retrieve whatever had fallen.

"You dropped something." Kirill reached down, his body blocking Viktor's view of whatever was on the floor. Then he straightened and held up a hotel key card. "It looks like you dropped your hotel key." Kirill handed it to Viktor.

A hotel key? "Thanks." Viktor slipped it into his pocket.

"Keep an eye on the skaters' bags," Kirill said. "Josef, I need you to translate with the rink manager. Coach Turgenev wants his skaters' music played so they can work on their routines."

"Yes, sir." Josef followed the guard.

Had Kirill truly left Viktor alone? Viktor moved closer to the benches where Sonya and Zoya had left their skating bags. When he glanced behind him, he caught sight of the second guard who had accompanied them. The man stared at Viktor as though he sensed Viktor had experienced a moment of freedom. Heaven forbid such a thing happen.

Viktor picked up both of the girls' skating bags and carried them to the rink's edge. If he was going to spend the next several hours babysitting athletic gear, he might as well watch the practice before him.

They had done it. Amaliya and Tyler had gone through their entire short program without making a single mistake. At least, they hadn't made any mistakes Amaliya was aware of.

"That may be the best we've ever skated our new short," Tyler said.

Amaliya lowered her voice to a whisper. "Pretty crazy, considering the whole time I wanted to look over to the side and see what was happening with Gordon and Viktor."

"I'm sure Gordon will tell us it's all of our hard work paying off."

"That may be part of it." Amaliya shook out her arms, both to loosen her muscles and to hide her nerves. Sonya and Zoya stepped onto the ice with their coach. They had barely begun their warm-up when Gordon skated to Amaliya and Tyler.

"How did it feel?" Gordon asked.

"Great," Tyler said. "I think it was our best yet."

"I'll have to take your word for it," Gordon said.

Amaliya looked to Gordon. "Did you—"

"Mission accomplished," Gordon interrupted before she could finish.

New hope rushed through her. "Really?"

"Really." Gordon pointed to the center of the rink. "Now, it's time to get to work. Next up, lifts. I want to see your signature lift before the Soviets start working on jumps."

"Sounds good." Tyler took Amaliya's hand. They moved into the sequence leading into their lift that had been fashioned after a ballet move from *Swan Lake*.

Tyler's hands gripped her waist. Amaliya bent her knees and pushed off the ice as he raised her over his head. She arched her back and held her position, counting off the beats in her head. Then she somersaulted back to the ground.

When Tyler released her, Amaliya caught sight of Viktor at the rink's edge, a wistful expression on his face. Were those tears in his eyes?

Gordon approached and gave them their next task as Sonya skated by. Sonya lifted her hand in greeting, and Amaliya waved back.

She took another look around the rink. "Are there really only two Soviet guards here?"

"At least, inside the rink," Gordon said.

"Who knows. There may be another dozen out in the parking lot." Tyler shuddered. "When we were in Leningrad, it seemed like they were everywhere."

"They won't have a reason to follow us here in Canada though," Amaliya said.

"They'd better not," Gordon muttered under his breath. He motioned to the far side of the rink. "Let's work on your figures. We'll wait until the afternoon's practice to go through your long program."

Amaliya skated to the empty space where Gordon indicated. She glanced across the rink again. Gordon had been successful in passing the note and hotel key to her uncle to facilitate her mother's reunion with him. She prayed the opportunity would arise for all of her family to talk to their Soviet relatives. Surely, they couldn't be so close only to be destined to simply see her uncle and cousins from across the ice.

Chapter THIRTY-ONE

The moment Viktor reached his hotel room, he pulled the paper from his pocket along with the hotel room key that wasn't his. Even though his door was securely closed, he looked over his shoulder to make sure he was really alone. Then he unfolded the single piece of paper.

Words written in Russian. Words written by his sister. His heart leaped.

> *Viktor,*
>
> *I am here, and I so desperately want to see you again. If you are able to slip away, this key will open room 403. When you get into the room, use the phone and dial 0 for the front desk. They will put your call through to me so I will know to come find you. The words you will need to say in English to be understood are at the bottom of this note. I hope to see you soon.*
>
> *Katerina*

Katerina was here, only one floor beneath him. His fingers tightened on the note. All the questions of how he was going to see Katerina dissolved into the new obstacle of how he was going to slip away. He glanced at the phone jack beside the bed. Had security not removed the phone from his room, he could have called from here. Then again, he had to assume someone could be listening to anything that happened within these walls. Katerina probably understood the security he was facing. She had lived it when she had toured with the Kirov.

The door clicked as a key unlocked it. Viktor quickly folded the note and stuffed it and the key into his pocket as Josef walked into the room.

Josef's gaze followed the movement. "What was that?"

"Nothing." Viktor wanted to trust his son, but the less Josef knew, the better. Not only was Josef less than enthusiastic about their American relatives, but if he remained unaware of Katerina's note, he also wouldn't be able to inadvertently slip up and tell anyone of Viktor's plans.

Plans. How would he get past the guards to go down to the fourth floor without risking his safety and the security of his family?

Not sure he was ready to face that question right now, he focused on Josef. "What have you been doing since you left the rink?"

"I had to finalize the times for our meal deliveries for tomorrow and then translate for Kirill. His hotel key stopped working." Josef sat on the edge of his bed. "I'm not going to be able to help with handing out lunch today. I have a meeting."

"A meeting for what?" Viktor made sure the paper in his pocket was no longer visible before he sat in the chair closest to him.

"It's a scheduling meeting for me and the other interpreter."

"It's hard to believe we need two interpreters for one competition," Viktor said.

"It's lucky for me we do." Josef looked toward the glass doors. "I never would have been chosen if it hadn't been for Sonya and Coach Turgenev."

"You also demonstrated that you mastered both French and English," Viktor said. "I guess reading all those books your grandmother had in different languages paid off."

"Maybe you should have read some too," Josef said.

"I don't need to speak English or French. Everyone I care about speaks Russian."

"I suppose that's true." Josef stood. "I'd better get to my meeting. I'll see you later."

"Are you coming to Sonya's afternoon practice?"

"Yes, I'll be there." Josef started toward the door. "Oh, I almost forgot. Izolda asked me to remind you that we need to help with the laundry tomorrow." Josef opened the door and disappeared into the hall.

The laundry. Maybe it would be possible for Viktor to get off the elevator on the wrong floor between carrying loads to and from the laundry room.

Hope took seed inside him and sprouted, his chest fluttering with anticipation. Tomorrow could be the day. Finally, the reunion he had dreamed of could become a reality.

Artyom walked into the empty hotel room that had been converted into the breakfast room for the athletes. The oversized bed had been pushed against the wall to create more space for the two extra tables that had been brought in from some of the other vacant rooms to create more seating.

Artyom steered away from the hard wooden chairs by the round tables, opting instead to sit on the couch. He opened his folder that contained his notes for the next meeting. What was this one for again? Media assignments?

Someone walked in, and Artyom glanced up. Josef Petrov. The young man looked down at his watch. "Am I early? I thought we were supposed to meet at 11:15."

Artyom checked his notes. "I have us down for 11:30."

"Sorry. I didn't realize I was so early." Josef took a step back. "I can come back."

Budimir appeared in the doorway. "No need for that." He continued inside and closed the door behind him. "I wanted to ask if your father has heard from his sister yet?"

Josef shrugged. "Not that I know of."

"Come." Budimir motioned toward the chairs scattered around the tables. "Sit down."

Josef complied. Had the young man truly messed up the time of their meeting? Or had someone deliberately given him the wrong time?

"Did your father talk to any of the Americans today?"

"Amaliya's coach, but it was only for a minute," Josef said. "And Papa doesn't speak English so I had to translate."

"What was said?" Budimir asked.

"Nothing. The American just said he was happy to see Papa, and he shook his hand." Josef's eyebrows drew together as though remembering something.

"There was more?"

"I don't know." Josef looked from Budimir to Artyom and back again.

Artyom sensed an awareness in the boy and had to fight not to warn him about sharing too much.

"What?" Budimir took a step forward. "What is it?"

"When I walked into my room a few minutes ago, Papa stuffed a paper into his pocket. He might have been hiding it from me."

"A note from your aunt maybe?" Budimir asked.

"I didn't see Papa receive any notes, but he did drop his hotel key right after the American left," Josef said. "I suppose he could have been putting a note in his pocket."

"I'm sure it was nothing," Budimir said, "but let us know if you find anything out about your aunt. We don't want your father to get into any trouble."

"Yes, sir."

Budimir checked his watch. "Our lunch should be arriving. Josef, can you go to the elevator and wait for it?"

Josef nodded and left the room.

Budimir sat in the chair beside Artyom. "A passed note. This could be what we were waiting for."

"Josef isn't sure Viktor received a note. It could be nothing."

"Perhaps, but it never hurts to be prepared." Budimir stood. "I'll let you get ready for your meeting. I have a few assignments to make."

A sickness filled him. "What are you going to do?"

"Don't worry about how I do my job. You have your own to worry about." Budimir left the room.

A moment later, Josef returned pushing a service cart loaded with food. "Is Budimir not eating with us?"

"No." Artyom swallowed the acid churning in his throat. "Not today."

Katerina paced the length of her suite. Viktor had the key. He had the note. He just had to sneak away. Would he be willing to risk it? The guilt she had been harboring since her defection rose inside of her, constricting her throat. She needed to see him.

In the bedroom area of their suite, Robert lay on the bed as he watched film on his upcoming opponent. The rented projector sat atop his bedside table, the bedside lamp now on the floor.

Katerina looked at the phone and willed it to ring. When it didn't comply with her wishes, she circled the room again, finally coming to a stop beside the balcony doors. Outside, the sun was quickly fading behind the buildings of the city, and it wouldn't be long before Amaliya returned from practice. Would Viktor be there again? And would Amaliya have the chance to speak with him or Sonya?

Katerina stepped away from the window and crossed to the kitchenette. She debated whether to eat an apple but decided against it. Tyler's parents should be here soon with dinner. She crossed back to the balcony.

Robert stopped the projector and flipped on the light where he was. "You're going to wear a path in that carpet if you don't stop pacing."

"I'm sorry. I can't stop thinking about whether Viktor will be able to sneak away to meet me." Katerina held up her hands and let them drop to her sides. "And then I feel guilty for wanting him to. What if he gets caught?"

"Trust Viktor that he'll know if the risk is one he can take." Robert swung his legs over the side of the bed and stood. "From what everyone has seen so far, it looks like the Soviet guards are mostly watching the main entrance and the elevators. He might be able to sneak away."

"They'll have someone guarding the stairwells too. Trust me."

Robert closed the distance between them and put his hands on her shoulders. "Relax. Everything is out of our control right now. The best thing you can do is find something to distract yourself while you wait for Viktor to call."

"How?" Katerina waved toward her book that lay untouched on the coffee table. "I don't feel like reading, and there's nothing worth watching on television this time of day."

"I'm sure we can think of something to get your mind off your brother." Robert slipped his arms around her and lowered his lips to hers.

Katerina leaned into the kiss, the familiar spark igniting inside her. She lifted her hand to Robert's chest, his heartbeat steady beneath her palm.

Knuckles rapped against their door, and Katerina pulled back.

Robert let out a disgruntled sigh. "That's probably our dinner."

Katerina stepped free of Robert's embrace. "I'll get it."

"Better let me." Robert put his hand on her shoulder as he stepped past her. "But first, tell me, was it working?"

Katerina's eyebrows drew together. "Was what working?"

Robert leaned forward for another kiss. "My distraction techniques."

Katerina's lips quirked into a smile. "Maybe."

"I'm happy to distract you again later." Robert wiggled his eyebrows, and Katerina couldn't help but laugh. Leave it to her husband to melt the stress from her entirely, if only for a moment.

Robert looked through the peephole and then opened the door.

Amaliya and Tyler walked in, and Robert closed the door behind them.

"Uncle Viktor was at practice again today," Amaliya said, skipping her traditional greeting.

"Did you talk to him?"

"Just a quick wave when he got there," Amaliya said.

"They only had two guards with them," Tyler added. "Maybe they trust Viktor isn't going to try to defect."

"I suspect the Soviets know he won't since he had to leave Ursula behind, but that doesn't mean they trust him," Katerina said. "He is my brother."

Another knock sounded at the door, and Tyler went to answer it. As Robert had a moment before, he checked to see who it was before he opened it.

"Dinner is here," Tyler announced. His parents walked in, their hands full. As soon as Tyler closed the door, he relieved his mom of the bag she carried.

"Gordon should be here in a minute," Nancy said. "We saw him in the lobby on our way up."

"What was he doing down there?" Robert asked.

"He was trying to see if he could borrow a projector from one of the meeting rooms downstairs," Grant said.

Katerina helped Nancy and Amaliya set out the food. They were just pouring their drinks when Gordon arrived, a look of frustration on his face.

"No luck downstairs?" Grant asked.

"No." Gordon held up a reel of tape. "This doesn't do me a lot of good if I can't watch it."

Katerina glanced at Robert. "Are you willing to share?"

"I guess I'll have to." Robert waved toward the bedroom. "I've got a projector over there. How much film do you need to review?"

"Only about an hour."

Katerina evaluated the space in the living room. "If we take that picture down, we could set it up on the table and watch while we eat."

"Dinner and a movie." Gordon set the film down on the kitchen counter. "I like it."

"Tyler, help Gordon move the table," Robert said. "I'll grab the projector."

Twenty minutes later, the lights were turned off, the film of Amaliya and Tyler was playing on the white wall of their hotel living room, and Katerina was seated beside Robert, her empty dinner dish on the coffee table in front of her.

Robert set his own plate aside and yawned. He leaned down and spoke in her ear. "I guess it would be rude for me to take a nap while everyone is here, huh?"

"Yes," Katerina whispered back and kissed his cheek. "But don't worry. The kids have a curfew."

Robert stretched out his arm and drew her closer. "Good."

Chapter THIRTY-TWO

Tyler walked down the hall to his parents' hotel room. The idea to stay at the same hotel as Amaliya's extended family had seemed like a good one, but this staying out of sight thing was getting old. His parents and the Donnellys had been alternating through the restaurant, the business center, and the lobby since the Soviets had arrived, but he and Amaliya couldn't risk being seen in the common areas. Instead, they were in their rooms, their parents' rooms, or sneaking in and out the side door when no one was looking.

Tyler knocked on his parents' door. It swung open a moment later.

"Hey there." His dad waved him inside. "How was practice this morning?"

"Pretty good." Tyler walked inside and chose one of the empty seats at the small table on the far side of the room. "Amaliya was a little distracted by her uncle and cousins being there, but I finally feel like we have our short program down."

"That's great," his dad said.

"It can't be easy on Amaliya to have her family in the same room and not be able to talk to them," his mom added, getting back to the difficult side of his current situation.

"Amaliya was able to say hi to Sonya when we skated by to get a drink, but she's afraid if she gets too close to Viktor that he'll have some extra restrictions that will keep him from being able to go to Sonya's competitions, among other things." Tyler didn't need to mention that those other things included sneaking out to meet Amaliya's mom.

"Is Amaliya joining us for breakfast?" his dad asked. "We ordered extra."

"No. She wanted to eat with her mom."

"In that case, let's eat."

"I guess you didn't wait to ask me what I want to eat, huh?"

"Gordon already gave us your breakfast selection."

"Yet another reason to go pro," Tyler muttered.

His mom sat at the table. "How are things with you and Amaliya? Any decision yet on what's next for your skating careers?"

"We're still at an impasse." Tyler took his seat. "With the Nike deal, if we win gold, we'll have enough to cover our training expenses if we decide to keep competing. We'd still have to teach lessons at the rink, but I think we could make it work."

"That's huge," his mom said.

"And a lot of pressure." His dad sat beside him.

"If money weren't an issue, what would you want?" His mom uncovered their plates and pushed Tyler's toward him. "I know you have to think about your financial future too, but being happy is more important than the balance of your bank account."

"Amaliya and Carolyn both asked me that too."

"If it weren't for the money, would you want to go pro?" his dad asked.

"I don't know." And he didn't.

"Sounds like it's time for you to take money out of the equation and get in touch with what you really want." His dad poured everyone some juice. "And if you decide to stay amateur, I'm sure we can help some with living expenses."

"Dad, I appreciate the offer, but I can't ask you to do that." Tyler leaned forward in his seat and rested his forearms on the table. "I'm about to get married. I need to be able to take care of myself."

His mom reached over and laid her hand on his arm. "Honey, getting married doesn't mean your family can't help you anymore."

"I can't expect you to help pay my expenses forever."

"It's not forever," his mom countered. "It's until the next Olympics or whenever you and Amaliya decide it's the right time to retire."

"We'll support whatever you decide," his dad added. "We just don't want you to step away from your dream if it isn't finished yet."

"I don't know what my dream is right now beyond marrying Amaliya."

"Maybe you need to pray about it," his dad said.

"And stop letting the dollar signs get in your way." His mom gave his arm another squeeze. "Listen to your heart."

Katerina sat inside her room next to the door leading to the balcony, the door cracked open an inch. She breathed in the crisp, fresh air and ached for the freedom she had fought so hard to earn.

For the past three days, she hadn't gone anywhere or done anything beyond plan, eat, and wait. Listening to Amaliya's reports after each practice gave her some solace that her brother was doing well, but she ached to see him herself.

Robert emerged from the bedroom and narrowed his eyes. "Why is the door open? Aren't you freezing?"

"I just wanted to breathe some different air." Katerina looked up at him. "Doesn't it seem stuffy in here to you?"

"Maybe a bit." Robert stepped behind her and massaged her shoulders. "We should get out of here for an hour or two."

"Leave the hotel?" Katerina shook her head.

"Amaliya and Tyler have left for every practice without any of the Soviets seeing them," Robert said. "And from what the Donnellys and the Lindens have said, the only Soviet guards downstairs are in the lobby and at the main entrance."

Temptation tugged at her. "I don't know . . ."

"I can go down to make sure the coast is clear before we leave the hotel." Robert leaned down and kissed her cheek. "Or better yet, we'll send Miles."

"I'd love to get out of here, but what if Viktor calls? I don't want to take a chance I might miss him."

"Amaliya said he's been at all of Sonya's practices. It'll be two hours before they all get back from the rink." Robert stepped around the side of her chair so he could see her more clearly. "We could use a little time away from here, and it's our last chance before Amaliya starts competing."

Katerina debated briefly. Despite the nerves fluttering inside her, she said, "I guess we'll want to make sure I can get out safely for the competitions."

"Great. I'll call Miles's room and have him make sure the coast is clear."

Katerina pulled the door closed and retrieved her shoes from the closet. "It's hard to believe I haven't had to put shoes on for three days."

"You're overdue for a dinner out."

"It's lunchtime."

"Lunch, dinner. Whatever." Robert punched Miles's room number into the phone. After a moment, he said, "Miles, I need a favor."

Robert proceeded to explain their plan. After he hung up, he said, "Okay, Miles will call us after he makes sure the coast is clear."

Less than five minutes later, the phone rang. Robert answered, his face lighting with a satisfied smile. "Great. Thanks."

The moment he hung up, Katerina asked, “We’re safe?”

“We’re good to go.” Robert grabbed his wallet and keys off the dresser and opened the door. He did a quick check of the hall before leading her out of the room and to the stairwell.

They made it to the third-floor landing before either of them spoke.

“You are going to come with me this time, aren’t you?” Robert asked.

The memory of the first time Robert tried to sneak her out of this hotel twenty-four years ago flashed through her mind. “I know now I can trust you.”

“You could trust me back then too.”

“Yes, but I didn’t know what freedom tasted like yet.”

“I’m glad you know now.”

“Me too.” They reached the first floor, and Robert peeked outside. After looking both ways, he reached for Katerina’s hand. “Moment of truth.”

Katerina pulled her sunglasses from her purse, drew a deep breath, and nodded. “Let’s go.” She crossed the few yards between the outside door and the rental car and slid into the passenger seat.

“Duck down in case anyone is watching us when we drive out of here.” Robert started the car.

She did as he asked, and he pulled out of the parking space. The car turned and then turned again.

“Okay, you’re good,” he said.

Katerina straightened and looked out at the busy road, snow visible on either side. A new sense of freedom washed over her. “Where are you taking me?”

“I’ll take you wherever you want to go,” Robert said. “As long as we can be back by four thirty.”

Katerina smiled. “I’m sure we can find someplace we’ll both like.”

Robert nodded. “I’m sure we can.”

Chapter THIRTY-THREE

Viktor made three trips to the laundry facility on the second floor, each time taking a different route to test security's reactions and to avoid creating any predictability.

He dropped off the fourth load and checked his watch. Sonya and her group should already be at the rink, which meant at least two guards would be with them.

He headed for the stairs and started his upward climb. If the room numbers on the fourth floor mirrored those on the fifth, the room he was looking for should be right next to the stairwell door.

He only needed a few minutes to slip into the hotel room, use the phone, and talk to Katerina. If all went well, she would be able to meet him on his next trip upstairs.

He passed the second floor and increased his pace. By the time he reached the fourth floor, his heart was racing both from exertion and nerves.

He stopped long enough to listen for anyone who might be in the stairwell with him. When he didn't hear any movement, he pulled the door open and found the correct room. As he suspected, it was only two doors from the stairwell.

Viktor reached into his pocket and retrieved the hotel key Gordon had given him. He slid it into the lock. Nothing happened.

He sucked in a quick breath, his heart beating even faster. He tried again. Still nothing. His third and fourth attempts were also unsuccessful.

Frustration and disappointment swept through him. Viktor quickly pulled the note from Katerina from his pocket and checked the room number again. The numbers matched.

Though he doubted Katerina would give him a key to her room, he knocked on the door. Perhaps someone was waiting for him inside. Perhaps Katerina was waiting.

No response.

A door opened behind him, and Viktor quickly looked over his shoulder. The hall was still empty. He could have sworn he heard something.

Eager to get out of sight, he knocked again. Still nothing.

Afraid someone would notice he was taking too long to get back upstairs, Viktor returned to the stairwell door. He opened the door slowly, taking the time to make sure he didn't hear anyone nearby. Once he was certain it was clear, he stepped inside.

Somewhere down the hall a door clicked shut, and Viktor quickly glanced behind him. Was that the stairwell door opposite him that had closed?

His pulse still racing, Viktor hurried up the last flight. He took a moment when he reached the fifth floor, attempting to slow his breathing.

He walked into the hall and headed toward the room where everyone had deposited their dirty clothes. A man emerged through the stairwell door opposite him, but he turned toward the guard at the stairs, his back now to Viktor.

A ripple of unease skittered down Viktor's spine. The man seemed familiar somehow, but Viktor couldn't recall seeing him since arriving in Canada.

Izolda approached carrying a basket of dirty clothes. "Here is the next load. You need to wait downstairs until they have clean clothes to bring back up to me."

Viktor nodded. He juggled the basket in his arms and headed back toward the stairwell. Maybe he could stop by the room on the fourth floor one more time, just to be sure his key didn't work.

Even though her sunglasses were firmly in place, Katerina ducked in the front seat of the rental car to remain out of sight when Robert pulled into the parking lot.

"Okay, we're here." He turned off the ignition.

"How close are we to the door?" Katerina asked, remaining where she was.

"Three spots away."

Katerina slowly straightened, her gaze sweeping over the parking lot. Relief flowed through her when she saw that it was empty.

The side door to the hotel opened, and a man in a long dark coat stepped outside, his eyes scanning, his mouth firm, his face nearly expressionless. Katerina froze. What had she been thinking? To anyone else, the man might look like he was waiting for someone, but Katerina knew the look. In addition to the unsmiling face and drab-colored clothes, the man had KGB written all over him. And he stood between her and her hotel room, between her and her family.

Robert tilted her head toward him and kissed her. What was he doing? Well, she knew what Robert was doing, but how could he kiss her now, when a KGB agent was only a few yards away?

Robert's hand slid up to cup the back of her neck. He pulled back slightly, but his face remained close. "If you're kissing me, he can't see your face."

Katerina leaned in, her lips meeting Robert's again. Her mind raced. What was a KGB agent doing at the side entrance?

Robert pulled back again and tilted his head slightly. "He left."

Katerina glanced around the parking lot. The KGB agent now stood at the corner of the building, a truck parked beside them partially obstructing his view.

"He'll still be able to see us as soon as we try to go inside."

"Maybe we should try to go in on the other side of the building," Robert said.

Katerina gave a subtle nod toward the guard. "If they have a KGB agent here, they may be watching all of the entrances."

"Hey, it's going to be all right." Robert put his hand on hers. "I'm sure there must be a reason."

Another bolt of panic shot through her. "Viktor."

"What about him?"

"What if he's the reason they have more security officers outside?"

"Don't worry about your brother right now. We need to get you safely to our room." Robert straightened. "I think our best bet is to walk in like we don't care about him."

Her eyes widened. "Just get out of the car where he can see me and go into the hotel?"

"I'll open your door for you and walk you inside," Robert spoke calmly. "I'll stay between you and him."

She drew in a deep breath and shook her head. "I don't know."

"You're an American citizen. They don't control you anymore."

In her head, she knew Robert was right. In her heart, she would always be Soviet; she would always fear the KGB.

"Come on. You can do this." Robert tucked a lock of her hair behind her ear. "I'll help you do this."

Though all she wanted to do was hide, she slowly nodded.

"Keep your head turned away from him." Robert opened his door and walked to her side of the car as though he didn't have a care in the world. Maybe he should have gone into acting instead of hockey.

By the time he opened her door, Katerina had already slipped her purse over her shoulder. Could she really make it to her room without being noticed?

Robert took her hand, and for an instant, she couldn't move. A gentle tug from Robert put her in motion. She stood, keeping her face turned away from the man still standing at the corner of the building.

Robert slipped his hand around her waist, his body creating a shield between her and the KGB agent. "Let's go," Robert whispered.

Together they walked to the curb. Katerina had to force herself not to stop when she reached the edge of the truck that lay between her and the front of the hotel. As soon as they reached the sidewalk, her instinct was to quicken her pace, but Robert held her close to his side, forcing her to match him step for step.

Panic rose within her and clawed at her throat until she could barely breathe. Robert's hand tightened on her waist, a silent reassurance. Then suddenly, they were at the side entrance. He opened the door, ushered her inside, and immediately entered the stairwell.

The thought struck that they could run into one of the Soviets on the stairs, but the elevator wasn't an option, not with someone watching the lobby all the time.

She and Robert hurried up the four flights of stairs. They reached their floor, her heart pounding. Robert peeked into the hall briefly and then rushed her forward. He slid his key into the slot, pulled the door open, and followed her inside, then closed the door. An instant later, she was in his arms.

"It's okay." Robert ran his hand down the length of her hair. "You're okay now."

She let out a ragged breath, holding on for a long moment. She was okay. She had Robert. And she was still free.

Their last regular practice before worlds, possibly the last of their amateur careers. After today, their practices would be intermixed with competitions, with their schedules and practice locations changing from one session to the next. Nerves and uncertainty jumbled within Amaliya, leaving her unsettled. The distractions her family had created had helped her hide from the looming decision she and Tyler had in their future, but today her desire to continue on the amateur circuit was magnified.

She and Tyler moved through a segment of their long program as their last few minutes came to a close. She checked Tyler's position when they both launched into their triple salchows. The sound of her blade hit slightly after Tyler's.

"Let me see the triples again," Gordon called out.

"That was on me," Tyler said. "I didn't have quite enough height."

Amaliya forced herself to ignore the other skaters on the ice with them. They circled their section of the rink and launched into their jumps again. This time, their blades hit in unison.

A thrill rushed through her. They were ready. She hoped they were ready.

"Okay, that's it for today." Gordon skated to them. "How do you feel?"

"Gordon, thank you for everything." Tyler swallowed hard as though he were fighting back his emotions.

"Don't start your goodbyes yet." Gordon held up a hand. "We still have three more days of competition before you can go pro. That's plenty of time for you to change your mind."

"You sound like you're hoping we will change our minds." Tyler glanced at Amaliya. "Or that I will."

"I am. You're the best athletes I've ever coached. I don't look forward to replacing you." Gordon pointed a finger at Tyler. "But if you do decide to go for the next Olympics, I'm going to deny saying that. I don't want any compliments going to your head."

Despite her own rising emotions and the tears trying to surface, Amaliya managed a smile. "Who us? Never."

"Just remember, you don't have to decide now to compete for the next four years," Gordon said. "You can take it one year at a time. The question beyond this weekend is, Do you still want to compete?"

Amaliya did want to compete next year. And the year after. If Tyler would agree, she wanted to continue through the next Olympics. She looked at him and searched for any sign that his feelings mirrored her own. His jaw clenched, a sure sign he was feeling something. What, she didn't know.

A deep yearning burned inside Amaliya, an excitement for her possible future rippling through her. She had found the certainty she had tried to ignore since learning of the job offers. Now she had to be brave enough to tell Tyler what she really wanted and be prepared to find a middle ground if he opted for a different path.

"Go cool down," Gordon said. "I'll meet you by the benches."

Tyler pushed off and rubbed at his eyes. In that moment, a new bolt of understanding shot through her. Maybe Tyler wanted to keep competing every bit as much as she did. Maybe his choices really were strictly born of his desire to establish their own financial security.

Amaliya pushed off and caught up with him. She took his hand and spoke in a gentle voice. "Tyler, this doesn't have to be our last competition."

"Amaliya, I can't do this right now."

Amaliya stiffened. Then she caught a glimpse of the tears shimmering in his eyes. He couldn't talk, but was it because he wanted to compete or because he truly was saying goodbye to a part of his life that had dominated his goals since his early childhood?

As they passed Sonya, she waved and called out in English. "Good luck tomorrow night."

"Good luck to you too," Amaliya returned in Russian. No point in letting the Soviet guards think they were saying anything they wouldn't approve of.

Amaliya and Tyler circled the rink once more and made their way to the benches where Gordon already waited.

Tyler swallowed hard. "Are you going to want to watch your cousin compete tomorrow?"

Before Amaliya could answer, Gordon shook his head. "Sorry, but I doubt we'll have time. Your morning practice won't end until close to when the ladies' figure competition begins."

"Will we get to watch her short program?" Amaliya asked.

"We'll see," Gordon said. "If she makes it into the top six, there's a good chance we can watch her before the two of you compete."

"Fingers crossed." Amaliya emphasized her words by holding both hands up, her fingers crossed on both.

"We've been crossing our fingers for a lot of things lately," Tyler said in a low voice.

Gordon nodded. "That we have."

Tyler walked into his hotel room and leaned against the door. The moment he was alone, tears welled up in his eyes. He drew a deep breath and fought against them. He wasn't going to cry. He wasn't going to let the emotions of today get to him.

Yes, this weekend might signify the end of his amateur career, but that could be a good thing. Right?

Tyler took another deep breath and then another until he managed to regain his composure. He crossed the room and sat on the edge of the bed. A bed, a small table, a dresser, his suitcase stored in the closet. Is this what his future looked like? Even after only a few days living in a hotel, he was looking forward to getting home and sleeping in his own bed. Could he last for months on end without having that opportunity? And where would home be once he and Amaliya stepped away from their amateur careers?

Travel and constant change, or stability and a predictable routine. Both held their own appeal, but which one was right for him? And what was right for Amaliya? If they won gold, Amaliya's wishes would be more feasible.

If they won.

Tyler let out a sigh. He didn't know if he should savor these next few days or if he should wish for them to pass by more quickly. It was time to make a decision, but he still had no idea which was the right one.

Chapter THIRTY-FOUR

KATERINA SAT ON THE EDGE of the bed as Robert packed his overnight bag. The figures competition would begin today, a competition she desperately wanted to go to, one she was desperately afraid of attending. With the exception of dinner the first night and her lunch with Robert, she had spent her entire stay in Toronto hiding out in her hotel room. The moment she went to any competition, she would be vulnerable.

She had no delusions that the Soviet skaters wouldn't be at the ice rink. And wherever the skaters went, the KGB would be shadowing them.

"Maybe it would be best if I stay here."

Robert retrieved his shaving kit from the bathroom and tucked it into the suitcase. "The Donnellys and the Lindens are prepared to sneak you out of the hotel and get you back in."

"I know, but what if the KGB starts watching the entrances again?" Katerina asked. "And what happens if Viktor tries to call?"

"I really don't want you meeting with Viktor alone." Robert zipped his suitcase closed and set it on the floor.

"He's my brother. He wouldn't do anything to hurt me."

"You have no idea how he may have changed over the past twenty-odd years." Robert sat beside her and took her hand. "Besides, Viktor probably knows that you wouldn't be here when Amaliya is competing."

"I guess."

"And you can always leave a message with the front desk to pass on to him."

"I could if he spoke English."

"Yeah, I keep forgetting about that," Robert said. "I just don't like the idea of you being here alone." He hesitated briefly before adding, "You could always come with me to my game."

"At least one of us should be here to support Amaliya."

Robert cocked an eyebrow. "Even if it's just from a hotel room?"

The regret from missing the Olympics surfaced. Katerina could watch the competition on television, or she could be there for her daughter and see her perform live.

Someone knocked on the door.

"That's probably Miles. He said he'd drive me to the airport." Robert crossed the room and opened the door.

Katerina followed him into the living room.

Miles stood in the hall. "Are you ready to go?"

"Come on in. I need to grab my suitcase."

"Katerina, Grant said to tell you he and Nancy are in their room in case you need anything while I'm gone," Miles said. "Linda and I will come pick you up when it's time to leave for the competition."

Though she couldn't quite battle back her fears, she said, "Thanks."

"So you are going to go?" Robert asked.

"You convinced me."

"Have you heard anything from Viktor yet?" Miles asked.

"Nothing. I think we may need to try for a new plan," Katerina said.

"Sounds like it's time to pull out some of those clothes you bought for him," Miles said.

"I know we talked about putting a note in his pocket, but what would it say?" Katerina asked.

"As soon as I drop Robert off at the airport, I'll go to the ladies' figures competition. Linda and I will watch to see where the Soviets are sitting so we can find a spot where he might be able to meet you tomorrow during the ladies' short program," Miles said.

Deliberately go to watch her niece in the hopes of seeing her brother. She supposed dealing with the presence of the KGB there wouldn't be any worse than when she would be watching one of Amaliya's performances. "Let me get the coat for you, just in case," she said.

"I'll get it." Robert set his suitcase down. "You write the note."

Katerina sat at the little table and retrieved a notepad and pen. She wrote two notes, one instructing Viktor on what to do when Miles gave it to him. In the other, she offered options of how she and Viktor might be able to meet. At the conclusion of the second note, instead of signing it, she wrote simply, *A gift*.

Robert returned holding the two overcoats. "Which one?"

"The brown one. It's the closest to what his current coat looks like," Miles said.

"Are the new gloves still in the pockets?"

"They are."

Miles glanced at his watch. "Robert, we'd better go."

Robert nodded. He took Katerina's hand. "Be careful. I'll be back tomorrow afternoon in plenty of time to go watch Amaliya's short program with you."

"Good luck at your game tonight."

"Thanks." Robert leaned in for a goodbye kiss. "Love you."

"Love you too." Katerina followed him and Miles to the door.

Her chest tightened the moment they walked out and closed the door behind them. She flipped the deadbolt closed and glanced at the phone on the desk. She could understand Robert's concerns about her meeting with Viktor alone, but despite the decades that had separated them, she knew her brother. And if the phone rang, she had to answer. The chance to see him might only happen once, and she wasn't going to miss it.

Viktor sat in the bleachers beside Josef and watched his little girl perform. Of the skaters he had seen compete so far, he hadn't seen any who had done better.

Even as that thought took root, he let out a sigh. Ursula should be here right now. She should be experiencing the joy of seeing Sonya compete. She should be spending her nights in a bed that didn't need a fireplace beside it in order to be warm.

A hollowness rose within him, a sort of ache that worked its way into his chest and continued upward until it squeezed at his throat. He blew out a breath and pushed aside his near-constant concern for his wife. He was here for Sonya right now. Ursula would want him to enjoy this moment and celebrate their daughter's successes.

Figures today, her short program tomorrow morning, and her long program on Sunday evening. At least she would have a bit of a break between the short and long. Amaliya and Tyler would compete for the next three days straight. He hoped he would be here to watch. Maybe then, he'd at least catch a glimpse of his sister. More importantly, he could make sure she saw the KGB coming if they sought to follow through with their threat of returning her to the Soviet Union.

He had gone through the motions of his duties for the rest of Tuesday and all of Wednesday, but not once did he find another opportunity to slip away to check the hotel room downstairs. He also didn't speak English well enough to ask the front desk for a new key to room 403. Seeing Katerina at a competition might be his only hope.

Sonya completed her third figure, and Viktor applauded with the rest of the crowd.

"She looked good," Viktor said.

"She did," Josef agreed.

The scores posted. Warmth spread through Viktor's chest as pride rose within him. "Those are better than her marks at the Olympics."

"If she gets another medal, maybe we'll finally be able to buy a heater for our house."

Viktor leaned back in his seat. "Our turn will come."

"It needs to come faster."

Not in the mood for the familiar argument, Viktor asked, "Are you coming back to the hotel after Sonya finishes, or do you have to stay here until after the pairs competition is over?"

"I'll be staying here," Josef said. "Grigori wants me to observe while Samuil helps with the interviews after the ladies' figures are over."

"I guess I'll be serving lunch without your help." Viktor glanced at the KGB agent standing at the top of their section of the bleachers. "Will you be able to get something to eat here? Or should I save something for you?"

"Best save me a plate if you can," Josef said. "Even when the organizers say we'll be fed, it doesn't always happen."

"I'll put a plate in the little refrigerator in our room."

"Thanks, Papa."

Viktor glanced at the KGB agent again. Would there ever be a time when he wasn't being watched? They were in Canada, for heaven's sake. That should give him at least a minute or two of freedom.

Josef stood. "I need to go to the media area."

"I'll see you later."

The KGB agent followed Josef toward the concourse, and for a brief moment, Viktor tasted freedom. He let out a sigh. It wouldn't last. Best not to get used to the sensation.

Viktor focused on the ice again, a skater in a pink dress working her way through one of the required figures.

Someone slipped into Josef's seat, and Viktor turned, expecting his son to have returned. Instead, it was another man who was around his age. Broad through the shoulders, athletic in his build. He folded his coat and settled it between them. A paper dropped to the floor, and the man bent to pick it up. He unfolded it, held it out, and asked something in English that Viktor didn't understand.

Viktor glanced down at the words on the paper, words written in Russian.

> *Take the coat. Check the pockets.*
> *My friend is asking if the note is yours. Don't take it.*
>
> *K.*

Viktor fought against his surprise and managed to shake his head. The other man shrugged and tucked the paper into his pocket before settling back in his seat. He remained there for several minutes, his focus on the ice. Viktor glanced behind him, checking to see if the KGB agent had returned. He hadn't.

Though tempted to search the pockets of the coat lying beside him, Viktor didn't dare. With his luck, the agent would return at the same moment Viktor tried to read the note.

A woman approached and spoke in English, pointing to the next section over. The man pulled his event ticket from his pocket and studied it. Then he shrugged and stood up, leaving the coat behind when he moved down the row and joined the woman.

The couple made their way onto the main concourse. A minute later, Viktor spotted them in the next section over taking their seats. As they did so, the KGB agent returned to his post.

Viktor feigned interest in the skater on the ice, counting down the last few competitors and checking the standings after each one. When the final standings posted for the figures competition, pride swelled in him once more. Second place. His daughter was in second place.

With today's competition concluded, Viktor debated between which coat to take with him. Could he possibly take both? Or would it be too obvious if he tried to put one on over the other? And would he even be able to? He ran a hand over the brown coat Katerina's friend had left. No holes, a thick lining, the possibility of a message in the pocket. If he had to choose, he would want this one. He picked up the new coat and slipped it on. Then he glanced at his old one. How would he explain the lack of holes in this new one? Would anyone even notice?

Viktor glanced over his shoulder at the KGB agent, who already had his coat on. No holes, no tears in the fabric. Maybe they would assume he too had started out with a coat in similar repair.

He quickly reached into the pocket of his old coat and retrieved his gloves and hotel key. Then he nudged the coat onto the floor so it would be out of sight.

"Viktor." The agent called from a few rows up. "It's time."

Ignoring the pounding of his heart, Viktor stood and, leaving his coat behind, followed the agent to the concourse.

"Go wait at the locker room to help the ladies with their bags. We will depart as soon as they are ready."

"Of course." The hotel key and his gloves still in hand, Viktor headed for the locker rooms. As soon as he was out of sight of the agent, he tried to put his gloves and hotel key into a pocket only to find it already full. He moved them to the other pocket, which was empty, and checked the contents of the first. He pulled out a new pair of gloves, and his eyes widened. Brown leather with a fabric lining. He couldn't afford something like this even if he saved for months. He quickly tucked them back into his pocket, and his fingers brushed paper. The other note, perhaps?

Sonya approached, a light of accomplishment in her eyes.

Viktor left the paper in the pocket and closed the distance between him and his daughter before scooping her into a hug. "You skated so well today."

"Thanks, Papa." She squeezed him tight before letting go. "I wish Mama could have been here."

"I know. We will tell her all about it when we get home." Viktor took Sonya's skating bag from her and slid it over his shoulder. He hoped the note in his pocket meant that by the time they returned to Leningrad, he would have his own success story to share with his wife too.

Chapter THIRTY-FIVE

Amaliya took her spot on the freshly groomed ice and proceeded to use her skate blades to draw the required design. Balance, precision, pacing. She concentrated on all three, Gordon's guidance echoing through her mind. She and Tyler were the Olympic champions. They could do this.

She reached the top of her first figure eight, adding the required intricate pattern before continuing. The daily practices of doing this exact pattern allowed her body to react instinctively as she and Tyler completed the first pass and began their second. Besides mirroring her partner and the position of her blades, Amaliya concentrated on her arm position and posture.

When she and Tyler finished their task, they exited the rink. Gordon was at her side a moment later. He handed them both their skate guards.

Amaliya lifted one foot and slid the guard into place and repeated the process with the other. "What do you think?"

"I'd say your practice may have very well paid off." Gordon put one hand on her back and another on Tyler's shoulder. "Well done."

"Thanks."

"I hope the judges agree with you," Tyler added.

The words were barely out of his mouth when the scores posted. Five eights and five nines across the board out of a possible six.

"Not bad," Gordon said. "That puts you in first."

With six more pairs to skate.

"Is it enough to keep us there?" Tyler asked.

"Let's go sit and watch your competition," Gordon said.

Amaliya followed Gordon to their seats and sat between him and Tyler. With the rest of today's results out of their control, she focused on the stands rather than the couple currently on the ice. She spotted her mom with Linda and Tyler's mom. Tyler's dad and Miles weren't anywhere to be seen.

She scanned the crowd for any other familiar faces. When she didn't spot any, she scanned again.

Tyler leaned closer. "Looking for your uncle?"

"I don't see him anywhere." Her gaze landed on a man near the entrance to the seating area where Popov and Sidrova had been sitting a moment ago. "Looks like they have some Soviet security people here though." Amaliya jutted her chin in the man's direction. "That guy down there. Dark hair, long coat."

"You knew they would have someone watching the athletes," Gordon said.

"It's funny that I never noticed that before we went to Leningrad," Amaliya said. "Now it seems like I see suspicious people everywhere."

"Being followed around for a couple weeks can make you paranoid."

The previous pair's scores posted, the scores averaging in the five six range. Popov and Sidrova stepped onto the ice and began their first of three figures.

"I really hate waiting," Amaliya said.

Tyler laughed. "When you go last, you always say you hate not being able to see our competition skate."

"I must be hard to please."

Tyler put his hand on hers. "That's not true."

Amaliya's thoughts flitted to what would come after this weekend and the uncertainty surrounding the decisions she and Tyler had yet to make. This could be their last competition, their last time competing in figures. She shook that thought away. Whether it was their last time or not, she needed to enjoy the moment, even if it did mean stressing through the waiting game.

"We're going to be in first after figures." Amaliya linked her fingers through Tyler's. "I can feel it."

Tyler let out a long breath. "I hope you're right."

First place. The familiar rush of accomplishment flowed through Tyler as he and Amaliya greeted his parents by the security station next to the athletes' entrance.

"You were incredible!" His mom embraced him before speaking to both him and Amaliya. "You both skated so well."

"Thanks, Mom."

"You really were amazing," his dad added. He nodded toward Amaliya. "Both of you."

Amaliya's face lit up. "Thank you."

The flow of participants and coaches continued toward the exits, their expressions ranging from accomplished to disappointed. Tyler had been on both sides of the equation, and he couldn't deny that he loved the rush that came from performing his best and receiving scores that confirmed he and Amaliya had come out on top.

Gordon approached from the adjoining hallway. "Okay, we're all set. I have our practice and warm-up schedules for tomorrow."

"Will we be able to watch the ladies' short programs?" Amaliya asked.

"We'll miss the first half, but we'll be here by the time Sonya competes," Gordon said.

Amaliya's expression brightened. "Good."

Tyler's dad lowered his voice and leaned closer. "Amaliya, your mom and the Donnellys already left. They're meeting us at the car."

"Did Mama have any problems getting here?" Amaliya asked, her voice barely louder than a whisper.

"Not that we saw."

"Glad everything went smoothly," Tyler said.

"So are we." Tyler's mom slipped her arm around his waist as Gordon reached them. "We were just telling Amaliya and Tyler how great they looked today."

"I agree," Gordon said. "These two may have forgotten how to lose."

Anticipation and excitement surged through Tyler. "Tomorrow will be the real test."

"We love a challenge, remember?" Amaliya squeezed his hand. "Otherwise, we wouldn't skate for Gordon."

Tyler chuckled. "True."

"Let's get you two back to the hotel," Gordon said. "You need to stretch and get some sleep."

"We're ready." Tyler said goodbye to his parents and walked with Amaliya and Gordon toward the reserved parking for the athletes.

Gordon started in on his typical post-competition pep talk, chatting about what they had done well, what he wanted them to focus on for tomorrow, what their schedule was for the next day.

"I'm a little nervous that it's Popov and Sidrova in second place right now," Amaliya said as they reached their rental car.

"You beat the Soviets before. You can do it again." Gordon unlocked the car and slid behind the wheel. As soon as Amaliya took her spot in the front seat and Tyler in the back, Gordon continued. "Focus on skating your best. You can't worry about everyone else."

Amaliya laughed. "That's what you always say."

"And look what happens when you listen."

When they listened to Gordon, they won. And they could keep winning. Tyler let that thought settle and enjoyed the rush of adrenaline that had yet to fade after tonight's performance. Would he feel like this after a performance with an ice show? Or was this sensation something he would lose forever once he hung up his amateur status?

At the moment, winning gold was his priority. Now he just had to find a way to settle down enough to sleep tonight.

Artyom had made it nearly two days without interacting with Budimir, and he appreciated every moment of the break. Granted, he had spent as much time in his room as possible. What better way to avoid the man's ulterior motives than to stay out of sight completely by dedicating himself to the desk in his hotel room?

Despite the paperwork and constant monitoring of athletes and juggling transportation schedules, the loss of his grandmother had consumed his thoughts more often than he cared to admit, and dealing with the possible kidnapping of a former Soviet citizen was a stress he didn't need. The gnawing ache in his center had become commonplace, as had his endless stream of regrets.

He should have spent more time with his grandmother. He should have visited more often. He should have paid more attention when she'd shared her stories. He should have written them down. The list went on and could easily duplicate itself for the other family members he had lost.

Alone. The word haunted him with annoying frequency, but it also described him far too well.

He pushed aside the latest practice schedule and leaned back in his chair. His conversation with Viktor on the balcony a couple days ago pushed forward in his mind. The man had done a good job of hiding his desire to see his sister, but Artyom couldn't miss Viktor's love for his family. That kind of love didn't go away.

He had no idea if anything had come of the tidbit Josef had shared. Artyom secretly hoped not.

The figures competition was already underway. He checked the bedside clock. Or perhaps the competition had already concluded. He had received word that Sonya had performed well and was in second place, a nice improvement to where she had started her Olympic competition.

A heavy-handed fist pounded on his door. His gut clenched. Budimir.

Artyom forced himself to stand and cross the room. He pulled the door open.

"Why was Viktor Petrov serving meals instead of attending the pairs competition?"

"I thought he was at the pairs competition." Artyom took a step back, not because he wanted to invite Budimir into his room but rather to prevent himself from being bowled over when the KGB officer pushed his way inside.

"Not only was he not there—Katerina Petrova was."

Artyom jolted at that news. "She's here? You saw her?"

"Only from a distance at the end of the competition." Pure evil flashed on Budimir's face. "She stayed away from her daughter, but one of my men spotted her leaving surrounded by her American friends."

"If she attended the figures, I'm sure she'll be at the short program," Artyom said. Even though the thought of Budimir being successful in his quest made him want to squirm, Artyom said, "I'll make a point of giving Viktor permission to attend the pairs events."

"See that you do." Budimir glared for a moment before he turned and left Artyom's room.

Artyom pushed the door closed behind him and bolted it. A tremor ran through him. Needing to put as much distance between himself and the KGB agent, he slipped on his coat and walked out onto the balcony. The room beside him remained quiet, but the parking lot below was bustling with activity.

Several cars vied for the few available spaces. One car circled twice before finally taking a recently vacated spot across from the side entrance. Beneath the wash of the parking lamps, five people climbed out of the car, two men and three women. One of the women hurried to the side entrance and opened the door. The rest followed, one of the women walking in the center of the others as though shielding herself from view.

Artyom's eyes narrowed. The petite build, the graceful movements as she walked. It couldn't be.

The woman looked around quickly as though expecting someone might be searching for her. Could that be Katerina Petrova?

One of the KGB agents appeared at the corner of the building, his gaze drawn to the foursome. He spoke to the man beside him for a moment. It took a second for Artyom to identify him as Josef. Both Josef and the agent watched the new arrivals until they disappeared inside. A moment later, the agent sprinted to follow them through the side entrance.

Josef remained by the front of the building for a moment longer, but then, he too rushed to follow the others.

Questions rambled through Artyom's mind. Would Katerina really stay at the same hotel as the Soviet team? If so, did the KGB now know how to find her? And did Josef Petrov have any clue what they had planned?

Chapter THIRTY-SIX

Katerina couldn't be prouder. She had stayed through the entire competition, long enough to see how her daughter and Tyler had ended up in the standings. Her heart swelled with joy, and she couldn't keep the grin off her face. "Amaliya and Tyler were amazing tonight."

"They always are." Nancy stopped in the hotel hallway outside of her and Grant's room. After the competition, she had convinced everyone to stop by a restaurant she had found for dessert to make sure they arrived at the hotel after the Soviets returned so they wouldn't have to worry about extra security outside.

"Aren't you glad now that you came?" Miles asked, he and Linda also stopping in the hallway.

"I am. It's not the same when I'm watching it on TV," Katerina said.

"It's too bad Robert couldn't be here tonight," Grant said.

"He likes the short and long programs better anyway." Katerina held up the takeout bag that held the chocolate éclair she had brought back for him. "And this will help ease the pain of missing out on our excursions tonight."

"Dessert tends to do that for him," Miles said.

"Well, I hate to be a party pooper, but I'm exhausted," Linda said. "I'm heading to bed."

"Me too." Nancy unlocked her door. "Good night."

"Good night." Miles motioned to Katerina. "Grant, I'll walk Katerina to her room."

"Great. See you all in the morning." Grant held the door open for his wife and then followed her inside.

Linda stopped at her room and waited for Miles to walk Katerina the last few yards to her door.

"Thanks for everything tonight," Katerina said. "I appreciate your making it possible for me to go."

"Happy to help." Miles waited for Katerina to unlock her door. "How about I check out your room for you before you go in?"

"You're just as protective as Robert."

"Yep." Miles stepped past her and walked into her room. A moment later, he reemerged. "You're all set. Do you need anything else? Ice? Something from the vending machines?"

A door opened and closed behind her, but when Katerina turned, no one was there. A ripple of unease shot through her, but she focused on Miles again. "Actually, if you don't mind getting me some ice, that would be great."

"No problem. Let me stop by my room and get my ice bucket too." Miles grabbed Katerina's ice bucket from her room. "I'll be back in a minute."

"Thanks." Katerina went inside and checked for herself that she was indeed alone. Then she slid Robert's éclair into the minirefrigerator.

A knock sounded on her door.

"That was fast." Katerina pulled the door open, but it wasn't Miles on the other side. She had never seen this man before, but she recognized the stance and the coldness in his expression. KGB? How could anyone have found her?

Panic shot through her. She shoved the door to close it, but she wasn't quite fast enough.

The man stuck his foot in front of the door to keep it open, and he pushed his way inside. Katerina squeaked in alarm.

"You need to come with me," he said in Russian.

Katerina backed up deeper into her room to put more space between them, but she had nowhere to go. She made it only a few steps before the man used his long stride to catch her.

He grabbed her by the arm to hold her in place. "Don't make this any harder than it needs to be."

"Let go of me." Katerina tried to jerk free, but his grip didn't falter. "I'm an American citizen. You have no right—" That was as far as she got before he pulled her toward the door.

"You are Soviet. You will always be Soviet."

"No, I'm not." Panic, helplessness, and fear overwhelmed her. She couldn't let this man take her away. She couldn't. She leaned back and dug her heels into the carpet. Her efforts did little to slow her progress as he dragged her out of her room and into the hall.

Another man's voice sounded behind her, the words spoken in Russian. "What are you doing?"

"This is none of your concern." Apparently frustrated with Katerina's continued efforts to keep from moving, her captor yanked her forward. He pulled her firmly against him, her back to his chest, his arm now firmly across her throat. "That's enough. You will cooperate, or you will not live to see tomorrow."

"Why are you taking her? She never saw my father. They never even spoke."

His father? Viktor? Was this Josef?

"Open the door to the stairs," the first man ordered.

"No, I won't help you with this," Josef said. "Let her go. She did nothing."

"She is Soviet. It is time for her to come back to Leningrad."

The words sent an icy chill through Katerina and spurred her into motion. She stomped her foot down, her heel landing solidly on his foot.

He grunted in pain, but his hold didn't loosen.

Katerina tried again, but this time, he jerked her body to the side and tightened his hold. His arm squeezed her neck, cutting off her air supply. Katerina lifted her hands to the man's arm and dug her fingernails into his coat sleeve. His hold didn't loosen. She tried to gasp, but she couldn't breathe. New panic jolted through her.

This man had threatened to take her back to the Soviet Union, but she wasn't even going to live long enough to see it—or anything ever again.

"You're choking her!" Josef must have done something because, suddenly, the man's hold loosened enough for Katerina to gulp in some air. She pulled down on his arm. Nothing happened. She jabbed her elbow into his ribs. He grunted, and his hold loosened enough for her to break free. She barely managed a step before he grabbed her again and jerked her toward the stairwell door.

She screamed.

The young man who had tried to help came into her view. Had it not been for the brown eyes, he could have been Viktor frozen in time from the day she had defected.

Katerina lunged toward him in an attempt to break free from her captor.

"That's enough!" The man grabbed a fistful of Katerina's hair with one hand and used his other to grab her around her waist. Her head jerked back, and her feet left the floor.

Josef reached out and grabbed his arm. Katerina's captor let go of her hair and punched Josef in the jaw. Josef staggered backward until he thudded against the wall.

"Katerina!" Miles's voice rang out as something hit the floor down the hall and footsteps pounded toward her. "Let her go!"

Before Katerina could draw another breath, Miles rammed into her captor and knocked both of them into the wall. Katerina broke free.

Her heart pounded, and she stumbled back several steps to get out of the way as Miles's fist flew at the man's face. Josef remained a short distance away, a dazed look on his face.

The KGB agent lifted his left hand to block the punch and jabbed Miles in the ribs with his right.

Miles grunted in pain, but he managed to put himself between the agent and Katerina.

"Run!" Miles shouted.

A door opened behind her. "Katerina! In here!" Linda's voice broke through the haze of the battle that continued between Miles and the other man.

Katerina rushed toward Linda's room, terrified of remaining in the hall but equally concerned about leaving Miles to deal with a man who was most likely armed. "Call the police!"

"I already did." Linda waved at Katerina to come into her room.

Katerina turned and looked behind her in the same instant the elevator dinged.

In a blur, two policemen rushed down the hall.

"Go inside," one called out.

Linda pulled Katerina into her room and closed them inside.

Katerina moved back several steps and just stared at the door.

Viktor paced his room, anxious to find out how Amaliya and Tyler had placed in the figures competition. It struck him how odd it was that he would care so much about a couple he hadn't known existed until a month ago. Family. Amaliya was family, and so far, she was the only connection he had to his sister. She also might be the only avenue for him to see Katerina.

His new coat now hung in his closet, away from anyone who might take notice that his elbows no longer poked out of his sleeves. The note had been simple enough. In addition to a repeat of Katerina's request that he use his hotel key to go to room 403 and call the front desk, she had also given him the alternative of passing a note back to her friend by putting it in the pocket of his new coat and allowing the friend to swap coats with him again.

Viktor wasn't thrilled with the idea of going back to his old coat, but at least he could keep the new gloves Katerina had given him.

His hotel room door flew open, and Josef burst inside, quickly closing the door behind him. He bolted the lock and leaned back against the door, a panicked expression on his face, a bruise darkening his jaw below his eye. His breath came out in quick bursts, and his eyes darted around the room before focusing on Viktor.

"What's wrong?" Viktor asked.

"Papa, I'm sorry. I didn't know . . ."

"Didn't know what?" Viktor took a step forward. "What happened?"

"It's your sister. Oleg tried to take her." Josef sucked in a quick breath. "He was going to make her come back to the Soviet Union."

"What?" Viktor grabbed Josef's arm and drew him away from the door. His fear of being overheard overshadowed his instinct to question his son further. He pulled his new coat out of the closet, slipped it on, and urged Josef outside onto the balcony.

Viktor lowered his voice. "Where is Katerina? Is she okay?"

"I think so. The police came before Oleg could drag her away."

Relief pushed aside the worst of Viktor's fear. "Tell me everything."

"I was downstairs with Oleg when he saw Katerina arrive with her friends. He followed her." He gulped hard. "Something didn't feel right so I followed him."

"Where did he go?"

"The fourth floor."

The fourth floor. Viktor could have been within a few dozen meters of his sister when he'd tried to access the room she'd sent him to.

"By the time I got there, Oleg had already pulled Aunt Katerina out of her room," Josef continued. "She was trying to fight him off. I tried to help . . ."

"She got away?"

Josef nodded. "One of her friends fought with Oleg, and Aunt Katerina ran down the hall. Then the police came. Oleg ran downstairs. I came up here."

"Who else knows you were there?"

"Your sister and her friend saw me. The police may have seen me, but I left as soon as I saw them coming." Josef's lower lip trembled. "Papa, I'm sorry. I'm so sorry. I didn't know they were going to do this."

Viktor reached out and pulled Josef into an embrace. "You have nothing to be sorry about. Thank you for helping your aunt."

Josef remained silent for a moment before he pulled away. "I don't deserve your thanks. I was trying to help them before I found out what they were really planning."

Viktor's eyebrows drew together. "You were trying to help who?"

"Budimir. Artyom Belsky. All of them."

Viktor took a step back, the railing of the balcony now right behind him. "What were you helping them with?"

"Budimir said if I would help them make sure you and Sonya didn't have the chance to talk to Aunt Katerina, he would move us to the top of the list for a new heater. He was going to give us new coats and blankets."

A slice of betrayal cut through him. "And all this just to make sure I didn't see my sister?"

Josef hung his head. "Yes."

"You would risk my sister's life? You would spy on your own father?"

Josef looked up now, a flurry of emotions darkening his face. "Your sister left us behind. She didn't worry about us or what her actions would do to our family." Josef lifted his hand and splayed it across his chest when he added, "She didn't care that I wouldn't get to go to university because I was the nephew of a defector."

"You've read her letters. Leaving us wasn't easy for her." Viktor shook his head. "I can't believe you would risk her this way. She could have been killed."

A voice carried from the adjoining balcony. "The boy didn't know."

Viktor whirled to face the newcomer. Artyom. One of the men who had turned his own son against him. "But you knew." Viktor drew a steadying breath. "You knew the KGB was going to take my sister back to the Soviet Union."

Regret flashed in his eyes. "Yes."

"And you were helping them?" Viktor fought to keep his voice low. "You were willing to ruin a woman's life because of something she did over twenty years ago?"

"Not by choice." Artyom's gaze met Viktor's, a silent pleading reflected in his eyes. "I was doing what I was told."

"Told by whom?" Viktor demanded.

"Sometimes it's best not to have all the answers." Artyom took a step back. "Don't be too hard on the boy. His heart was in the right place."

Forgiveness didn't come, but understanding surfaced regardless. Josef had tried to help the family. Viktor prayed Josef's efforts to provide for their home in Leningrad wouldn't turn into a disaster and cost them everything they had left behind.

Chapter THIRTY-SEVEN

Katerina jolted when the door opened. Miles strode inside, a determined look on his face and a smear of blood at the corner of his lip. He closed the door behind him and focused on Katerina. "Are you okay?"

Katerina offered a shaky nod. "Thanks to you."

"Did the police catch that guy?" Linda asked.

"I don't know. They haven't come back yet." Miles bolted the door closed.

"You're bleeding." Linda moved toward the bathroom.

"So's the other guy."

Katerina shuddered at the image of Miles grappling with the man who had come after her. "You're lucky you weren't killed. That man was likely KGB."

Miles swiped at his lip. "Maybe he's new. I've taken more of a pounding playing hockey than what that guy dished out."

Linda returned from the bathroom holding a wet washcloth. She pressed it against Miles's lip. "Thank goodness he didn't pull a gun."

"He didn't want to deal with me. He only wanted Katerina." Miles took the washcloth from Linda, pressed it to his face briefly, and then tossed it through the open bathroom door into the sink.

"I never really thought the Soviets would try to take you away," Linda said. "Not after all these years. I was wrong."

"I had hoped they'd forgotten about me too." Katerina drew a shaky breath and let it out. "My wishful thinking didn't come true."

Someone knocked. Katerina startled.

Miles strode to the door and looked through the peephole before he pulled the door open. A police officer stood on the other side.

"Did you catch him?" Miles asked.

"May I come in?"

Miles waved him inside and promptly closed and bolted the door.

Linda sat on the bed beside Katerina. "What can you tell us?"

"One of them ran upstairs, but he must have a room because I couldn't find him in the halls," the officer said. "The other one got away. He had a car downstairs and took off. My partner is in pursuit right now."

Two men. One of them must have been Viktor's son. "Which one drove away?" Katerina asked. "The older one or the younger?"

"The older one. My partner and I will do a room-by-room search to find the one we believe is still in the hotel."

"That won't be necessary. He wasn't trying to hurt me," Katerina said. "He was trying to help."

"Are you sure?" the officer asked. "The way he took off, he looked like he was guilty of something."

"He was. He's Soviet. I'm sure he wasn't supposed to be down here."

"You know who he was?" the officer asked.

Katerina debated how much to say. If she gave Josef's name, he could be sent home, possibly punished for his involvement in her rescue tonight.

"Katerina?" Miles asked. "Who was he?"

"I think he was my nephew."

"Then he will know who the man was who tried to kidnap you."

"Yes, but he will be severely punished if anyone finds out he helped me."

"Do you know why the man came after you?" the police officer asked.

"He wanted to take me back to the Soviet Union." Taking in the confused look on the man's face, Katerina added, "I defected from the Soviet Union twenty-four years ago."

"Why would someone come after you now?" he asked.

"Probably because this is the first time they've known where she was and had access to her," Miles said. "Katerina, you can't stay in your room. We need to move you to another hotel."

Katerina started to agree. Then she caught sight of the ticket stubs that lay on the dresser from tonight's competition. "If I move hotels, we'd need to take Tyler and Amaliya with us. I can't make them pack up and move in the middle of their competition."

"Sure you can," Miles said.

"Not without upsetting them," Katerina countered. "They're in first place. They have a chance for another gold medal."

"Ma'am, I have to agree with your friend here. It would be best if you stayed somewhere else," the police officer said. "We can put a police officer on site here for the next day or so, but many of the Soviets staying here have diplomatic immunity. We can't guarantee your safety if they know where you are."

"See?" Miles motioned to the policeman. "Besides, Amaliya and Tyler can still win, even if we move to another hotel."

"No." Katerina's fear competed with her resolve, but she pushed forward. "I don't want them to spend the next two days worried about me when they need to stay focused."

"If you won't move to another hotel, then you need to stay here with Linda tonight. I'll go crash in the extra room you booked."

"Miles is right." Linda put her hand on Katerina's arm. "You shouldn't stay in a room alone."

Katerina didn't try to argue. "Thank you."

The officer pocketed his notepad and retrieved a business card. "Here's my number. I'll let you know when we have more information on your attacker."

Katerina stood. "Thank you, officer."

"I'll be in touch." He slid the bolt free and opened the door.

As soon as the officer left, Miles secured the door again. "Do you have Robert's number at his hotel in Montreal?"

Katerina nodded.

Miles motioned to the phone. "You'd better call him. He won't be happy if he comes back and finds the police here without knowing why."

"You're right." Katerina moved to the phone. She would call her husband, and maybe, just maybe, he would be able to come back earlier than he'd planned. The sooner, the better.

Tyler couldn't sleep, and his head was pounding. He had stretched after returning to his hotel room and gone through his typical bedtime routine, but he couldn't convince his mind to shut down. Lying on his bed, he linked his fingers behind his head and stared at the ceiling.

He and Amaliya had performed every bit as well today as they had in the Olympics, but what would tomorrow hold? They had managed to go through their short program only a handful of times without mistakes. Would tomorrow be a repeat of a good performance or one of the many when he and Amaliya had failed to execute their new choreography cleanly?

He pushed off the covers and climbed out of bed. Too restless to sleep, he grabbed the empty ice bucket on his dresser and the hotel key and headed for the door. He didn't particularly need ice, but it was a handy excuse to escape the hotel room for a few minutes.

He walked the length of the hall to the small room where the vending machines and ice machine were located. He filled his ice bucket and headed back to his room. A glass of ice water, a Tylenol to get rid of his pounding headache, and then maybe he could finally escape into sleep. If not, the chances for a clean short program would fall from questionable to impossible.

A door opened a short distance away, and Gordon stepped out. "What are you still doing up? You should have been in bed an hour ago."

"I was in bed." Tyler shrugged. "I couldn't sleep."

"What's on your mind?" Gordon folded his arms and leaned against the wall across from Tyler's door.

"Just worried about tomorrow. We haven't had a lot of clean runs since we got here."

"You've had more clean practices than not," Gordon countered. He pushed away from the wall and took a step closer. "You know as well as I do that your performance tomorrow will depend as much on your mental preparation as on the physical. You need to believe you can perform your new program without flaw, and you need to help Amaliya believe the same thing."

"Amaliya is the one who is convinced we can do anything."

"She's right, but that doesn't mean she hasn't picked up on your doubts," Gordon said. "Trust yourself, and trust your partner."

Tyler nodded. He didn't know what the future held, but no matter what he and Amaliya decided, that was a piece of advice they needed to follow.

"Now, get to bed. You need your rest."

Tyler nodded. "I'm going."

"And, Tyler?"

"Yeah?"

"Positive thinking can go a long way."

Tyler nodded. He unlocked his door and went back into his room. Positive thinking. Gordon was right. They could skate a clean program tomorrow. And if they could manage that feat, they had a shot at another gold medal. They also had the potential to skate for many more competitive seasons beyond this weekend.

He took a deep breath. One thing at a time. Sleep first, perform tomorrow, and think about the future later. But right now, it was time to take a Tylenol. His head was killing him.

Chapter THIRTY-EIGHT

ARTYOM'S HEAD POUNDED, THE PRESSURE worsening with each passing hour. Through the window, the early-morning light filtered through the curtains. If only the sun could chase away the gloom that had been hanging over him since he'd learned of the incident with Katerina and Josef.

He had managed to doze a few times during the night, but he hadn't dared dress for bed in case he received more information about Oleg. So far, the only details he had received were from what he had overheard when eavesdropping on Viktor and Josef. How in the world had Artyom ended up in the middle of an attempted kidnapping?

Admittedly, he hadn't wanted Katerina Petrova to be dragged back to the Soviet Union, but he hadn't anticipated what would happen if a failed attempt occurred. Had Oleg managed to get away before the police could arrest him?

His clothes rumpled from his restless night, Artyom debated whether he should attempt a quick shower before breakfast. He had yet to make a decision when a knock sounded on his door.

He answered it. Budimir stood on the other side.

"We need to talk." Budimir pushed his way into Artyom's room.

Resigned, Artyom closed the door. He debated briefly if he should play dumb about the incident last night or not. Thankfully, Budimir didn't give him the chance to speak first.

"Katerina Petrova was spotted here in this hotel last night, but now we have a situation," Budimir said.

Artyom sat on the edge of his bed to hide the trembling of his knees. "What kind of situation?"

"Oleg was chased by the police. Now he's trapped inside the Soviet embassy."

He escaped. Would he implicate Josef in the failed attempt? Artyom swallowed his questions and asked, "What will happen to him now?"

"If he leaves the embassy, he risks being taken into custody." He slashed his hand through the air. "It's in the diplomats' hands now, but that doesn't change our objective."

"Surely you aren't planning to go after Katerina again." Artyom gripped the edge of the bed. "The attempt alone will likely rattle the American pair."

"Maybe, but that doesn't change the fact that Katerina Petrova has been using the skills we gave her to undermine our athletes. She needs to come home."

A chill ran through Artyom. "What do you plan to do?"

"I have men watching the exits. Eventually, she will leave the hotel. When she does, my men will follow."

"And do what?" Artyom asked. "It's doubtful she will go anywhere alone."

"She had her chance to come home. If she makes things difficult the next time my men approach her, she can be dealt with a different way." Budimir's eyes darkened. "The roads are slippery this time of year."

Murder. He was planning a murder.

"I need you to set up a meeting with Viktor and Katerina."

"I thought you didn't want them to see each other."

"I don't, but the promise of seeing her brother will bring Katerina out of her hiding place," Budimir said. "Did you already give him permission to attend his niece's competition tomorrow?"

"Not yet."

"Make it happen."

"I can arrange for him to stay, but I doubt it will make a difference. I don't think Viktor will try to see his sister, not after what happened last night."

"Viktor and Josef trust you. You can make them think we're allowing a visit."

More lies. More manipulation. "Josef knows Oleg tried to take Katerina by force."

"I'm well aware of Josef's involvement. He can either help or be punished."

Punished. Artyom didn't want to know what Budimir meant by that.

"Tell him whatever you need to in order to make this happen," Budimir demanded. "And set it up today, before the short programs."

"That's impossible. I need more time." The look on Budimir's face caused Artyom to add, "I want to make sure we don't have another failed attempt."

A muscle twitched in Budimir's jaw. "How much time do you need?"

"Until tomorrow. That will let me create a believable compromise with Katerina and Viktor. If we try too quickly, they won't believe I'm sincere."

"You have until two o'clock tomorrow. After that, I'm taking matters into my own hands."

"I understand, but in order for this to work, you need to tell your men to let Katerina go to today's competition without threatening her," Artyom said. "We want her to let her guard down in order for her to fall into your trap."

"Ah, you're starting to think like me." Budimir scratched his chin. "I will tell my men, but you had better not fail me. Siberia is quite cold this time of year."

Artyom swallowed hard. "So I've heard."

Robert was coming back. Katerina had spoken to him last night after the police had left, but hearing his voice on the phone wasn't the same as having him here beside her. Now here she was, sitting at the table in Linda and Miles's hotel room, her breakfast still untouched.

Nancy and Grant had brought them food this morning, but Katerina wanted a hot shower and her own clothes. The mere thought of going back to her room to get her things, though, was enough to paralyze her.

"You need to eat something," Linda said.

Katerina broke off a piece of her croissant and took a bite. Even that little bit of food was enough to cause her stomach to churn.

Someone knocked on the door, and Katerina's body jolted.

"I'll see who it is." Linda crossed to the door and looked through the peephole. "It's Robert."

Relief and myriad other emotions flooded through Katerina. She stood as Linda opened the door. The moment Robert spotted her, he rushed inside and pulled her into his arms.

Katerina burrowed into his chest, the comfort of his presence chasing away the worst of the nightmare she had lived the night before.

After a long moment, Robert pulled back and looked down at her. "You're okay?"

"I'm better now that you're here." Katerina tilted her head back so she could see him more clearly. "How did you get here so fast? I thought your flight didn't land until this afternoon."

"I caught an earlier flight." Robert kept his arm around her and turned to face Linda. "Where's Miles?"

"He stayed in the extra room next to yours." Linda crossed to the phone on the bedside table and picked up the receiver. "I'll let him know you're here."

Robert focused on Katerina again. "Have you heard anything from the police since I talked to you last?"

"Nothing yet." Katerina's fingers clutched the back of his shirt. "Maybe Miles has talked to them."

After a brief conversation, Linda hung up the phone. "Miles will be here in a minute."

By the time she crossed to the door, Miles was already using his key to come inside.

Robert didn't bother with a greeting. "Anything from the police?"

"Yeah, but you aren't going to like it." Miles closed the door behind him. "The guy who tried to grab Katerina is holed up in the Soviet embassy. Seems he's claiming diplomatic immunity."

"You've got to be kidding me." Robert's voice rose.

"I'm afraid not." Miles jutted his chin toward the balcony doors. "The police are camped outside the embassy to make sure he doesn't try again, but from the sounds of it, the diplomats are involved now."

A new wave of anxiety crashed over Katerina. "It doesn't matter if he's in the embassy or not. If the Soviets know I'm here and they want to take me back, someone will try again."

"We need to take you back home," Robert said.

Katerina shook her head. "The airport is the first place they'll look for me."

"Then what do you suggest?" Robert asked. "The Soviets know you're here. We need to move to another hotel."

Miles shot Katerina an I-told-you-so look. "That's what I said."

"I don't want all of this to upset Amaliya and Tyler."

Robert took a step back so he could see Katerina more clearly. "They don't know what happened?"

"No. Neither does Gordon."

"Amaliya will know something is wrong if you aren't at the competition today," Miles said.

"You can't go." Robert gripped both of Katerina's arms. "It's too dangerous."

"I agree," Miles said.

"How do we get Katerina out of the hotel, make Amaliya think she's at the competition, and avoid the Soviets?" Linda asked.

"If I switch hotels, Amaliya will know something's wrong," Katerina said. "We need to wait until tomorrow, assuming we decide to move at all."

Miles stroked his chin. "You know, it could be easier to sneak Katerina to another room here in the hotel than to get her out of here."

Robert fell silent, but Katerina recognized the expression on his face. It was the same determined look from when they had first planned her defection.

"You have an idea," Katerina said.

"I think so." Robert crossed the room and dialed a number on the phone. A moment later, he said, "Yes, I would like to know if you have any suites available, preferably on the top floor." Robert turned his head, and his eyes met Katerina's. His lips curved up slightly. "Good. I'd like to reserve it starting today. The name is Donnelly."

After a short discussion with the front desk, Robert hung up. "We're all set."

"Want to tell me why I have another hotel room?" Miles asked.

"I just didn't want the Soviets to track the reservation in case they know Katerina's married name." Robert moved back to stand beside Katerina. "Katerina and I will move up to the new suite when it's time to leave for the competition."

"Why then?" Linda asked.

"Because that's when the Soviets will likely have most of their people watching the exits," Katerina said, cluing in on her husband's plan. "We'll have to make an excuse to Amaliya and Tyler about why I'm not at the competition though."

"We can just say you left early to avoid the Soviets," Linda suggested. "They already know you need to be careful."

Katerina sighed. "I hate that I can't watch them compete live."

"They'll understand when they find out," Robert said. "We can tell them what happened after they win their next gold medal."

"I'm so sorry this all got so complicated," Katerina said.

"We'll be at the rink to make sure Amaliya and Tyler have a live cheering section. So will Nancy and Grant."

And Katerina would be locked up in her room. She focused on Robert again. "How long do you expect me to hide upstairs?"

"Until the Soviets leave."

Until Viktor left. Her insides withered. All their efforts and still she had failed. She would never see her brother again.

Viktor sat alone in the stands, his new coat lying on the empty seat beside him, his focus on everything but the skater currently on the ice. His mind still couldn't quite reconcile the events of last night with Josef's involvement. And Artyom. How could that man simply stand by while their government manipulated people and their lives?

The last question repeated, and he recognized the answer quickly: they were Soviet. The government owned their lives.

A new seed of fear planted inside him. What would happen to Josef now that he had interfered with the KGB's plans? And would Ursula be punished in their absence? If only he could call and warn her. Even if he could, where could she go? What could she do?

When Sonya's name was announced and she stepped onto the ice, Viktor welcomed the distraction. He was here for his daughter. If she did well enough in this competition, perhaps her success would provide some level of protection for the rest of the family.

Viktor hated that they were in a position where they had to rely on her to have the simple comforts of enough food on the table and a roof over their heads, but that was the reality.

Sonya took her starting position, and her music started. Viktor let himself get caught up in the moment, his pride swelling as she executed her program with power and grace. The Petrova grace. From what Viktor had seen of Amaliya on television during the Olympics and at her recent practices, she had been blessed with that gift as well.

Sonya completed her routine, and Viktor instinctively rose to his feet as he applauded her beautiful performance. He looked around to see he wasn't the only one standing. The audience was giving her a standing ovation. His little girl had captured the crowd, and they approved of what they had seen.

By the time everyone sat back down, the scores were already posting. The marks were good, and the updated standing proved it. Sonya was still in second place, still contending for a medal.

Someone picked up Viktor's coat and took the seat beside him. For a brief moment, he expected to see the man from yesterday. Instead, it was Artyom sitting beside him.

"She looked good." Artyom handed the coat to Viktor.

"Yes, she did." Viktor focused on the ice again.

"You have been approved to stay at the competition so you can watch the pairs competition."

A trap. Viktor sensed it.

"Why?" Viktor lowered his voice, venom filling his whispered words. "Are you using me to get to my sister?"

"I'm not."

"If not you, someone else?"

"They will try but not today."

If not today, tomorrow. Viktor absorbed the implication. Tomorrow, the KGB would capture Katerina and take her back to the Soviet Union. At least, they would try.

"You know this is wrong," Viktor whispered.

Artyom stood. "Enjoy the competition."

Viktor muttered his thanks because it was expected.

Artyom took a step but then turned back. "One more thing."

"Yes?"

"After you get back to the hotel, it would do you good to take in a bit of fresh air." Artyom tilted his head slightly. "Might as well take advantage of having a balcony while you can."

Chapter THIRTY-NINE

Amaliya's nerves stretched thin, the music coming through the earphones of her Walkman doing little to block out the hustle and bustle of the backstage area of the competition rink or the couple who had just taken the ice. She and Tyler would be up third in the final group of competitors tonight. In only minutes, they would find out if the gamble to change their short program would pay off or if the new routine she choreographed would become their downfall.

From where he stood beside her, Tyler took her hand and squeezed. The gesture gave her little comfort. If they messed up, it would be her fault. This could be their final competition, and everything was now riding on whether they could execute the moves they had been working on for only a few weeks.

Gordon approached and tapped his ears with both hands to signal them to remove their headphones. As soon as they complied, he said, "You're in first place. You have a solid routine. Just focus and have fun out there."

Amaliya couldn't stop her doubts. "What if our new program—"

"Your new program is exactly what the judges are looking for," Gordon interrupted. "This shows that you have versatility, that you are respecting the world championships as its own entity rather than a repeat of the Olympics." Gordon put a hand on her shoulder. "And you're ready."

"He's right." Tyler lifted her hand and kissed the back of it. "We can do this."

The confidence in Tyler's voice, especially after he had expressed so many doubts over the past few weeks, sparked a new resolve. If he believed they could still win, maybe they really could.

"You're in first place," Gordon reminded them again. "Go out there and show everyone why you should stay there."

"No pressure." Amaliya blew out a breath.

"Concentrate on what you've practiced," Gordon said. "You can do this."

The scores from the couple who had just skated were announced, and a rink official opened the door in the rink barrier. "Linden and Marcell."

Tyler squeezed her hand again. "Let's dance."

Some of her stress eased, and Amaliya nodded. They took off their skate guards and handed them to Gordon. A moment later, their names were announced, and they took the ice.

The applause was instant. The crowd came to their feet. Amaliya didn't know how it was possible, but the noise level went from deafening to off the charts.

Tyler led her around the rink once before circling to the center. He stopped and faced her. "You ready?"

"I'll let you know in two and a half minutes."

Tyler's grin was instant, and Amaliya couldn't help but smile back.

They took their starting positions. The crowd quieted. The music began.

Amaliya put her body in motion, the first dance moves coming as naturally as if they had practiced them for months instead of weeks. Tyler grabbed her hips in preparation for their throw triple twist. She gripped his wrists and bent her knees to help him elevate her over his head. Then suddenly, she was airborne.

Three twists over Tyler's head, her body angled as she came back down, Tyler's hands on her waist. Her own hands rose in victory as the crowd applauded.

They moved into the core of their program that had remained the same from the Olympics. New confidence rose within her with each move, with each jump.

A little spurt of adrenaline shot through her as they entered their combination jumps. She fought to keep her moves in time with Tyler's. They took to the air in unison. Triple lutz. Double toe loop. Their blades hit the ice in tandem. The crowd roared again.

Tyler took her hand, and they transitioned into their pairs camel spin. Only another forty-five seconds.

Tyler's hand gripped her waist as they spun together. The connection between them magnified, and they moved as one. She concentrated on what came next, willing her body to perform the moves that were still so new to them.

Seconds ticked by, the music nearly drowned out by the crowd. Double axels. Perfect. Adrenaline and excitement rose another notch as they moved into the final dance sequence. They hit their final pose, and Amaliya held her position, stunned. They had done it. They had skated a clean program.

The crowd came to their feet, the volume once again reaching deafening volumes.

Amaliya straightened and curtsied as Tyler bowed. They repeated the process once more, and then Tyler swept her into his arms.

"That was amazing." His words were barely audible despite his nearness.

"I can't believe we pulled it off." Amaliya waved to the crowd. Tyler did the same. A minute later, they were sitting in front of the cameras with Gordon, awaiting their scores.

Their technical marks illuminated the screen, five eights and five nines.

"Those are going to keep you in first," Gordon said.

The artistic marks came up a minute later. A five eight, several five nines, and two sixes. Two perfect scores!

Gordon nodded his approval. "And those will increase your lead."

"One more program," Tyler said. "We might just pull this off."

"I'm counting on it," Gordon said. "Whether this is your last competition or not, I expect you to finish this season on top."

Amaliya pushed aside her uncertainty of what would happen next and let herself get swept away in the joy of the moment. Finish the season on top. She liked the sound of that.

Katerina leaned forward to stretch her back, a combination of joy and frustration flowing through her. Amaliya and Tyler were in first place, but she hadn't been there to see them compete. She was so tired of watching her daughter's competitions on television screens.

Robert reached out and rubbed her back, applying enough pressure to ease some of the knots that had formed in her muscles. "You doing okay?"

"I'm sorry you were stuck here with me tonight."

"I like being stuck with you." Robert shifted and used both hands to massage her shoulders. "Besides, it's not like we've never seen Amaliya compete in person before."

"We've missed more competitions than we've been to," Katerina said, her frustration spilling out. "And for all we know, this could be their last one."

"Your safety and freedom are a lot more important than us being in the arena to watch," Robert said.

The phone rang, and Robert leaned over to answer it. "Hello?" He paused for a moment. "That's fine, but tell them they need to get off the elevator on the fourth floor and take the stairs up from there." Another pause. "Thanks."

As soon as he hung up, Katerina asked, "Who was that?"

"The front desk. Someone from the diplomatic corps is here to see us."

"You're making them walk up three flights of stairs?"

"Absolutely. We don't know if someone might be watching the elevator to see where he goes. He'll know if he's being followed in the stairwell."

"You've been watching spy movies again, haven't you?"

Robert shrugged. "Sometimes they pay off."

"I wish we weren't in a position for them to play out in real life."

"Me too." Robert leaned in and kissed her. "You would make a cute spy though."

Katerina rolled her eyes, some of her jitters easing.

Robert stood and crossed to the door. He waited only a minute before a knock echoed through the room. He answered it to a light-haired man in his midforties, a set of credentials in his hand.

"Nelson Thompson, Global Affairs Canada," he said. "Are you Robert Marcell?"

"Yes." Robert checked his ID and then waved him in. "This is my wife, Katerina."

"I recognize you from your photo."

"My photo?"

"We have a file on you from when you planned to defect in Montreal."

A missed message from Robert had resulted in a failed attempt on that night in Canada. "That was a long time ago."

Robert motioned for Nelson to sit before joining Katerina on the couch again. "What's the latest on the man who tried to kidnap my wife?"

Nelson sat in the chair across from them. "He's still in the embassy, and the Soviets are claiming diplomatic immunity."

"Have they offered any explanation for his actions?" Robert asked.

"Something about Mrs. Marcell being a cousin who wanted to return to the Soviet Union," Nelson said. "He claims he was helping her, but someone prevented her from leaving with him."

"That's a lie!" Katerina said. "All of it."

"We suspected as much, but I needed to hear that from you." Nelson retrieved a notepad and pen from his pocket. "Do you have any idea why that man came after you?"

"He said he was taking me back to the Soviet Union." Katerina shuddered at the memory of the cold words and the fear that had ripped through her.

"Why now? You defected twenty-four years ago."

"I don't know." Katerina shrugged.

"Maybe it's because this is the first time they've known where to find her."

"Possibly, but I suspect there's more to it than that."

"Like what?" Katerina asked.

"Your daughter is the reigning Olympic champion. Their skaters came in second."

Katerina's eyebrows rose. "You think they came after me to get even with Amaliya?"

"Or they hoped to interfere with your daughter's potential success in the world championships."

Protectiveness and fear tangled inside her. "They could go after Amaliya."

"Our police have a detail assigned to protect them. Your daughter won't even know they're there."

"What about my wife?" Robert asked. "Do we have to hide here until the Soviets leave?"

"That would be my suggestion," Nelson said. "We are negotiating with the Soviets to have your attacker deported back to the Soviet Union, but we can't guarantee another agent won't take his place."

"What about Josef? You need to make sure they don't hurt him."

"Who is Josef?"

"My nephew. I'm pretty sure he's the second man who was at my room last night," Katerina explained. "He helped me get away. The KGB won't be happy when word gets out."

"I can't believe we went through all of this and you never even got to see Viktor."

Nelson's eyebrows drew together. "It sounds like I'm missing a few details about what's really going on here. Maybe you should start at the beginning. Who is Viktor? And what were you planning?"

Katerina let out a sigh. "This may take a while."

"That's okay. Gathering information is my specialty."

Robert shifted beside her. "I hope you also specialize in knowing how to use it."

"As a matter of fact, I do."

You always have a choice. His grandmother's words echoed through Artyom's mind for the hundredth time as he stood beside his balcony door and stared into the darkness. He did have a choice, but was he willing to suffer the consequences? Live with the guilt of knowing he had ruined a woman's life, or face the possibility of exile to Siberia or even death. Neither option appealed to him. Difficult decisions were never easy, but this one was nearly impossible. At least he didn't have any family the KGB could threaten. The cold truth flowed through him. He was alone. Katerina Petrova wasn't, nor was Viktor.

Movement on the balcony beside his caught Artyom's attention. He slipped his coat on along with whatever courage he could muster before stepping outside.

Artyom took in Viktor's rigid posture, Viktor's hands in the pockets of his coat. Artyom took a closer look. Was that the same coat he had worn when they'd boarded the plane in Leningrad?

"I'm here. Why did you want to talk to me?" Viktor asked.

"I want to help you." Artyom did want to help. He just didn't want to die because of it.

Viktor scoffed. "Why should I trust you?"

"Because if you don't, your son will be punished and your sister may not survive the week." Artyom slipped his own hands into his pockets in an effort to find more warmth. "I don't know how you feel about her defection, but I doubt you want her dead."

"No, I very much want her to live."

"Tomorrow when she leaves for the competition, she will have an accident unless we find a way to protect her."

"What makes the KGB think she will be there?" Viktor asked. "I didn't see her at the competition today." If Katerina took the safe route and didn't try to attend her daughter's competition, would this fruitless endeavor finally end? "Why is the KGB after her? She is too old to perform. She hasn't done anything to threaten the Soviet Union."

"She has helped her daughter become a champion, someone who can beat Popov and Sidrova."

"They would hurt Katerina to get to Amaliya?"

"They succeeded in hurting Amaliya at worlds last year," Artyom admitted.

Viktor's face paled. "They wouldn't try again, would they?"

Ice filled Artyom's veins. Would the KGB go after Amaliya if Katerina didn't show herself?

Viktor reached out and grabbed Artyom's arm. "We have to warn them."

They did have to warn them, but how? Even though they suspected Amaliya and Tyler were staying in the hotel, Artyom had no idea which room either of them was in, nor did he know if Katerina was still here.

"Their practice," Artyom said as the lightbulb went off in his mind. "Amaliya and Tyler are in the same practice as Sonya. You can talk to them there."

Viktor sighed. "I can save their lives but only if I upset the chance for them to win."

Though the Americans falling in the standings would benefit Artyom, the integrity instilled by his parents and grandparents surfaced. "Maybe you don't have to choose."

"I can't risk their lives," Viktor said.

"No, of course not, but you could talk to their coach."

"He doesn't speak Russian."

"No." Artyom shook his head. "But Josef speaks English."

"You have put Josef in a difficult enough situation. I don't want to jeopardize him any further."

"I have an idea. If it works out, we can not only protect Amaliya and Tyler from harm, but we may be able to protect the rest of your family as well."

"I'm listening."

Chapter FORTY

THIS COULD BE THE LAST time. How many times over the past few days had those words flowed through Tyler's mind? The last time competing figures, the last short program, the last practice with Gordon.

Tyler took off his skate guards and let the most recent possible last sink in. One more practice. One more long program. After that, they had to make a decision.

Amaliya looked around the rink before following him onto the ice. Undoubtedly, his fiancée was experiencing her own lasts today, only in her case, it was also potentially the last chance she would have to talk to her uncle and cousins. Once Tyler and Amaliya competed tonight, their practice time would shift to give priority to the men and the ice-dancing pairs. The likelihood of being granted the same practice time as Sonya for the next few days was unlikely, at best.

Gordon skated onto the ice behind them. "Get warmed up. I'll keep an eye out for Viktor."

Amaliya nodded and put her hand in Tyler's. "I hate that Viktor and Mama are both here in Toronto and they still haven't seen each other."

"I know." Tyler started around the rink in step with Amaliya. "Have you talked to your mom today?"

"No. I tried calling her room, but no one answered."

"That's odd. Maybe she and your dad went out to breakfast."

"I didn't think she would try to leave the hotel at all except to come watch us compete."

"Once we skate tonight, I'm sure they'll catch us up on whatever has been going on."

"I wish I knew if they'd had any luck passing notes to Viktor or if Mama might have even talked to him."

"I hate to say it, but I doubt that's happened, or you probably would have heard about it by now."

"I know, but I keep hoping."

They rounded the corner of the rink as several people walked in—the Soviets, including Sonya, Viktor, and Josef. "Looks like your family is here."

Amaliya's face brightened despite the two Soviet security officers who accompanied them. Sonya's coach said something to her and steered her and her teammate to an area on the far side of the rink where they could stretch.

"I need to talk to Viktor, to make sure he knows Mama is here and trying to see him," Amaliya said.

Tyler debated the wisdom of Amaliya's plan. He understood her need to make contact, but he also knew how easily they could lose their focus if they weren't careful. More than once, he had finished the short program in first place and then failed to make it to the arena to compete the long program. He didn't think he would survive that kind of disappointment again.

They completed their warm-up, and Gordon approached. "Amaliya, concentrate. I can see you losing your focus."

"This could be my last chance to talk to my family."

"This could be your last practice as an amateur," Gordon countered. "You have one more long program to get through. After that, I'll camp out in the hotel lobby with you to help you talk to your uncle."

The last long program. The last chance for a medal.

The magnitude of the moment washed over him. This could be it, the end of his competitive career, the culmination of over a decade and a half of practices, of sacrifices, of highs, and of lows.

"Would it really hurt to let me talk to Viktor for just a minute?" Amaliya asked.

"Yes." Gordon pointed at the center of the rink. "You two finish warming up. I'm going to get your music queued up."

Tyler executed a half spin so he was in front of Amaliya. His gaze landed on where Gordon now stood beside the skating office. Viktor and Josef approached him, and Josef said something to Gordon. Tyler glanced at the Soviet guards. One stood by the door, out of sight from where Gordon stood with Viktor and Josef, and the other was speaking with Sonya's coach.

Tyler started to comment about the scene in front of him but stopped himself. Focus. They needed to focus, and talking about Amaliya's family was guaranteed to prevent that.

He pushed aside his curiosity. Tonight, after their long program, he would indulge in asking Gordon about the conversation.

"I hate it when he gets into this whole focus thing," Amaliya grumbled.

"You hate that he's right," Tyler corrected. "We do need to focus."

"It would be a whole lot easier if we could decide if we're keeping our amateur status or not."

Pressure welled up in his chest. He couldn't do this right now. "We can talk about this later."

"Tyler, it is later." Amaliya placed both hands on his arms. "I'm sorry, but when we step out on the ice tonight, I need to know if this is the last time I'll be competing for a medal. I need to be able to appreciate tonight for what it is, whether it's a new beginning or the end."

"You already said you don't want this to be the end."

"Yes, I did, but whether I like it or not, my decision is tied to yours."

An unexpected hurt surged and was quickly masked by anger. "So I'm the one holding you back?"

Amaliya dropped her hands. "I'm simply asking you to give us both the gift of stepping out onto the ice tonight knowing where we stand."

Tyler blew out a breath and tried to settle his emotions.

Amaliya skated backward. "I'm going to get a drink."

Tyler watched her go. What she was asking of him wasn't unreasonable, so why did he feel like he'd just been put in a corner he had to fight his way out of? He shook his hands to loosen his tight muscles. Was it nerves causing him to tense up? Or was it fear? Or perhaps it was a sign. Amaliya was right. One way or another, he had to decide. If only he could be certain which option would take them where they needed to go.

Katerina soaked in the bathtub and tried not to think about the past two days or the disappointment and guilt that continued to gnaw at her. The sound of Robert's voice in the living area of their hotel room pushed her out of her stupor, and she forced herself to climb out of the cooling water to get dressed.

When she emerged from the bathroom, lunch was on the table, and Robert once again had the phone to his ear.

"Take the stairs. I'll see you in a minute." Robert hung up.

"Who was that?"

"Gordon. He said he needs to talk to us."

"How did he know we changed rooms?" Katerina asked.

"Miles told him." Robert lifted the cover off one of the plates and picked up half a sandwich. "The kids still don't know what's going on."

"Does Gordon?"

"Not that I know of." Robert took a bite of his lunch.

Knuckles rapped against their door. Robert set his food back on the plate and went to answer it.

Gordon walked in, his expression grim.

"Is everything okay?" Katerina asked.

"The kids are fine. For now."

"What is that supposed to mean?" Robert asked.

"I had a chat with Josef today."

"The Soviets let you talk to him?"

"For a few minutes anyway." Gordon raked his fingers through his hair. "Long enough for me to learn we have a problem."

"What kind of problem?" Robert asked.

"From what Josef said, one of the reasons the Soviets were going after Katerina was to distract Amaliya. They wanted to make sure she wasn't in the frame of mind to win another gold medal."

Robert held up his hand. "The Soviets tried to kidnap my wife because of a skating competition?"

"Yes." Gordon swallowed hard. "Not only that—Josef and Viktor believe they may try to hurt Katerina when she's on her way to the competition today."

"What?" Katerina grabbed Robert's hand as panic streaked through her. "Are you sure?"

"Not only that, if they can't get to Katerina, Viktor thinks they may go after Amaliya at the competition."

Katerina's grip tightened on Robert's hand. "We can't let that happen."

"Agreed." Gordon nodded. "I don't know how Viktor and Josef found out about this or if someone is just trying to rattle us, but Viktor has a plan."

"What's the plan?" Katerina asked.

"And can we trust him?" Robert added.

"I don't know." Gordon pulled a folded piece of paper from his back pocket. "That's for you to determine, but this is what Viktor gave me."

Katerina took the folded note and opened it. She read through the words written in Russian, words written in her brother's handwriting. In the note, Viktor repeated what Gordon had just told them. He also outlined a plan.

Katerina read the note twice, her heartbeat quickening. Viktor had a plan to protect Amaliya, but part of that plan would be to put Katerina at risk.

Katerina read the note a third time before she looked up at Robert. "Do you still have the phone number for Nelson Thompson?"

"Yes, why?"

"We're going to need his help."

"What exactly does the note say?"

"I'll translate it for you." Katerina held it up. "But you aren't going to like it."

Artyom had the perfect view from his balcony. Even from four floors up, he couldn't miss Katerina Petrova. She carried herself with the same grace and elegance as her daughter, and her appearance was strikingly similar to Amaliya's.

Katerina glanced over her shoulder, but whether the gesture was for show or she was really looking for the KGB officers who were watching for her, he couldn't be sure. The man walking beside her put his hand on her back and escorted her to a car a short distance from the side door. He opened Katerina's door and took a quick look around before taking his place behind the wheel.

This was it. If Katerina had gotten the message, she would know which route to follow, and so would the police. If she hadn't received the message, the woman likely wouldn't survive the drive to the arena.

Artyom had suffered through two meetings with Budimir to gather the information he'd needed to interfere with Budimir's plans. And as much as Artyom wanted to believe no one would learn of his involvement, he suspected it was only a matter of time before the KGB put two and two together.

The car pulled out of its parking space. It had barely reached the hotel exit before two cars followed. The KGB.

Katerina's car made the turn onto the main road. The two KGB vehicles crept forward. The one in the front reached the exit and waited a moment, as though giving Katerina a false sense of security on purpose. Then, as though a starting pistol sounded, both cars zipped onto the street in pursuit of the former Soviet ballerina.

Would Katerina Petrova survive the day? And if she did, was he about to take her place as the KGB's next target?

Katerina looked over her shoulder, and a chill ran through her that didn't have anything to do with the subzero temperatures. "Someone is following us."

Robert glanced in his rearview mirror. "I see him." He glanced again. "Both of them."

"There are two?" Katerina watched behind her until she saw the second sedan pull out behind them.

"Don't worry," Robert said, the tightness in his voice betraying whatever confidence his words may have instilled. "Just a couple of turns and the police will be there to intercept them."

Katerina watched the cars close the distance between them, slowing when the lead vehicle came within a few car lengths.

Robert sped up briefly before making the first turn onto a four-lane road. Their car fishtailed, nearly hitting the vehicle beside them. Katerina gripped the dashboard, and her heartbeat quickened. Memories of a winter night in New York flashed in her mind. She and Robert had survived a serious car accident once. She didn't want to tempt fate by going through another one.

She looked behind her again as the two cars pursuing them whipped around the corner. They passed the single car that now occupied the space between them. The two sedans held their distance for a moment. Then the lead car accelerated as though the driver were unconcerned that a car was in front of him.

"Robert, watch out!"

Robert pressed on the gas. He increased the distance between them briefly, but it didn't last. The car accelerated again and rammed into the back of them.

Katerina jerked forward. The car skidded.

Robert turned the wheel and drove onto the shoulder before returning to the main road. Someone honked. Another car pulled off the road.

"Are you okay?" Robert asked.

Katerina nodded, but she doubted Robert saw the gesture. His gaze was entirely focused on the road. A crossroad came into view a half mile away.

"That's the turn up there," Robert said, his voice tight. He sped up again. They were rammed from behind again.

Panic shot through her. "We aren't going to make it."

"We're going to make it." Robert pulled into the left lane, passed a pickup truck, and cut back to the right lane. Then he sped up once more.

"Can you see them?"

Katerina glanced in the car's side mirror. When she didn't see anything, she turned her body so she could see over her shoulder again. "I don't see them."

"Hold on." Robert reached the crossroad, hit the brakes, and quickly made the turn.

The instant he was clear, the two sedans appeared again, only this time they were both closing in on them, one in the right lane of the four-lane road and one in the left.

The one in the left accelerated with surprising speed and pulled beside them while the other crowded them from behind.

Katerina gripped the dashboard again. "They're going to run us off the road."

"Where are the police? They're supposed to be here." The words were barely out of Robert's mouth when a siren sounded and a police car came into view in front of them.

The vehicle beside them swerved, heading right for them.

"Robert!"

Robert hit the brakes as they approached the next intersection. Their front fender collided with their aggressor's rear bumper. Another siren rang out, this one from behind them.

The car trying to push them off the road immediately turned left. The one behind them turned right. The two police cars split off to pursue both vehicles.

Katerina let out a relieved breath. "I don't want to ever do that again."

"Me neither." Robert pulled into a restaurant parking lot.

"Now what?" Katerina asked.

"We stay here until we're sure the police have taken care of those guys."

"What if they come back?"

"The police won't let them," Robert assured her, though she suspected he was saying the words because that was what she wanted to hear.

Katerina scanned the intersection for any sign of their pursuers. Several minutes passed before a police car pulled off the road and parked beside them. The officer approached, and Robert rolled down the window.

Katerina leaned closer to the window and asked, "Did you catch them?"

"We caught one of them," the officer said. "The other took refuge at the Soviet embassy."

"Not very subtle," Robert said.

"No. We have plenty of evidence that the Soviets are behind Mrs. Marcell's attempted kidnapping," the officer said. "This should give the diplomats the leverage they need to protect you."

"Thank you."

"I can escort you wherever you want to go," the policeman said. "Did you want me to take you to the arena?"

"Thanks, but no. You may have chased off those guys, but I know for sure they'll have friends at the competition." Katerina let out a shaky breath. "Heaven forbid one of their athletes experience any sense of freedom."

"We'll go back to our hotel," Robert added.

"Yes, sir." The officer motioned to his car. "I'll follow you."

The police officer climbed back into his car, and Robert put their car in gear.

Regret surfaced, and Katerina let out a sigh. "I hate that I won't be there to watch Amaliya."

"I know." Robert glanced at her. "We may not be able to go to the arena, but with the help of our friend there, we can make sure Amaliya knows we're thinking of her."

"How?"

Robert wiggled his eyebrows. "We just need to make one quick stop on our way."

Chapter FORTY-ONE

Amaliya followed Tyler off the ice. Their final warm-up. Her hands fisted at that thought. Was it so unreasonable for her to want a decision? Only five more performers until they would skate. Their time was nearly up. And how was it that she and Tyler always seemed to end up skating last?

Gordon held out their skate guards. "Go listen to your Walkmans and try to stay loose."

Amaliya nodded. Maybe some music would distract her from Tyler's lack of conversation since their last practice. She slipped a skate guard onto one blade and then the other.

Popov and Sidrova exited the rink behind them. Sidrova stopped a few steps past them and tilted her head toward Amaliya before speaking in Russian. "Look at her. She thinks everything is just fine."

Amaliya ignored the words. Gordon had warned her often enough about the mind games other competitors tried to play to rattle their opponents.

"She probably has no idea her mother is dead," Popov added.

Amaliya gasped and whipped around to face them. Mind games were one thing. But what they said couldn't be true.

Could it?

Had there been another accident? Had the Soviets found her mother? Would they stoop to taking her life?

"What are you talking about?" Amaliya demanded in Russian. "Why would you say something like that?"

"Just stating the facts." Sidrova gave an unapologetic shrug. "Icy roads can cause terrible accidents."

Popov tilted his head toward Amaliya. "I guess she knows now."

"Don't let them get to you," Gordon said in English.

Ignoring him, Amaliya took a step closer to the Soviet pair. "Who told you this?"

"Does it matter?" Popov asked. "Everyone knows. The officials must have been trying to protect you from the news until after you compete."

Amaliya's heart squeezed in her chest, and she turned toward the ice, her gaze scanning the crowd in search of her family.

"Amaliya, what's wrong?" Tyler asked. "What did they say?"

His words barely registered. She continued her search until she found Tyler's parents sitting in the stands with the Donnellys. Her own parents weren't anywhere to be found.

"Amaliya." Gordon said her name with his coach's voice, breaking her out of her stupor.

Amaliya turned numbly. Popov and Sidrova had moved across the ready area to join their coach. Sidrova glanced her direction, a light of victory visible in her eyes.

"Tell us what they said," Gordon said.

Tears surfaced at the mere possibility of the Soviets being correct. "They said my mom is dead."

"What?" Tyler's face paled. "How would they even know that?"

"It's a sick mind game," Gordon said. "This is low, even for the Soviets."

Amaliya motioned toward the stands. "But my parents aren't out there. Neither one of them."

"I'm sure there's a logical explanation . . ." Gordon said.

A short distance away, a police officer approached the security guard at the entrance to the ready area. The officer held a vase of red roses that contrasted against his dark uniform.

The guard pointed at Amaliya.

"Oh no." Panic streaked through Amaliya. What Sidrova said had to be true. Why else would a police officer be looking for her?

Tyler slipped his arm around her waist. "Everything will be okay."

The officer approached. "Amaliya Marcell?"

All Amaliya could manage was a weak nod.

"These are for you. They're from your parents."

"Are they okay?" Amaliya asked.

"They're fine."

Relief washed over her.

"Why is a police officer delivering flowers?" Gordon asked.

"Mr. and Mrs. Marcell knew they wouldn't be permitted in the backstage area." The officer handed the roses to Amaliya. He then reached into his pocket and retrieved an envelope. "This is for you too."

Amaliya took the envelope and ripped it open.

"What's really going on?" Tyler asked.

"We had some security concerns. We thought it best if the Marcells didn't watch the competition from their intended seats."

Amaliya pulled the paper out of the envelope and read the note from her mother, the words written in Russian.

Milaya,

I'm sorry we can't be there in person, but we will be watching. Don't let anyone or anything get in the way of your success. Your dreams are there for the taking. Don't be afraid to chase them. Papa and I will celebrate with you when you get back to the hotel.

Best of luck to you and Tyler. Remember, your best will always be good enough.

Love,
Mama

Amaliya unfolded a second note, this one written in French.

Amaliya,

Just a quick note to wish you and Tyler good luck.

And whatever you do, don't let those Soviets play any of their mind games on you. Your mama and I are fine, and we'll be watching from our hotel room. We know you will be amazing. You have your mother's grace and the heart of a champion. Enjoy this moment. Make it a memory you will always treasure.

Love,
Papa

"Any idea why Popov and Sidrova would have told Amaliya her mother died?" Tyler asked.

A light of awareness and determination sparked in the officer's expression. "I have an idea of why they might have thought that would be the case." He focused on Amaliya. "I assure you, both of your parents are fine. If you would like, I can arrange for you to speak with them."

As much as Amaliya wanted to believe the policeman was telling her the truth, she needed to hear her mother's voice for herself. "I'd like that."

"We only have twenty minutes until you perform," Gordon said.

"There's a phone in an office right over there." The policeman pointed. "Come with me."

Flanked by Tyler and Gordon, Amaliya followed him to the security post and then a short distance down the hall to an office. A minute later, she had a phone in her hand, and her mother's voice came over the line.

The Soviets had been lying. They had been playing mind games. "Mama. I'm so glad you're okay."

"I'm fine," her mom said. "Why are you calling though? Aren't you about to compete?"

"In a few minutes. I was worried about you." Amaliya dropped into the office chair, the adrenaline in her body still flowing.

"I'm fine. Papa is fine. You need to go get ready. You have a gold medal to win."

Her dad's voice sounded in the background, another source of relief.

"I'll do my best."

"Good luck, milaya."

"*Spasibo*." Amaliya ended the call and looked up at the three men staring at her.

"You good now?" Gordon asked in his no-nonsense tone.

"I think so."

"Good. I want you to walk back into the prep area and make it clear that the Soviets' little game didn't work."

"How am I supposed to do that?"

"You speak their language." Gordon shot her a conspiring look. "I'm sure you can come up with something."

They walked back to the ready area, and the police officer stopped beside the guard. "I'll inform the competition officials of what just happened."

"I doubt they can do anything about it, but thank you," Gordon said.

Amaliya and Tyler led the way into the ready area. Popov and Sidrova's names were announced by the rink official as they passed between them and the rink entrance.

Amaliya stopped and waited for them to approach, her mind transitioning from English to Russian. "It's a shame you feel you can't beat us without help."

Amaliya took another step forward. "For the record, my mother is just fine. I just talked to her—and she is very much alive. Better luck next time."

"What did you say?" Tyler asked.

"I just wished them luck."

"Why do I get the feeling you're leaving a lot out?"

"Because you know me so well."

"You can tell us all about your run-in later," Gordon said. "For now, I want you to focus. Walkmans. Now."

Oddly settled by the order, Amaliya reached for her skating bag. "Yes, Coach."

Tyler willed his emotions to settle, the music from *Swan Lake* playing through his headphones. He had managed to keep his focus away from the ice and the other competitors, but more than once, the cheering of the crowd had overshadowed the notes playing on his Walkman.

In her seat beside him, Amaliya fidgeted, her leg bouncing as though she couldn't contain all her energy. He wondered if the fear she'd experienced earlier would derail her concentration, if the Soviets' mind games would pay off. He had to admit, they had succeeded in rattling him. Of course, he and Amaliya had already been a bit off since their argument after practice.

Tyler closed his eyes and drew a deep breath. Slowly, he let it out and forced himself to look once more at the options laid out before him. As much as he hated being pushed into decisions, he couldn't fault Amaliya for wanting some closure tonight. He wanted it too, but what choice was the right one?

He opened his eyes and looked at Amaliya once more. She glanced at him briefly before looking down at the ground. This wasn't leftover emotions from the Soviets she was working through now. It was remnants of their argument and the lack of plans for their future.

Gordon approached and grabbed the folding chair from beside Amaliya, then dragged it so it was in front of them. He sat and motioned for them to take off their headphones.

"Is it time?" Amaliya asked.

"Almost." Gordon leaned forward and rested his elbows on his knees. "I know you had a scare today, but you need to put all of that aside. Skate like this is your last chance for a gold medal."

Amaliya looked at Tyler. "It could be our last chance."

"Whether it is or not is up to you to decide," Gordon said. "You're ready for this. You are the best figure skating pair in the world. Your long program is beautiful. Go skate it just like you did in Leningrad."

Tyler drew in a deep breath. They had skated last in the long program at the Olympics too, but on that day, he and Amaliya had been truly unified. He wanted that feeling again today.

Gordon stood. Tyler and Amaliya followed suit, both of them shaking out their arms and legs to get the blood flowing again.

Tyler focused on the ice, where the Canadian pair was currently taking their bows. His body trembled with nerves and new beginnings.

"Are you as nervous as I am?" Amaliya sighed. "I must be crazy to want to keep doing this for the next four years."

Four more years of skating every day with Amaliya, of planning new programs, of stretching their abilities to become even better. The clarity of that image brought with it a sense of unexpected calm. It sounded perfect.

Perfect, except for the living-with-Amaliya's-parents thing.

Tyler weighed that inconvenience against the possibility of months on the road, of squeezing time in to get married, of having others dictate their routines.

Amaliya had demonstrated an aptitude for choreography. Based on the employment contracts offered them through the Ice Capades, she would no longer have the option to use that skill.

Tyler drew in a deep breath and let it out slowly. Amaliya was right. He had let the dollar signs cloud his decision. He evaluated the two paths before them, weighing each before making a decision. "Will it be easier for you to focus on today's long program if you think this is our last competition or if you know it isn't?"

"I already told you I want to know what we're doing next before we compete today." Amaliya took a step to the side so she was directly in front of him. Her gaze met his as understanding dawned. "Are you saying you're willing to keep competing with me?"

Tyler shook his head, and the hope in Amaliya's eyes dimmed. The clarity of what Amaliya wanted combined with his own desires. "I'm not just willing to compete with you. It's what I want."

Both of her hands gripped his arms. "Really?"

"Are you sure, Tyler?" Gordon asked. "You don't have to decide right now."

"I'm sure," Tyler said. "That is, if you'll keep coaching us."

Gordon fought against the smile trying to form. "I guess I can stick around for a few more years."

"Yes!" Amaliya threw her arms around Gordon and squeezed before she turned and repeated the gesture with Tyler.

Tyler drew her close, the friction between them melting away.

As soon as he released her, Gordon put a hand on each of their shoulders. "I'll keep coaching you, but first, go out there and win the gold. I have a reputation to uphold."

Tyler's own lips quirked. "We'll see what we can do."

The announcer called their names, and Amaliya slipped her hand into Tyler's.

His heart lighter than it had been in weeks, he escorted her onto the ice. This was a new beginning. Very soon, he and Amaliya would embark on a new quest for Olympic gold, they would start their married life together, and somehow, they would turn their kitchenless apartment into a home.

He shook the thoughts of the future from his head and focused on the now. They were the Olympic champions. It was time to prove, once again, that they really were the best in the world.

Chapter FORTY-TWO

Amaliya's throat clogged with emotion as she skated onto the ice with Tyler. She had experienced so many ups and downs over the past thirty minutes that her mind could barely keep up. Her family was safe. Her future was set. She struggled for calm.

Tyler squeezed her hand as though he knew she needed a reminder that he was beside her, that they were a team. A smile bloomed on her face. They were a team in skating and in life.

They reached the center of the ice and took their starting positions. Gordon's words echoed through Amaliya's thoughts. She and Tyler were the best in the world. It was time to prove they deserved that title.

Her gaze lifted to meet Tyler's, and he gave her a subtle nod. They were ready.

The music started, and Amaliya let herself get swept up into the dance. They moved into their signature lift, Tyler raising her over his head as she arched gracefully, her arms reaching toward the ice. The applause was instant and didn't stop when Tyler lowered her back down. They moved through the next bit of footwork before launching into their most difficult move, the triple twist lift. Amaliya combined her power with Tyler's to send her airborne. The buzz of the crowd faded beneath her concentration—three twists, a slight angle of her body as gravity pulled her back down. Tyler's hands gripped her waist as her own hands lifted gracefully. More applause, this time the volume nearly overshadowing their music.

Amaliya let the music play in her head as she continued. After a moment, the noise died down enough to ensure that she was indeed skating in time with the music.

Her stomach lurched when they entered their combination jumps. She leaped into the air, completing three rotations. The scrape of her blade against the ice was lost beneath the roar of the crowd. She immediately launched into her double toe loop, relieved when she landed cleanly and Tyler was where she expected him to be.

The dance continued. Their death spiral. Perfect. Double axels. Clean landings. The choreography they had practiced so often flowed smoothly.

They reached their final major element, their throw triple lutz. They came together, the excitement visible on Tyler's face. Was it possible they could skate another clean program?

Tyler gripped her waist, and Amaliya fought against the pressure mounting inside her. She bent her knee, positioned her skate, and pushed herself into the air with Tyler's help. She flew upward, her body rotating once again. One, two, three. Her blade connected with the ice, her back leg swung out to help her maintain her balance, and her arms rose skyward. They'd done it! Only one more sequence.

Amaliya circled Tyler, the two of them meeting in the center for a pair's camel. Then they took their last few dance steps and struck their final poses.

The crowd came to their feet amid the deafening applause. Roses rained down from the stands. Tyler bowed, and Amaliya curtsied. They reversed direction and repeated the gesture.

This time when they straightened, Amaliya surrendered to impulse and threw her arms around Tyler. He pulled her close and pressed a kiss to her temple, then grinned at her and took her hand. He said something, but the crowd drowned out his words. They both accepted bouquets of flowers from the young skaters who were currently clearing the ice.

Amaliya raised her bouquet of roses above her head to gesture her thanks to the audience. With Tyler at her side, she skated to the opening in the barrier wall.

Gordon met them at the bench situated in front of the cameras, where they would receive their scores. They took their seats, and Amaliya gripped Tyler's hand, her nerves humming. Were they good enough to win gold? More importantly, had they beaten the Soviet pair?

"You both skated beautifully." Gordon sat beside Amaliya.

"How do you think we'll measure up?" Tyler asked.

The first set of scores posted before Gordon could answer. A five eight, with the rest five nines.

The crowd shared their approval.

"That's a nice start." Gordon gave a satisfied nod.

A moment later, the next set of scores illuminated the screen. Three perfect scores. Amaliya's jaw dropped.

"Did we just . . . ?" Tyler waved his hand toward the monitor.

"Three perfect scores?" Wonder filled Gordon's voice. "Wow."

Amaliya was still reading the numbers when the final standings posted.

Linden and Marcell. Number one.

"We won!" Amaliya hugged Tyler. Gordon hugged them both.

As soon as the two men released her, she looked at the rest of the standings. The Canadian pair had taken second, and the Soviets had fallen to fourth behind the French couple.

"Popov and Sidrova didn't medal?"

"Sidrova put her hand down on her double axel. And they had a timing issue on their side-by-side spins."

"Even with that, I'm surprised they dropped out of the medals," Tyler said.

"The Canadians and the French had great performances." Gordon allowed a slight smile. "You two are just better."

"We won the gold medal," Amaliya said with a sense of wonder.

"If I have my way, you'll be winning a lot more over the next few years."

Tyler squeezed Amaliya's hand. "I like that plan."

Artyom turned off the television, resignation hanging heavy over him. Popov and Sidrova hadn't medaled. The Soviets had been disgraced. And Artyom had played a part in it.

Siberia was no longer a possibility. It was a surety. And if he didn't work fast, the Petrovs would be in just as much danger as he was. Together they had exposed their countrymen and the extremes they would use to get what they wanted. How quickly he and the Petrovs would be identified as the source of the trouble was another question.

A heavy-handed knock rattled his door. Artyom startled, and a wave of panic streaked through him. So soon? He had expected the KGB would wait until after they returned to Leningrad before taking any action against him. His panic mingled with fear.

He drew an unsteady breath and straightened his shoulders. He had made his choice. Now he would have to live with it. He only hoped he could keep his promise to Viktor that he would help his family.

Artyom opened the door. Budimir moved past him and slammed the door closed behind him.

"Did you hear?" Budimir asked at an uncomfortably high volume. "This is a nightmare."

Artyom didn't answer. What could he say?

"Oleg has already been sent back to Leningrad." Budimir lifted both hands in frustration. "Now I have two men sitting in a cell at the police station. Two more are hiding inside the embassy."

KGB agents arrested? Others in hiding? Was this because of what Artyom had done? The situation was worse than he'd thought. Or perhaps it was better. He fought against the lump in his throat and asked, "What happened?"

"The police showed up when my men tried to take care of Katerina Petrova." Budimir furrowed his eyebrows. "It was almost as though they knew we were going to be there."

"I don't know how that would be possible," Artyom lied.

"Someone interfered. When I find out who, they will be held accountable."

The lump in his throat expanded. He swallowed. "What will happen now with your men?"

"The embassy is sending some officials over to discuss the situation, along with some extra guards to keep an eye on our athletes. They should be here anytime now. The athletes will arrive in a few minutes."

"So soon? The results just posted."

"Kuznetsov left as soon as Popov and Sidrova fell into fourth place." He moved to the door. "You will need to stand at a post in the hall while my remaining men ensure they are escorted to their rooms."

"Of course." More guards on their way. Artyom's insides churned.

Budimir led the way into the hall and pointed. "Stand here and make sure everyone gets to their rooms." Budimir headed down the hall to the elevator.

Within minutes, the elevator dinged, and the two sets of pairs skaters approached with their coaches. The air of disappointment and frustration hung over all six of them.

Without any conversation, the skaters made their way to their rooms.

A moment later, Josef appeared with Viktor. When they reached their door, only a meter from where Artyom was standing, Viktor glanced behind him, evidently to make sure the hall was empty. "My sister?" he whispered.

"She's fine. I'll do what I can to make sure she stays that way."

"What about you?" Josef asked.

"I made my choice. Eventually, they will learn what I did." Artyom motioned to their room. "The embassy is sending some people over. If I'm able, I'll go onto my balcony after they leave."

Though his reluctance was evident on his face, Viktor unlocked his door and ushered Josef inside.

Their door clicked closed as the elevator dinged again. This time, Budimir emerged with two well-dressed men in their late fifties. Not guards. Diplomats.

Budimir motioned to Artyom. "Come with us."

Artyom followed Budimir. They entered the spare hotel room that had been used as the breakfast area. As soon as the door closed behind them, Budimir said, "This is Nestor and Denis from the embassy." He waved at Artyom. "Artyom Belsky is our director of figure skating."

"And you are aware of tonight's situation?"

"I know that some of our men were arrested and others are at the embassy."

"Yes, and now Global Affairs Canada is making demands." Nestor sat down.

"What sort of demands?" Artyom asked.

"They are threatening to reveal our country's involvement in what they are calling an attempted kidnapping if we don't grant Katerina Petrova access to her family."

"They want us to allow them to defect?" Budimir's hands lifted in an I-can't-believe-this gesture. "We can't allow this."

"Not defect," Denis said. "Simply the opportunity to visit."

"A visit can lead to a defection," Nestor countered. "We all know this."

Artyom mustered his courage to speak. "If I may, I don't think the Petrovs are interested in defecting. Viktor's wife is still in Leningrad. It's unlikely he would stay here and leave her behind."

"What do you think?" Denis asked Budimir.

"The man appears devoted to his wife, but I don't like this."

"Nor do I, but if our men's involvement comes to light, our athletes could be banned at the next Olympics," Nestor said. "We can't afford to have that happen."

"Is this all they are asking for?" Artyom asked.

"No, but they have yet to submit their full demands," Denis said.

"I don't trust them," Nestor added.

Budimir folded his arms. "Neither do I."

Chapter FORTY-THREE

Katerina couldn't contain her joy and relief when Amaliya walked into her suite with Tyler and Gordon.

"Congratulations!" Robert scooped Amaliya into a hug.

"Thanks, Papa."

Robert released her, and Amaliya stepped into Katerina's outstretched arms. "I'm so proud of you. And I'm so sorry we couldn't be there."

Amaliya held on for a long moment before stepping free from her embrace. "What happened?"

Katerina glanced at Robert, not sure how much they should share.

"She's old enough to know the truth," Robert said.

Robert was right. Katerina motioned to the couch. "Come sit down."

Once they were all seated, Katerina and Robert explained the message they had received and the events of the night.

When they finished, Tyler let out a low whistle. "Thank goodness you're okay."

"I can't believe you didn't tell us what was going on," Amaliya said, a touch of accusation in her voice.

"We didn't want you to worry," Robert said.

Tyler stretched his arm along the back of the couch, his hand resting on Amaliya's shoulder. "What happens now?"

"We're waiting to hear back from Nelson Thompson from Global Affairs Canada." Katerina glanced at the phone. "I was hoping we would have heard from him by now."

"Maybe now is a good time to share our news," Tyler said.

Amaliya's face lit up.

"What?" Katerina asked.

"Tyler and I decided tonight," Amaliya said with a wide smile, "that we're going to keep competing."

"Really?" Katerina's heart lifted. Her little girl was staying home. Granted, she would soon be her married little girl, but keeping her close by was what mattered.

"That's assuming you're both okay with us living in the apartment over the garage once we get married," Tyler said.

Robert glanced at Katerina before he answered for both of them. "I think we can handle that."

"I'm sorry we'll still be invading your kitchen all the time," Tyler added.

"It will be like when I was still living in Leningrad." Katerina offered a wistful smile. "My brother and his wife moved in with my parents after they married."

"I'm so glad they still live in the house where you grew up," Amaliya said. "I love that Tyler and I were able to visit it."

"Even though we practically froze while we were there." Tyler gave a mock shudder.

"That's true," Amaliya said. "Visiting Viktor's house when we were in Leningrad made me appreciate the little things, like having a working heater."

"You'll have heat," Robert said. "You'll also have a kitchen."

"What?" Amaliya asked.

"I may have called a contractor last week to see about expanding the apartment," Robert said. "I don't have the plans yet, but I told him adding a kitchen is our top priority."

"Really?" Amaliya stood and crossed to her father. She kissed his cheek. "Papa, that's incredible."

"Consider it an early wedding present." Robert tilted his head toward Tyler. "Sorry, Tyler, but you're about to live in a construction zone."

"That's okay." Tyler's expression vacillated between embarrassed and grateful. "I can't believe you're doing this."

"It's for us too," Robert said. "If a bit of remodeling will keep Amaliya close by, it's worth it."

Someone knocked on the door. Robert checked through the peephole before answering it.

Tyler's parents and the Donnellys walked in, all of them grinning.

Miles looked past Robert and spotted Amaliya. "I heard there are some gold medalists in here somewhere."

"I still can't believe it." Amaliya embraced Miles and Linda in turn, before hugging Tyler's parents. "Thanks so much for being here. It means so much to us."

"We wouldn't have missed it for the world." Linda glanced at Katerina. "Have you two decided what comes next for you?"

Amaliya's smile was instant. "We're going to keep competing."

"Well, I am thrilled to hear that." Nancy said.

"Me too." Linda reached into her purse and retrieved an envelope. "And now that you've made your choice, this is for you."

Amaliya took it from her. "What is it?"

"It's a little contribution from my family to help cover your living costs."

Amaliya opened the envelope and skimmed the document she pulled out. Her jaw dropped.

"Amaliya?" Tyler stepped closer and read over Amaliya's shoulder. His gaze whipped up to focus on Linda. "You're giving us an apartment?"

"You have a choice of living in an apartment in one of my father's buildings in Virginia, or you can have a monetary stipend equal to it." Linda glanced at Katerina before adding, "If you decide to live with the Marcells, the stipend will be enough to cover the rest of your living expenses until you decide you're ready to retire from competition."

"They're going to stay in the apartment over the garage," Robert said quickly. "Right?"

Amaliya turned to Tyler. "If Papa really remodels the apartment, it would be the best of both worlds."

"I agree," Tyler said, "but Linda, I don't understand how this is possible. This much money each month adds up to a lot, especially if we go all the way to the '88 Olympics."

"Yes, but my family can afford it," Linda said. "My father's company has been very successful over the years, and he's come to be a big supporter of the arts. It didn't take much convincing for him to see you two as promising artists who could use a little help."

"Thank you, Linda." Amaliya reached out and hugged her.

"You're welcome." Linda turned to Katerina. "Any word yet on your brother?"

"Nothing yet." The phone rang, and Katerina snatched up the receiver on the table beside her. "Hello?"

"Mrs. Marcell, this is Nelson Thompson. I have some news."

"Good news, I hope?"

"I believe so," Nelson said. "I've been negotiating with the embassy personnel at the Soviet embassy."

"And?" Katerina asked.

"They have agreed to allow your family to meet with you."

Hope and fear both rose within her. "Are you sure it isn't a trap?"

"You will be meeting them before the ladies' long program tomorrow night, and we will have police present to ensure that no one tries to take you anywhere you don't want to go."

Hope took flight. "Thank you so much."

"I should warn you that the Soviets will also have some of their security personnel to ensure that your brother doesn't try to defect."

"But the police will be there."

"Yes, ma'am."

"In that case, I want to try."

"That's what I needed to know," Nelson said. "We'll work out the final details tomorrow."

"Thank you." Katerina hung up, her emotions rising as tears filled her eyes. *Finally.* She was finally going to see Viktor. She could finally apologize for leaving him behind.

"Well?" Robert asked.

"Tomorrow." Katerina sniffled. "Tomorrow, I get to see my brother."

Viktor hovered by his balcony door, watching for any sign of movement from the room beside him. Nothing. Over an hour had passed since he and Josef had returned, yet not even a flicker of light had come from Artyom's room.

Viktor's own light was also off, a concession to the lights-out rule given by the security forces. Viktor should have retired to bed some time ago, but the possibility of news regarding Katerina had his mind racing.

Behind him, Josef paced the room as though trying to keep himself awake. Midnight had already come and gone, and Josef had been on his feet for hours, translating for the skaters and the coaches during the competition.

Viktor fought against his disappointment in Josef's involvement with the KGB and motioned to him. Josef crossed the room to stand at Viktor's side.

Viktor lowered his voice to a whisper. "You should sleep. You have work tomorrow."

"So do you."

It was true. In a matter of hours, both he and Josef would need to be up serving breakfast before leaving for the rink with Sonya.

Despite his turmoil of emotions regarding Josef's earlier actions, his paternal instinct rose within him. "You can't afford to make any more mistakes while we're here."

"Helping your sister wasn't a mistake."

A piece of the wall between them chipped away. Josef may have been naive, but when it had mattered most, his values had shown through.

"You're right."

Knuckles rapped against wood. Was that someone knocking at their door? Viktor and Josef exchanged a confused glance. The sound repeated.

Viktor moved to the door and looked through the peephole. Artyom. Why would he be coming to their door instead of their joined balcony?

With some trepidation, Viktor opened the door. "Is everything okay?"

"Arrangements have been made. You will see your sister tomorrow."

Viktor grabbed the edge of the door. Had the impossible really happened?

"A meeting has been approved," Artyom continued.

"With permission?" Viktor asked.

"With permission." Artyom nodded. "It will happen tomorrow before the ladies' long program."

Viktor gripped Artyom's hand. "Thank you."

An intense emotion flashed in Artyom's eyes. Was that regret? "You're welcome." Artyom stepped back and moved to his room. He glanced at Viktor for a moment before disappearing inside.

Viktor closed his door and slid the chain back in place. Though there was no reason to assume Artyom would have more to tell him, he moved back to the balcony window and picked up his coat from where he had left it on the back of a chair.

Only a few seconds passed before the faint noise of a sliding door opening carried to him. Viktor slipped on his coat and quietly opened his door. Josef followed.

Artyom already waited beside the narrow railing separating their two balconies.

"What didn't you tell us?" Viktor asked.

"Global Affairs Canada is negotiating with the embassy. Your meeting with your sister will be supervised by the KGB and the local police to ensure everyone's safety."

"It's not a trap?" Josef asked.

"No."

"What about Josef? What will happen to him when we return home?"

"That was discussed tonight. I made the argument that Josef was acting instinctively to protect a family member, that he was unaware of the plan to return Katerina to the Soviet Union."

"Was that enough to protect him?" Viktor asked.

Vulnerability flashed on Josef's face. "I don't want to go to jail."

"Neither do I," Artyom said. "There is little hope for me, but if you have the chance, I recommend you ask Global Affairs Canada to ensure your safety as one of the negotiating points in exchange for their silence."

"Why would you go to jail?" Josef asked.

"Because he helped Katerina." Viktor studied the man before him in a new light.

"Yes." A quiet resignation hit Artyom's voice. "The KGB already suspects someone leaked their plans to the police. I'm one of the few who knew of them besides the KGB. Eventually, the truth will come out."

"What of your family? Are they at risk too?"

"I have no family."

"Then you have nothing to go home to." Viktor glanced from Artyom to Josef and back again. His sister's defection had taken years to recover from, and the stigma still followed his family. Was it possible he could reclaim his family pride while also helping Artyom?

"Tell me exactly where we are meeting tomorrow. I have an idea that could help both you and Josef."

"What kind of idea?" Artyom asked.

"The one that turns you into a defector and Josef into a hero."

A spark lighted Artyom's eyes. "You have my attention."

Chapter FORTY-FOUR

Katerina laced her fingers as she gripped her hands together in her lap. The large practice room was lined with mirrors on two walls, a thick mat covering the floor. A handful of chairs had been set up in the corner of the room opposite the room's single entrance. She sat in the center with Robert on one side and Amaliya and Tyler on the other. Two policemen stood beside the door, and Nelson had assured her that two others would be positioned outside in addition to one of the arena's security guards.

Beyond the guards, Miles and Linda also stood nearby, both of them holding cameras. Linda had taken control of the Polaroid, ready to snap photos for her when Viktor arrived, while Miles held the Nikon she typically used when capturing family memories.

Time stretched out, every second passing by as though it were several minutes.

Finally, the door opened, and a KGB agent walked in.

Katerina stiffened. Robert's hand reached over to rest on top of hers. Another man entered, but this one didn't have the hardened look of someone in security. He stepped aside to make room for the two men who followed. Josef. She recognized him from the night of her attempted kidnapping. Beside him was the older version of her brother. Viktor. He was here.

Katerina shot to her feet, her emotions churning uncomfortably. Did he hate her? Could he ever forgive her for what she had done?

Questions were still circling through her head when Viktor rushed forward, his arms open. Katerina reacted in kind. She rushed into her brother's welcoming embrace, her eyes watering, her heart full. She breathed him in, the scent of hotel soap and the underlying scent that was uniquely his.

A knot formed in her throat, blocking any words she might have offered. Tears spilled over.

Viktor held her tight for a long moment before he stepped back to look at her with damp eyes.

"I'm so sorry," Katerina managed. "I wouldn't have defected if there had been another way."

Viktor looked past her to where Robert stood. "This is your husband?"

Katerina nodded. She reached out a hand to Robert, and he stepped forward. "Viktor, this is Robert." She switched from Russian to French. "Robert, this is my brother."

Robert extended his hand. For an instant, Katerina worried Viktor wouldn't take it, but he stepped forward and reached out to shake hands.

"It's good to meet you," Robert said.

Viktor offered a similar sentiment in Russian.

Viktor motioned his son forward. "This is Josef. I hope you will meet Sonya later."

"I would like that." The question that had hummed through Katerina for weeks spilled out. "What happened to the other child? The one Ursula was carrying when I left?"

"A miscarriage." As though reading her thoughts, Viktor squeezed her hand. "It wasn't your fault."

"I'm so sorry."

"We have been blessed with two wonderful children. They make us proud."

Katerina shifted her focus to Josef. "Thank you for everything you did."

Josef glanced at the guard behind him before opting to answer in French instead of Russian. "I was partially at fault for what happened. I am sorry."

Katerina didn't know what his involvement may have been, but she reached out and put her hand on his arm briefly. "It all worked out."

"Almost." Josef lowered his voice, still speaking in French. "We need your family's help."

Katerina glanced at the KGB agent at the door. Eager to avoid suspicion, she turned to Linda. "Can you take a picture of us?"

Linda held up the Polaroid. Miles stepped beside her and lifted his camera as well.

"You ready?" Linda asked.

Katerina nodded. Linda took two photos and handed one of the Polaroids to Katerina and the other to Viktor.

"This is so you can take a memory back to Ursula," Katerina said in Russian.

"I don't understand. What is this?"

"It's a Polaroid," Katerina explained. At his blank look, she added, "It's an instant photograph."

A look of wonder filled Viktor's expression as the image took form. "This is wonderful. Thank you."

Katerina glanced at the KGB officers again and then motioned to the chairs behind her. Again, she spoke in Russian. "Come sit down." She put one hand on Josef's arm and the other on Viktor's. "We have so much to talk about."

Viktor nodded. "Yes, we do."

Artyom stood at the top of the bleachers beside Budimir, his heart pounding. He had a choice. He could risk his life now, or he could face whatever punishment his government would mete out when he returned to Leningrad. His grandmother's words echoed through his mind again. *There is always a choice.*

The reunion between the Petrovs and the Marcells had moved from the private room in the stadium to their reserved seats in the bleachers a few rows ahead of where he and Budimir now watched over them.

"What has this world come to?" Budimir shook his head. "Katerina Petrova should be back in Leningrad, and instead, she is sitting here like she can have everything she wants."

"We are fortunate the Canadians were willing to negotiate," Artyom said. "The two guards who were arrested didn't have diplomatic immunity."

"Our superiors seemed more concerned with our athletes losing their ability to compete under our flag than they were about my men."

"National pride is important to those back home," Artyom said. That same pride could cost him his job after Popov and Sidrova had failed to medal. Of course, that was assuming he was going back home.

Sonya Petrova took the ice for the final leg of her competition. Excitement rippled through her family, her cheering section now significant when including the Marcells and their friends.

Her music rang over the loudspeakers, and she started her skate. She moved through each jump and spin with precision, her grace adding another layer of perfection to the performance.

Despite his own nerves, Artyom couldn't help but get caught up in the excitement. Sonya performed a triple toe loop with such grace she made it look easy.

The crowd applauded with each successful maneuver, and Artyom suspected Sonya could walk away with a medal by the end of the night.

When she concluded her program, the crowd came to their feet. Artyom joined in the applause. She really had performed beautifully.

"Will she get a gold?" Budimir asked.

"I don't know, but she has an excellent chance to medal," Artyom said. He bolstered his courage and took a step toward freedom. "I need to check with the officials about the medal ceremony."

Budimir nodded. "Be sure to let me know when we have the timeline. I'm still shorthanded. We may need to have everyone wait until after the medal ceremony to return back to the hotel rather than go back in two groups." He lifted his chin in the direction of Viktor. "We don't want to chance the Petrovs getting any ideas about staying behind with the defector."

The defector. Artyom was about to be one himself. He hoped. "I'll be sure to get the information to you." He walked down the bleachers until he reached the concourse. He spotted one of the KGB agents who had been temporarily assigned to keep tabs on the athletes. The man had taken position only a few meters from the door that led to a rear exit. More specifically, he was only a few meters from Artyom's door to freedom. According to Viktor, a Canadian diplomat and a police officer would be waiting right outside. But could he trust that they would really be there? All the arrangements had been made by Viktor's sister, a woman he didn't even know.

"Where are you going?" the KGB agent asked.

Artyom lifted his head higher to feign an air of authority. "I need to speak with the competition organizers." He held up the badge that hung from his neck that allowed him to access the restricted areas in the arena.

Without waiting for permission, he continued forward, past the hallway he was supposed to walk through.

His heartbeat quickened as he considered the consequences of what he was planning and what would happen if something went wrong.

To maintain the illusion that he was still operating in an official capacity, he stopped beside the judging table to speak to one of the competition administrators.

"What time will the medal ceremony be held tonight?" Artyom asked in Russian. Of course, the man didn't understand.

For the sake of anyone nearby who might speak Russian, Artyom added, "I'll get my translator." Artyom turned back and studied the KGB agent who was now focused on Sonya and her coach. Artyom quickened his step and approached the door. Go, or don't go? He didn't hesitate. He pulled open the door and slipped inside the tunnels that connected the rink to the locker rooms and various offices. The moment the door closed behind him, he ran.

In the seat beside Amaliya, Tyler watched to see if anyone followed the Soviet named Artyom through the doorway where he had disappeared a moment ago. It was like watching a spy movie. The plan to help someone defect had sounded exciting in the moment, but now, with a man's life and freedom at stake, Tyler's heart was pounding as though he were the one responsible for the man's success or lack thereof.

Tyler's own future had fallen into place so neatly, he almost felt guilty for having so many options to choose from. He and Amaliya were free to marry whenever they chose. They had so many career opportunities ahead of them. They could travel as they chose without anyone restricting them—other than having to deal with concerned parents and an overprotective coach, of course. Tyler had his freedom, and the Soviet was risking everything to gain his.

In the seats in front of Tyler and Amaliya, Viktor leaned close to Josef and whispered something in Russian. Tyler really needed to learn the language.

"What did he say?" Tyler asked Amaliya.

"He said it's time."

Josef glanced behind him as though looking for someone. In fact, he was verifying the person he was looking for wasn't there. Then he stood and crossed to the menacing-looking man standing at the top of their section.

Josef rattled something off in Russian and pointed toward the scoring table.

Tyler was about to ask for a translation when Amaliya leaned closer and said, "Josef asked the KGB agent where Artyom went because he was supposed to translate for him."

Amaliya fell silent until after the older man responded. "He's telling his men to find Artyom."

"He only left a minute ago. Do you think he got away?" Tyler asked. "Maybe they should have waited longer."

"It's risky, but it's best if Josef tells on Artyom soon after he disappeared to make it look like he's trying to turn him in."

"And this makes him look like a hero?" Tyler asked.

"A loyal Soviet citizen, anyway."

"I really hope this all goes according to plan."

"Me too."

Artyom's breathing quickened as he made another turn down the dimly lit passageway. Where was the exit? Surely there had to be a door around here somewhere.

A door banged open and shouts carried to him.

Josef had talked to Budimir too soon. Artyom was going to get caught.

His heart raced, but he pushed forward, praying he would find the way out before it was too late. He reached the end of the passageway where it intersected with another hall.

Footsteps echoed toward him.

He made the turn, a red exit sign illuminating the space above a door.

He raced forward, his breathing coming in rapid gasps. He reached the door and burst outside.

A man wearing a gray wool coat stepped forward. "Artyom Belsky?"

"Da."

In heavily accented Russian, the man said, "Come with me." He waved a hand, and a car engine came to life.

A police car pulled forward and stopped beside him. The man opened the back door of the car and waved him inside. Artyom got in. A moment later, the man climbed into the passenger side.

The door Artyom had emerged through burst open, and two KGB agents rushed outside. The policeman pressed on the gas, and the car lurched forward as the two agents raced toward them.

Artyom ducked down. The car picked up speed and rounded a corner. A minute passed and then two.

The man in the front seat spoke again. "We lost them."

"Are you sure?" Artyom asked.

"Yes." The man offered a smile. "Mr. Belsky, welcome to Canada."

Relief flowed through him and merged with a sensation he had never before experienced. Could it be freedom? He fought against the sudden surge of emotion and nodded to the man who had helped make this moment possible. "Thank you."

Chapter FORTY-FIVE

KATERINA STOOD IN THE HOTEL lobby surrounded by her family. She really hated goodbyes.

For the past three days, they had been granted time to visit, always with a KGB agent and a police officer watching over them.

Tyler stood beside Amaliya, his hand resting gently on her waist. Her family was expanding, yet Viktor and his family would soon be out of reach.

"I wish we knew when we would see you again," Katerina said, her focus on her brother.

"We'll all have to make worlds so we can see each other next year," Sonya said.

Viktor glanced at the KGB agent by the door. "Let's hope they'll allow me and Josef to come too."

Katerina linked her arm through Viktor's and forced confidence into her voice. "With all the negotiations taking place among our diplomats, it should happen. The Soviets promised your family won't be punished for your association with me, and they said they will permit you and your family travel for Sonya's competitions."

"All of my family?" Viktor asked hopefully.

Katerina smiled. "Yes, everyone, including Ursula."

Viktor's eyes lit up. "That would be incredible."

"Fingers crossed," Sonya said.

"I never thought that Tyler and I deciding to stay in competition would give us these opportunities," Amaliya said. Aware that Tyler and Robert were unable to understand the conversation in Russian, she repeated the sentiment in English.

"Tyler, you and I may need to learn more Russian," Robert said.

"I think you're right." Tyler nodded. "It would be nice to not need a translator."

"As long as someone always needs one," Josef said. "I don't want to lose my new job."

"We may be seeing you more than anyone else," Amaliya said. Not only had the negotiations yielded protection for Viktor's family, but Josef had also been promised a permanent position as a translator for the Soviets' athletic department. Katerina prayed those promises would be kept.

The memory of Josef's actions rose within her and clogged her throat. She was free because of him. Had Josef not interfered, she could have been long gone before Miles had arrived. Her voice trembled when she spoke. "Josef, thank you again for everything. Truly, I am forever grateful."

Josef shifted his weight from one foot to another as though suddenly uncomfortable with the recognition.

The KGB agent approached. "It is time to go."

"We have a few things we need to send back with you," her mom said. "My friends are bringing everything down right now."

"What things?" Viktor asked.

"Just a few gifts." Her mom hugged Viktor and held on for a long moment. "I want to share some of what I have been blessed with."

Viktor tugged at the lapel of his coat. "You have already been generous."

"I'm glad you think so, but there's more."

The elevator dinged, and Tyler's parents emerged with the Donnellys, each of them carrying a large suitcase and a backpack, except for Linda, who had a stack of blankets in her arms.

"Here they are," Amaliya said.

The moment they set the luggage down in front of Katerina, all of Viktor's family stared wide-eyed. "Not all of this is for us."

"Yes. All of it." Katerina remembered the days of having little and wished she could do so much more. "We packed a suitcase and a backpack for each of you. You can sort out who gets what when you arrive home."

Viktor shook his head. "This is too much."

"Sorry, but that's not quite all of it." Amaliya took the blankets from Linda and handed them to Sonya. "You'll each be able to carry one of these on the plane with you without it counting against your luggage."

Before they could protest further, Amaliya reached out and hugged Viktor. "I'll miss you."

"I'll miss you." Viktor kissed her forehead. "I want to see wedding photos when we meet next."

"I wish you could be there."

"So do I. Maybe someday, things will change so we can travel more freely."

"I pray that's the case,"

Katerina stepped forward, "But for now, I'll look forward to the next world championship."

Viktor pulled her into another hug. "As will I."

Home. Amaliya's heart lifted the moment her house came into view. Still sitting in the back seat of her father's car, she slipped her hand into Tyler's. With so many questions regarding their future lingering when they left, she hadn't considered how much living here meant to her.

"I have to say, one great thing about staying amateur is living with this view for a few more years," Tyler said.

"I agree." Amaliya squeezed his hand.

"My view of the woods isn't so bad either," Gordon said.

"I, for one, am thrilled that you aren't moving away," her mom said.

"Me too." Her dad turned into the driveway before glancing in the rear-view mirror. "I'm not sure I could have handled you living in hotel rooms for months on end." He pulled the car into the driveway and shut off the engine. Everyone climbed out, and they unloaded the luggage from the car.

"Tyler, why don't you leave your suitcases here for now," Robert said. "I have something I want you and Amaliya to look at inside."

"What is it?" Amaliya asked.

"Just grab your bags and follow me."

Amaliya lifted one suitcase and reached for her second.

Tyler beat her to it. "I can take that."

"Thanks." Amaliya followed her parents and Gordon into the house.

Eleanor looked up from where she stood at the kitchen counter. "Welcome home!"

"Thanks." Amaliya set her bag down and breathed in the scent of cookies. She inhaled deeply. Chocolate chip cookies.

"Robert, the papers from the architect are on the table."

"Thank you, Eleanor." Robert set his suitcases beside the wall and retrieved the folder in the center of the kitchen table.

The kitchen timer buzzed.

"You have perfect timing." Eleanor donned an oven mitt. "Seems to me, Gordon promised you could each have cookies after worlds."

"Only two," Gordon said. "They start training again tomorrow."

"I had a feeling that's what you were going to say." Eleanor grinned.

"I am so ready to try these cookies I've heard so much about," Tyler said.

"They are amazing." Amaliya's mouth watered. "And fresh out of the oven. Mmm."

Eleanor opened the oven door and pulled out a baking tray filled with enormous chocolate chip cookies.

Tyler's eyes widened. "Wow."

Gordon pointed at the tray. "Those aren't normal-sized cookies."

"You said they could each have two." Eleanor grabbed a spatula and dished two of the huge cookies onto a plate. She then repeated the process. "You never said anything about how big they could be."

"Lesson learned." Gordon eyed the remaining cookies on the tray. "Do the rest of us get some too?"

"Of course."

"And while you're enjoying your reward, come take a look at this." Her dad sat at the table and opened the folder.

"What is it?" Amaliya sat beside him.

"Your new home." He pulled out a floor plan diagram. "The architect drew up some plans to convert the rest of the attic space over the garage."

Amaliya leaned closer. The drawing included a full kitchen, an expanded living room, and a large second bedroom. "This looks amazing."

"We have some options to talk over, but once we chat with the architect, he thinks he can have the permits approved by the end of the month."

"So it will be done before we get married?" Tyler asked.

Robert nodded. "That's the plan."

"Since you're going to have a construction crew out here anyway, you could build a rink in the backyard." Gordon pointed toward the back of the house.

Her dad cast a hopeful look at her mom. Her mom shook her head. "Sorry, but I rather like having a traditional backyard rather than looking out the window at a building."

Gordon looked at her dad and shrugged. "I tried."

"We can keep practicing at our current rink," Amaliya said, "even though a rink in the backyard would be awesome."

"We may want to keep working at the rink anyway so we can build up our savings," Tyler said. "With living here and the money from the sponsorships, our income should cover any other expenses we have."

Her mom stepped behind her and put her hand on Amaliya's shoulder. "It sounds like you two are well on the road to your happily ever after."

Amaliya looked at Tyler, her love for him spreading through her. She was getting married. They were going to keep competing. Her life couldn't be more perfect. Happily ever after. She really had found hers.

Chapter FORTY-SIX

VIKTOR HURRIED UP HIS FRONT porch steps, a suitcase in each hand, his new backpack hanging from his shoulder, and a blanket draped around his neck.

Josef and Sonya followed, each hauling similar loads as their driver pulled away.

The front door opened, and Ursula's face lit up. Her gaze swept over the extra suitcases. "What's all of this?"

Viktor simply dropped the suitcases and pulled Ursula into his arms. "I missed you."

"I missed you too." She reached up and kissed him. "Come in, come in. It's so cold outside."

Viktor leaned down and retrieved his luggage. He stepped into the warmth of their home and set the suitcases down again, this time beside the table. He lowered the backpack onto a chair and turned back to his wife. She looked just the same as when he had left. He tried not to resent that he and his children had experienced so much while Ursula had been forced to remain behind.

"Did you see Katerina?" Ursula asked.

Viktor couldn't contain his smile. "I did." He motioned to Josef and Sonya, who now stood inside the door with their pile of luggage. "We all did."

"I'm so glad." Pure delight illuminated her face. "She is well?"

"She's doing very well." Viktor pulled the photo Katerina had sent home with him out of his backpack and handed it to Ursula. "This is her now."

"Oh, she looks wonderful. And so happy."

"She is happy." Viktor motioned to the mountain of luggage. "And she sent gifts home with us."

"What kind of gifts?"

"We aren't sure." Sonya moved to a chair by the woodstove and collapsed onto it.

"Our backpacks have food and some books." Josef took off his coat.

"Katerina also sent an envelope filled with American dollars," Viktor said, still awed by his sister's generosity. "We didn't have time to look in the suitcases before we left."

"Security let you bring food and books home? And money?"

"They didn't check our bags," Viktor said. The oddity of it still didn't make sense to him. Could that simple freedom have been part of what the government had agreed to grant his family in exchange for the release of Katerina's attackers?

Viktor sensed the impatience in his children and tipped one of the suitcases on its side. "Let's see what we have here."

Viktor's words must have been the magical cure for Sonya's jet lag. She popped back up to her feet, leaving her coat and gloves behind.

Viktor opened the first suitcase, his eyes widening when the contents were revealed. Levi's filled one side. The other side contained an assortment of socks, gloves, and scarves.

"Oh my." Ursula lifted a pack of socks. "I can't remember ever seeing so many clothes in the same place."

Josef picked up a pair of Levi's and held them up. "Can I keep these?"

Viktor understood the root of Josef's question. While the Levi's would provide a good alternative to Josef's few pairs of pants, they also would fetch a good number of rubles on the black market.

"You may do with them what you choose," Viktor said. He rifled through the stack of jeans. "It looks like there are sizes that will fit all of us."

"This was so generous," Ursula said.

"Open another one," Sonya insisted.

Viktor slid the suitcase aside and opened the next. Sweaters, yarn, knitting needles. T-shirts with American logos, shoes. One by one, they opened each bag. The contents ranged from clothing to accessories to toiletries. When Viktor opened the final suitcase, his emotions clogged his throat. Coats for every member of the family, a new dress for Ursula, two aprons, a new set of kitchen knives, a frying pan, an assortment of spices.

Ursula picked up the coat that appeared to be her size. "This is for me?"

"It's for you. Try it on." Viktor took it from her and held it out so she could slip her arms into the sleeves.

Ursula donned the coat and turned so Viktor could see. She ran a hand down the front. "It's so warm."

Viktor furrowed his eyebrows. "You weren't wearing a coat." He scanned the room. His coat and gloves on the table, Sonya's coat on the chair, Josef's coat hanging over the edge of one of the suitcases. "We have heat?"

Ursula smiled. "For two days now."

"How did this happen?"

"I don't know. Two men came in a truck and said it was our turn. They put a heater in and installed vents so the heat will carry to all the rooms in the house."

"I can't believe it." Had Katerina arranged for this? Or perhaps Artyom had set the installation in motion before he'd defected. Or someone in athletics had determined that Sonya's recent success was worthy of a reward. Regardless of the source of their good fortune, Viktor couldn't have asked for a better gift.

He glanced at the abundance flowing out of suitcases in front of him. "We have been truly blessed."

"You are all home," Ursula said. "I couldn't have asked for anything more, and yet, look at all of this."

Viktor slid his arm around Ursula. An abundance of the necessities of life, his family safe and healthy, and the promise of seeing his sister in the future. Truly, Viktor couldn't ask for more.

Author's Note

THE WORLD OF FIGURE SKATING has evolved tremendously over the past several decades. In the 1980s, when this story is set, the Winter Olympics and Summer Olympics occurred in the same year. In 1986, the decision was made to separate them to bring more attention to the Winter Olympic Games, but the change didn't go into effect until 1992.

Figure skating also included figures as a competition element. Figures were discontinued in competition in 1991.

Although there were other ways to advance for experienced skaters, such as placing in the previous world championship, most athletes advanced to the national championships by first competing in one of nine regions in early October and then in one of three sectional championships in late November or early December. In the 1983–84 season, skaters needed to place in the top four in each of these competitions to advance.

For the sake of the story, I changed the locations of some of the competitions in the 1984 championship season, but here are the dates and locations as they were actually competed to help visualize the timeline:

- United States Figure Skating Championships: Jan. 18–22, 1984—Salt Lake City, Utah
- 1984 Winter Olympics: Figure skating competed Feb. 10–12, 1984—Sarajevo, Yugoslavia
- 1984 Winter Olympics closing ceremonies: Feb. 19, 1984
- 1984 World Championships: Mar. 20–25, 1984—Ottawa, Canada

About the Author

Traci Hunter Abramson was born in Arizona, where she lived until moving to Venezuela for a study abroad program. After graduating from Brigham Young University, she worked for the Central Intelligence Agency, eventually resigning in order to raise her family. She credits the CIA with giving her a wealth of ideas as well as the skills needed to survive her children's teenage years. She loves to travel and recently retired after spending twenty-six years coaching her local high school swim team. She has written more than forty best-selling novels and is a seven-time Whitney Award winner, including 2017 and 2019 Best Novel of the Year.

She also loves hearing from her readers. If you would like to contact her, she can be reached through the following:

www.traciabramson.com
Facebook group: Traci's Friends
bookbub.com/authors/traci-hunter-abramson
twitter@traciabramson
facebook.com/tracihabramson
instagram.com/traciabramson.com